LA FICTION ANTHOLOGY

LA FICTION ANTHOLOGY

SOUTHLAND STORIES BY SOUTHLAND WRITERS

edited by

JOHN BRANTINGHAM & KATE GALE

Red Hen Press | *Pasadena, CA*

Book design and layout by Selena Trager

ISBN: 978-1-59709-542-6
eISBN: 978-1-59709-596-9

Library of Congress Cataloging-in-Publication Data

Names: Brantingham, John, editor. | Gale, Kate, editor.
Title: LA fiction anthology : Southland stories by Southland writers / edited by John Brantingham & Kate Gale.
Description: First edition. | Pasadena, CA : Red Hen Press, [2016]
Identifiers: LCCN 2015050365 | ISBN 9781597095426 (paperback)
Subjects: LCSH: Short stories, American—California—Los Angeles. | Los Angeles (Calif.)—Fiction. | BISAC: FICTION / Anthologies (multiple authors).
Classification: LCC PS572.L6 L25 2016 | DDC 813/.01083279494—dc23
LC record available at http://lccn.loc.gov/2015050365

The National Endowment for the Arts, the Los Angeles County Arts Commission, the Los Angeles Department of Cultural Affairs, the Dwight Stuart Youth Fund, the Pasadena Arts & Culture Commission and the City of Pasadena Cultural Affairs Division, Sony Pictures Entertainment, and the Ahmanson Foundation partially support Red Hen Press.

First Edition
Published by Red Hen Press
www.redhen.org

ACKNOWLEDGMENTS

"Burying Ellie" by Lloyd Aquino. First published in *East Jasmine Review*, Volume 1, Issue 1. Copyright © 2013 by Llyod Aquino.

"California" by Sean Bernard. First published in *The Portland Review*, Issue 58.1. Copyright © 2011 by Sean Bernard.

"The Relive Box" by T.C. Boyle. First published in *The New Yorker*, March 17, 2014. Copyright © 2014 by T. Coraghessan Boyle.

"Yoshimi and the Robot" by Michael Buckley. First published in *Miniature Men* (World Parade Books, 2011). Copyright © 2011 by Michael Buckley.

"The Pirate Story" by Ron Carlson. First published in *Clackamas Literary Review*, Spring 2000. Copyright © 2000 by Ron Carlson.

"Terminal Island" by Stephen Cooper. First published in *Hot Type: America's Most Celebrated Writers Introduce the Next Word in Contemporary Literature* (Collier Books, 1988). Copyright © 1988 by Stephen Cooper.

"The Appropriation of Cultures" by Percival Everett. First published in *Damned If I Do: Stories* (Graywolf Press, 2004). Copyright © 2004 by Percival Everett.

"Wertheimer in the City" by Judith Freeman. First published in Absolute Disaster (Dove Books, 1996). Copyright © 1996 by Judith Freeman.

"Under the Radar" by Suzanne Greenberg. First published in *West Branch*, Number 64, Spring/Summer 2009. Copyright © 2009 by Suzanne Greenberg.

"The Snack Bar" by Grant Hier. First published in *Word Riot* (Wax Statues, 2011). Copyright © 2011 by Grant Hier.

Elsewhere, California (excerpt) by Dana Johnson (Counterpoint, 2012). Copyright © 2012 by Dana Johnson.

"Frozen Yogurt" by Gerald Locklin. First published in *The Vampires Saved Civilization* (World Parade Press, 2010). Copyright © 2010 by Gerald Locklin.

"Preparing to Photograph My Grandparents" by Paul Kareem Tayyar. First published in *Follow the Sun* (Aortic Books, 2010). Copyright © 2010 by Paul Kareem Tayyar.

CONTENTS

LA FICTION ANTHOLOGY

Los Angeles stories bite the dust, sail through the air like oversized spruce planes; they tumble to the shore like waves, they fall like palm fronds, they float like orange blossoms, they drown in the thickets of golden heat and then rise again like surfers at Zuma Beach. Even in winter sunlight, these stories shine. Stories of tattered homeless, of pirates, of weirdos, of creeps and strange bedfellows, make you glad you entered the narrative of Los Angeles. This collection includes famous writers and new writers; it gives the reader a way of understanding West Coast stories, but especially Southern California where the air is drier, the pools wetter, and the artificial is everywhere. These stories are raw, salty, wild; they find their way into your consciousness. You'll have the time of your life. Welcome to Los Angeles fiction.

The Pirate Story

RON CARLSON

First hear this: we are pirates, and as always, from the days when wind first filled a handmade sail made from jute coffee sacks unto these latter days when it is all pleasure yachts and jet skis, we are proud of it. So, it is not the word to which we object. We are pirates. But there is so much in the general picture to which we do take offense.

There is too much loose talk about what we actually do as pirates. We conduct our business, most of it, on the open sea (we don't call it the bounding main), and that is part of why we are misunderstood. Have any of the historians been along for the ride when we interact with other vessels? The answer is no. But these folks, who have never even been on a ship of any size in the harbor, let alone on the high glassy waters of a real sea, feel free to write these godawful accounts of pirates this and pirates that. Swashbucklers! Buccaneers! Then they slap a picture of that insane looking criminal caricature on the front cover, waving a sword which looks more to me like a snow shovel than anything I've held in my hands, and publish the thing so that the American public can be exposed to the most wrongheaded view of pirates imaginable.

Let me try today to rectify this crazy picture. Piracy, first of all, is business. People put it down as violence or some kind of evil entertainment, which it is not. We are business people and our methods and our problems are those shared by most hardworking men and women in this country. So this is what we do. We venture out onto the uncertain waters of the world's oceans and do business. We meet new people. A lot of this involves cold calls. We come across a vessel and they don't know us. Personally. They recognize the franchise flag, which we do run up the flagpole. We merge and we acquire. Like all entrepreneurs, we're out to make a killing, but we rarely have to. We board our target vessel, explain our business to the client, because information is key in all commerce today.

In such negotiations we suggest our clients transfer their cargo to our hold. It is a good deal for everyone, a definition of the win-win scenario. We are able to procure their two tons of necessaries and luxuries, and they are able to stay alive, stay afloat, essentially live to quibble another day.

So, given that, can you imagine us conducting such an interaction wearing that ridiculous hat or a hook, stabbing around on a peg, and all this with one eye covered?

To be portrayed this way, frankly and simply, offends and hurts us. Do you see? We don't wear that hat. Nobody wears that hat. A lot of times the material we're acquiring from our clients has been carefully stowed below decks, and most of these upscale summer holiday yachts have small passageways which are tightly fitted, and that hat would get absolutely in the way.

We don't say *shiver me timbers* and we don't *say shiver your timbers*. We don't say *shiver anybody's freaking timbers*. We lay out our plan and when it is completed and stowed securely in our hold, we say *thank you very much*. Who doesn't do that? No one is raised on the yardarm and no one walks the plank. We don't have a plank. Why would we carry around a plank? We have the center leaf from the long oak mess table we sometimes bring topside if our negotiations get difficult or thorny, and yes, we've had some clients walk this. But they don't walk very far, and it is not an extended or particularly unpleasant ceremony. But when we finish and the last item is transferred onto our ship, we say *thank you*. Do you ever hear about pirates saying *thank you*? I don't. I don't *see thank you very much* in any of these Harvard educated historians' big book of lies about the pirates. I'll just say this: when you write your book, put *thank you* in there.

And the peg leg. Let's consider that. Look at me closely; let me turn around. Does anybody see a peg leg? No? What about a big wooden leg about this long protruding from my rolled up trousers, something with which I could pin a flounder to the floor? So, if I may be so bold: what's that about? Let me tell you. There was one guy. That's right, some of us knew him. It was one guy and his name wasn't Peg Leg Pete or Peg Leg Fred or Peg Leg Matthew, Mark, Luke, or John. His name wasn't Peg Leg Anything. His name was Anthony Ingram, and he did have trouble with his leg, more than trouble really, got it infected from a tennis blister, several years ago, twenty, after the Captain's Open on Madagascar, and he had too much of the Chardonnay at the reception and he fell asleep without getting it treated. And he lost the leg, most of it, and he did wear a temporary device for a few years around the Indian Ocean and the Venezuelan Basin. That's all it takes: bingo! We're all stumping around the decks like Thumper and Bumper. It is not fair and it is not accurate. You should see Anthony Ingram today. He walks without a limp, and he still plays in the annual Caribbean Senior Doubles every year on St. Barts.

In all my years doing business in the way of a pirate, I have only met one soul who wore that hat, had the eye patch and ever said, *Aye, matey*. I've sailed the Seven Seas (of which there are really twelve if you count them by their true character), and I've boarded vessels at every longitude with the two dozen crews who have worked with me, (more than a hundred men and women), and I've only seen that stupid hat once. It was a hat you'd remember. Regan Peterson, one of the best female pirates to have ever worked with us, wore it.

Telling her story might help.

Regan was really something. I mean, she wanted to be all of it. At the end, she had the hat, a big black tri-corner with a lavender ostrich plume, a silk eyepatch which she wore as an accessory, she said, because her eyes were perfectly fine, twelve tattoos, and for the last year she had Ensign Happiness, a blue Brazilian Parrot who could actually say, *Aye, matey*, and *Avast!* Ensign Happiness wore an eye patch too. He was a good bird to have in a tough negotiation.

Regan Peterson and I joined at the same time. I had been in Baltimore seeing my uncle about a job in his auto body shop; this was a long time ago. It was more of a junkyard, really, where people came to get parts of the two hundred wrecks my uncle had piled up. I was there an hour and we both knew it wasn't for me. My uncle took me out to the pub and told me to go back to school. It was a tough time for me; who knows what they want to do with their life? I knew I wasn't going back to school, and I knew I wasn't going to climb around in death cars with a wrench removing carburetors. So, I was confused and stayed on after my uncle went home, having a few more beers than I should have.

Anyway, about midnight there's a ruckus and in come a dozen blond girls, not all blond, but young and shiny like that, especially in this dive, where there isn't a barstool without a crust of grease around the edge and the bar is unfinished plywood. It's a Greek thing, sorority rush, and the pledges each have to get matchbooks from every pub along the waterfront. Well, the only matchbook they're going to get from the Anchor Chain is that generic white one in a box by the register, the only thing printed on that is going to be the thumbprint of the criminal who hands it to them. They don't care, these girls. They're *oohing* and laughing, and I mean, it is kind of fun to watch. They're idiots, but better to look at than the four guys passed out around the room. In five minutes they're gone, and in the new sharper silence created when they leave, I can hear a noise I guess has been there all along: the ocean. I can hear the water lapping at the harbor wall, which is right outside. It was a moment I remember, because in ten minutes my life went that way forever.

What happened was this. First, a girl comes back into the bar and looks around. She's been in the head, and her friends have left without her. She shrugs at me and calls to the bartender, Set 'em up! Drinks all around! Then she sits down with me with a grin I would see a thousand times in the years to come, and she says, I've always wanted to say that. But before the bartender can even lift his head from the bar, six guys enter the front door and swoop us up, relatively gently, and out around a corner we're in a dinghy. It was confusing. A moment later we were on the solid deck of the Jolly Merger, and that fine ship was already moving out to sea. It was the first time I ever heard the snapping of the big sheets as they gathered the small breezes.

That was a long time ago. The two of us were bound and gagged until morning. By then the Jolly Merger had cleared harbor and the coastline of America was a faint illusion, and then it was gone. When they brought the two of us up on deck, I was still a little apprehensive. But the girl got right into it, laughing with the men, pushing and hauling with them, and finally sitting on the rail and cutting her khakis off at the knee and slipping the rope they'd used to bind her through the belt loop and cinching a knot in it. Before the day was over, she was right at home. Even down in the galley where I started my life as a pirate, cleaning dishes and pouring coffee and rum, I could hear her voice every five minutes as she called out the new vocabulary she was learning: *mizzenmast! Starboard! Crow's nest!* After saying each one, she'd add, Aye, matey! and laugh. I heard her say, I've always wanted to say that. I kept my head down and did what I was told, afraid that when they found out she was ridiculing them, they'd think I was too.

But by that first night, she had a blue tattoo on her shoulder, the grinning Jolly Roger, and a purple scarf wrapped around her head, tightly with all her hair in it. She sat in her bunk and admired her new boots, a big pair of black brogans with a folded stovepipe. They were crazy, yet she looked at them as if they carried all her magic. When she'd pulled them off and swung her legs into the small bunk, she lay down and looked across at me. I hadn't moved and my eyes were open the width of a playing card. I'd been in bed half an hour not moving, just feeling the Jolly Merger work the ocean. I could feel sleep in each trough our ship assumed. Regan Peterson was looking at me from her tiny pillow in her tiny bunk. My eyes were closed. She was grinning. Isn't this wonderful, she said.

Well, I'm not going to tell the whole story, our history, just that we stayed on and prospered. I worked my way up through the ranks, and I liked all the work, and I liked my colleagues. Our captain was a man named Jason Nelson, a man who wore tortoise shell glasses and sweater vests. He was a calm, pipe-smoking gentleman who assumed a philosophical posture toward piracy, and looked more like a professor than any pirate the popular press has created. Captain Nelson liked my earnestness and I advanced. There was no question that once I had boarded another vessel and dealt with our clients and their cargo, that negotiation was my forte. I have a direct, though not unpleasant manner, which is highly effective with nervous and uncertain folks. I'm relatively well groomed, and I don't carry a visible weapon. I learned these things from the Captain. Our clients were glad to see me, and they come right up and start asking questions: What's going on here? Who are you? What are you doing? Things like that, basic things for which I have the answer.

Regan and I advanced together and we became friends. That phrase, became friends, is thrown about these days like confetti at a wedding (of which there are way too many), and its meaning is as thin as river fog, but friends on a ship are something necessary and steady. She went at piracy with the kind of energy and verve you don't see twice. She learned the ship and its every part faster than I did, serving double watches, and getting to know the crew and their assignments. She was a bright thing on the Jolly Merger. Regan wanted to work with me in inter-ship negotiation, but she was a touch wrong for it, too chatty, and she stimulated the delicate meetings with our clients too much. Our clients flirted with her, breaking the mood I was trying to create. She eventually joined one of our three-person batteries and ran the biggest cannon; she also coordinated our holds and was responsible for fresh cargo rotation.

One September as we rode at anchor in Nickelhook bay, which is where we always went to regroup and do our accounting, I saved her life. We'd made a last acquisition with Captain Nelson before he retired to Bermuda, where he still takes tea every afternoon on the porch of the Ivory Orchid, and we'd sailed hard and were resting. Regan Peterson always ran a diving contest, which all the pirates enjoyed, and after a beautiful two and a half from the stern rail, she did not come up. Well, I knew what she was doing, and I dropped off the other side and found her snagged in the tiller, which she tried to swim under to come up on the other side of the ship. Her stupid belt rope was cinched into the tiller hinge tighter than a wet knot, which it was, and I looked into Regan's worried face in the blue water and cut the rope with my knife. We blew bubbles to the surface. On deck she put her head against my shoulder for half a second, grinned thinly, and said, Thank you, Captain.

You understand she was an unusual person, and bore an unusual personal beauty, which we all acknowledged. But listen closely: do not imagine the two of us sitting on deck in the moonlight chatting as the big wheel of stars turned overhead. The entire ship asleep below decks on a bright night as we whispered and dreamed and parted the purple seas. It didn't happen. As tender as it might have been and as lonely as I was, it had no place in the workplace, and a pirate's lot, as even the bad bookwriters know, is a pirate's lot, and I accepted mine.

As for Regan, she bought herself that bird, a giant blue parrot on our one stop in Brazil, and she taught it several phrases. She named it Ensign Happiness, another of her little jokes, and late at night sometimes when I steered the Jolly Merger through our oceans, I could hear them talking.

What happened to us finally, happened to us aboard the Yuppie Days off the coast of Venezuela. We could see it was a prime pleasure yacht, and the bright brass trim blinked brightly from half a mile. She was riding low, which we loved to see, meaning she was newly stocked and ripe and ready for successful interaction with the Friendly Merger. We came alongside and greeted the half dozen occupants of the craft. Our flag was up, the Jolly Roger, big as life, but for some reason they still weren't aware of the nature of our visit. I stepped over and shook hands all around; American women love to shake hands. They were three couples and made a handsome crew; the men's wristwatches alone were worth a fortune, but we never, ever as pirates took personal effects from our clients. Business is business, and we kept it that way. We were all standing there in the tender midmorning sunlight on this yacht, which was perhaps the prettiest jewel of a boat I'd ever boarded, and I could see the questions on their faces. I mean, they didn't understand what we were up to. One of the handsome women, her auburn hair shining like money, looked at us expectantly the way you anticipate having won the sweepstakes. At this juncture, I always begin a quiet explanation of what would transpire over the next three hours, that we'd be taking all their stores, except those they needed to get back to port; in effect: their plans have changed.

Before I could even begin this discussion, there was a noise behind me and in a red and black blur, Regan, sweet Regan, flew by my head, swinging on one of the mast ropes, and she dropped to the deck in the middle of our little uncomfortable circle. She was in full regalia, the floppy boots, the pantaloons, the billowing ruby shirt, the black satin eye patch, and behind her in the air, her idiotic tricorne hat which had been blown off her head, and Ensign Happiness, the blue parrot, sweeping behind her in the air like some minor demon from the jungle. I saw it all as the anathema of standard business practice, and I saw it correctly as a threat to the natural order of things and their procession today. And now, Regan had done her stunt, the kind of theatrics I should have anticipated, and she was moaning lightly, holding her hip where she had evidently cut herself falling on her redundant oversized saber.

My god, one of the handsome women said. They're pirates!

Regan was crying now. She looked at me and I knelt and gave her my kerchief and I held her in my arms for the first time, and I realized how long I had wanted to do it. At this point I saw one of the men backing up from our circle and moving into the unmistakable posture of someone on the telephone, and I lay Regan down and I went to him. One of the women was screaming now, which undermines the quality of the meeting in a hurry. Many members of my crew had boarded and were mingling uncomfortably with our clients. One of the gentlemen was invoking legal terms, which is many times the case. There is nothing so pathetic, really, in the civilized world than a man or a woman invoking their lawyer or any of his wondrous abilities. Meanwhile the man with the telephone was ardent about making his call, and I had to terminate that attempt. As I tell so many of our customers, it is rude to make a call in a meeting (as well as in a movie or restaurant) and it really spoils the focus. Mr. Telephone, however, wasn't going to take this information passively, and he stuck me above the eye with his little toy telephone. One of my officers witnessed this event, and his reaction, plus the woman screaming, several sudden movements by our clients, the appearance of our injured angel Regan there on the deck, and the man declaiming a litany of legal terms, led to the rest. The scuffle. It was not a sea battle, but it was an unpleasant little conflict.

We on the Jolly Merger only resort to restraining our clients during cargo transfers in rare circumstances. We take no pleasure from carrying boxes of the world's finest goods past the pained faces of our clients as they stand and moan bound to the masts, rails, and hatches. It takes the little joy right out of one of the central pleasures of being a pirate. Most often, the people we encounter, when they understand the nature of our meeting, go below decks and wait until we cast off. Here on the Yuppie Days, a beautiful yacht which I now hated, we did tie up these three handsome couples, and we did empty their hold of half a ton of sumptuary delights, including thirty-two cases of Perrier and four of Dom Perignon.

I am not proud of the way I conducted the matter. The sight of Regan bleeding on the deck had influenced me, that is, I was angry, and anger has no place in any deal. I instructed my crew to take all the linen on the ship, pillows and such, and every fork, knife, and spoon from the galley. I led our clients, bound as they were before me, to believe that I was certainly planning to sink the Yuppie Days, and I described in rich and effulgent detail what it would look like down there nestling into the sandy bottom. Oh, I behaved badly. I described to them how far the smoke would travel if I burned their silly boat and how sweet that smoke would smell to the vacationers on St. Thomas which was ninety miles westward. Do you see? I was a bully.

I'd never done such a thing before, delivered gruesome speeches with animated hand gestures, and I gave myself to the moment too fully. My own crew watched me warily as they marched by with crates and boxes. I was on fire, and I knew by the way each glance at the wounded Regan Peterson inflamed me that I had developed and concealed for these years powerful feelings for her, feelings that would certainly be the end of me as a pirate. Love has no place in such a world; I had known that from the beginning. Captain Nelson had told me all about it. Love has as much place in a pirate's life as that insane floppy hat, or the stupid boots, or ludicrous eye patch.

Ultimately, I got hold of myself, and when my crew was all aboard the Jolly Merger, I stepped back on the yacht and untied my unfortunate clients, apologizing to each and giving them back some sheets and silverware. I told them which way to strike for land. The apology is always important, but it was my lowest moment as a pirate.

We sailed south hard to the hidden bay at Nickelhook, which had been our plan, but I could see my men watching me, giving me a wider berth. I'd behaved in a less than professional manner, and we all knew it. It was a sober two days, quiet and apprehensive, hardly the tone you want on a pirate vessel. Riding anchor in the glowing teal waters of Nickelhook, where we'd spent so many fine full hours together counting our blessings and pallets of dry goods, and planning our coming campaigns, things were different for us all. We fell to making necessary repairs, polishing our brass and mending the sails; many of the crew swam and slept upon the beach, and we had meals, long groaning boards of fresh fruit and fish, and the filet mignons fresh from the Yuppie Days, and barrels of wine and sparkling water. Regan did not appear and when I sent the doctor to see her, he reported her wound was infected and he had cleaned and treated it, sewing seven stitches to close the wound which was on the bottom of her right hip. But there was something else, he told me, a tattoo. There was a tattoo there, close to the place, a mark only he and the person who inscribed it had seen. What is it, I asked him. It is your initials done in Old English, he said.

Finally, one morning Regan Peterson asked to speak to me, in private, and we took the smallest of our day boats and pulled the oars a quarter mile to the second island in Nickelhook Bay, five acres of rock, palm jungle, and sand. She was in her pirate getup, the coat, the hat, the patch, the boots. Ensign Happiness stood on her shoulder like a sentry. His great orange beak twitched when he heard the wild parrots calling. Regan herself looked healthy again, a faint grin riding her face, as it always did.

On the island we opened our lunch kit and spread it in the grassy shade. You're a good captain, she started. We were drinking light rum tonics and spreading Dutch cheese on crackers from Portugal. And I know that life on the Jolly Merger will be amazing. You are so good at what you do. She toasted me and we drank. But, she said, climbing to her knees to speak to me, I'm not right for this, and I've known it for a long time, and . . . I tried to interrupt her then, but she put her hand on my shoulder and held forth. And what I did the other day, it ruined the whole deal. I'm not good at it. Ultimately, and I've thought it out. I'm not a good pirate. Look at me. Here she held her arms out in display. It's all wrong.

I can still hear those words and I wish every dreamer who wants to draw a picture of a pirate or write a little pirate story could hear them and watch what Regan Peterson did next.

She pulled the monstrous hat from her pretty head and peeled her eye patch off, stuffing it inside. She removed the coat and pulled her boots, with some difficulty, from her lovely feet. Quickly she pulled the billowy red satin shirt over her head, and the girl who sat before me in her bikini top and dungarees looked like a sophomore at Pepperdine. All of this transformation had Ensign Happiness confused. He didn't know where to stand.

Can I borrow your knife one more time, Regan Peterson asked me. When I handed it to her, she turned deftly and clipped the bird's minor tendon under each wing and took his eye patch. This had the effect of surprising him and he stood very still and very tall now opening his wings, both of his eyes open to his new home.

When she handed back the blade, Regan said, Can you drop me in Charleston when we go by there next month? I have to resign as a pirate. While she was speaking she was scooping a hole in the sand between us deeper and deeper. The big blue bird had backed to the edge of the jungle. Regan laid her pirate regalia into the hole, hat and all, and she buried it there and patted the spot triple. The she grinned at me and drew an X over the place.

I know what you're going to say, I told her.

Then I won't have to say it, she said, lifting her glass again to me. After a moment, we heard a bird call and turned to find the Ensign gone. I know the Doctor told you about my tattoo, she said. I had that done in Guadeloupe when we stopped right after that time under the Merger when you saved my rear. I meant it as a tribute. You saved it and thereby had some claim.

She looked this old pirate in the eye, and I said what a pirate says. I put my glass down and stood up and brushed the sand from myself, and I nodded at her in that island sunlight, and I said, I renounce the claim.

Three weeks later the Jolly Merger stopped for two hours off Fort Sumter and let off one of our crew. She was a good pirate and we wish her well on the mainland. Said she was going to go on the stage and I'll bet she does. She buried the hat, the eye patch, all of it, and now I want the rest of you to do the same. We're pirates, by god, and we deserve better.

Discussion Questions:

1. What seems to be the narrator's main complaint about the way he is treated?
2. What are the names of the various pirate ships, and how do these names reflect the self-image of the pirate?
3. To whom does the pirate refer as clients, and why does he use this term?

Essay Questions:

1. The humor of this story relies in large part on point of view. How does the point of view help to enhance or even create one or more of the themes of the story?
2. Compare and contrast Ron Carlson's story to any or all of Grant Hier's stories. For both of these authors, voice is an important part of the storytelling process. How do both of these authors use voice to help the readers understand their meanings and messages?

Yoshimi and the Robot
A Bedtime Story

MICHAEL BUCKLEY

Yoshimi's vast potential for robot killing was first discovered by her gymnastics professor, Dr. Atakai.

"You are quick, Yoshi, and strong. I see in you all the makings of a great Robot-Killing Karato."

And he was right. At the R.K.K. try-outs in downtown Long Beach Yoshimi surpassed every other hopeful in speed, ferocity, and smile-wattage. At the end of the afternoon Wexworth Stall, the greatest sensei in Long Beach and a hero of the robotic conflict, regarded the crowd of contestants. The try-outs were meant to fill two vacancies in the city's team of Robot-Killing Karatos. A recent skirmish near the salt marshes had resulted in one death and one clipped-off arm; two personal friends of Stall's were off the team, and he was loath to choose two new karatos. But even in his dark glower he couldn't deny the obvious superiority of Yoshimi.

"You, step forward," he said to her. "You are chosen to train for the team. And, um . . ."

Stall scanned the shining faces. As far as he could tell they were all the same, hopeful and mediocre. At random he pointed to a moonlike face.

"You," he said. "Excellent work. Step forward. Thanks to everyone here for offering to help in our endless war against the robots. These two will get the chance to train with us. Names?"

"Yoshimi," she said, eagerly.

"Stencil," the moonface said. He didn't look happy.

"The war between man and robot has raged for ages," was how Stall began his lecture on the first day of training. Yoshimi and Stencil sat before him, each in crisp running suits. Wexworth himself was clearly hungover; he had spent the night before drinking high balls and wrestling with his boa constrictor.

"As you know," he continued, "the robots are programmed to do us evil. Fortunately, much of their technology is frozen at a mid-1950s level..." Stall continued on with everything the students needed to know about the robot-human conflict. It began back in the mists of time, perhaps twenty-five years ago, when the robots mercilessly turned on their human creators. It was a dire betrayal; Wexworth himself had seen pictures of humans in double-breasted suits sharing coffee cake with robots, and it was well known that human kindnesses were again and again rewarded with robotian cruelty. They'd made their city in the ruins of the oil refineries that lie on the far side of the salt marshes. Day and night the oily housewives of southern Long Beach could hear the robots building more robots, attaching and testing buzz-saw hands and roaring in their strange language while testing clampers and clippers and defenestrators. They attacked once or twice a month, when their complex, evil plans came to fruition. Only one weapon was proven effective: karate fighting. The specific mixture of violence and back-flips, chops and rooster calls, seemed to dazzle the robotic brain. The raging karate wars that spanned the salt marshes were the stuff of legend, and Yoshimi glowed as she heard about them. Stencil played with a shoelace.

Stall was a ferocious teacher. He demanded their training suits be perfectly clean, he required them to stretch and breakdance for two hours a day, and he fed them panoplies of vitamins at each mealtime. Other rules were not mandatory: he preferred students to cultivate hoary lamb chops like the ones that nearly touched his own lips, and he asked that they paint their faces bright blue for lecture period. Yoshimi's body was made for karate and Stall found it difficult to demand her to do things she could not do. She could high-kick, tiger-strike, back-flip, and screech like a parrot all the while. Her grasshopper stance was second only to his own, and although she was bony and young, dwarfed by her own big black eyes and ponytail, Stall was, he realized one afternoon, afraid of her.

Stencil was the opposite. He was a round little guy and reprehensibly soft on the inside: Stall had made him cry three times just describing the inscrutable, flame-belching evil of the robots across the marsh. If he can't handle that, how will he do in an all-out karate war? Stall thought. But he had chosen Stencil himself and could not, without looking foolish, reject him.

"Why did you try out for this?" Yoshimi asked Stencil one night. They lie on their cots as the sun went down, spent from a training session.

"My uncle wants me to."

Stencil's uncle, one of the latest casualties, had told Stencil of his long held dream that the boy become a famous karato; as he did this he tested his new prosthetic arm in front of the mirror, unwrapping Twinkies with difficulty.

"And look for that bastard robot with the red eye." Uncle held up his plastic hand when he said this.

"You don't want to be a Robot-Killing Karato?" Yoshimi asked.

Stencil thought.

"It's alright. I like the running suits."

"What about the robot war?"

"I'm scared!" Stencil said. "There's a robot out there cutting arms off! What if he recognizes me?"

Stall attended a champagne and weenies reception for city employees. Every reception in his spotty memory was the same: boring conversation, burping, and a headache. It was true that his younger days as a karato (or Robot Confrontation Technician, RCT-1, as the city's designation went) saw him rudely gulping champagne and forcing palmfuls of weenies into his maw, to end the night barfing pink foam, but since his fame as a sensei had grown he'd put effort into controlling his darker urges. The other RCTs were congregated near the bucket of iced champagne. The most recent combat had involved a twelve-foot tall, green-eyed robot, equipped with the latest defenestration technology. It had come after Stall himself, and even defenestrated him quite handily; thank God they can't climb stairs yet, he thought. Get thrown out of, say, a *second* story window and there could be trouble.

"How are the new recruits?" one of the karatos asked as he approached. The man's name was Bixby and Stall considered him too theatrical to be taken seriously as a Robot-Killing Karato.

"One of them is great."

"One?"

"I'd put her up against you." Or even myself, Stall thought. He felt drunk.

"When do they join the team?" Bixby asked.

"Next week," Stall replied, and arm-looped the passing waiter.

That night, their night off, Yoshimi ditched Stencil and went to the salt marshes. It was, of course, forbidden. The land was frequented only by robots, karatos, and flocks of dirty seagulls, but Yoshimi couldn't resist going.

The barest traces of dusk still hung over the marshes and she made her way carefully through the fifty meters of reeds. The ground was soft sand, and once or twice it tried to grab her shoes in a muddy suction. Beyond were dwarf palms, planted years ago in the pre-war excess, and also rusted oil derricks in various states of profile and prayer. Yoshimi hadn't imagined the salt marshes would be so peaceful; there was a gentle scent of the sea and then she came upon a flock of seagulls, perhaps five hundred of them, at rest in a field of churned sand.

Yoshimi stood still and watched the birds.

Suddenly, as one, they burst into flight. The noise was horrible and the birds caused their own strong wind that stung Yoshimi's eyes and moved her hair. And then they were gone, a wide black mass in the sky, leaving an empty field before her.

Her heart kicked her in the sternum; she could see something moving at the edge of the field, its eyes glowing, faint and purplish. Yoshimi crouched down and watched. There were no other robots she could see, and even though Stall's voice warned her ("Don't be a fool, Yoshimi!"), she crossed the field.

The robot was acting strangely, rummaging in the low bushes, shuffling like a miser. She approached within attack distance, just under ten feet, and leapt erect.

"Huzzah!" she said, and the robot turned.

Yoshimi flashed a dizzying array of hand signs. This technique was known to fire up the robot's cerebral vacuum tubes, allowing it to flip through punch cards to decipher the meaning of the hand signals. Stall had warned her: "Never use nonsense hand signals, Yoshimi! It is an item of trust between us and the robots. As long as they know that everything we do means something, it keeps them curious." Yoshimi flashed these signs: a peace "V," a Vulcan live-long-and-prosper, an English schoolboy salute, a Girl Scout honor oath, and a war flag from a gang known as the Tre-Lo Crips. The robot chuckled and booped, computing the visual input. Now was the time to strike, Yoshimi knew. A side kick to the neck could decapitate the thing. Or maybe a power chop or head scissors—

And then the robot signed back to her: A peace "V," which it then reversed to a British "fuck you." Yoshimi stared in amazement. This had never happened before; the very fact that the robot had human-like hands instead of automated cleavers or spiked pincers was remarkable, and here it was signing . . . And then it spoke.

"Olé!" it said, in a deep metallic timber.

Yoshimi had just met a robot called X-8A8. He'd been born just to the left of the abandoned smokestacks, where the conveyor belt spit out new robots at the rate of two a day. If forced to say something about himself, X-8A8 would say:

"I feel there is something profound in the universe, something that understands me even though I do not understand it."

It was typical of X-8A8 to say something philosophical like this. In fact, of course, 8A8 was correct: the robotic race had a "C.U.R.," or Central Understanding Receptacle, which collected, collated, categorized, and channeled knowledge to all robots. There were flaws in the system, though, and 8A8 had received snatches of music from C.U,R., bits of television broadcasts from the human world, even offers for real estate seminars and sexual performance enhancers. All of these came to him like surreal revelations of rash beings at once quite robotic and quite illogical. 8A8 often watched the other robots as they loitered about the ruins of the refinery, waiting for a human to wander into their sights so they could hamstring or robo-clamp or auto-spank him, and wondered: Is this all there is?

This was what brought him to the salt marshes. It was a contemplative place: the low light that glowed a very gentle purple in his thermo-vision, the old oil derricks that stood like drunken cousins.

And then Yoshimi surprised him.

She appeared in his vision like clusters of heat bound together by black cord. The strange hand signals were confusing. He'd heard stories from other robots and wondered: Are they trying to communicate? Is it a threat?

He mimicked her peace "V," then spoke a word he'd heard in a salsa commercial he'd intercepted, a word he hadn't translated and felt meant "hello," "I love you," "let's dance," and "sky" at the same time.

"Olé!" he said.

Yoshimi's decision to not kill the robot and to begin a hand-sign conversation with him was one that, for the rest of her life, she did not understand.

She began: thumbs locked, her hands formed a seagull.

The robot responded with two pairs of rabbit ears, moving across a field.

Yoshimi formed a dog's profile, and when she moved her pinky, she barked out of the corner of her mouth.

8A8 formed two canine profiles, barking at each other with a sound like a cheap tin gong.

Yoshimi gave thumbs-up to show she approved.

8A8 formed his hands into a diamond shape over his crotch, a sign of conversational power that he'd seen human sensei use with karato inferiors.

Yoshimi responded with the black power salute, then bolted. She looked back one last time and saw 8A8, his purple eyes following her.

Graduation, and status as true RCTs, was only a week away. Stall upped the tempo of training, introducing cheetah roars and disco shouts into the panoply of *kiaps* Yoshimi and Stencil could use, introducing savage biting techniques meant to sever robot lube lines, and revealing the secret weapon: to bend the robot's antenna, warping his connection to C.U.R., the equivalent of kneeing him below the belt. This intensified pace took its toll on Stall. One morning he woke up, a glass with a sip of whiskey left in it in his hand, and his boa constrictor lying in front of him waiting for the dawn to come so it could resume the wrestling match they'd left off the night before. He knew it wasn't healthy.

It was one day watching Yoshimi ax-kick a combat dummy that he fell in love with her. He couldn't explain it himself; he had known women who were more beautiful, but Yoshimi made him feel something much like tenderness. It was a feeling he hadn't had for anyone or anything in a long time, except maybe his boa, whose black eyes turned his heart to putty.

At about the same moment—through the human mystery of our own C.U.R., maybe God or pheromones or pack thinking—Stencil fell in love with Yoshimi. He felt deflated looking at her, an empty skin next to her flamboyant kicking and *kiaipping.*

That night, as Stencil and Stall tried to come to grips with their feelings, Yoshimi returned to the salt marshes. She had resolved to kill the purple-eyed robot. Somehow she knew he would be there, where he had been before. The reed beds concealed her approach, and she crouched by a dwarf palm to spy on the robot. Sure enough he was there, staring out over the same grounded flock of seagulls, deep in thought. Yoshimi cracked the knuckles on her left hand, the killing hand, and made her approach.

8A8 turned when she was within a few feet of him, preparing to strike. His perceptiveness surprised her, but more surprising was the oily-looking panel on his chest. It was difficult to make out, and then she saw him gesturing. He gestured. It was the sign for dawn. Yoshimi got closer. 8A8 signed *dawn* again and she saw what it was on his chest: a mirror. As he signed *dawn*, she saw her face reflected in his chest panel. She was confused for a second then forgot all thoughts of killing him, and only wanted to understand the robot, his history, and his mind. They spent the rest of the night there, Yoshimi and the robot, signing to each other and eventually waltzing in the sand next to the seagulls that this time did not fly away but slept, beaks under their wings, standing on one foot.

The graduation ceremony was a spartan affair. After an address in which Stall openly wept when describing Yoshimi's brilliance, and after his reading of Shakespeare's Sonnet 28 and the lyrics to "Sweet Child O' Mine" by Guns n' Roses (during which his crying broke afresh on the line: "Where do we go now?") the karatos cracked open cans of generic beer and plainly spoke about the upcoming mission. Stall himself took Stencil and Yoshimi aside.

"You two have been a great class. Best in a long time. I could even see two karatos like you turning the tide in the robot war."

"Me too," Stencil said. Yoshimi looked beautiful and fresh in her new official karato uniform, strands of her black hair floating in the ambient breeze and holding sunlight like gilding. She didn't speak.

Their conversation continued like this, the two men telling Yoshimi things they desperately wanted her to believe about them ("I like to kill robots because I am brave and suitable" or "Now and then when I see her face it takes me away to that special place and if I stay too long I'll probably break down and cry"). Yoshimi was not interested.

Although it was daytime, Yoshimi went to the salt marshes. She crawled through the reeds to conceal herself from both the karato guards and the robots that undoubtedly patrolled the place during the day then shimmied up an oil derrick. Her thin shape was indistinguishable in its profile, and she looked off towards the distant robot city. I wonder what they do there, she thought. Are all of the robots like 8A8? Of course Yoshimi had seen robots do bad things, but most of the images she could conjure were not robots at all but public service announcements about them: "The Inhuman Menace!" series was famous, and the most recent one she'd seen that morning, with a close up of a robot's demonic, rusty-toothed face and the words "STEEL DOESN'T FEEL."

I don't know anything, she thought.

From the top of the derrick Yoshimi could see an old wildcatter's shelter, concealed between dwarf palms and rusty, cast-off machinery. Until that moment she did not understand what she was going to do, but then it went off like a stick of dynamite burning away in her heart, and she shimmied back down the derrick and slipped away.

Six hours later, when night was fully upon Long Beach, Yoshimi belly-crawled back into the reeds. She made it quickly to the spot where she knew 8A8 would be standing. He was waiting for her, holding a rough-hewn eucalyptus branch as an offering. Yoshimi accepted and began dragging it towards the wildcatter's shelter. 8A8 followed. The salt marshes were quiet, unusually so, as if thoughts and eyes on both sides of the war had turned away from the other; because Yoshimi was excited she didn't hear the two figures creeping behind her and 8A8.

When they got to the shelter Yoshimi kicked the old, worm-eaten door in. It looked like the place had been used by kids in the days before the war; old bottles littered the planks, labels bleached and peeling. It smelled like the ocean and oil and old wood.

Yoshimi turned to 8A8 and took a deep breath.

(Interlude: Yoshimi had learned about sex the way everyone does: reconstructing secrets with rumors. She formed her likely scenario: a man and a woman connected their bodies in some event that lasted anywhere from six to fourteen hours, and when finished, were more in love than before. This scene was warped by Dr. Atakai's matter-of-fact description of sex during a health class: it was shorter, messier, and of a depressingly certain purpose. But now she understood, and from such a strange source. It reaffirmed to Yoshimi that something about her experience with 8A8 was miraculous. What would probably happen now is the fourteen-hour experience, a cross between a concert, church, a massage, and a tornado.)

Yoshimi reached out to touch 8A8's cheek panel. For a moment, his purple eyes glowed.

Then he cut her hand off. It was a spring-loaded limb shear that had popped out from under the mirror on his chest. Yoshimi didn't react for a moment; at some level, she reflected later, she believed this to be the beginning of sex; that ended when 8A8 snipped off her other hand. It was a good limb shear and didn't hurt much and before she even began to bleed, shock hit Yoshimi like a heat wave. She kicked at 8A8 and he chopped her leg off at the knee, and when she fell, stooped to chop the other one off mid-femur. She was now bleeding very badly, and she screamed.

Wow, 8A8 thought. (Or, in robot, F13.) He'd believed she must've finally decided to attack him. A great karato, as he knew Yoshimi to be, would make short work of him. But she went down so easy that he realized he may have made a mistake. It struck him: this thing humans call sex, the thing they sell enhancers for, the thing that happens as music swells and couples disappear behind billowing sheets, might involve touching. Perhaps she wasn't trying to attack him. F13, 8A8 thought as he looked at Yoshimi bleeding on the floor, I need to get another one.

Outside, Stall and Stencil heard Yoshimi screaming. They jumped out of the reeds and recoiled from each other, because neither had known the other was there, then burst through the door of the wildcatter's shelter. They saw Yoshimi lying on the floor bleeding, the slickness of her muscle and the shock of her exposed, hewn bone. Stall went crazy and in a flurry of limbs and wood he clubbed 8A8 to pieces with a baseball bat he was carrying. Stencil's shock broke as the robot's eyes went into a disco flash, and he attacked also, stomping the ruined machine as it convulsed and vomited hydraulic fluid out of its various apertures. When 8A8 was finally still, the two men turned to Yoshimi. Her breathing was weak and blood surrounded her, creeping towards their feet, but she was still alive. They slid and slipped in her blood while they tourniquetted her limbs then lifted her and left the wildcatter's shed. They splashed through the reed beds and made it out of the salt marsh quickly, each believing Yoshimi would die before she got to safety.

She didn't. Yoshimi made it to the karato hospital, where they'd seen countless evil amputations. The karatos collected and stood in the upholstered lobby, quiet with shock, developing rumors. How could it be that a new karato, just graduated, would be in the salt marshes? And why was she by herself? Is it possible that her heroism, like her natural talent, bordered on the ridiculous? Perhaps she'd gone alone to wage a singular, passionate war, something that each karato in the circle agreed that they'd wanted to do their whole lives.

Stencil and Stall stood and listened. Neither said anything as the stories got better and better; Yoshimi fought, flipped, flew, Yoshimi the teenage hero; and the sensei got the impression that Stencil was waiting to follow his lead. But still he was quiet. What could he say? He wasn't even sure what he'd seen.

Finally Stencil clarified it. When he could no longer wait for Stall, he told the story in an arterial rush of impressions: Yoshimi had fraternized. Yoshimi had led the evil robot to the wildcatter's shelter for incomprehensible, probably impure reasons. Yoshimi had accepted a gift from the robot.

"What was it?" Bixby asked.

"A eucalyptus branch!"

The team booed. Yoshimi could hear the noise from her room. A nurse stood by her bed and flipped the pages of a thick prosthetics catalogue.

That night, Wexworth Stall went home and got drunk. He forced a happy face for his boa, but it didn't last and in a fit of rage and despair that he neither expected nor understood he strangled the boa constrictor and hung himself with its carcass. It wasn't just the tragedy of Yoshimi that brought it on; it wasn't just the bat that leaned against his glass wall, slipping again and again because of the hydraulic fluid that coated it, which had been meant as a gift for Yoshimi; it wasn't just the innocent black eyes of his boa (Bruce was his name) either. Stall suffered the realization that the robot war would change: one day the robots would develop knife-shooters or flame-throwers, and karatos would start to carry guns, the robots would develop armor and the karatos would invent radiation weapons that would warble metal where it stood, the robots would begin to fly and produce other robots that looked like babies and ticked like bombs and karatos, now defused of all karate grace and just simple soldiers, would dust off the nuclear weapons in the oil baron basements of downtown Long Beach. It made Stall tired.

Stencil, by contrast, thrived. After Stall's repticide-suicide, the young karato rose fast, always fighting the specter of his ex-classmate's perverse betrayal. He was known for his competent if unimaginative grasshopper style and he retired at the apex of his pay grade, bought a speed boat, and disappeared.

If you're much of a historian, you know that fifteen years after Stall's suicide and just before Stencil's retirement, Bigfoot monsters descended from the San Bernardino Mountains. They brought with them their ancient, imperial ambitions, and after enjoying a brief literary fame characterized by tell-alls and performance poetry, they attacked the robots. The battle was short. Apparently they knew something we did not, and the once-thriving robot city has been reduced to two double-wide mobile homes, inhabited by a family of sad, confused robots. The Bigfoot monsters, of course, attacked us shortly after their victory; as of this writing they are the worst enemy man has yet faced. In recent months they have led vicious raids on bookstores, and although psychiatrists have had trouble penetrating the motivations of their proto-simian minds, I believe it is the memory of the hollowness of literary fame that haunts them. The point here is that if you are in a bookstore now, especially a corporate one (they favor the bathroom facilities and sales displays), look around. Do you see a man who looks cagey? Is he tall, does he have shaving cream behind his ear? He is their scout. Find the largest book in the reference section and throw it at him. Run. Scream. You are in danger.

MICHAEL BUCKLEY
YOSHIMI AND THE ROBOT

REVIEW

Discussion Questions:

1. This story is a reference to a song by The Flaming Lips. Does knowledge of the song and an understanding of how the story is situated in popular cultural enhance the story?
2. Does the humor of the story enhance or undercut the message and themes of the story?
3. Why does Buckley call this "A Bedtime Story"?
4. Why are Bigfoots introduced at the end of the story?

Essay Questions:

1. How does Buckley use popular cultural references to things such as The Flaming Lips, classic horror films, and martial arts films to create a discussion of mainstream perceptions of the world?
2. Referring to at least three different stories, how do different authors in this book view the idea of isolation? Does Buckley's vision of isolation seem to be more or less dark than others'?
3. The facility where the robots are made is based on a real and very large power plant in Long Beach on the San Gabriel River. Buckley seems to be making a comment on the differences between the natural and unnatural in our world. What do his main arguments on this point seem to be?

Burying Ellie

LLOYD AQUINO

I was just sitting down to dinner for one when Ellie knocked on my apartment door, insisting that I let her in. The beef stew I'd cooked, much more stew than beef, would have to wait; I knew from the timbre of Ellie's knocks and the pitch of her voice that this was no mere stop-in. Before answering the door, I put a kettle on the stove and uncovered from among stacks of canned cheap-something-or-others two bags of jasmine tea, Ellie's favorite.

"Didn't you hear me?" A blur left the fragrance of Chanel in its wake on its way into the living room. "Was I not loud enough?"

It was an innocent question, more curious than accusatory. Still, I knew Ellie. "Not really. Hey, next time, just bring an axe. Or maybe a battering ram."

"Ha, ha," Ellie said as she glared at me from my ratty old couch. She used her thumb and index like forceps to pick up the sweater I'd left lying there, dropping it onto the floor. It was her special way of throwing down the gauntlet, but I was tired from a double dose of a double shift and a two-hour art class.

"Want some tea?"

Ellie accepted the peace offering, and when I returned from the kitchen, my sweater was sitting on the arm of the couch, neatly folded. Ellie watched as I put the tray down on my duvet, olive green to mismatch the navy blue couch, ready to pounce on the smallest misstep. But I'd made many a cup of tea for her over the years and had prepared this one perfectly. The next few minutes passed without a word, Ellie sipping from her cup, me trying to stay awake above mine.

Then Ellie said, "I think my roommate's trying to kill me."

Those words perked me right back up. For a moment, I thought I'd only imagined Ellie had said them, and was about to explore what such a fantasy said about my psyche when I realized that she was staring at me, waiting for a response.

"Come again?" I said, sitting up a little straighter.

"I said, Em, I think my roommate is trying to kill me."

"Oh-kay," I said, emphasizing both syllables, and inhaled a sigh. "Talk to me."

In the years since we'd become adults—Ellie just a year before me—we'd remained close enough to discover that the qualities we both had growing up were only amplified. There were no changes, only infinitely more of the same.

For Ellie, that meant melodrama all day, every day. Fantastic highs were inevitably followed by near-suicidal lows, every event becoming an adventure no matter how mundane. And Ellie sure knew how to weave a story, a trait that served her well as she flitted from job to job, always accumulating more gossip about the people unfortunate enough to work with her. She would regale coworkers and bosses with tales so colorful, she ought to have charged them for admission and a two drink minimum.

I was the only one who could navigate through all the fireworks and accompanying smoke to get back to level ground again, oftentimes dragging Ellie and her flights of fancy down with me.

I also knew what it was like to suffer the occasional indignity, but at least I knew how to suffer quietly. Everything Ellie did was loud. Our mother had said the same about her birth, and I predicted that someday—with any luck, in the very distant future—Ellie would meet her very voluminous end, kicking and screaming.

"Talk to me," I repeated, trying to get Ellie to focus through the tears now streaming down her face like they were on fast-forward. I glanced down at the teacup in my hand and the bowl of beef stew on the coffee table and just knew both had gone cold. The orange glow coming through my threadbare curtains had been drained to dull black.

Finally, Ellie calmed down enough to say, "She—she threatened me wi—with a knife."

My mind immediately recreated the scene, and I was too tired to stop it: an Amazon of a woman towering over Ellie, who was huddled in a corner—no, in her bed, the high thread-count of her blanket not nearly enough to protect her, and now the Amazon brandishing a machete, cackling in a voice almost too deep to be feminine—

"Go on," I said, placing my teacup down on the coffee table.

Ellie spoke fast. "We were cooking dinner the other night—build-your-own-tacos because we were having some people over—and I made a joke about refried beans, and Dee just lunged at me like a maniac."

"With a knife."

Ellie dabbed at one tear-soaked eye with her fingers. "Uh-huh."

"What was the joke?"

"What?"

I tried to get my sister to look me in the eye, but settled for staring at her scalp as she eyed the coffee table. "What did you say to Dee about the refried beans, Ellie?"

"All I said," Ellie explained, rearranging the bills and junk mail that had been piling up for the last few weeks and were now threatening to topple over onto her teacup, "was maybe she should think twice before having some, especially if she wanted to impress the guys coming over. Unless she thought they'd find explosive flatulence impressive."

"Oh, Ellie."

"What? It's my fault she's so sensitive? Everyone knows I'm a kidder, Em."

"What was she doing when you said this?"

"Chopping up lettuce."

"Ellie, did she really attack you with a knife?"

"Why would I lie about something like that?"

"Ellie."

"Okay, then, tell me if you believe this."

Rolling up one sleeve, Ellie showed me her forearm and the thin red cut running down the middle of her forearm, stretching from her wrist to an inch or two below.

"Sweet fucking Jesus," I breathed, leaning over the coffee table to get a closer look.

"Language, Em." Ellie rolled her eyes at me and sighed.

"Sorry. But, seriously, what the fuck?" I reached out to take her arm, then stopped myself. The cut looked bad enough without my fumbling grip to upset it.

"Is it bad?" Ellie asked.

As I replied, I noticed that my sister was no longer crying. In fact, it looked like her eyes were damn near twinkling. I tried to convince myself I was just imagining things. "El, this looks pretty serious." I was being honest. Regardless of what had happened, whatever had led to the serious cut I was looking at, it definitely wasn't good. "You swear your roommate did this to you?"

"Jesus Christ, Em," Ellie shot back. "Why would I make something like that up?"

I could think of more than a few reasons, but saying any of them out loud wasn't going to make this conversation any easier. I sighed. "Okay. I believe you. So what do we do about it?"

"I'm glad you asked," she said, and as she stood and paced back and forth, hands flitting about excitedly as she spoke, I got a sinking feeling in the pit of my stomach. "I'm thinking Dee wouldn't dare try anything if there were another person in the condo. An eyewitness. I want you to come over to the house. Tonight."

"I don't know," was all I said. The sinking feeling had now grown to roughly the size of a black hole. "Why don't you just, you know, stay here?"

The nervous chuckle to punctuate the question was certain to convince her. Almost certain.

An hour later, after enduring Ellie's endless makeover tips and general hen-pecking, I got out of her Audi, dragging an overnight bag with me, and followed her up the stairs to her second-floor condo, just off Beverly. I could hear Belle and Sebastian playing on someone's stereo, and the sound was getting closer. It was either that or the sounds of the late night crowd at the Tommy's on Rampart, just down the street, that set me off.

Ever had a panic attack? Where you start hyperventilating, just keep leaking the air you're sucking in? Try that while walking up a flight of stairs. Let's just say I don't do well in most social situations.

Ellie must have noticed I wasn't right behind her. She gave me a look, like I was somehow shaming her and the family name. "Jesus Christ, Em. What's wrong now?"

"Nothing." I didn't look her in the eye for a second, then a thought occurred to me. Shooting her a glare, I said, "You could've told me you were throwing a party."

She rolled her eyes and clacked her tongue. "It's just a few friends from work, you big baby." She put both hands on her hips. "Look, you promised you'd help me do something about my psycho axe-murderer roommate."

I was about to retort that I'd said no such thing, but that's when she yanked me by the arm and pulled me up the rest of the way, taking all the indignant wind out of me. Before I knew it, we were standing in front of her condo.

She still wouldn't let go of my arm, and my mind flashed back to a random memory: being scolded by my mother when I was six for running around the house with scissors. Actually, more accurately, I had been chasing Ellie around with scissors. I smiled.

Ellie's corresponding frown melted away quickly. "All right, here's the plan." She snapped her fingers at my face to get my attention. I wiped the smile off my face. "I'll distract Dee while you sneak into her room and find, I don't know, in-criminating evidence or whatever."

"Yeah, no," I said, certain that Ellie was just repeating something she'd half-heard on one of those *CSI* shows. "I'm not doing that. That's stupid."

Ellie blinked once, twice, a dozen times. I wiped the smile back onto my face.

"Why do you insist on being so difficult?" Ellie said, and I swear to God, her eyes started to well up with tears. "What if she kills me in my sleep? I just hope you don't make stupid jokes at my wake."

"Oh, great, guilt tripping," I said, deadpan, but a second later I found myself waving my hands for Ellie to continue.

Surprisingly, she recovered from the metaphorical knife I'd apparently stuck in her back without too much trouble. "Okay," she said, clapping her hands, "new plan: just follow her and make sure she doesn't get anywhere near me. Sound good?" It didn't at first, but then I realized that meant I wouldn't have to stay anywhere near Ellie, either. "Deal," I blurted out, grabbing Ellie's hand and shaking it vigorously.

Before opening the door, Ellie gave me a wary look.

Then the door opened, and all my senses failed. Or rather, they were overloaded and broke down. Faces. Faces everywhere. Shoegazing music. But loud. Too loud. Strobe lights. Why strobe lights? Alcohol. Red cups.

Danger. Danger. Danger.

I was vaguely aware of gritting my teeth through the endless procession of shouted introductions, unfamiliar hands reaching out at me. I nearly cracked a molar as Ellie's nails dug into my arm where she had been holding me, like a prison guard making sure her prisoner didn't try anything funny. The swarm of people practically parted as Ellie's roommate approached. I had just enough time to register her black hair that hung over her shoulders in stylish curls, the pink shift she wore with a white flower sewn to one shoulder, and the greenest eyes I've ever seen before Dee was upon us. We'd only met once or twice, very briefly, so the smile of recognition she gave me sent a sensation up the back of my neck.

"Hey," she said.

"What is up?" I replied, waving weakly with a withered claw.

Dee snorted, and even through the fear-induced fog, I could feel a twinge of annoyance pinball inside me.

Ellie fake-laughed beside me. "Hi, Dee," she said, her voice so thick it was practically dripping from her lips. "Okay, everyone, back away and give Em some space."

She pantomimed pushing everyone aside, and they all obeyed, even Dee. Then Ellie yanked me back towards the front door. "What the hell is wrong with you?" she whispered at me.

I wanted to punch her and run out of the condo, screaming. But that would probably look bad. "I want to go home and throw up."

"Here," she said, thrusting a plastic red cup into my hand. "Drink. Now," she added, sharp enough to force the cup to my lips. I swallowed, then felt my body relax in the wake of that awful taste.

"What is this?"

Ellie smiled. "Courage juice. Be strong, little sister."

And she disappeared into the swarm of party guests.

I spent the next hour tailing my sister's roommate, trying to decide whether or not she fit the profile of a homicidal maniac. One time, I watched her standing next to the hallway that connected the living room to the rest of the condo, doing her best wallflower impression as people eased past her to get to the bathroom. Experts say that it's the quiet ones you have to watch out for. So there was that.

Another time, I saw her somehow holding three conversations with five different people at once. And she was damn good at it, too, the proverbial center of attention. Experts say that sociopaths are exceptionally charming.

My conclusion: the experts are idiots.

The truth was I was having a hard time getting any kind of impression of Dee, my sister's maybe-would-be-killer. Maybe it was the strobe lights. They hurt my eyes and made my chest feel all stabby. It might have also been the alcohol. I had taken to sipping whenever Dee looked even remotely in my direction—kind of like a drinking game, now that I think about it. I'd lost count of how many of those plastic red cups I'd swallowed, and now the world was spinning all pretty.

Those two factors might have played an integral role in my losing track of Dee, I'll grant you, but with the benefit of 20/20 hindsight and the clarity of sobriety, I'm going to blame Ellie's friends.

It started with CeCe, Ellie's coworker at Forever 21, stumbling over to where I was standing next to the rubber fern between picture frames and asking, the lethal combination of alcohol vomit and cherry red lipstick wax pouring out of her mouth, "Is it true you called our store Ex-Ex-Eye Forever?"

To my credit, I knew how to deftly deflect such an asinine question.

"Huh? Get away from my face! You smell like poopy breath."

Thus, I strode away, head held high.

And fell face-first into Ellie's leather couch. It was sticky. I heard girlish tittering as I picked myself up, slapping away the helpful hands that came out of nowhere, and when I looked up, I could see Dee and her fellow conversationalists covering their mouths. Bitches.

A couple of someones whose faces I couldn't make out gasped nearby. That's when I realized I'd said the word out loud.

More laughter. Uproarious. High-larious.

I retreated into the hallway, groping in the stuttering dark—those motherfucking piece-of-shit strobe lights—for the bathroom door. It was locked. And, apparently, there was a line of disgruntled would-be patrons, one of whom tapped me on the shoulder.

"What?" I could hear my voice echo off what I knew were Ellie's pink hallway walls. It sounded like evil.

Not that that phased the mouth-breather facing me one bit. He looked half-baked out of his brain. "You're Ellie's kid sister, right?"

"Fuck off."

"All right," he said, nodding like the Grateful Dead was playing in the next room. "I heard you beat the shit out of your math teacher. Bad-fucking-ass, man."

"Go to hell, *ma'am*," I shot back. I shoved my way back towards the living room, sending anyone in my way bouncing off those fucking pink walls with a satisfying *thunk*. I caught a glimpse of jet black hair and pink dress but kept on moving. All I'd wanted was a semi-quiet space so that I could collect myself, but now I wanted something else. Blood. And I wanted it now.

It was Teddy—T-Dog, as he preferred to have others call him—that helped me make up my mind. Teddy was a "friend" from the old neighborhood who'd transplanted himself to Los Angeles around the same time Ellie and I moved here after high school. You could say he "followed" Ellie and that he was "stalking" her; I wouldn't disagree. But although Teddy was an asshole, he was harmless.

So when he stopped me on my way to the kitchen and said, "Are you okay?" I had to stop.

"No touchie," I said, swatting at hands that never came.

"Easy, babe," he said. "T-Dog's got you."

I nearly slapped him. "What did you say?"

"C'mon," he said, all slime and thinly-veiled innuendo. "We've all heard the stories. Let T-Dog take care of you."

Now I did slap him. Three times. Maybe more. By the time I walked away, he was a cowering, huddled mass on the floor. I left him there, and a part of me felt guilty. Like I said, Teddy was harmless. He didn't deserve to be humiliated like that.

But another, much bigger part of me dismissed that thought. As I passed through the condo and found my way into the kitchen, all I could think of were my sister's pretty face and the color red.

Ellie and Kay, Ellie's current BFF, didn't hear me walk in. They just kept on sitting with their backs to me, picking at two plates of some kind of salad. And talking.

"I'm not going to set her up," Ellie was saying. "I don't care how much you keep bugging me about it."

"I'm just saying every time I've seen her lately, she's riding solo." Kay picked up an olive, but didn't put it in her mouth. "It's not normal."

"Yeah, well, that's Emma for you."

They were talking about me. I could feel my face burning.

Then Kay said, "Standing offer: I can set up your sister with my boss's niece anytime. One quick phone call and we'll get little Emma good and laid."

That's when I snapped.

One other difference between Ellie and me is how we express our emotions. Ellie's all knee-jerk while I'm blueprints. Ellie's hot; I run cold. Ellie's animal instinct. I'm a fucking machine.

So when I picked up the giant knife sitting by the sink, I knew exactly what I was planning to do with it. The voice in my head started speaking right then. *Open up. Just open up.* It spoke slowly, seductively as I inched towards my sister, still deep in conversation with Kay, still completely ignorant to my presence.

Rip. Tear. Rip. Tear.

The knife felt good in my hand. It felt right.

Open up. Just open up.

So I did.

The knife went in faster than I expected, cutting a near-perfect line as I dragged it downward. If there was a sound, I didn't hear it.

Whenever I hear someone talk about blacking out while doing something horrible, I always want to call bullshit. Then again, I don't remember pulling the knife back out. I don't remember the scream.

What I remember is the look on Ellie's face when I dumped all the contents of a ripped-open trash bag all over her. What I remember is the open-mouthed silence. It was beautiful.

I didn't even give Ellie a chance to get the first word in. "I can't fucking believe I let you convince me to come to your stupid-ass party with your stupid-ass friends just so they could—"

There were still some bits of trash, mostly paper plates of half-finished chips and guacamole, so I shook them free to make sure they found their way atop my sweet sister's head.

"—all gawk at Ellie's weirdo sister live and in the flesh, and don't you dare say you're telling Mom because—"

I took out my phone and took a picture of Ellie in all her trashy, drippy glory.

"—I will post the shit out of this." I became aware that I was holding a giant knife in one hand, my phone in the other, so I made my eyes cartoon-big and made my voice a low growl. "Just go ahead and try me."

Ellie stared, frozen.

When I left her condo a few seconds later, I walked out with all the calm of a Sunday drive. And I was still carrying the knife with me. People gave me a wide berth.

It wasn't until I'd walked a block's distance that I remembered Ellie had been my ride. "Shit," I muttered to myself, half turning back in the direction of the complex. I could still hear the strains of ceaseless chatter over faint indie rock. I really didn't want to go back there, not unless it was to demand Ellie's keys at knifepoint.

I was contemplating the merits of that approach when a string of headlights cruised past me. When I turned my attention back towards the complex, Dee was standing there. Watching me.

Neither of us said a word for a while.

Then she said, "Huh."

"What?" I said, practically baring my teeth at her.

She took a half-step back and held her hands up. They were, in fact, empty. "Nothing. It's just the way El talked about you, I was expecting you to be a mess of a puddle."

She reached into her jacket pocket and showed me a little packet of Kleenex.

"Huh," I said. "I'm going to take a walk around the block. You can join me if you want."

"Sure." The suddenness of her response surprised me a little. "But only if you put down the knife."

I looked down at the sharp object in my fist. "Oh."

"Yeah. It's no big deal. I'm just allergic to stainless steel is all."

Dee pushed a few strands of hairs out of her face and smiled, and I smiled back. I tossed the knife into a dumpster butted against the side of the complex, and we walked and talked, mostly about Ellie's party at first, then, as we found our route gravitating towards an empty but well-lit community park, about Ellie.

"How can you stand living with her?" I asked as we passed a fenced-in pool that glowed aqua blue.

Dee snorted and kicked aside a pine cone in her path. "You tell me. You had to do it for much longer, right?"

I followed after the skittering pine cone and gave it the stiffest kick I could. It felt good to watch it fly off into the darkness. "Well, yeah," I said, coming back to the path, "but that's because we share the same blood, and for reasons I won't even pretend to understand, that's supposed to mean something."

I saw Dee hide her mouth behind her hand, not enough to hide upward-curving lips and a hint of teeth. "Do you have something you'd like to share with the rest of the class?" I asked.

"No," Dee said. Then she burst out laughing.

And didn't stop for a long while. I looked on, trying to hold on to the lump of annoyance I could feel in my gut, folding my arms, trying my hardest not to join in. At least one of us was having a good time.

When Dee had calmed down enough, I said, "What's so funny?"

"Methinks thou dost protest too much, fair lady," Dee said, curtseying.

I frowned, folded my arms even tighter. Was this bitch admonishing me by quoting Shakespeare?

At least Dee seemed to notice my discomfort. Her face and voice softened. "Sorry. It's just—" She paused to consider her next few words. "You sound like you wish you or she were adopted, but I noticed how protective of her you were at the party." She stopped, glancing off to where a brick wall separated the park from some condos. All we could see from where we were standing were the rooftops, but Dee moved off the path and started walking through the grass. As I followed her, she added, "You know, before you turned her into a walking garbage pile."

I tried to suppress a smile as the image of Ellie, open-mouthed and frozen, came to mind again. I did so enjoy seeing my big sister suffering. That's what little sisters are for, right? It didn't mean that I cared about Ellie and her ridiculous get-togethers and way-too-expensive clothes and especially her exasperating oh-woe-is-me attitude. She was just someone I had to tolerate being related to. I tried to scoff away Dee's insinuation.

"I mean, that's why you were following me around, right?" Dee asked, quickening her pace a little towards that brick wall.

"I was trying to be inconspicuous," was all I could muster as I tried to keep up.

"Well," Dee said, turning her head and letting that jet black hair toss like a curtain, "you kind of suck at it."

Before I could stop myself, I snapped back, "Or else you're really paranoid. The world doesn't revolve around you, you know."

Dee barely had time to react—already she looked like she'd been gutshot—before I was saying, "I'm so sorry. I'm still pissed at my sister. I shouldn't take it out on you like that."

To my relief, Dee relaxed, letting her shoulders slacken. "It's okay. I understand."

"Do you have an older sister?"

"Three."

"Ouch." I winced. "Condolences."

She just smiled and pushed the hair out of her face again. She did that a lot.

As we reached the wall, I felt my sneakers kick up against something round. Looking down, I saw that the grass was littered with blood oranges. Right on cue, Dee gestured at the tree from which said oranges had fallen and said, "The owners don't care if people take them."

We spent the next few minutes picking the best blood oranges, leaving behind their lesser brethren. I took three oranges and started juggling.

Dee tilted her head, which made her smile look a little lopsided. "You can juggle?"

"I've been known to juggle," I said, nonchalant as can be. I started walking, keeping the three oranges moving in perfect rhythm. When Dee started clapping, I tossed each orange high in the air and caught them in the lapels of my skirt one after the other.

We kept walking across the grass, which was slick and cool, towards a small playground set in a pit of sand.

"So," I said, tossing Dee the blood orange as if it were a softball, "did you really try to murder my sister?"

Dee caught the blood orange in one hand and, as she crushed it and let the juices spill down the length of her forearm to stain the playground sand, said, "Yes. And the bitch deserved it."

I wouldn't be surprised if our laughter woke up the city.

So that's how I stole my sister's roommate. Dee moved in a month later. And I didn't regret it once, not even the morning when I woke up to see Dee standing over me, wearing a Raggedy Ann apron that was two sizes too small and smeared with what looked like blood, holding a knife directly above the space between my eyes.

A ring was wedged over the knife's edge.

Of course I said yes.

A few of the stories Ellie tells about me are true.

Of course, these days, she's always happy to tell anyone who'll listen the story of how she helped her inept little sister find the love of her life. I let her. I'd never say it to her face, but she tells it pretty well.

But I always make sure she includes the part about the garbage bag. After all, it's my second favorite part of the story.

REVIEW

Discussion Questions:

1. How does the voice of the narrator help to develop the story? How does it help to develop the character?
2. How are the sisters different?
3. To what degree is Ellie's falseness mirrored in Emma?
4. To what degree can we trust the narrator's assessment of what happens in the story?

Essay Questions:

1. Compare this story to Stephanie Barbé Hammer's "Encore Plus." What are the two authors suggesting about the way women deal with body image? You might carefully note the last line of Hammer's story.
2. "Burying Ellie" explores the theme of sexual identity. Analyze the characters' attitudes towards sex and sexual orientation.
3. Ellie is the protagonist of this story, but to what degree is she the hero of the story?

Elsewhere, California

DANA JOHNSON

Summer *way* sucks if you're working. But at least I have some money saved. I haven't spent that much of it. I only saw *The Blue Lagoon*, *Fame*, and *My Bodyguard*, and then I bought a pair of black Dickies and some red jellies. Still, though, if you're not working and after you've bought a bunch of stuff and saw some movies, it gets to be boring. You end up just staring out the window sometimes. Dad's mowing the lawn. Come here, Ave, he says. You want to go to a game tomorrow? Double-header on Sunday? He says, You and Keith been working hard. Me too. Everybody needs a break. He's got five tickets. One for him, and then tickets for me, Brenna and Keith. Mom won't go. She never goes. And she's not talking to Dad anyhow. There's some other woman calling the house and hanging up now. So there's one more left. Carlos. I want to bring Carlos.

Dad stops pushing the mower and leans on it. Who is Carlos?

I can tell by the way he's asking me that he thinks Carlos is somebody who wants to make out with me or something. I wish. Yeah Dad. Carlos has ulterior motives. I drive him mad with desire. I go, He's just a friend at school. He's nice.

He Mexican?

Yeah, I say. He's Mexican.

Dad stares down at the grass. There's this one patch that's a perfect triangle. It's the only piece left. He looks at me with one of his eyebrows raised. What kind of people are his family?

I bite my nails for a second. I don't even know what kind of question that is. I think. *Kind of people*. I know what Dad is asking me, but I guess I'm just wondering how should I know? I only met his sister once and she was mega awesome. So.

Dad says, He not one of them cholos, is he?

Dad, I say. I don't know. Why would he be a cholo?

The thing is, he is kind of a cholo, but I think cholos are cool and I don't want to get into a whole thing about it because Dad always thinks he's right about everything, so don't even try.

I'm not saying he is, Dad says. I'm just asking if he is. Because you don't need to be running around with people driving around in cars and doing whatever it is they're doing.

I wish. I wish I could ride around in Carlos sister's glitter green car listening to oldies. But I just say, Dad. He's really nice. You can see for yourself. If he comes to the game.

All right then, Dad says. He can come if he want to.

I go to Carlos's house that day and ask him. I know where he lives because I followed him home one day. He's watering the lawn, when I get to his house, standing in tan cut-off Dickies and a white T-shirt. I go, I got a ticket to the Dodgers tomorrow. Want to come? He goes, For real, Avery Day? Don't play girl. And I know he's coming. He doesn't say yes or no, that's all he says. And I'm so nervous about the game today. I figure out an outfit to wear. Tan Dickies that are going to be pressed straight down the middle. Cuffs sharp like blades. My blue Sassoon polo shirt and my green jellies. I can't go full-on cholo because dad will have a cow. But it's close. It's my version.

Nice threads, Brenna says when she sees me. I'm so confused, she says. That outfit is confused.

But *I* put it together with the parts that *I* wanted. I'm not confused. Carlos is riding up front with Dad and all I can think of is I hate our car. It's crap. It used to be green, but now it's brown and yellow and green. And it's trashed inside. Dad's a maniac about a clean house, everything has to be spotless all the time. But his car. Man. Newspapers everywhere, books, Kentucky Fried Chicken wrappers. Jack in the Box. And the lining on the roof of the car is torn so it's hanging down in the middle of the back seat. Also, Dad never fixed that piece of metal that sticks out of the passenger side door and sliced my ankle open last summer. Keith and Brenna don't care anything about how the car looks, but I'm sorry. It's embarrassing. After I know Carlos has noticed the three different colors on our car, and the trash in it everywhere, when Carlos is getting into the car, I have to tell him, Carlos. Watch your leg. That metal thing can cut you. And then I want to kill myself.

It's cool, Avery Day, he says. My dad drives a bucket too. Yeah, I think, maybe. But at least your sister doesn't.

Dad turns up the radio so he doesn't have to talk to Carlos. This is what he always does when somebody's in the front seat with him and he doesn't feel like talking. Vin Scully and Jerry Doggett are announcing. Bobby Castillo is pitching today. I'm sitting in the back behind Carlos. Keith and Brenna are sitting together, of course. I lean forward and look at the shiny tip of Carlos's ear. If I kissed it, Dad would never even know, and Carlos would maybe think it was on accident, since I had to lean in to talk to him. But I'm chicken. He'd probably turn around and say Avery Day what up with you? I stare and stare at his ear, all shiny and brown with just a little red underneath. I say, I miss Sutton. Last time I saw him pitch he was on fire!

That's right, Dad says. He likes Sutton. Sutton's his man. But now he's always talking about a player named Valenzuela. Dad says that dude is bad and we're going to see a lot more of him, watch and see.

But Carlos is stuck on Sutton. So why you like Sutton better Mr. Arlington? Carlos asks. He totally scores points for just adding Mr. Arlington at the end of that sentence.

Well, Dad says slow.

No! I know that when he says *well* all slow we're going to get a long-ass story. He turns down Scully and Doggett. Oh no. Here we go.

He says, Sutton comes from *nothing*. And I mean nothing. A tarpaper shack. You all know what a tarpaper shack is? Oh no! We're getting ready to get a definition, *too*. Somebody just say they know what it is so we can move on. But Dad's got the definition ready. He goes, Tarpaper is just paper that's got tar in it. It's tough. But you think it's tough enough to keep the wind and cold away from you? You think it works as good as a real wall?

Nobody says anything.

Sutton is a hardworking dude, Dad says. Hasn't missed an opening yet, not cause he's sick, not cause he's hurt, not cause of nothing.

Okay Dad, I'm thinking.

And let me tell you something else. He was telling the truth when he let everybody know that Reggie Smith is the money on that team, not that pretty boy Steve Garvey. Smith work hard like Sutton. Born on the same day, Sutton and Smith. Bet ya'll didn't know that.

Brenna looks at me and rolls her eyes. Like this even has anything to do with baseball, she says low, so Dad won't hear her. But I totally get it. Dad hates lazy asses and people who get other people's credit just for looking like they ought to. Everybody thinks Garvey and Cyndi are all perfect and pretty. But they actually are to me, though. I don't tell Dad that.

All American, Dad says. Folks don't know what American is if it's just gone be some dude with a pretty face.

Nobody can say anything until Dad is done with this whole Sutton thing. And I'm sorry, but Steve Garvey happens to be a fox *and* a good first baseman, so why blame him for anything? Like it's his fault people like him.

Dad turns up the radio, so he's done with all that anyway.

Traffic is slowing down and we're almost to the stadium. It only takes about 45 minutes from home and then you're eating a Dodger Dog and peanuts. You can always tell when you're almost there, because of the old wooden houses with their paint peeling off on the right side of the freeway. White houses with blue paint underneath or a red house with yellow underneath or a green house with brown underneath, right in the middle of apartments too. Bars on all the windows. I like those old houses because they don't seem to fit where they are, right next to the freeway, looking like they're from a million years ago or someplace else that's not L.A., like Cape Cod. I don't even know what Cape Cod is, exactly, but that's what those houses seem like they are.

Then I hear something that sounds like it fell off the car.

What's that noise? Keith says.

Yeah, Brenna says. She sits up straight. Turns around to look out the back window like she's looking for something behind us in the road. The car is coughing and then there's a rattle. Our eyes are all big and Dad eases off to the side of the freeway. Then, the car just stops. Dad turns the key but the car just screams without moving.

Dad says, Shit. He gets out the car and opens the hood and we all sit in the car watching other people get to the stadium.

Rad, Brenna says. Really. This is awesome. Great ball game.

Keith slides down in his seat. I don't care if we get to the game or not he says. I'd rather play than watch these other fools play. But Carlos is bumming like me. He turns around in the front seat so he can shake his head at me. Avery Day, he says. *Man.*

Dad leans into our side of the car. Y'all might as well get out the car. It's hotter in there than it is out here. He takes his Dodger cap off so he can wipe his head and then he puts it back on. Bring the radio so you can listen to the game while you're out here. Let me try to figure out what's wrong with this car.

We all get out the car and sit on the freeway ramp. Carlos has the radio and turns it up as loud as it will go. It's still hard to hear, though, because of all the cars, and the game is going to start in like five minutes. We're going to miss the beginning of the game I say. I kick a smashed Burger King cup that's by my feet.

Einstein, Brenna says. Does it even look like we're going to make it to the game? Call your chauffeur, why don't you. Tell him to pick us up.

Yeah, Keith says. He puts his hand on top of Brenna's. Tell him to have some refreshments waiting for our asses, too.

Shut up, eh, Carlos says. He's got the radio up to his ear. I can barely hear the game, he says.

BFD, Brenna says and Keith gives her a kiss on the cheek but only because Dad's head is under the hood and can't see us. They better watch it. They totally better watch it.

Now there's a truck pulling up behind Dad. A rusted-out truck that looks even crappier than our car. It's a Fix Or Repair Daily. A Ford. A man gets out. We all stare at the guy. Even Carlos stops listening to the game. The man's kind of crazy looking. A long ZZ Top beard. A t-shirt that's got stains all over the chest like he just wipes his hands on it all day long. He says something to a little girl sitting in the front and then gets out of the car. His belly's sticking out from underneath the shirt and he keeps pulling up his jeans. He's got a long blonde ponytail sticking out the back of his Dodgers cap. He ignores us and goes straight to Dad. It's Avery's husband, Keith says. Moron.

Hey man, the fat dude says to Dad. What's wrong with your car?

Don't know, Dad says. Can't figure it out. They both take off their caps and stand with their hands on their hips. They stare at the car. Let me check it out, the man says. He's not under it long. Can't tell what's going on, he says. Well, Dad says.

You going to the game? the man says.

We was, Dad says.

I'll give you a lift in my truck, the guys says.

Dad looks at him, thinking about him, I can tell. Dad looks at all of us sitting on the side of the freeway. Brenna leans into me and whispers, Total serial killer.

Yeah, Dad says. I'd appreciate that ride.

Yes! We are going to make the game. That's all I care about. We all get in the truck and the man puts the kid in back with us so Dad can sit in the front. She's scared of us since she's so little. She stares at us with her mouth open and holds on to this baseball like we're going to grab it from her. Keith pretends he's going to steal it. No! she screams and we all laugh. It's pretty funny. A Dodger's going to sign it, she says.

What's your name, kid, Brenna says.

Monica. Her blonde hair is swirling all around her face from the wind. She holds her ball up. Like her name's on it or something.

Which Dodger's going to sign? I ask her.

She stands up and almost falls back down because the truck's moving. She turns around so we can see her shirt. Scioscia. Nice.

Hey, Brenna says. Sit down kid before you bust your ass.

She listens to Brenna and sits down holding on to that ball real tight.

Carlos isn't paying attention to the kid. He's listening to the radio. His head is bent close to the radio and his black shiny hair looks like it's got blue in it, it's so black. I love you Carlos, I want to make out with you so bad. Hopelessly devoted to you. I'm going to totally transform myself, for reals. Not halfway like today. And then you're going to be way into me.

I pull the radio from Carlos. They start? I put my ear to it. What's this? I frown but I don't mean to. All I hear is in Spanish.

Yeah, foo. Jaime Jarrin mo fo. Carlos winks at me. You like Scully, he says. I like Jaime.

I pass the radio back to him. Well tell me what's happening, at least.

He holds his finger up. Lopes at bat, he says. He hits real good off of Steve Rogers. He keeps his finger up to tell me to be quiet. Yes! he says and smiles real big. What I tell you Avery Day? Base hit. He's on first now.

Keith and Brenna don't even ask about the game. They don't even try to act like they're not into each other. They sit there holding hands and talking to each other. They better not let Dad see them, I swear to God.

We are at the stadium now. Finally. The man parks his truck and we all jump out. Brenna helps the kid out and holds her hand until the man takes her. Dad shakes the dude's hand. I really do appreciate the ride, Dad says. The guy goes, Nah. Glad to do it. He's holding the little girl's hand and he picks her up, puts her on his shoulders. Double-header with this one, he says. He pulls on her foot and she laughs. I thought I wanted a boy, the man says, but old Monica's all right. For now. He smiles real big when he says that, and he's got the whitest most perfect teeth. How did he get those teeth? He looks at all of us. Enjoy the game, he says, and then he walks off with the kid on his shoulders. Hurry up, Dad says. Come on, ya'll.

But what are we going to do about the car, Dad?

Don't worry about it, he says. We'll get towed home. Cost a damn fortune but it was gone cost a fortune whether or not we see the game. May as well get our money's worth. We done drove all this way. Keith and them walk in front of us, like they even know where they're going. They don't know the stadium.

I ask Dad. Who was that guy?

I don't know. Nice fella, though.

I mean, you didn't even get his name?

I didn't ask, Dad says. Don't matter no how. Looked a little rough, but he was just as nice as he could be. Dad looks at my hands. Who's got the radio?

Carlos, I say.

Good, Dad says. He squints at Carlos's back like he's trying to see him even though he's right in front of us.

Something just happened because the whole stadium is cheering. I love hearing that sound, a whole bunch of people sounding like they all agree that whatever's happening is the best possible thing for everybody here.

DANA JOHNSON
ELSEWHERE, CALIFORNIA

Discussion Questions:

1. Dana Johnson uses a strong and specific voice in this short story. How does the voice, specifically the word choice, help us to understand who the character is?
2. What is the narrator's father's concern about Carlos entering his daughter's life?
3. The narrator's father has a long discussion about Sutton's work ethic that frustrates the narrator. What is the point of this discussion from the father's point of view?

Essay Questions:

1. Compare and contrast the voice of the narrator in Dana Johnson's excerpt to the voice of the narrator in Marcielle Brandler's story.
2. How does the last line of the piece, "I love hearing that sound, a whole bunch of people sounding like they all agree that whatever's happening is the best possible thing for everybody here" help us to understand theme of the entire work?

Preparing to Photograph My Grandparents

PAUL KAREEM TAYYAR

I

We would walk all over the city, his decades as a downtown surveyor providing an anecdote for every area we passed through, every street sign whose name I read aloud, every intersection we stopped at, waiting for the light to turn.

"I met your grandmother for our first date right here," he said, looking up at the *1932 Summer Olympics* sign that rose above rickety stadium seats and a filled-in pool.

"You took her swimming on her first date?"

"Across the street," he answered, laughing. "There used to be a restaurant."

"We traveled with security when we re-paved this street. The Manson trials were going on, and some of the family would show us the newspapers on their way into the courthouse, pointing out their faces in the grainy photographs that ran on the front pages. Death threats everywhere."

"Why did our family go to the courthouse?"

"No. The Manson Family. They were murderers. Crazies."

"Humphrey Bogart lived here. He used to wave to us as he pulled out of his driveway. Always had a cigarette in his mouth."

"This was a USO dance hall back during the war."

"Were the nurses pretty?"

"They had nothing on your grandmother."

The streets of Exposition Park, its failing football stadium that the *Raiders* would soon abandon, the billboards advertising the *Lakers* and the *Dodgers* and the *Trojans*, the buses never running on time.

The streets of downtown Los Angeles, the courthouse in need of a paint job, the *Re-Elect Bradley* placards attached to the streetlights and placed in barber-shop windows, the pretty women in business suits and the gray-haired men carrying attaché cases, the smell of gasoline and the sounds of Teddy Pendergrass and Prince sidling out of open car windows.

The streets of South Pasadena with their Old Hollywood estates, their art deco bridges, their guard dogs growling from behind black gates.

The Miracle Mile, the Fabulous Forum, the pony rides in Griffith Park, the games of HORSE at the public courts next to the City Reservoir.

We walked all over the city, his voice in 4/4 time his only submission to modernity—his flannel shirts in the middle of summer, his cowboy hats, his black boots all vestiges of some lost West where WWII had just ended, where Jackie Robinson came to the coast with the rest of the Brooklyn squad, where Gary Cooper was still king.

II

A lost West where my grandmother was thirty-one years old, pregnant with my mother, her unborn child pushing her above one hundred and ten on the bathroom scale for the first time in her life.

She bought those shirts for him. Those hats and boots too. She'd rub sunscreen on his nose before we'd head out on our walks. She'd pack our lunches. She'd pass the afternoons with a jigsaw puzzle, with a rerun of *Perry Mason*, with a biography of John Kennedy, with a roast in the oven we'd devour when we returned.

She was so good I was certain she'd invented solitaire, the sewing machine, the ability to cut through the chaff of the National Convention speeches to tell me what was what. She should have been a baseball analyst if not a mother, a television script writer, a voter on the board of decency for American Film, a regional historian for her Ohio hometown.

"Your mother is right to hate Reagan."

"Your father was lucky to have left Iran when he did."

"Mayor Bradley has his hands tied."

"The South should be ashamed of itself for leaving the Democratic Party."

"Johnson did the right thing."

"Dukakis has no chance."

"Edward Kennedy is still a good man."

"Hersheiser is no Koufax."

"Valenzuela's throwing motion is going to cut into his prime."

"*Magnum, P.I.* is first-rate *Streets of San Francisco*."

"*Ironside* is second-rate *Perry Mason*."

"They could have made that movie without all of the cursing."

"My mother fed everyone who came to our door, black or white."

"My aunt owned the one pair of scissors in three neighboring counties."

"Your parents are lucky to have you."

If he was a man of the streets, comfortable only when he was walking, talking, searching for stray cans to return for a few cents or a discarded switchblade he could add to his collection, she was his opposite.

The inside of that house *happened*, it vibrated, its photographs rattled from their perches even when there had been no earthquake.

He'd get my knees dirty encouraging me to dive for the ball when we were playing one-on-one to twenty-one on the basketball court.

She would wash the dirt away.

When I wore shorts on our hike to the Catholic Cross at the top of Pasadena Hill, he carried me the last quarter mile when my legs began to itch from the tall grass.

She covered the itches with a bar of rough soap and some calamine lotion when we returned.

He led her around the square dance floor. She knew the places where the dances were held.

I helped him load the food she had bought for the down-on-their-luck living in the SROs a few blocks south of the Civic Center.

They voted Democrat, he liked Sinatra, she tolerated Bob Hope.

They loved the *Lakers*, they liked the *Dodgers*, they rooted for the *Trojans*, they felt nothing for the *Bruins*. The *Angels* were too Disney, the *Rams* were losers, the *Raiders'* owner was nuts.

They buried their third child in a cemetery off the 710 Freeway when she died of a hole in her heart when she was three months old.

"There was nothing we could do," he said.

"Six months later they invented the surgery that would have saved her life," she said.

III

It's like photographing the earth from space. The dignity of oceans in the way they lean their heads towards each other, the white flair of clouds threaded like skin over spirits, the blue hum of sky a song whose melody one can't hear through distance, the lens swallowing history into stilled narrative, impervious to dreaming sound.

REVIEW

Discussion Questions:

1. What kind of relationship does the narrator of "Preparing to Photograph My Grandparents" have with his grandparents?
2. What kind of clues does the narrator give as to the sort of people his grandparents are and the philosophical stances they take? How would you describe his grandparents?
3. Explain the simile in the last paragraph of the story.

Essay Questions:

1. Chances are that you do not understand all of the popular culture references throughout the story. Is this story meant to be read by the few people who can understand them, or are you able to gain meaning even though you cannot fully understand what he is talking about?
2. Compare and contrast the writing style, especially as it relates to the way the idea of memories are relayed in "Preparing to Photograph My Grandparents" and Grant Hier's three vignettes.

Lifestyle

STEPHEN JAY SCHWARTZ

"Why play in a mansion in Woodland Hills when you can play in a mansion in Beverly Hills?" The advertisement on the Lifestyle home page said it all. Tyson and Cassie Cooper attended parties at both locations and they couldn't complain about either one. But the ad had a point; the house in Beverly Hills was a classic movie star mansion with imposing Greek columns and a cherry oak deck that extended off the second-story master bedroom, hovering like a magic carpet over the glimmering lights of Hollywood and downtown Los Angeles. The last time they were there, Tyson fucked his wife over the balcony railing while two dozen couples whirled on a great master bed behind them, tumbling onto arabesque ottomans and silk cushions that saved their soft white, black, yellow, and brown skin from the burn of the tight, berber carpet.

The Beverly Hills event was sponsored by The Pleasure League, a premier promoter of the Lifestyle scene. They advertised their events as "catering to the playful, under forty crowd," but the Coopers met plenty of rule-breakers, like themselves. The Pleasure League made its guests submit photographs to ensure they met the required age, weight, and body-proportion criteria, and it retained the right to refuse admission to anyone who didn't measure up.

The results were impressive. Pleasure League parties were the best in the city. The women were mostly spry, athletic types from their mid-twenties to early forties, while the men were often older and somehow carved from stone, with muscled, cobra-shaped backs that funneled into polished torsos supporting impossible erections. Tyson and Cassie were just happy they'd made the cut. At forty-four, Tyson was three years older than Cassie, but most couples thought they were in their mid-thirties.

The Coopers made the commitment to get back in shape after joining the scene six months earlier. Since then, their friends on the "outside" commented on how good they looked, and they both knew there was more than just the gym to thank. They gained something from the scene, a confidence absorbed through osmosis, a vibrancy derived through the exercise of their animal needs. They didn't just appear younger, they *were* younger. Full of life and purpose, counting the days between one party and the next, looking at the Lifestyle profiles of other guests online for pre-coital glimpses of the bodies they'd soon be seeing in the flesh.

Their decision to enter the Lifestyle came as an outgrowth of Tyson's desire to spice up the marriage. The passion had gradually drained from their eighteen-year union, coinciding with the gradual aging of their daughter into puberty. Fourteen-year-old Kari Cooper was a lot like her mother, a sharp, independent red-head, complete with Cassie's freckles and green eyes. As the two women grew closer, Cassie and Tyson drifted apart. Sex went from three times a week to three times a month, and they seemed more like siblings than husband and wife. The simple things they used to do for one another were lost to daily routine. Tyson no longer wore the itchy sweater she bought him for his birthday, the one that matched his dark hair and complimented his deep, brown eyes, and Cassie stopped rising early every morning to see Tyson off to work.

There were times when Tyson saw opportunities for office romance. But as a teen he had watched his parent's marriage dissolve under the weight of his father's infidelity, and he promised himself his own marriage would not fail similarly. A litigator by profession, Tyson knew there were always ways to bring two parties together on mutual terms.

It took him a full year to get Cassie onboard with the strip clubs. He was overjoyed when she finally agreed to go. They became regular customers at *The Body Shop* on Sunset Boulevard, where a few dollars dropped gave them front-seat tickets to the ultimate tease. Tyson was further elated when she agreed to join him for lap dances in the club's VIP room. Cassie encouraged their newfound adventure for a time, but watching Tyson wet his pants under the grinding asses of each new girl eventually grew tiresome. The strippers actually thought they were doing her good, saying things like, "You'll get sex tonight, honey" or "He'll be thinking of me but fucking you." Cassie might not have minded so much if their words held true. The unfortunate fact was that their nights at the strip club left Tyson satisfied and Cassie wanting more.

Then one day Cassie came home to say she'd been hit on by a girl at the gym. Invited to join her and her husband at a local club for a sex party. The Coopers later learned that Cassie had been "vanilla hunted," a term used to describe the way Lifestyle members introduced the scene to people on the outside. Cassie said she was straight and had a husband, and the girl said the parties were for couples interested in exploring the sexual boundaries of their relationship with others. No pressure, Sherry, the girl from the gym said, handing Cassie a business card with her Lifestyle member name, ROCKIN'TIMELOVERS.

Tyson and Cassie logged onto the Lifestyle home page and found Sherry's profile. "That's her," Cassie said, as Tyson ogled the thin, muscled blonde in her thirties. She wore a pink, Frederick's of Hollywood nightie over fishnet stockings and stiletto heels. Tyson clicked an icon and additional photos of Sherry, in various stages of undress, appeared. The last five photographs showed Sherry having sex with her husband and a gorgeous, dark-haired woman. Tyson wondered if Sherry's real objective in approaching Cassie was to invite her into a three-way with her husband. It was the one thing Tyson always dreamed about, bringing another girl into bed with his wife. He couldn't believe there were couples who actually lived that way, their relationships surviving unscathed.

"She's beautiful," Cassie said, her eyes fixed on the screen. Tyson didn't know if she was referring to Sherry or the other girl and he didn't care, he was just happy she considered two women having sex appealing. Both women had attractive, natural breasts and were completely shaved. This surprised Tyson, who thought the "Barbie doll thing" was just for strippers. He was more surprised to see that Sherry's husband was shaved as well.

"All the guys in the pornos are shaved," Cassie said, clicking back through Sherry's photo gallery for another look.

Tyson watched her get lost in the imagery. "So, what do you think of it all?" he asked, innocently.

"I think it's insane," she said, smiling.

There were things he knew she considered insane, like the all-terrain triathlon in Maui and the bungee-jumping in Costa Rica. Both things she did without hesitation. "Insane," he said, "as in, you want to give it a shot?"

She turned from the monitor to study his face. "You're not serious, Tyson."

His eyes suggested otherwise.

"I thought we were just looking," she said.

"Maybe that's what we should do. Just go and have a look."

She tapped her finger absently on the arrow key, returning to images of Sherry's ménage à trois. After a moment she sighed, turning to give him her full attention.

"Is this what you want, Tyson?" she asked.

Tyson swallowed. He couldn't believe they were actually having this conversation.

"I do," he said. He felt his cheek twitch involuntarily.

"We'll need to set some boundaries," she said.

He felt a wave of relief. "Okay."

"We don't touch anyone and no one touches us."

"Yes," Tyson said, thinking of Sherry and the other girl, wondering if Cassie would bend the rules someday and consider doing a three-way.

"I don't want to share you," she said.

"All right," he agreed.

"Are you okay having sex in front of others?"

The question surprised him. It was more than what he thought she'd consider. In truth, he didn't know if he had it in him. He didn't think he could handle other men watching Cassie get off.

"We'll just watch," he said. "And if we decide to do anything, we'll go in a corner or some place private where we can do what we want."

"If we do this, Tyson, it's got to be about us. It's got to be something that adds to our relationship, that strengthens it." She seemed almost desperate to get her point across. "Above all, we have to stay connected. You understand, don't you?"

"I do, I get it. We have to stay connected," Tyson said, careful not to say anything that might derail this train. She stared silently into space while he waited for her to make a decision. He imagined her mind pitting each scenario against its ultimate consequence. Finally, she turned and, with a gentle, almost disappointed smile, nodded her approval.

They clicked over to the Lifestyle home page and created their own account, paying fifty dollars for a one-year membership. This gave them access to the profile pictures of hundreds of other couples. They read through the message boards and learned what they could about the scene. They discovered that the parties were for couples and single women only. Single women added intrigue to the mix, especially since most of the coupled women were bisexual, or at least bi-curious, an adder that played particularly well for the male partner's ego. Single men were not allowed because single men were basically scoundrels who made everyone else uncomfortable. The only exception to the rule was when arrangements were made by a couple to include the single male as their *third*. Sometimes a woman made it clear to her husband that she needed something more than he could give. The third was the fantasy man, the one with the spectacular penis and all the right moves. The one who thought about her orgasm before his. The one who delivered.

Tyson and Cassie were required to list their sexual preferences for their Lifestyle profile page. Under sexual orientation, Tyson wrote "heterosexual." He felt an electric jolt when Cassie typed "bi-curious." They were asked to choose from a list of sexual activities in which they engaged. Items on the list included foursomes, gang-banging, bondage, creampies, double penetration, facials, fisting, squirting, deep-throating, group sex, strap-ons, bareback, and additional categories they would need to Google to comprehend. They felt square listing the only activities that applied: voyeurism and exhibitionism.

They learned the rules and etiquette of the parties, specifically that "no means no," and that members would be asked to leave if they were identified as a threat to the community. Some of the parties occurred at bars or Hollywood clubs, and those parties generally didn't allow "on-premise play," which meant that no one was getting fucked. These parties served as playful get-togethers for couples to meet before hooking up at the local hotel. Hotel play seemed too intimate for the Coopers. They were only interested in the on-premise parties, where dozens of anonymous couples came to play. The last thing they wanted was to develop a real relationship with anyone other than themselves. For this reason they chose not to take Sherry up on her offer.

The day of their first party Tyson found Cassie in the bathtub with a disposable razor between her legs. She pulled him into the tub and asked him to do the honors. Tyson didn't know where to begin. She massaged conditioner into her pubic hair and guided the razor in his hand. She pressed hard and the hair came off neatly without causing any harm. A clean mound of soft flesh was left when they were done.

She spread conditioner on his torso and turned the razor around. He pushed her hand away.

"Trust me," she said.

He relented and she made the first stroke, tackling the wild hair just below his belly. She continued down to the base of his shaft. She shaved around and beneath his balls, careful not to nick or cut his skin. The attention excited him and made him hard. Harder than he'd been in a long time. Tyson leaned over and slipped into his wife in the warm tub as water spilled over the edge and onto the floor.

When they were done he dried himself and looked between his legs. He said he felt like a shorn sheep, but she said he looked good, and tidy, and presentable.

The party was at the mansion in Woodland Hills. They parked on a side-street a half-mile from the house, as instructed by the email invitation they received after registering for the party. Cassie wore the third outfit of the six she had purchased at Victoria Secret the day before. They all looked great, but the ultimate decision was determined by which top most easily peeled away from the shoulders to expose her breasts, while still managing to cover the razor-thin scar from her Cesarian section. Tyson didn't know why his wife felt so insecure about the scar; to him it was just another characteristic that defined her, like the perfect smile she had in candid photos and the way she tugged at the ends of her hair when she concentrated on performing a complicated task.

They waited by the car for ten minutes before a private van pulled up, the sliding door opening from the inside. Two couples were already there, the men in designer jeans and the women in short skirts and lingerie. The men each held a bottle of booze in their hands. Vodka appeared to be the drink of choice: Tyson with a bottle of Skyy, the others with Grey Goose and Kettle One. The Coopers stepped awkwardly into the van and were met with coy smiles.

It was a beautiful house with a grand entryway, marble floors and bronze statues. The main room had been cleared of furniture and converted to a dance floor. A popular local DJ mixed tunes while girls danced half-naked tetherball circles around recently planted poles. Cassie and Tyson went to the bar where a numbered sticker was attached to their vodka bottle and a matching number written in ink on the back of Tyson's hand. The bartender poured heavy vodka cranberries and sent them on their way.

They wandered the property, poking their heads into empty bedrooms designated as "play areas." Paper towels and wrapped condoms had been placed on end tables, countertops, and footstools. About a hundred couples were in attendance, each moving slowly with the flow, friends chatting with friends, everyone eyeing everyone else. Cassie and Tyson's nervous smiles were met with broader, playful smiles and hands that slipped out to touch and pat their arms and legs and asses. Tyson was tense, but for some reason Cassie moved along with ease. She reached out to touch the hands that touched hers, letting the tips of her fingers brush against thighs and bellies and chests. One man's hand moved for her chest, prompting Tyson to steer her away and into one of the play areas.

It was a moderately-sized, tastefully-decorated bedroom. A California king-sized bed sat center stage, wearing tight, clean sheets and an auburn comforter. Two loveseats hugged the wall. Three couples were there ahead of them, and there wasn't much room for anyone else. The couples sipped drinks and quietly commented on the artwork that graced the walls. Despite a sense of heightened sexual awareness, no one was having sex, not anywhere in the house. It was as though everyone was waiting for a starting gun to set things off.

Or maybe it was all hype. Maybe the couples came only for the tease. Tyson leaned against the wall, prepared to wait it out with the rest of them. And then Cassie led him to the bed.

She pulled her blouse up and over her head, letting her breasts hang free.

"Let's get this party started," she said.

Tyson stood frozen as she peeled off her skirt and panties. She lay back on the bed wearing only a garter belt, stockings and high-heeled shoes. She seemed not to care about the C-section scar that had been the source of such insecurity in the past. She tugged at his belt until he was compelled to help. He removed his clothes and placed them on the floor beside an end table. When he looked up he saw that two other couples had joined Cassie on the bed.

Tyson resisted the urge to hide his growing erection as he moved to join her. She pulled him close and, grabbing the shaft of his penis, guided him between her legs. He had a tough time at first; she was dry and he had trouble staying hard.

He couldn't think for the distractions, the bodies beside them, the women on all fours, their men above them pumping, the mix of sweat and perfume, the quiet noises growing louder. She was wet before he was hard, and so he focused, working to maintain his erection. He glanced at one of the women beside him, stared at the curve of her back, her ass in the air, the sway of her breast behind her arms. Her hand reached out and touched Cassie's breast, and Cassie reached across to stroke her cheek. They stared into each other's eyes as Tyson pumped from above; Tyson feeling like he was interfering in a private moment. Or maybe it was the vodka fogging his mind. Male hands appeared on Cassie's arms and face, and she grabbed one and held it to her breast, and Tyson pumped harder, listening to her moaning grow into something he'd never heard, her sounds encouraging the vocalization of others until the entire bed was a cacophonous, perpetual motion machine. Cassie's insides contracted around him, milking him, until, exhausted, he fell flat against her stomach and chest.

They lay in each other's arms, slowly settling, while the couples around them continued at a frantic pace. Tyson noticed that the couple to his left was more than they seemed. It was a woman with her husband—two matching Celtic Claddagh wedding rings—and another man, younger, stronger, more handsome than the man with the ring. The other man had a sharp, Errol Flynn jawline capped with a tidy goatee. The two men gave the woman equal attention, but the woman favored the one with the goatee, the lover, the *third*. He took her from behind and his movements caused her to bellow as she turned her head to face him, her lips pursed, the husband forgotten. She stared deep at her lover, but his gaze was elsewhere. Tyson followed the man's look to his point of interest and found that it was Cassie.

Her eyes were on the man as well, following the curve of his hips as they drilled into his lover. Cassie's shoulders trembled and her breathing increased. Tyson noticed the slow, circular movement in her right shoulder. His eyes followed her arm to where her hand disappeared between her legs. Cassie, alone with Tyson still inside her, came simultaneously with the *third* who came inside the wife of the man who watched from the sidelines.

It was past three in the morning when they arrived home. Cassie checked on Kari, who had fallen asleep on the sofa with the Wii control in her hands. The teenager was getting used to her new weekend schedule, which consisted of regular sleepovers at her girlfriends' houses or late nights playing video games and watching romantic comedies on Netflix. Tyson re-heated the previous night's spaghetti while Cassie led Kari back to bed.

"So, what's on your mind?" Cassie asked, joining Tyson at the kitchen table. She could always tell when Tyson was pondering a question. He couldn't help but smile—these were the same words she spoke the first day they met. They were students at USC, Tyson in the graduate program studying business and Cassie getting her BS in marketing. She found him outside the student union with that look on his face, pondering a question. She asked what was on his mind and he told her that he was considering going to law school, but it would deplete his finances and put him in debt for years. A free spirit in her early twenties, Cassie was reckless and joyful and ripe for adventure. She advised him to make the jump. "It's not like you're dropping everything to study improv with the Groundlings. It's law school. No matter how much it costs and how long it takes, it's basically a sure thing, provided you don't fuck it up with distractions like getting married and having kids." She made it seem easy. Of course, their meeting led to marriage and pregnancy and Tyson had to juggle that with law school and the stress of financial ambiguity, but he felt that as long as he listened to Cassie everything would be all right.

All this flashed in his mind when she asked what was on his mind.

"I thought we were trying to stay connected," he said.

She seemed surprised by his words. "I thought we were connected."

"They had their hands all over you."

"Well, I don't think there's much we can do about that. It's a Lifestyle party, that's what they do."

"I just thought it was kind of strange. That you didn't seem to mind it."

"It didn't mean anything. I was there with you."

"What happened to us going there just to watch? Or making love in a corner by ourselves?"

"I don't know, it just didn't go that way. If it's a problem, we can stick with being voyeurs."

"No, it's not a problem. I'm just surprised by how comfortable you seemed. I didn't expect that."

She thought about his words. "It felt like it was about you and me, and we were connected. Was it different for you?"

Tyson grew silent. It's like they had two entirely different experiences. Maybe he was being too restrictive. Maybe he should trust Cassie's judgement on this, as he did with so many other facets of their lives.

"Let's take it as it comes," Tyson said. "We'll do what feels right."

She kissed him lightly on the cheek. "I love you, Tyson. I won't ever do anything to hurt you."

The next weekend Cassie and Tyson found the party in Beverly Hills. There were a few familiar faces, but most of the guests had not attended the party in Woodland Hills. Tyson was nervous, having only maintained the one erection the weekend before, and then only until the quick ejaculation that finished him off. Most of the men in the Lifestyle were Energizer bunnies, holding off their ejaculations until their women were over and done. Or, if they ejaculated early, they were hard again instantly and continued fucking late into the night. Some men were satisfied with one or two orgasms, but the women always needed more.

This time, Tyson prepared by taking a 50 mg dose of Viagra. The pill was left-over from a bottle his primary care doctor prescribed for him a year earlier after he'd hurt his back training for the LA Marathon, an injury that resulted in an embarrassing case of erectile dysfunction. When his back healed, the ED went away and the pills were retired to an empty place in the back of the medicine cabinet. Tyson also brought a small, rubber cock ring to the party, purchased from an adult gift shop near his law office on Wilshire Boulevard.

The Beverly Hills party boasted a topless female DJ best known for working the New Year's Eve sleepover at the Playboy Mansion. It also featured an S&M fire show where a stud in a loincloth blew fire through his teeth between the legs of blindfolded female guests. Cassie watched with interest, her eyes memorizing the details of the fire breather's muscular legs and ass.

They found the large playroom upstairs, the master bedroom with the cherry oak balconies. They fell onto the floor with the beautiful people, a pulsating sea of curves in shades of white, black, yellow, and brown. This time when hands reached for Cassie, Tyson reached out as well, doing the things he'd wanted to do since his first trip to the strip club. His fingers found full, unnatural breasts that felt more like over-pumped inner tubes than natural flesh. He pinched broad, round nipples and soft areolae. He let his hands crab-crawl drum-tight bellies to rest in the spongy, hairless clefts underneath. One woman took his hand from between her legs and pushed it away with disgust. It shocked him; he thought all play in the bed was allowed. Her partner, whose cock she was sucking, smiled at Tyson and let out a quiet laugh.

"We think it's about us, right?" he said. "Then we get here and find that it's all about them. The girls have the power. They get exactly what they want."

The man pressed his partner's head into his cock, his fingers tightening around a clump of her hair. Tyson realized that the man's other hand was lost in the soft, newly-shaved mound between Cassie's thighs. Cassie did nothing to discourage him.

Tyson rose to his knees on the bed and observed the spectacle around him. A crowd surrounded a corner of the bed where one woman was being fisted by another. In a corner of the room a woman in a spiked collar struggled to breathe as her lover forced his enormous penis into her throat, striking her ass with a black, leather paddle in the process. Most people on the bed were involved in garden variety doggy-style or missionary, with enough full-swap to keep things exciting. The environment made him anxious and overwhelmed and somehow deflated. All the women with their Barbie doll pussies and altered breasts and bleach-blonde hair looked vaguely the same. The passion he thought he'd feel wasn't there. The play seemed desperate, if not downright clinical.

Tyson didn't know what had come over him. He was the luckiest man in the world; he should have been counting his blessings. He thought of his partners at the firm and how any one of them would have traded their lot for his, and how their wives would have filed for divorce or called the marriage counselor if their husbands even suggested joining the scene. No, Cassie was special. She trusted him and cared enough to let him explore his fantasies without feeling threatened. Tyson had it good and he was determined to enjoy the ride.

He bent down and gently pushed the man's hand from between Cassie's legs, then proceeded to give his wife oral for the first of what would be many times that night.

Months passed, each week filled with an anticipation relieved by the fulfillment of their weekend plans. Every Saturday night an armada of flesh. Tyson felt at last that he had stepped outside his simple box to taste what life had to offer. They laughed when they heard vanilla couples talk about the "wild" parties they attended, the ones where the odd couple drank too much and got kicked out for "dirty dancing." *Yeah*, Tyson thought, *but did the whole party strip down naked and have sex on the pool tables?* Because that was the new normal for Tyson and Cassie Cooper.

What began as one party a month turned to every other week and ultimately every weekend. There was always a Lifestyle party going on somewhere, although sometimes the venue was not as nice nor the crowd as upscale. Once they attended a party in downtown LA where all the guests were members of local street gangs. Tyson and Cassie still managed to play, but at any moment they felt they could be attacked or gang-raped. Eventually, they put together a schedule of core parties they felt comfortable attending on a weekly basis.

Still, Tyson began to feel a desperate anxiety pursuing them from playroom to playroom, party to party, as they sought out the "perfect" Lifestyle experience. They were always the first to arrive and the last to leave, anxious for the evening to begin and reluctant to see it go. Cassie stared hard into the shadows of lovers in motion, searching for more, as if by witnessing these events she would become them, she would understand them, or understand herself, or acquire some magical insight into the mystery of her life. Tyson felt the pull, too. He recognized the addictive nature of the thing, which was why he felt it was time to make a change.

"I'm ready to slow down a bit," he told her one Friday night.

She held him in bed the way she always did the night before the night they went to party. These were the warm times, when nothing more was needed but the feel of their own bodies in the covers.

"It doesn't make you happy?" she whispered.

Tyson had to think about that. He wasn't sure if happiness had been his objective. He'd done everything he wanted except bring another woman into their relationship. His fantasy to have a third had not materialized, and yet he didn't feel the need to push it any further. Maybe it wasn't meant to happen. Maybe it would have been the thing that killed what they had. It was probably best for some fantasies to remain fantasies.

"I've kind of done what I needed to do," he said. He exhaled, growing calm and relaxed. Accepting what he'd been feeling for some time.

She took his fingers and placed them in her mouth and sucked them, kissing gently between each knuckle. "I did it for you, you know," she said. "You needed something I couldn't give."

"It was good for us both, right?"

"Let's do it one more time," she said, mischievously.

He smiled and held her chin in his palm. "At least."

"No," she said. "Just one more time."

Something in her voice told him she wanted to stop. She needed someone to close the door, and she knew it couldn't be her.

He nodded. "One more for the scrapbook."

"As long as we stay connected," she insisted.

"As long as we stay connected," he agreed. He gripped her neck in his hand and pulled her face to his own. He deep-kissed her and pushed her back onto the bed. They made love and it was quiet and peaceful and passionate and good.

The next night they went to Club Deviant, a refurbished warehouse located in an industrial park in the city of Van Nuys. It didn't have the warmth of the mansion in Woodland Hills, or the movie star sizzle of the mansion in Beverly Hills, or the hip, frenetic energy of a Hollywood club takeover. But what it had was *everything else*. It was Lifestyle from the ground up, with a dozen play areas, each crafted to accommodate the moods of its guests. At the club's entrance, Cassie and Tyson encountered an outdoor jacuzzi surrounded by burlap cabanas of the kind seen in Hollywood films of the 1940s. They checked their coats and continued to the bar, where they handed their bottle of Skyy to the bartender who poured fast and strong. They drank a cup and refilled, looking to get a buzz before losing themselves in the scene. A dance floor opened beyond the bar, with a raised stage that included the ubiquitous stripper pole, used by professional and amateurs alike. Part of the stage included a large, open shower, for the more playful exhibitionists.

The first room they saw held two long sofas under a large, flatscreen television playing XXX porno films. A heavy curtain separated the room from an adjacent play area where a comfortable bed held the weight of a muscled black man and three black women. Cassie pulled the curtain open and stared hypnotized at the scene. The man fucked one of the women from behind while kissing another on the mouth and fingering the third in the ass.

"Isn't it beautiful?" Cassie whispered to Tyson.

The black man looked back and smiled. "Plenty of room on the bed," he said, his eyes taking in Cassie's school-girl skirt and tight, see-through blouse. She smiled bashfully, and Tyson took her hand, leading her away.

They climbed a long stairwell to the second floor where they discovered rooms decorated like Ali Baba's hut and Dracula's lair. Each scene laden with fresh towels, Kleenex tissues, bowls of condoms, and a box of wet wipes. Club Deviant catered to the needs of its clientele.

Tyson and Cassie entered the Dragon Room, where black light fixtures illuminated decorative, iron lattices featuring twisted scenes of medieval battles. A large bed made of black foam sat in the center of the room. Tiny, white flecks in the foam glittered in the eerie light, turning the bed into an image of galaxies in the night sky. The room was empty. Tyson grabbed his wife's hand and held it tight. He stared into her face, *seeing* her, unobstructed by others. She felt his desire and took him to the bed. She unbuckled his belt and lifted his shirt over his head. He let his pants fall to his ankles. She stripped naked. She dropped to her knees and reached inside his underwear, taking his penis into her hand. He slipped the tight, rubber cock ring over the tip and maneuvered it to the base of his shaft, pulling out pubic hair in the process. She took him into her mouth and deep-throated him. He was harder than he'd ever been.

Others came through the door. They stood watching, enthralled by the spectacle of authentic passion in the room. Tyson lifted Cassie onto the bed and took her from above. She stared into his eyes, her hands kneading his shoulders and arms and chest. They felt the room's atmosphere shift as the voyeurs moved in, the observers becoming participants. Tyson ignored them, focused on his wife, remaining *connected*.

He felt the heat of bodies, smelled fresh sweat and expensive perfumes. He stared at Cassie's eyes, which were closing. Then her mouth, her short, quick breaths. Then the trickle of sweat that formed on her chin, slipping down the length of her neck. Then her breasts, full and soft, with large, burgundy areolae and erect, pink nipples. They hadn't engaged in foreplay, so she was tight. He pumped hard, and he knew it hurt her inside, could see it in the twitch of her jaw and the movement of her pelvis, the rising arch of her back.

The bed was crowded. Tyson didn't notice until he saw Cassie's gaze shift to a set of lovers on her right. Her mouth opened slightly, a hint of recognition in her eyes. Tyson looked and saw a man on his back getting oral from his wife. He remembered them from before, the couple with the matching Celtic Claddagh wedding rings. Then he saw the other man making love to the man's wife from behind. This was where Cassie's gaze had gone, to the *third*, the man with the classic good looks and tidy goatee. And, just as before, the man stared at Cassie as he moved inside the other man's wife.

Tyson looked back at Cassie and tried to reconnect. But she had gone somewhere else, her eyes on the third. Tyson focused on her lips, on the lower lip clenched between her teeth.

He thrust harder, and she began to moan. Her back arched further, and Tyson thought it might snap. He held her, enthralled by her rising voice. He felt it coming, just around the corner, and began vocalizing as well. He tried holding off, tried to be indifferent, like the others. The vodka helped, made it harder to stay hard. He looked between their legs, at the point where their hips met, the piston in the machine. He looked to her face, but her eyes were still on the third. The man moaned, his rhythm and tempo matching Cassie. It was they who were connected.

Tyson felt his erection give way. Cassie turned to face him, her eyes widening.

"No, no . . ." she whispered.

"I can't," he said, shame and apology tainting his voice.

"No . . ." she pleaded.

His penis slipped out and was too soft to penetrate her again. Cassie pushed him onto his back and took his penis in her mouth again. She worked hard, the way she did when they were dating. When they were young she could come by giving him head, he excited her that much. When they were young she was wet all the time. He placed his hands on her head and let his fingers move through her long, fine hair. She began to moan again, and it turned him on, this focus, this connection they shared. His sounds matched Cassie's sounds, and as he moved his pelvis he felt her body moving along with him. He stared at the top of her head, and when she looked up he saw a passion he recognized from a lifetime ago.

She came as he came. And in that moment Tyson saw a hand on her ass, and as Cassie's head whipped back he realized she'd been pulled by her hair, and the third was behind her, and he was penetrating her, had *been* penetrating her since the moment she dropped her face in Tyson's lap. And he was coming, too, the *third*.

Cassie finished with a deep, breathy groan and collapsed into Tyson's arms, and when Tyson looked up the third had disappeared, had slipped into the blur of bodies behind and around them.

She wore a dreamy half-smile. He smelled vodka on her breath. Cocooned in her arms and in the fog of Skyy, Tyson wasn't sure what had gone on. Maybe his perception was off, maybe the third had been behind a different girl all along. Maybe it was someone else he'd been fucking.

They returned home around three o'clock in the morning. Kari had spent the night with a friend, so they had the house to themselves. Tyson waited for Cassie in bed while she boiled water and poured a cup of tea. She brushed her long hair at the vanity while she drank it, humming a tune he hadn't heard in years.

She drew the covers back an hour later and lay her head on his chest. Cassie caressed Tyson's shoulders and arms while he stared into the gray ceiling a thousand miles away.

"You were wonderful, Tyson," she said, releasing a slow, content sigh.

He could smell the party in her hair. It smelled of sweat and lust. And youth. It smelled like the *third*.

Tyson's hands fell to his side. His breath shallow, his body cold. He pushed Cassie off his chest and curled into a fetal position, holding back the tears that welled up in his eyes.

Her hand found his head and gently stroked his hair.

"Next time," she said, slowly drifting off to sleep, "we get one for you."

REVIEW

Discussion Questions:

1. What does the title refer to?
2. The story makes the point that the Lifestyle has a positive effect on a person's health. Why is this? Why do the main characters seem younger than they are?
3. Why does Tyson believe that the Lifestyle is really about women?
4. Explain the final scene. What does Tyson learn about the Lifestyle?

Essay Questions:

1. "Lifestyle" is a story of a subculture as is Robert Roberge's "Torn and Frayed." Compare and contrast the subcultures of these two stories. What are their dangers and difficulties? How do their members take care of and damage each other?
2. What is the theme of the "Lifestyle"? What is it that Stephen Schwartz seems to be saying about the nature of human experience?

Burt the Martian

CYNTHIA ADAM PROCHASKA

Many people ask me why I started dating a Martian, and my first response is that I didn't plan it. It was just one of those things that happened. One minute I was standing at the Eat Right health food store minding my own business, and the next I was dating a Martian. The first thing that attracted me was his looks, sort of male model looks. I'll admit it. Burt the Martian looks like a male model, maybe not the top tier A-list sort of Tyrese or Calvin Klein Underwear guy, but a Sears underwear guy, kind of good-looking, but not too sexy, with a thin chest and eyes that cross ever so slightly. Wholesome sexy. He has nice buns, if that's what you're wondering. And a porn star mustache and a chin that is best described as chiseled. I guess the Martians wanted him to look attractive to humans in a pleasing, safe way, and they got most of it right.

As I said, I met him in the health food store, and I was struck immediately by not only his good looks, but his social awkwardness. Even though I have a job at the art museum a few storefronts away and have to schmooze people all day long, when I am on my own time, I'm shy and a little tongue-tied. So when Burt the Martian halted a little on the pleasantries of my food purchase, a bagel if you must know, saying "The clouds seem to portend ominous amounts of sunshine," I was immediately struck.

"You don't like the sun?" I asked, amazed to meet a fellow traveler in this seaside town.

"It can be oppressive," he said, "to have so much of the same weather."

His courtly language made me smile and he tilted his head and smiled back like we were playing some sort of game. I liked it that he was odd and a little spontaneous, taking the dollar I handed him and licking it. His tongue lapped the side of the bill and he smiled at its taste, as if he was licking my hand. I can't remember now if he asked for my number or just read my mind, but that night

I got his phone call and it seemed wholly unsurprising after our exchange that afternoon.

"This is Burt," he said, "from the health food store that you frequented today. I would like to ask you on a date."

It surprised me how forthright and serious he was, and I when I said "yes" he gave a pleased little yelp.

"This pleases me a great deal," he said.

What I didn't know then that I know now is that Burt dated by committee and I was the first girl to be approved by his crew: Durai, a Sufi dancer he had met when he first arrived, Oscar, a rent-a-cop, and William, his coworker at Eat Right. Who all just happened to be in the store that day.

We decided to go to a movie, whose title I have now forgotten, at the local university, about an obsessive and doomed love. Then, Burt talked about his penchant for operas about dead presidents and underground music.

"The more industrial, the better," he said. I was smitten.

I felt I was doing something important, because of his hopeless nihilism and the way, as arm candy, he rated at least an eight.

When the evening of our date came, I was saddened by how dark the movie for our first date was, ending as it did with a double suicide and the poetic falling of dead leaves. Burt, however, was elated. It was as if he'd only seen the most trite of Hollywood movies with the sappiest of endings, and that a movie could end badly was a revelation to him.

"Such death," he said, "without massive amounts of firepower is unusual."

He was saying he mainly liked movies about cyborgs and the occasional dog, when I was about to volunteer my secret love of *Benji*. Before I could say it, he bent down to kiss me. The sky was full of stars, and we were standing outside of the auditorium in the grass. I felt a small electric spark (which I thought was due to the surprise, and have found out since is a Martian thing) when his lips touched mine, and he kissed me in the shaky way new and eager lovers do. I could feel the tension in the way he held me to him and the chemistry that is both right and a little wrong. When he finally came up for air, he was smiling so that every tooth in the front of his mouth showed.

"That was fantastic," he exclaimed, "It was even better than I imagined."

When he held my hand afterward, I knew it would be hard to get rid of him later, when and if the time came.

As I lay in bed later replaying the kiss, there was a knock on the front door. It was well past midnight, and there on the porch was Burt and Durai, the Sufi dancer.

They stood there as if there was nothing unusual about their timing, as if people just dropped by in the middle of the night all the time. Burt seemed to glow a little with a slight green cast, a kind of chartreuse that some people describe as lemon-lime or neon. It was faint, and somehow, I thought the porch light was playing a trick on me. As I stood there in my Camp Beverly Hills nightshirt and leggings, Durai scanned me with his dark eyes.

"I was telling Durai about your beauty and the kiss, and I wanted him to see you again for himself," Burt said.

Durai smiled, and I was struck by the whiteness of his turban and flowing shirt.

Then Durai took my arm and began twirling me around the front yard in large sweeping circles. I felt dizzy and breathless as he swung me around, covering almost the entire surface of the grass. Burt stood to the side and smiled as a bridegroom might, and I thought this was some odd and joyful marriage dance, a kind of welcome to their tribe. After an hour of dancing, I felt flushed and ecstatic, and happy in a way I hadn't been in awhile. It was past two when they left, waving their goodbyes even as the wind stirred behind them. I leaned into the tree and wondered just what I had gotten myself into.

The next day I was at work thinking about the night before when Katrina, my boss, tapped my desk.

"Waaaake up, Selene," she said in her rich person's lockjaw coming down hard on the "c's" and "d's." "Don't forget, *we* have an image to uphold."

She used the royal "we" like I was sullying the image of the museum with my poor posture and less-than-perky demeanor. Every day she watched me from the other side of the office we shared and in the months we worked together I'd started the lockjaw thing, too. It was unconscious; somehow, I just picked it up.

"You need to have the Ellsworth proposal done by tomorrow," she said, as if I had somehow forgotten the thirty-five page request for $50,000 to exhibit the work of some crappy French artist no one cared about.

"I'm on it," I told her, "It's in the baaaag." I imagined a man in a polo shirt and madras shorts when I said the word "bag," drawing out the "a" when I said it, thinking I had become like one of them.

I was preoccupied by Burt and then Timothy, the photography curator, who had asked me to pose for him. Timothy said I had an interesting look, like a maid one day and like I owned the place the next. He liked the scar on my stomach from the time I fell off a tree when I was a kid and had to be cut open. The juxtaposition of my sweet and wholesome face and the savage scar. He wanted me to pose at his house, which was bad enough, and he wanted me to pose naked. They would be arty nudes, I knew this, in black and white, but I was not ready, shy in a way that shocks me. Frightened that being naked would be more revealing than I could even guess. That I wouldn't be good at it, that I wouldn't be open enough to make it work.

When I got home, there was a present from Burt waiting on my doorstep. A raw organic chicken wrapped in plastic. There was no note or anything, just the raw bird, steeping in its own blood. I looked at it, and I wondered if this was some kind of message, that I would be gutted and naked after going out with him—or if he meant to buy chocolates, but forgot, or if he really has no sense that this was an inappropriate gift. I left it there, glistening in the sun, not knowing what to think.

An hour later he called and asked with excitement whether I received his gift.

"You looked like you needed protein," he said.

And I told him he was the strangest person I knew.

"Selene," he said, "I would like to kiss you again."

After our second date, I noticed I was starting to glow a little. Not in the blushing bride way, but in the greenish, muted glow that sometimes occurs in off-brand stores under the wrong kind of fluorescent light—fluorescent, that's it, the way I looked. I started thinking that the museum was doing this to me, since my office looked out on a wall, and the light was more artificial than real, but then I remembered Burt having the same glow. And he was such an avid kisser, in fact, he was more avid about kissing than anyone I have ever dated, that maybe he had passed some radioactivity to me. Seated as we were in the bar of the Rusty Scupper, a nautical themed restaurant that was out on a pier over the water, I looked at him and he smiled back. We were watching the luminous fish light up below us, in the dark churning water and I wondered if there was something he was not telling me.

"Burt," I said, "I am glowing."

"That happens," he said, "with the exchange of molecules."

"Back up," I said. "Exchange of molecules? What's going on?"

This was when he sprang it on me, noting that he knew I might figure it out sooner than later.

"I have something I have to tell you," he said, "that might dismay some people, but you have been selected, in part, because of your ability to synthesize information."

"Huh?" I said, because this was usually what men said when they sprang the information that they were married on me.

"Selene," he said, "I am not from this biosphere."

"Excuse me."

"I am from another planet."

I sat there thinking this was a new one, not the "I'm just in town for a convention" or "I live in Iowa" but a whole other planet.

"Which one?" I asked, blinking out at the harbor lights.

"Mars."

Jesus, Selene, you know how to pick them, I thought to myself.

"It doesn't mean anything," Burt said with his arms around me, "Just that you'll have a slight green cast to you. Wearing brown usually helps hide it."

Suddenly, I felt very tired and told Burt to take me home, that I would call him in a few days.

He seemed more distressed than I could say, but he acquiesced.

Over the next several days, I noticed that butterflies seemed to hover around me, as if my new coloring had drawn them to me or as if Burt had sent them. Other things started happening, too, bizarre things, like traffic stopping just as I approached the crosswalk even if there wasn't a light, clouds parting over me, if I walked under them. Men in muscle T-shirts seemed to appear on corners where they never were before like Secret Service. I got the Ellsworth grant in, and it seemed to levitate above the post office counter.

More strange gifts appeared. High fiber cereal. Batteries. A leg of lamb, which I hated. Flax seed. Bamboo plates. Open toed huaraches, which were surprisingly stylish. Except for the lamb, his gifts were strangely timely, each almost anticipating what I needed. But I was not sure about this Martian business, because, in the words of the old song, "I fall in love too easily." Give me the right combination of oddness and eloquence and I am done for. And I had sworn off men after each time I got hurt: the reggae drummer, the TV weatherman with a sink fetish, the coked up city redevelopment guy. And I usually lasted two weeks in these swearing off cycles until the next highly-literate social misfit comes along. More than anything, I hated being alone, ever since Antonio my first love disappeared in a catamaran that got lost at sea.

So I did what I always did when I needed to think. I went to the ocean and tried to skip rocks. Once, I skipped a rock five times, all the while whispering to Antonio's spirit to give me an answer. But today I didn't feel like fooling with the rocks and I just sat there, digging my toes in the sand, eating a vegan fig bar that Burt left.

I saw children with a kite near the water and the kite had a Martian face on it. It was one of those big-eyed creatures with an oval green face, and I smiled at it and the way they were struggling to get it to fly. There was a dog, worrying a piece of seaweed in his teeth, and the seagulls circling and looking for treats. It felt good to be alone and away from everything—and I knew that I didn't have to have all the answers now, that they would come with time. And when I saw the Martian kite crash, I was sad in a way that had nothing to do with the kite, and I knew that I would call Burt later. And I knew he would pick up and say how good it was to hear from me.

Discussion Questions:

1. What is added by making Burt a Martian? This is a story about the awkwardness of romantic relationships. How is that theme strengthened by his otherness?
2. What kind of gifts does Burt leave Selene? What do they say about Burt?
3. Why is Selene interested in Burt?
4. The ending of the story is enigmatic. Do you think Selene will leave Burt?

Essay Questions:

1. This story explores the differences between partners in a romantic relationship. What do you think "Burt the Martian" is saying about the nature of two very different beings coming together in a relationship?
2. Many of the stories in this collection explore the idea of otherness or outsiders. Compare and contrast this story to several others. What are these stories saying about what it means to be an outsider?
3. Is there something about Selene's life that makes her need to find a partner who is much different than all the people she knows?

Wertheimer in the City

JUDITH FREEMAN

I. The Arrival

It had been a long time since Wertheimer had been in the city. During his absence his apartment stood empty, as it always did when he was away. Coming home to it was always the same: he opened the door and there it was, his old forsaken world, unchanged except for the little ghostly feeling that haunted the place whenever he left it empty. The apartment was by no means luxurious, but it had always been adequate for his needs. He kept it more out of habit than necessity for he had increasingly fewer occasions to use it now that Michael was gone and his life had undergone a great change.

Usually his visits to the city lasted only a few days but he expected to stay longer this time. There was a family matter requiring his attention. Before leaving his house in Sante Fe he had called Mrs. Cochran, his housekeeper of many years, and asked her to air out the apartment and watch for a package from his doctor which might arrive before he did.

He drove into Los Angeles at dusk on a clear and beautiful evening after a long trip across the desert. The aria from Wagner's *Tristan and Isolde* was playing on the radio as he pulled off the freeway at Alvarado and it ended just as he reached the apartment. It seemed to Wertheimer a perfect moment—the exquisite music finishing exactly as he arrived, the sight of the old two-story building in the golden evening light—and he was momentarily flooded by feelings of familiarity, affection, and nostalgia, that combination of emotions peculiar to homecoming.

Only when he'd unpacked and finished his first drink did he call Nadia.

"Who is it?" she said instead of offering a hello. He was used to her abruptness, and said simply, "It's me."

"Oh, it's you. When did you get in?"

"Just now."

"How was the drive? I don't know why you don't fly like everyone else."

"The drive was very pleasant." He started to describe his trip across the desert, how beautiful the ocotillo had looked, but she cut him off.

"The question is, what are we going to do about Arthur?"

"Did you tell him I was coming?"

"Of course. He's expecting you to have lunch with him tomorrow. He plans on bringing her to meet you."

"Ah, yes. What is her name again?"

"Bea. Didn't you get their Christmas card? It was on the card."

Wertheimer had gotten the card from his son. And of course he did remember it. He hadn't ever gotten a Christmas card quite like it. It showed a picture of a partially-naked blonde with the words, *I'll be your perfect fantasy.* The girl was wearing some sort of bustier and had formed her mouth into a kittenish little pout. The image was still quite vivid. The card had been signed, *Happy Holidays, Bea and Arthur.*

"She's a hippie," Nadia said. "A hippie who makes pornography."

"I was under the impression she was an artist."

"An artist who makes pornography is no artist, just another purveyor of smut." This last word, colored by her German accent, came out as *schmut.*

"Well I don't think . . ." Wertheimer began. And then he stopped himself because he didn't want to get into an argument with his ex-wife over someone he hadn't even met.

"You'll see when you meet her. Arthur has lost it this time."

"Lost what?" He had become momentarily distracted by the dogs barking in the alley below his window.

"His head—he's lost it completely. He's decided to marry her. Remember? That's why you're here. To talk to him. He listens to you. He doesn't listen to me. Are you even listening to me?"

"But Arthur's an adult now, Nadia. He's thirty-five—"

"Thirty-seven," Nadia said. "You never remember your son's age."

"Anyway, he's old enough to make his own decisions."

"I'm not asking you to work miracles here. I just want you to convince him to get the prenuptial agreement. He doesn't think he needs to do this."

"Maybe he doesn't." He thought such agreements were silly: they showed bad faith.

"He's sunk if he doesn't get an agreement. I know a gold-digger when I see one, and this Bea is only looking for a rich ore to mine."

For a moment he thought Nadia had said *a rich whore to mine* and he felt shocked thinking Nadia would refer to herself that way since it was her money

Arthur had lived on for years, although recently he'd come into his own trust. Then he understood what she'd really said and laughed.

"This is funny to you?" she snapped.

"No, no," he mumbled.

"It shouldn't be. It won't be so funny when she dumps him and takes him for all he is worth."

"It's his money now." He did feel he should point this out to Nadia.

"The problem is she's not serious about him."

He suddenly felt weary. "Look, Nadia, why don't I call you tomorrow? I'm rather tired after the long drive."

"Don't bother calling. Just come and see me after you have lunch with them. Arthur's expecting you at 12:30." She named a restaurant where he was to meet his son, the one restaurant he himself would have picked if anybody had bothered to consult him on the matter.

II. A Morning Walk

Wertheimer awoke early on his first morning back in the city and went out for a walk just as the sun was rising. He strolled down Rampart and made a right on Sixth Street, heading toward the old granite church on the corner of Common- wealth where he'd often attended the free organ concerts on Thursdays. He was struck by certain changes in the neighborhood, most of them unpleasant. As he approached Lafayette Park, he was sorry to see that the local branch of the public library had finally been closed. For years the graceful little library had been in a state of decline. Still he was sad to see it boarded up. The Felipe de Nueve Branch Library. Shuttered now.

It was the park itself, however, that shocked him most as he passed through the gate and began strolling down the uneven path that led to Wilshire. The homeless had completely taken over. Everywhere he looked he saw the unfortu- nates, clumped under blankets on the grass, sitting slumped at the picnic tables, looking defeated and bored. Most of the tables had been tented with tarps and blankets to form crude shelters. The grass was gone, now worn to dirt. Wild para- keets screeched from the tops of the trees, thick in the upper branches. He walked slowly along the path, glancing occasionally at the people stirring in the morning light—an elderly man folding his filthy blankets carefully, a young couple with a tiny dog sharing a cigarette, an old woman ranting to herself, wandering in circles. Insane, he thought, meaning the woman, but it also applied the scene sur- rounding him. What sort of shitty society, he wondered, let its people sleep in the rough? A Third World country, he thought, or an indifferent rich one.

He crossed Commonwealth, heading for the Sheraton Townhouse Hotel where he intended to buy the morning paper, but instead he saw a boarded-up building. The hotel, too, had closed. It had been such a lovely little hotel. He and Michael used to swim there and use the sauna and often entertained friends by the pool. He looked at the shuttered windows in disbelief. At the dead canna lilies, the graffiti on the walls. Already it had begun to look like a ruin.

He wondered how so much could have changed in such a short time. That was the dispiriting part. Ugly things managed to survive while the old and the beautiful—the carefully made, he thought—simply disappeared.

In the old days he would have walked on down Wilshire to the Ambassador Hotel and had an early breakfast in the hotel coffee shop but that hotel had been closed a number of years ago. Even Bullock's Wilshire, with its old-world tea room—a place of many wine-blessed lunches with Michael—had gone out of business. Looking around him, Wertheimer felt he simply didn't recognize his old neighborhood anymore.

He started for home, aware of a pain in his chest. He wished he had thought to take a pill before he left the apartment. He had to stop for a moment to get his breath at an intersection. Sound came at him from all directions. Somewhere far down the street, a siren wailed. Everywhere he looked he could see trash. He wondered why they didn't pay unemployed people to pick it up. Give some youths a job. Had the city really become so much harsher in his absence? Or had he simply forgotten what it was really like?

He felt dispirited as he headed for home. He did not see how civilization could endure such decay. Libraries closing, parks in ruin, people without a place to live, the insane left to fend for themselves, with garbage everywhere. What sort of life was this?

Then, as he rounded a corner and began passing Casa de Cleaners, he stopped in front of a sight that lifted his spirits it seemed so extraordinary. At least he found it extraordinary to see the mushrooms poking out from a layer of damp leaves right next to the sidewalk.

He stopped and bent over to examine the mushrooms. They were edible, just as he thought. *Coprinus atramentarius* growing right in the city! He had never seen more beautiful inky caps. And they were at the perfect stage for harvesting.

Wertheimer grew excited. He began thinking of the meal he could make out of such lovely mushrooms. But soon he was confronting the problem of how to carry them back to his apartment. He didn't want to bruise them, to spoil them in any way. What he needed was a basket or a paper bag, but he had neither. At last he decided the thing to do would be to return later and gather them. Surely no one else would spot the mushrooms. But just for safety, he piled a few handfuls of leaves around them and hurried away, happy with his find.

III. The Luncheon

He arrived at the restaurant a little early and killed some time by browsing in a bookstore next door.

Only a few minutes passed before he saw his son arrive in the company of a young woman. They came down the sidewalk hand-in-hand and stopped in front of a magazine rack outside. Arthur was wearing a suit, and he looked as if he'd gained a little weight. The woman with him did not look like the woman on the card that said *I'll be your perfect fantasy*. She wasn't wearing sexy clothes. She was wearing a simple outfit, sweater, slacks, sandals. She seemed very young—much younger than his son. Wertheimer thought she was rather pretty.

He stood watching them through the window for a moment. He wanted to observe them while remaining hidden himself even if this did amount to a kind of spying. He noticed how relaxed his son looked. He couldn't remember the last time he'd seen his son looking so happy.

"There you are," Arthur said as he approached him. "I was about to look for you in the restaurant."

He embraced his son, and then stepped back and extended his hand to the young woman.

"How do you do—Bea, I believe, isn't it?"

"Nice to meet you," she said, and gazed at him with a serious expression. She looked like the sort of girl you'd like to know but who might not want to know you. *Difficult*. This was the word that came to mind. It wasn't so much a first impression as a fleeting thought, irrational, unprompted. The hand she extended was cold and very thin.

"Shall we go inside?" Arthur said, leading the way into the restaurant.

He followed his son, who even at that moment didn't feel like a son so much as a fond acquaintance he hadn't seen for a while. To his regret, Wertheimer had never felt much like a father. He hadn't exactly taken his duties lightly: he thought in many respects he had carried out his responsibilities admirably. He had tried to see that the right decisions had been made in regard to Arthur's life. Yet he lacked something—not love exactly, not feeling, for he had always been very fond of Arthur. He simply felt none of the requisite authority most people associated with parenthood, that instinct to dominate he had so often observed. He'd certainly been supportive of Arthur in all the crucial ways. He'd intervened with Nadia on his behalf on many occasions—when Arthur had decided to spend a few years traveling, for instance, instead of immediately entering law school as Nadia had wished. "You don't know what it means to be a father," Nadia had said to him at the time in a voice full of emotion, and he'd found that comic coming from her. He'd done his best, that was all he could say, but he knew his role had been limited. Sometimes he had wondered if Nadia wasn't right—he didn't know what it meant to be a father. It wasn't only the fact that after the divorce he had lived apart from his son. He had also lived most of that time with Michael. He had always been grateful that Arthur had accepted this arrangement without noticeable difficulty.

"Well, Arthur," he said when they were seated, "what have you been up to since I saw you last?"

"I've been falling in love," Arthur said and gazed fondly at Bea.

"Always an admirable undertaking!" he said.

"You know we're going to be married?"

"Yes. Nadia told me. Congratulations to you both."

"I'm afraid Mother is against it," Arthur said.

Wertheimer glanced at Bea to judge her reaction to this comment. But her expression didn't change. She gazed calmly at him with large dark eyes that had been heavily outlined in black. She exuded a toughness he found somewhat intimidating.

"I know mother asked you to come here to try and talk us out of it," Arthur said.

Wertheimer cleared his throat, feeling suddenly uncomfortable.

"I'm sorry if you came into the city just for this because nothing could change our minds."

"Yes, yes, of course," he said. "Nor should it."

"It's the money," Arthur said. "With mother, it's always the money, I'm afraid."

"She thinks I'm a gold digger," Bea said. "She thinks I want Arthur only for his money." This was said without malice or any visible emotion, as if she were simply stating a well-known, if tiresome, fact.

"I'm sure she doesn't mean anything against you personally," Wertheimer said.

"Of course she does," Bea replied. "She means it *only* against me, in fact. She hasn't liked me from the very beginning, from the moment Arthur and I met."

He sensed an opportunity to take the conversation in a different direction and seized upon it.

"How *did* you and Arthur meet?" he asked. "I'm just curious . . ."

Bea laughed and looked at Arthur. "Shall I tell him?"

"Of course," Arthur said. "He might find it amusing."

"We met in a porno shop. I was buying something—"

"A dildo," Arthur said, rather too loudly judging from the way the woman at the next table suddenly looked over at him.

"Let me talk, sweetie. Yes, I was buying a dildo for a piece I was doing." She was interrupted by the waiter who approached the table and asked if they were ready to order yet. They all decided quickly and when the waiter left, Bea continued eagerly, as if she'd been waiting anxiously to get on with her story.

"I'm an artist, maybe you already know this. I make videos of myself acting out roles. You might say my work is an investigation of women and desire and power. I needed some things for a new work, so I went to a porno shop on Sunset where I met Arthur. He was looking at a rack of movies, trying to decide what to get. But instead of a video, he got me!" She smiled and touched Arthur's arm and he covered her hand with his.

"Interesting." Wertheimer laughed. He could not quite picture the whole thing—Bea's videos of herself, the sort of art she was describing. And he was also thinking of Arthur, whom he would not have previously suspected of being all that interested in pornographic movies.

"When—and where—do you plan on being married?" he asked, thinking it wise to focus on specific details.

Arthur said, "We thought we'd go to Vegas. We haven't set a date."

"I see." He did not actually see the thing at all. The idea of getting married in Las Vegas was appalling to him.

"Bea likes the idea of getting married in Vegas, don't you darling?"

"I *love* the idea," she said in her throaty voice. "I'm going to rent a dress at one of those Mexican bridal stores. We'll get married by an Elvis impersonator. No witnesses, no family, no reception—no bullshit in other words. It should all be over in half an hour." Bea looked flushed with happiness as she described their plans.

He wanted to say, why bother? Marriage was enough of an anathema to someone like himself, let alone a marriage that sounded like theater, or a costume party.

"I can tell you don't like the idea," Bea said, frowning.

"No, no," he protested. "It's just . . . it's just that I often don't see the point of marriage at all. I mean, in our day and age, when it's perfectly acceptable to live together as a couple—"

"Like you and Michael did?" she said, interrupting him.

"Yes, I suppose," he said a little stiffly. He was surprised to hear his deceased lover's name come from her lips. Surprised, and a little put off. It seemed presumptuous of her to speak about Michael, someone she'd never met, someone he had yet to mention in this conversation. He realized his life must have been fully raked over by the two of them.

"I wouldn't think that Michael and I would have provided a model for anything, least of all a relationship between you two." He was unable to keep the chilly tone out of his voice.

"I've upset you? Haven't I?" She looked stern and put off, as if she'd just been told bad news.

"On the contrary, I'm just . . . surprised."

"You must still be mourning him, aren't you? Arthur told me how horrible it was at the end, with the AIDS."

This was too much. He felt dismayed by the impropriety of it all. The presumed intimacy. Talking this way. Raising this difficult subject when they'd only just met. And in a restaurant! He looked at his son, hoping for help, but instead, Arthur said, "Look, Dad, we've never really discussed Michael's death. You guys hid his condition for so long. He was already in the hospital and dying by the time I found out. Afterward, you said it wasn't the time to talk about it."

He frowned and shook his head. "Nor do I think it's the time to do so now. I think the subject at hand is marriage, isn't it? I mean am I wrong about this?"

"Why do I always say the wrong thing?" Bea stood up suddenly.

"Where are you going—?" Arthur looked at her anxiously.

"Home. You guys have things to discuss and you don't need me around to do it. Only . . . I just want to say . . ." Here she stopped and bit her lip, and Wertheimer saw that she was about to cry.

"My dear," he said, half rising and at the same time extending his hand. "Sit down, please." She looked so young and distraught: Her mouth began to tremble. He'd been wrong about her firmness. The presumed toughness. He could see that now.

"Only I just want you . . . I think you should know, I meant to say something good."

At that point she turned and left the restaurant.

For a few moments Wertheimer and Arthur said nothing. They stared at the doorway through which she had disappeared.

"Oh dear. That was a bit of botched business, wasn't it?"

"Botched business? *Botched . . . business?*" Arthur gave him a disgusted look. "You didn't give her a chance. Not a chance. You're worse than Mother!" He was seething now with anger.

He had never experienced this sort of anger from his son. He couldn't think of anything to say. He realized they were going to have a fight, right here in the restaurant, about Bea leaving, and it had been his fault. It only made matters worse when the waiter arrived bearing three plates. As he set the first plate down at Bea's spot, Arthur said, "Take that one away."

"I could put it in something if you wanted to it take with you later—"

"I don't," Arthur snapped. He flicked the back of his hand toward the plate. "Just get it out of here," he added rudely.

When the waiter had gone, he said, "Look, Arthur, I'm terribly sorry."

"You would be," Arthur answered. He lifted his wine glass and drained it, then filled it again.

He looked down at his plate, picked up his knife and fork and cut into his fish, trying to ignore his son who was staring baldly at him with an unhappy look, and began eating. Arthur did not touch his food. This went on for some time. And then he spoke up.

"Why did you and mother get married? I've never asked you before. I'm just curious."

He set his utensils down and looked up at his son, a fair-haired, rather round-shouldered man going a bit soft around the middle. He looked like the lawyer he was, somehow both pampered and proper.

"Is this actually important to you?" he asked.

"I'd just like to know. It's something I've always wanted to know and never felt I could ask."

"I suppose we were in love. Isn't that why most people get married? Because they think they're in love?" He didn't bother to give his answer much thought. What would be the point of trying to explain?

"So you didn't marry her for her money?"

He looked away, embarrassed now. It was as if sudden holes were opening up, little tics radiant with vanishing consolations and swelling anxieties. How depressing, he thought, to sit here in this bright noisy place, to feel such misery at what he thought would be an ordinary lunch. He saw the waiter staring at them from the corner of the restaurant. He saw the woman with the gaudy jewelry who was clearly eavesdropping.

"You didn't marry her because it would make you seem . . ." Arthur faltered for a moment, but quickly added, "I mean . . . you weren't just trying to cover up what you really were?"

"And what do you think I really was?" he said quietly, trying to indicate to Arthur that he should lower his voice. He knew very well what his son was saying but thought, why not play the thing out?

"Well," Arthur said, "didn't you know you were gay? And if you did, why else would you marry her unless it was for money or because you were trying to appear normal?"

He felt humiliated now. Not just embarrassed but humiliated. Who was this man sitting across from him? Talking this way in a voice others could hear. He did not seem like the son he had known for thirty-seven years. Where had the impudence come from? The rude manners? What had he done to deserve this?

"What a quaintly reductive picture of human nature you have," he said. He lifted his hand to his mouth and gently stroked first one corner of his lips, and then the other.

"It's just that I have a hard time even picturing you and mother together. I can see mother. I can see you. I just can't see you *together*."

"I believe there are photographs of us from that time. When we were young, just before we were married. Perhaps a visual aid might help you . . . *picture* us, as you say."

"I've seen the photographs. And you know that's not what I mean."

"I'm afraid I only know too well what you mean. I suppose I'm just trying to avoid facing the ugliness of your remarks. The implication that I used your mother for some unsavory purpose. For money or to conceal something I was afraid of admitting. I believe that's what your insinuating, isn't it?"

"Well—"

"And the worst part is—" He found he could not finish his sentence and actually say what the worst part was. But the thought continued to run through his head: *the worst part is I came here to help you, and I find myself accused of the very thing you and Bea resent . . . of marrying for money*! He realized at that moment the tables had been turned: it was his life now being questioned. How, he wondered, had this happened?

He said very little during the rest of their lunch which ended rather hastily. After paying the bill, he assured Arthur that he would do whatever might be required of him. He promised to speak to Nadia. He encouraged him to get a prenuptial agreement only if it was something he wanted to do and otherwise forget it. He said he regretted getting off on the wrong foot with Bea and he hoped there would be a chance of seeing her again before he left. She seemed, he said, a very *interesting* person. He knew interesting was the weakest adjective he could have chosen but he was tired and beyond caring. He simply wanted to end the conversation.

Out on the sidewalk, he turned to his son and said, "Well, then." He meant to add something, but Arthur spoke up first.

"You know, Bea's had a hard life. She's had none of the advantages I have. No education. No money. None of that. And yet she seems to know things I don't. She has a better feel for people than I do. I trust her and she makes me happy— very happy."

"Then I bless your happiness," he said. He patted his son's shoulder, and then turned and walked away.

IV. Recapitulation

The events at lunch left him exhausted. Furthermore they brought on a bout of discomfiting recollection. He didn't bother going to see Nadia as promised—it would be altogether too depressing to attempt to report on his lunch—but instead went to bed early and lay in the dark thinking of Arthur's questions: Why had he married Nadia? Why hadn't he ever discussed Michael's death with his son?

He found himself going back over the years, in particular those first years with Nadia. What Arthur didn't understand was what a shy and awkward young man he had been, how he lacked any sort of experience with women or sex, how Nadia—ten years older, from a wealthy Berlin family transplanted to LA—had seduced him with her worldliness and confidence, her European manners, her free and casual approach to sex, especially quick, spontaneous sex in public places, something he soon developed a taste for. But before long he found himself seeking out men for the same thing. And once he discovered men he felt as if he had found the part of himself that had always been missing.

Still Nadia was his first affair, and it was as if she had enabled him sexually, thrown some erotic switch. He had only recently begun teaching music at a private boy's high school when he met her. She amused him. She took care of him, she was high-spirited and fun. There seemed no point in not getting married, especially after she got pregnant. Michael, who he'd first noticed at a school concert, was a senior at the time, just seventeen. The boy had definitely seduced him. Not the other way around. Though this would have made no difference whatsoever to the school authorities if their affair had come out. And then Michael had graduated, and suddenly they were free to do whatever they wanted. He left Nadia. He left Arthur, who was only two at the time. He'd always been grateful that Nadia had accepted his defection without much fuss (*I always suspected*, she'd said in her thick accent, and left it at that). But now, all these years later, he could see how upsetting it might be to Arthur. Why he might wish to finally make his own fuss.

He went out early the next morning, carrying a basket and a small paring knife. It had rained during the night. The city was damp and smelled of clay. Cool, refreshing waves of air drifted up from the wet ground. He headed directly for the spot near Casa de Cleaners where he had seen the mushrooms and was delighted to find them still there. He picked them carefully, checking to see that each one was free of insects, and headed back to the apartment.

When he reached the top of the front stairs he saw her. She was sitting on his porch, her knees pressed together with her chin in her hand. She took him by surprise. She was wearing an old wool coat and sneakers without socks and her long pale legs looked spindly and coltish.

As he approached she stood up and put her hands in her pockets. "I hope you don't mind, but Arthur told me where you live, and I decided to just come over."

"No, of course I don't mind." He wanted to add, *I'm glad you came.* He found he was actually happy to see her.

She followed him into the apartment, into the kitchen filled with warm light.

"Nice apartment," she said. "How long have you had it?"

"Forever," he said, setting his basket down on the kitchen table. "How old are you?" he asked suddenly.

"Twenty-four."

"I moved to this apartment before you were born then."

"The neighborhood must have changed a lot."

"Oh yes. All downhill, I'm afraid."

"I used to buy drugs around here," she said. "MacArthur Park."

"Really?" He was surprised by the casualness of this admission. "What sorts of drugs?"

"Oh, the usual stuff. Pot, mostly." She rubbed her nose with the back of her thumb.

"I went through a period when I enjoyed cocaine quite a bit," he said, feeling emboldened by her honesty into making his own little confession. "You know about Freud and cocaine of course. He used it for a number of years. He once said something like, 'It can be taken regularly with no apparent habit-forming consequences. In fact, the more one takes the less one is interested in consuming.' Ha! Some shrink."

"I never did cocaine," Bea said. "Couldn't afford it. What's in the basket?"

"Mushrooms! I found them right here, in the city. I thought I'd cook them for breakfast—delicious sautéed and served on toast. Can you stay for breakfast?"

"Well—"

"Please do."

She peered into the basket. "Are you sure they're edible? I mean you just picked them up somewhere?"

"Of course they're edible. Inky caps. I *do* know my mushrooms. I won't poison you, my dear, if that's what you're thinking. I may have left you with a rather bad impression yesterday, but I'm not that sinister—"

"It was really my fault," she said and sighed, looking up at him sadly. "I've been pretty depressed lately."

"Really? What's troubling you?"

"My nerves are shot. I had a bad experience with a friend on a project. What's this stuff?"

He turned to see where she was pointing and saw she was looking at the rows of his medications lined up on the counter next to the table. Before he could answer, she said,

"You're sick, aren't you?"

Should he lie? Or tell the truth?

"I knew you were sick, I could tell, but Arthur said you were fine. He said that when Michael died you told him you were okay. Are you okay? Really?"

He took a moment to answer. "It depends on what you mean by okay."

"Do you have AIDS?"

He looked at her and she gazed back at him, direct, calm, waiting. It could be he had wanted this. It could be he was tired of pretending. It could be if he spoke up now it might all come out, lift him up and lighten him. But he could not speak up.

Instead he began cleaning the mushrooms with a little brush. When he looked over at her, she gazed back at him serenely. She held her chin in the palm of her hand. Her blonde hair was black at the roots and none too clean. Her fingernails had been painted a dark purple and it gave her hands a bruised look, a damaged quality. It didn't seem she'd bother to comb her hair that morning.

"The thing about mushrooms is," he said brightly, "one may be poisonous and one perfectly wholesome, and only by knowing the distinguishing characteristics of each can one separate the good from the bad. Yet it's not as difficult as people might think."

"You don't have to tell me the truth," she said. "But you'll know I know."

Again, he said nothing.

She drew her coat around her, holding it closed at her throat. It was an old coat, frayed at the collar and cuffs with raggedy fur trim—some vintage thing from the forties. "My problem is I get upset so easily. I shouldn't have gotten so upset yesterday and left like I did. I've had to admit I'm high strung. That's my shrink's word by the way. High strung."

He put several tablespoons of butter in a pan with some garlic and soon the room was filled with the smell that always cheered him. Then he began slicing the mushrooms.

She helped herself to a glass of sherry from the sideboard and sat down at the table again.

"I just got out of a treatment program—something I had to do for a DUI—and I'm not supposed to drink, but . . . one thing I know is I'm not an alcoholic." She lifted her glass and took a sip. He glanced over at her, and she smiled and brushed a wisp of hair out of her eyes.

"You're thinking, gee, she looks different than yesterday, aren't you? I dressed to impress yesterday. Didn't see the point today."

She took another sip. "Do you think I'll be any happier when Arthur and I are married? Or do you think I'll just make him as unhappy as I am?"

He didn't know how he could possibly be expected to answer such a question—such a *troubling* question.

"You're probably wondering whether I'm right for Arthur, aren't you?"

"I couldn't possibly judge as I don't really know you, do I? "

"We're so different. But they say opposites attract. So maybe it'll be okay."

"Perhaps it will. I hope so."

He dished up the mushrooms, dividing them carefully between two plates. What she said actually bothered him. Was she right for Arthur? This admittedly unhappy person? This high-strung girl? Perhaps Nadia was right and this marriage was a bad idea.

As they ate, Bea began talking about her work. She mentioned she was working on a piece called *Three Stories about Men*, a video about a woman who picks up strangers. Not that the encounters were necessarily intended to end with sex. The point was to be in charge, the way men are in charge when they pick up women or hire prostitutes or do any number of other things men do. It was all part of her continuing investigation into desire and power. She had been depressed lately because she'd had a fight with someone who had been helping her with her film. Someone she thought of as her best friend who turned out not to be her best friend at all. This person's name was Sylvia and she'd done something quite terrible, quite unforgivable.

He could not bring himself to ask what the terrible thing was, but he didn't have to. Bea launched into the story voluntarily, some long account having to do with a scene she'd been shooting in the Valley and all the terrible things her friend Sylvia had done to sabotage the shoot, out of jealousy she was sure, but he found it difficult to follow her story because he was absorbed with his own thoughts.

The more he learned about Bea, the more worried he felt for his son. Here, he thought, is a troubled person—a person not quite in control. Drugs, depression, a treatment center—films about erotic encounters with strangers. What sort of situation was Arthur getting into? If it was true that he had acted primarily as an intercessor in his son's life, should he not intercede now to protect him from someone who might prove disastrous to his future? And yet he could not forget the way Arthur had looked at him yesterday and said, *she makes me happy*. How he'd seemed to be pleading with him to understand how essential this happiness was to him.

"Anyway," Bea said, taking the last bite of mushrooms remaining on her plate, "I shouldn't have told you all that. I'm sure it doesn't make you think good of me. You're probably feeling right now that you should discourage Arthur from marrying me, aren't you? Just tell me the truth. That's what you're thinking, isn't it?"

He took a few moments to answer. He wanted to meet honesty with honesty, but it frightened him to think of doing so.

Finally he said, "I've never been one to rush to judgment, and I'm trying not to do so now. I want nothing more than for Arthur to be happy. He seems to love you deeply and to think you'll make him happy. I suppose the question is, do you also love him?"

She looked down at her hands and didn't speak. Tears began puddling sloppily against her lids and then fell in fat drops. It upset him to see her crying. He had a great urge to give her a pep talk, as he used to do with his students, to tell her to pull herself together, to forget about making videos about desire and power and encounters with strangers. Above all he wanted to say, don't even think about marriage until you're older, until you have a better grip on life.

That's what he wanted to say. But instead, he got her some Kleenex and waited for her to stop crying.

Which she did after awhile. And once she had gotten control of herself, she looked up at him with her large, brown eyes—so sad! So full of the anguish of life!—and said, "I do love Arthur. He knows I do. And I'm going to marry him because I think this is my best chance at happiness. So that's all I have to say."

At the door she hesitated a moment. "You know, I didn't have to tell you any of this stuff, about my problems and all. For some reason I always want people to see the worst side of me so they won't feel deceived later. I guess it's a sort of test I put people through. If they can look at the worst side and still accept me then maybe when they see the best side they'll even learn to like me." She drew her coat around her and stepped outside.

He wanted to say something kind to her, such as *my dear, I already like you.* But, as usual, he waited too long to speak up and she began walking away.

"By the way," she called back at him without turning around, "Thanks for the breakfast. I've never had mushrooms like that before."

If she turned sideways and looked back, he thought, she would see him for what he is—the pale forehead and receding hairline, the heavy eyebrows now gone gray, the deep-set, light-colored eyes, a man showing his age, with a failing heart and a variable T-cell count. But she did not look back. She put a hand on the railing. She descended the steep steps lightly. Did he know what was happening? She knew, yes. And he knew. And to know what you think—and, for a while, hope—is either the absolute end or the start of something else. He felt his lightness and happiness and surprise. He felt it deep within himself.

JUDITH FREEMAN
WERTHEIMER IN THE CITY

Discussion Questions:

1. What is the attitude of Wertheimer to Bea by the end of the story? Why does he feel this way about her?
2. Compare and contrast Wertheimer's attitude toward Arthur and Bea to Nadia's. Why do they each feel the way that they do toward their children? Is one more right than the other?
3. Wertheimer feels ambivalent about what his role in his son's life should be. What should it be?

Essay Questions:

1. Each character in this story has a different view on what the role of marriage is and should be in society. Explain each point of view and why they seem to have this point of view.
2. Compare and contrast the views about marriage and relationships in Judith Freeman's story to those in Dana Johnson's story.

California

SEAN BERNARD

Summer evenings we gather in newly restored craftsmans, extended ranch houses, post-and-lintels built in the sixties; these are our homes. We have money and mortgage now, children who swim in carefully-fenced backyard pools. We grill chicken and fish, corn on the cob. We sip wine and eat cheese and grapes and speak of life and weather. Sometimes we bring out the guitar, strum a few chords and laugh, waiting for the air to cool, the sun to set, the kids to bed down.

Then we look at each other, wondering if it's time, if we're ready. Always, we are.

We go with slick, refilled glasses of wine into the living room; we sit on sofas and chairs, on the floor like children. The lights dim. A screen is pulled. Tape flaps, a fan whirs, a soundtrack clears its throat, and we watch film from an old projector. The projector reminds us of moments we've seen in movies, a nostalgia for a time we never knew.

None of the clips we watch have made the Internet. At work, when we vaguely mention their existence to colleagues, we draw blank stares. No one else knows of them. The clips pull us here—partially—because they are so rare, they are private, only ours. And it's also that our lives are so ordinary, we're not disappointed in this exactly, just cheerfully resigned.

The clips are something else entirely, new, unexpected. Nothing about them has been explained. They are mailed to us intermittently. No return address. We recognize people in them we don't know personally. We feel they are moving us somewhere, propelling to a climax we cannot guess. And we sit forward in our seats, hungrily, waiting for the next clip to begin.

The footage is especially grainy in #4, the sound cluttered. Immediately we hear the whine of the diesel VW Westphalia. The public television show host is on the road again, we see, precisely what the voiceover says as the clip begins, "The public television host is on the road again, ho-hum, always on the road, hum of engine, hum of road, rectilinear agricultural fields, irrigation canals, mountains, deserts, etc., etc., look at him, the host, so solemn, so distracted."

The camera zooms in on his face. His chin and jaw are strong. His white flat-top seems gray in the footage. There are wrinkles deep around his eyes, like an old surfer from quieter days.

He stares out a window, chin on fist. The voice says, *The host ruminates over a recurrent nightmare: empty deserts, the vast central valley with nothing but oil derricks and bones and him standing alone in denim shorts and boots and a white muslin shirt, sunglasses missing and microphone in hand, but not a soul to speak to. It's a nightmare a mind could get lost in.*

On the screen, audibly, the host sighs.

"What could it all mean?" asks the voice. "Does emptiness forespeak of great miseries?"

The host laughs shortly, "Ha!" and turns from the window. He looks directly at the camera, at us, and it is this moment that always disarms us—that he knows he's being filmed.

He smiles. What does he see? Who is behind the hand-held camera? Why is he smiling?

The camera pulls away as he looks down and taps his hiking-booted feet against the bus's floorboards. The host smiles, the voice exclaims, *Floorboards, he thinks! Such an antiquated word! Were cars truly once fitted with floorboards, actual pieces of wood that somehow did not cause fires? combustion? is there an auto museum in this state with an auto museum docent who can say if once cars had floorboards do auto museums have docents? attendants? a pit crew? there is the Internet of course, but we don't use the Internet, we use real people, That Is Who I Am, thinks the host happily, He Who Speaks to Folks, this is how we learn about the world thinks the host how we experience life here in the western Americas, here on the road, and yes! there is indeed one of course the auto museum on museum row in downtown Los Angeles, what a fool,*

The film flaps, the clip is over.

Early on we choose favorites, usually the purer ones lacking voice-over. #10 for example is amusing, behind-the-scenes, the host and his cameraman in a bright studio, sitting at an older PC, editing segments from their television show. They speak in the monosyllables of men who know each other well. "Too long." "Yep." "Cut here?" "Cut here." "Chatty Cathy, isn't he?" "They all are." #5, too, is enjoyable, the host standing outside an office building (in Studio City, we all agree, though we're only guessing) paying for a delivery of gyros. "Are the fries in there?" he asks in his soft drawl. "I gotta have my fries, delivery man!" He laughs and clearly tips well—the delivery man thanks him twice. The office door shuts, the clip ends, warm, light-hearted.

The majority of us prefer #6. It is long and simply shows the host making coffee. He seems aware of the camera but not distracted. He glances up, nods at us, doesn't speak. He is deliberate: he opens his refrigerator, removes a bottle of water, pours it into an electric kettle, flips a switch. He opens his freezer, removes four bags. He smells each, shutting his eyes tenderly with each sniff. He lingers over one bag, nods. Measures three scoops into a black grinder. Seals and returns the bags to the freezer. He presses a button and grinds the coffee. The kettle begins to steam. He flips a switch. The steam recedes. Onto the counter he sets a coffee mug fitted in what looks like a wet-suit; on this, he sets a perfectly fitted filter. Spoons grounds into the filter. Last he pours the steaming water slowly, incrementally, everything precise, just so.

He removes the filter, blows steam from the lip, sips, smiles. And so the clip ends.

We laugh over the phone, over email, over text—simultaneously we've realized that we've each been reconsidering our coffee habits, how much we tip, our interactions with coworkers.

After the laughter dies down, we start to wonder if this is no accident.

#23 begins with the host sitting forward on a brown leather sofa. On the wall behind him hangs a mirror. There is reflection of neither camera nor crew, a crack in logic that disturbs us.

"But *how* was it done? An f/x program? How much money was spent on this, really?"

This is what Don always wants to know. The strangeness worries him greatly.

Hush, we tell Don. He sighs, sits back, sighs again, frustrated.

In the clip, the host leans over a clear glass coffee table set upon iron claw feet. On one side of the table is an enormous mound of walnuts, still in shell.

The host pilfers the pile. Eventually he thumbs a single nut into his palm, shuts his eyes, and squeezes. The cracking of the shell is audible. He opens his eyes, his palm, and reaches in for the meat, which he sets on the opposite side of the table. The shell bits he wipes to the floor.

The voiceover says, *The host cracks walnuts just like the Godfather or more to the point, Brando. He never tells anyone of this ability though it is a source of great pride. He cherishes the strength of his hands. It makes him feel of the land. Self-reliant. He could have been an arm-wrestler, he thinks sometimes, and is surprised at his regret in not having been an arm-wrestler.*

The host is wincing, eyes squeezed, two hands around a nut.

He looks at his palm, frowning, and suddenly throws the shelled nut across the room.

He is six feet four inches, strong as most any man, even at sixty, and when his cameraman of eighteen years (whom he still calls "cameraman") cuts off his feet or hair in close shots, the host cries, "Least you got my guns, cameraman!" flexing his biceps.

The host, reaching over again, begins cracking walnuts again, one nut at a time.

From the start we recognize the host, of course. We have all lived in this state longer than expected—some of us born here—and so we all know the public television show, the ebullient host interviewing this person and that, exploring the magnificent wonders of California. The first clip, marked #2, we think has been mailed mistakenly: it shows the host washing his hands in an anonymous white bathroom. The clip is shot through a stall in the bathroom. It is barely twenty seconds long. We watched it and wondered what it meant, ignored it, laughed.

Two days and the second clip, #3, arrives: the host in a Ralph's grocery store, considering maple syrups, seemingly unaware of the camera, again the clip short, a minute at most.

Then the third, the fourth, and so on. Sometimes two, even three, four in a week.

We don't yet know what they mean.

After each ends, we go outside and it is cool, even in summer, the ocean breeze only half-warmed by the breath of millions between us and seas, we sip the harder drinks we've moved onto, the gins and scotches, or those of us still driving home our simple glasses of tap water. The kids sigh in sleep through screen windows. We are barefoot in grass. Some things like stars resound above the city skies. Wonderings about the host. Does he know? Is he part of it all? The more modern of us imagine that the clips have been found by an enterprising PBS intern, a film student with a taste for the avant-garde, amused by the potential in these odd and casual outtakes.

This is our early, innocent theory, when all the clips seem that way, innocent.

"What if he *doesn't* know?" Don says. He always worries. "What if it's a threat?"

We laugh Don off—certainly the clips are a prank by someone's distant cousin at the public television station. A joke with us. It's all simple fun, and one of these early nights, drunk, enjoying ourselves, someone brightens and suggests, "Let's call him! See what he knows!" We applaud the concept. Quick research is done and we find an extension at the television station attributed to the host. Maybe he's in! It is decided we'll use a pay phone—Don insists, no cell phones, no home numbers. We think this very hip, very noir. Cynthia, our only smoker, recalls once using a pay phone at a nearby convenience mart. Being a water-drinker, I'm sent as driver.

We don't speak on the drive, not at first, those balmy winds blowing through my window.

I have the air conditioning on, but she doesn't seem to care.

Finally I ask if she's lived in California long, if she's from Los Angeles.

"No one's from here, everyone knows that." She seems bored. Smokes without asking.

I ask if she's excited about making the call.

She shrugs.

I stay in the car while she puts in quarters, dials the number. She speaks into the phone. I lean forward to eavesdrop. She cups the mouthpiece and turns away. Her face, first smiling, shifts to alarm—and I, so late in the night, so excited, imagine that she's paled in fear. I step from the car, worried, but she's hanging up, saying into the phone, "Goodbye," almost breathlessly.

She looks at me steadily. "Wrong number," she says. She tells everyone else the same.

I'm too nervous to contradict her story, to describe the faces she made.

We all go home disheartened. All week I worry, what has happened, what it means.

Late Thursday the call comes. Another clip. We must gather.

We sit with unusual anxiety, sundown, curtained windows, breath held.

We lean forward as the lights dim.

This clip doesn't show the host. It's me. I'm in my car, staring anxiously from a window.

A female voice-over says, "He doesn't know what to do with all his learning, is paralyzed by education, by the choices before him. Does he go to her? Does he sit quietly? Does he—?"

I gape, confused, worried. What will happen next? What will happen to me?

Then I realize everyone in the living room is watching me, holding in laughs, exploding.

It's a pretty good prank, I agree, but it upsets me all the same.

That's the night, you'll remember, we go home early and I refuse to speak to you.

Some of us think Clip #27 has been unjustly overlooked. It is the briefest of all, a photograph of the host pinned to corkboard. The camera trembles as it zooms in. In the photograph he wears a tuxedo and holds a microphone, addressing an audience we cannot see. One arm swings wide in story-telling grandeur. The voice-over tells us, *At gatherings he says, "How about ol' Marlon Brando? Cracking those walnuts? Ever seen anything so amazing?"*

No one has seen anything so amazing.

He feels overjoyed by this.

And then sometimes you call, which must cost you effort, pride. I appreciate that, I do.

"We haven't seen you," you say. "They miss you."

Sometimes the patience in your voice irritates me.

"I haven't been by," I agree. "You're very perceptive. You should be a private detective."

"You've been drinking." You always sound more tired than angry.

"I don't have to be drunk to be angry," I say.

"Are you ever going to explain it all to me?" Now your voice is sad.

"I saw her in Whole Foods today," you say. Sadder.

Maybe I should explain it all, the *her*, the *they*, the *you*, the *me*. But does any of it matter anymore? All that remains from these stupid pronouns are your voice and its many shades, sad, angry, distant, forlorn, calm, pensive, brusque, bitter, small, and hurt. And hurt.

#9 confirms our unspoken suspicions. No more can we pretend it's all simply a prank.

The clip begins with the host inside a ranch-style home—certainly in the foothills, we agree, above Pasadena, we can tell by the plant-life, the yard, the architecture, the curve of earth, sun. The host sits at a kitchen island. Newspaper spread before him. The wet-suited coffee mug.

This time the camera is outside the house, looking in.

Inside, a phone rings very lightly, muted. The host picks it up, we hear and read his lips as he gives a (muted) booming Hello. "Hello!" cries the voice-over.

We see the host's lips repeat, "Hello!" We see his mouth form the words, "Who's this?"

"The host!" says the voice.

In his kitchen, the host frowns, pushes a button, sets the phone down. He looks annoyed.

The phone rings again. He checks the number, sets it back down. Now he is worried.

After a moment, though, he answers it.

"Hello?" whispers the voice-over. "Hello? Hello? Hello?"

And we can see, quite clearly, the speaker's breath against the kitchen window.

Then we stand out on the porch, itchy, it is summer, allergies, invisible pollens swell the air.

"We having fun yet?" Cynthia says to no one, to everyone, lit cigarette wanding the air.

#15 is one of the longest and most unsettling clips. It begins with a black screen and that ever-present voice-over: *The host has always felt restless, he is a jittery man, he understands that all his life he's been waiting for a grand moment.*

That most people bore him is the great irony of his work. All he wants is what we all of us want, a shift, an opportunity to prove himself.

The screen lights up, is blurry, comes slowly into focus. The host and his cameraman sit in a booth in a diner. Plates of half-eaten eggs and toast. A jar of dark syrup that looks black. Glasses of either milk or orange juice. The two men eat without speaking.

The voice-over explains, "Today they film an Indian and his old oak tree."

"They don't smile!" the host says suddenly. "They totally creep me out, cameraman!"

"The host quietly distrusts Indians," explains the voice-over.

The cameraman looks worried. "You can't say that!" he whispers. "People will hear!"

The host waves at the empty diner. "Hello, everyone! I'm racist!"

The camera pulls away from the men and zooms in on the front door. After a moment a shadow appears. The door opens. (Does the camera know this would happen? It seems so.) A man in brown uniform walks to the table. "Sir?" he says to the host. He holds out a sealed envelope. The host takes the envelope and tosses it aside. The man walks away.

The cameraman watches this all but says nothing.

The host pokes at the liquid yolk with a crust but does not eat.

The clip goes dark—but after a moment it is light again, we've moved outdoors, time has passed. The host and another man stand beneath what the camera reveals to be a remarkable oak tree, a canopy almost fifty yards in diameter and so thick with branches that it is nearly pitch-black beneath. "Remarkable!" exclaims the host. "What significance has this for your people?"

The Native American is wearing jeans, an ironed Polo shirt. His hair is combed neatly.

The voice-over says, *The host can see that this man before him has crazy eyes.*

The Native American talks a little about how his people were persecuted and some even hanged here beneath this sacred ancestral tree, and the host mumbles sadly. The Native American says, "There will be a turning point, of this we are certain. A day of reckoning in this land. There is too much history of violence. Old angers are bone deep. All the blood has not yet bled."

The voice-over says, *The host is worried. Does this madman think this will make an actual episode? Does he care? This is a wasted trip, the host thinks. But let the man keep talking.*

The Native American calms down and speaks more about the tree, the host asking questions, smiling. Their voices are muted as the voice-over says, *Think about his words, host. A day of reckoning. Interesting, isn't it? After all your hands are strong, you'd be fine, if the world tilted crazy couldn't you lead us into alpine valleys where we would thrive in the climates as once we were meant to in peace and harmony? Couldn't you be the one to save us all?*

In the clip the two men walk away from the tree. The cameraman follows.

The image lingers on the tree. Slowly it zooms to the base of the oak.

We see a torn envelope—one we all agree is the same delivered in the diner.

Beside it, a sheet of paper. The camera zooms in and we read in block letters: I NEED YOUR HELP. I WILL CALL WITH INSTRUCTIONS.

We sit on the porch in the cool air. Was the man in the delivery uniform part of the plot?

Every time we watch the clip his face is lowered, obscured by the bill of a cap.

How could the host, the cameraman, *not* know they were being watched?

How could they *not* see a second camera filming their every step?

Why the talk of destruction? Of blood?

"It's a treasure hunt. We're Hansels and Gretels picking crumbs off the forest floor."

That's what Cynthia says, softly, before she leaves.

She means it lightly but words don't reassure.

You seem distracted. Somewhere else.

Where am I? I'm on a cell phone. You don't know where I am.

You say that as if you're angry, like you need to win a fight. *You* hurt *me*, remember?

No, that's not it at all. You think I did the damage, but it's always the other way around. Don't you know that when a person is angry it's only because they were hurt first? Who in this world gets angry without being hurt first? No one. No one. Certainly not me. I'm not crazy.

You don't make sense anymore.

Nothing does and it never did. Who thinks it should? Who came up with such a theory?

Certainly not a person with open eyes. Living in this world. Not him. Not her.

#24 begins in a darkened house, a camera stepping through fluttering curtains and an open sliding door. The footsteps of the invisible cameraman are barely audible, a faint shuffling on wood floors. The camera enters a room and there's a lumpen shape in a bed.

A digital clock says it's three a.m.

The phone rings, the camera pulls back.

A hand reaches from the bed, hits a button. The host speaks softly to the phone. "Hello?"

The voice-over says, *Go to Silver Lake, swim to the fountain, find the next clue.*

And then, as always, darkness.

Our theory is that Clip #8 follows #24, at least chronologically. #8 is a long and quiet night sequence, filmed from a car we cannot see. We are following tail-lights—presumably the host's—and that is the only visual. The voice-over speaks softly, *Los Angeles at night, the 110 freeway, always puts the host in a pensive mood. This is the hidden freeway, curving through hills, past homes where men once raised cows, planted corn and squash, didn't care about the gleam of Dodger Stadium, Chavez Ravine a canyon named for a hacendado from the nineteenth century, an old husband of a daughter of a son-in-law of a conquistador who killed Indians with muskets and put plow to land and lived by that one word all men in this land once lived by: Build. The host knows this, reflects on this now, during his late night drive. He knows that the landowners died, that the land was parceled, the ranch house fell into disrepair, was razed, the land scooped by up speculators, Broad and Bren, Kaufmann and Argyros, Emmerson, Roski, great place for a ballpark! The history as it always is in this state—vanished. Gone. Amazing.*

Amazing. Amazing. The word is his now. Several years ago he interviewed an etymologist who explained the word's origin. It was unsurprising, after all—maze, labyrinth, to be confused, confounded, caught in a world of unseen connections . . . but still there is a logic to mazes, isn't there? The spool of thread in the first labyrinth, Ariadne, spider's web. Amazed.

Night brings back memory, how he was taunted once as a child back home in Tennessee squalid Tennessee where to dream to delight to awe was not correct. Smoky Mountains sunset, sad, evocative. He had an old Pentax G10 rigged to a fencepost as tripod and took time-elapsed photos of dying light. He showed the pictures at school. Isn't it amazing? he whispered.

The teacher and the older kids beat him after class. He has admitted this to no one.

The voice quiets but the taillights keep moving, pulling further away, until the clip's end.

"What it is is a meditation on the nature of television, of film," Don suggests one night. We've all had too much to drink. Now we're frustrated—this week's clip, #62, is blank. Nothing. Angrily we blame the creators of this absurd virtual chase that never leaves our living rooms. We assign petty motives. "Bored rich kids," we agree. "Avant-garde assholes," we say.

But Don has a larger and more complex point; he's an academic. "Isn't television after all the great medium of our time? Our country? This state? We live fifteen minutes from Hollywood. We *are* the image, not the thing itself. We are the gaze *and* the object. Why trust these clips as real? They are *film*! *Two*-dimensional!" Don spills his drink and swears loudly. He's under pressure. Up for tenure in the fall, struggling to complete his book, to find a publisher. Normally we cut him off but tonight we let him ramble. "What do we know about the host? He is like us—like us, he loves television. He remembers moments—moon landing, Watergate, Ali-Frazier, Munich, those transcendent moments offered only by television. Television is one-way immersion without obligation. You sit, you flip a button, you look away, you read the paper, you look up, you mute, you change channel, take piss, heat pizza, wander house, push-up, sit-up, phone call, text. The Internet? You can't wander from it, it's too needy. Only television is so accommodating!"

He's almost shouting. "It wouldn't work on the Internet! This is film, this is community! Here we are in other worlds—real ones, real people! The world used to be parks! Then it was benches! Then it was sofas at home!" He stares at us, desperate. "I've seen gaming chairs in Target, speakers built in and wires for kids to sit in for hours!" He looks madly. "Quick! I need to write!" Someone passes him a pen and napkin, he grasps them, begins jotting furiously.

We pity and loathe Don. I hold Cynthia's elbow as we walk to our cars. She smiles sadly.

"Now calm down, that was an ocean of gin you drank, cowboy."

She blows me an air kiss, is gone.

In Augusts I take to night-driving, Mulholland, very quick, very romantic, clichéd, stupid.

You know how it goes, of course—the strange things that matter don't go on forever.

First we get a call: there is a new clip, yes, but we will not be watching it.

Why? The police have been contacted. The host has been notified. Much grave concern.

We move harried through the week. Worried at each police car, flinching at each phone ring. Don dutifully sends panicked emails at the top of each hour. The police call some of us in, those who've hosted screenings. One, at the police station, being led to an interrogation room, sees the host. "Of course I'm concerned!" the host is yelling at a detective. "Who wouldn't be?"

Enraged, he looks at our passing friend. The host's face is red, wild, incensed.

A few of us meet in a bar Friday night, sitters for the kids, those with kids. Cynthia can't make it. I tell you as much later. You don't believe me. Another goddamn fight. Over drinks we murmur, booth-cramped. What we know—thanks, police—the clips aren't old. They're made each week. The host has recognized several—he knew where he was, what he was doing. The detectives want answers but the consensus is they don't suspect us. As if that reassures us.

"Why *should* they suspect us?" we protest. "We're not suspect!"

We drink our drinks and agree that police are fools. Someone else is the guilty party.

Or maybe we just can't bear suspecting each other—your cruel theory all along.

You tell me they like monkeys so Saturday, monkeys. Of course a gorilla escapes its cage.

Really. I need to piss so I leave them in the cotton candy line. Too much water in me, it's too hot in this city, this state. Thirty-five million people roasting three months a year. Madness.

I wash my hands and outside lean over the water fountain. I hear a snorting, a snuffling.

I turn. A gorilla is staring at me. He's much larger than me. Wider. Firmer base. His eyes are dilated, he looks stressed. His muscles are enormous and shagged with coarse hair. Such fingers. He could destroy me. We turn at a siren coming through trees. He grunts, scoots along.

They are at a picnic table, lips coated in pink puffed sugar, and what do I say to them to explain the police swarming the zoo? That those peaceful gorillas can get loose and maybe if you're lucky you won't get hurt? Is that the lesson here? Instead I tell them a story about a father who invents magical glass boxes for his children, all they have to do is push a button and whoosh, glass walls all around, safe and sound. They say what about air? Food? Xbox? I reassure them. These are advanced glass boxes! Totally decked out! They exchange skeptical looks.

I drop them off and you say to me, "Hear the one about the escaped gorilla?"

I tell you the gorilla was me and you don't understand how such a thing could be true.

On Monday night, in my mailbox, a large yellow envelope. No return address.

I open it inside, lights out, feeling nauseous.

A film canister.

Clip #49 begins as many do—nothing but darkness. Then a voice from the void.

"Like Genesis," murmurs Cynthia, fanning herself with the business section.

I ask for quiet and listen to the words.

He has seen and touched every part of this state, literally traveled every paved road, been to every county seat, every damn landmark and boy there are a few thousand, aren't there, has spoken to professors and town folk to historical society ladies and blue-collar workers, to illegals and Border Patrol, to vigilantes and human rights crusaders, has sat with mayors and senators and oh so many civil engineers, dam builders, bridge builders, highway designers, public transportation consultants, architects and other assorted mad men, the oldest living woman in the state, and when she died the next one, and the next, and the next, plucked fruit with original fruit-pickers, packed crates with original crate-packers, flipped patties with original burger-makers, made fries with the sad McDonald brothers and once talked with Ray Kroc himself before that rich and sleazy salesman kicked the bucket, has surfed with surfers, dived with anemone divers, flown with kite fliers, sand volleyball players, racecar drivers, rock climbers, artists of every color, ate donuts with Sonny Barger, Sonny Bono, a very young Arnold and so many cultural representatives, schnitzel, tabbouleh, pupusas, cricket tacos, Oaxacans, Basques, Guatemalans, Romanians, Filipinos even Tasmanians all here in this Popeye-arm-shaped state.

At this point the darkness recedes. Light enters the frame.

It reveals a swastika.

"Holy shit," says Cynthia.

The camera pulls back further. The swastika resides on the face of a deranged man.

"Whitman?" wonders Cynthia.

The voice continues, *And still the most famous, the one above them all, the firmament over this state is and always has been him, the single most unsettling person the host has ever spoken to, and the host believes that there is something of this man in us all, in the water, in the air, we are all this man, a derangement not as the rest of the country thinks, not Californians as hippies and crystals and free love but anger to the bone that anchors on Popeye's arm swinging round and round, the chain digging into the skin of the palm, that pressure that needs burst.*

Staring at us steadily is Charles Manson.

That's it. That's the last of the clips.

You leave voice messages via can-and-string, say they're worried about me, you are, too.

Stop working. Take a break. Come inside. Dinner's ready.

But mustn't we believe that if we can unravel just one thing the maze will come undone?

I dream of walking at night in the dark.

I see a large man ahead of me, saying, *Who are you? Why are you following me?*

Carter Sullivan and Jack Benny, oh Jack, *Your money or your wallet . . .* golden silence.

California gold? Television! That clever image, those flashing lights! We are all moths!

I lie awake tonight, thinking of mankind fleeing darkness, flapping at bright screens.

It's not a lightly-thought thought.

The State of California. Been there. Not sure I made it back.

Cynthia blocks my number. Don gets tenure. Everyone sort of tolerates me but they don't hide it well. I move out of the city, to an apartment in Eagle Rock. We don't see each other anymore, them, me, you, us. We were part of the group of smart people, so smart, our group of smart, clever smart people, and then you and me baby we split and sure we tried to make up, but we split again and they all chose you. No, no, that's not exactly what happened but it's close. I call Don late the way I used to, drunkenly smoking on our porches, but he's married now, has to sleep, notes for tomorrow's lecture. "Those were some strange days," I tell him, my voice thick, I can't help it. He's polite. "Yes, indeed. Strange days. Like in that The Doors song," he says. *That the.* Always smart, Don. "Gotta tuck up, bud," he tells me. "We'll get together soon."

Some days I sit watching re-runs of the host's television show. How cheery he is! How sated! I know that TV-him isn't real-him, that he's a different man with his own fears, his own struggles, I know I need to stop, need to let go of Cynthia/her the kids/them you/you so I/me can move on but the words trip me up every time, "move on" isn't moving on just moving back? Yielding? A surrender? I've never liked this state, it's always felt uneasy to me, trembly, on the verge of explode, it's the air, the winds, the fires, tides under ocean, deserts, I don't know, such foreboding, just a sense is all. You can come to the west what you can do is you can come to this land of grand scale and learn to think in shadows, in shadows men will pan for gold backroom deals buy all the land steal the water forces align, it's obvious, look around, such tremendous forces after all. Look, that dome, that volcano, that geyser. That beach. That bear. Eagle. Whale. Ronald Reagan. Woolly mammoth. Joshua Tree. Death Valley. Donner Party. Neverland Ranch. John Muir. Manson. To think no forces are conspiring would be to be a fool! Sometimes I think I could learn a bit by reading up on Manson but what good would that do? It'd only make me obsessive and it's bad to obsess over crazies. Obsess over normal things. It's healthier.

Unpacking boxes this week, I find these words in an old notepad:

Go to Silver Lake, swim to the fountain, find the next clue.

I laugh about it. So silly, all that, the days of magical mysterious clips, when everything was so cosmic and fraught. Nostalgic, I take a drive to the area. I walk the path that loops the reservoir. There's live music from a bar. Young people laughing. Couples walking past, smiling.

I consider swimming to the fountain. Instead I sit on a bench in sight of the fountain.

A man walks past me. He pauses. Of course I know who it is—of course it's the host.

We stare at each other.

You're the one, he says. I dream about you. You're always following me.

I shake my head in denial.

Why are you here? he asks. Who are you?

I'm no one, I say.

His voice is soft. He sounds tired. I feel bad for him. He's old. You did all this, he says.

All what?

He sighs. He's confused. Exhausted. Something falls from his hand. I pick it up. A photo. On the back is written "#1." It's a Polaroid of a chalked word on blackboard:

California

I rise and hand it to him. He nods thanks. For a minute we stand there together. Looking at the photo, then around us, at everything. What is this, the host asks softly.

All this time I thought you'd know, I admit.

We stare out. It's dark but we know what's out in the darkness. The valleys below us. The seas. Hills and roads. People. Silence. Trees. I'm pretty sure we can hear waves crashing in the bay.

REVIEW

Discussion Questions:

1. How does the narrator of "California" feel about the state of California?
2. Why is the narrator ostracized near the end of the story from his friends?
3. How would you characterize the relationship of the narrator and the host of the show at the end of "California"?

Essay Questions:

1. "California" explores the ideas of fame and intrusion. The host has lost his privacy, and the narrator feels uncomfortably like an outsider in this world. What does "California" suggest about the role of fame and privacy in the state of California?
2. Define the term "privacy" using "California" to develop your ideas. Does the story capture the reality of our lack of privacy in the 21st century?
3. Compare and contrast the relationships in "California" to those in "The Jizo Statues," "Palimpsest," and/or "Burt the Martian." What difficulties do these characters face in their relationships and how do they resolve those difficulties or fail to resolve them?

Lot's Wife

MICHELLE DOWD

A thing is mighty big when time and distance cannot shrink it.
—Zora Neale Hurston

Mark mesmerized me with his sadness, of a weight and texture so familiar, it almost felt like mine. I told him early on that I would leave, that it's what I do, but he didn't believe me. I don't even know if I meant it, but it seemed like a fair warning.

"I'll leave, you know," I said to Mark, the first time he took off my shirt, "even if I love you, even if you think whatever we have is working."

"Maybe you won't this time," he countered, reaching to unhook my bra strap, "Did you ever think maybe I'm different?"

I shrugged, and arched my back to make it easier on him. I spoke to his softly lit reflection in the car window, opening my breasts to the empty field in front of us, idly curious at the way he fumbled at my back. "Maybe," I said, "But I don't know if I am."

We hadn't seen each other in almost fifteen years, since we were teenagers swaddled in a cult, and he said he regretted we hadn't been sexual back then, suggesting perhaps we had unfinished business. I didn't argue, since I hadn't even said goodbye back then, when I abandoned everyone I knew at the Field and hightailed it to a liberal arts college that welcomed and financially supported my cultural diversity. I didn't tell him about the Council meeting, or explain that I don't like goodbyes, not even casual ones, how I would rather slip away unnoticed, even from parties, searching for escape routes upon arriving, so that when I get that panicky feeling, I know where and how to bolt. I didn't tell him how I wanted this option more than caffeine, alcohol, music, or sleep, craved it more than coming in tandem, needed it more than I need love.

Mark stayed at the Field longer than I did, but even now I don't know the terms of his exodus. He was reluctant to talk about it, and I accepted this without complaint. He had never married, never lived with a woman, never had a child or attached to the world through those relatively predictable milestones we call settling down, and eventually I would see in the way he avoided eye contact, and the subtle slump of his shoulders, that his confidence was a ruse, that he never got over the shunning. Having everyone you've ever known stop speaking to you is a harsh ritual. It gets inside of you like a bad dream and wears down the joints and muscles and sinews of what you think of as your corporeal being until you're not sure where you end and anyone else begins.

When Mark contacted me after so much time had passed, he breathed a brokenness I recognized, and I wanted so badly to heal it, I returned his affection almost immediately. I fingered the fear behind his eyes, a palpable pain that resonated more effectively now than it had when I had last seen him at seventeen. I assured him we wouldn't have to talk about our pasts, that we could pick up as we were, that right now was all that mattered.

Mark still resided in the San Gabriel Valley, which held a basin of memories that yanked to roots I thought were buried beyond recollection. When I drove from the high desert to see him, the view of jacarandas and the smell of eucalyptus assaulted me from the freeway, through the surface streets to his Pasadena condominium, permeating even the pastrami sandwiches we shared at The Hat. Walking through Huntington Gardens on his annual membership pass and feeding the ducks at the Arboretum made me weep in ways he assumed were joy. There we were, two adults trapped in the ghosts of adolescence, unable to communicate in anything but the present tense. This philosophy works well in meditation or a yoga class, but we didn't attend either, and one day he climbed on top of me and I had no idea who he was. I felt accosted by this stranger and I got nauseous and stiffened, turning my head to the side, clenching my eyes shut, while he kept undulating, as if casually copulating a corpse. When he came with no complaint, slid off, and went to the kitchen for water, I threw up over the edge of the bed.

So I left him too, via a text message the next morning, and I never explained why.

———————————

The Meeting Room floats above a football field in Arcadia, balancing on the base of the scoreboard and two rickety wooden pillars, attached at the rear like a pier. I am seventeen and have known every face in this room since before I knew what knowing meant. I was born and raised here, on the border of El Monte, in a hollowed out former city dump, leased by my grandfather in 1946, burrowed into the end of a cul-de-sac, now forged into a basin of athletic fields, a scoreboard tower, and a clubroom we call a church. Each member of the Council of Elders belonged to this community back when my mother was born in 1947, the first daughter of the Leader and his wife, my mentally compromised grandmother, with whom I now live.

I want to leave our faith community to go to college, but the Field's Council has expressly denied my request. As instructed, I signed a "commitment for life" form when I was twelve, and the Council interprets this as legally binding. I don't comprehend the distinction between the Field's version of communal law versus state or federal judicial systems, but I tell them I will come back when I am done with my education, that I will sign in blood to devote myself to the Field, its members, all of whom are my clan, and I genuinely believe this can happen. They have been conceptually clear about the unmistakable tainting that transpires from contact with Outsiders. "We are all disposable," my father says, "paper cups worth only what we are filled with. Fill yourself with the Holy Spirit of the Lord our God, and you will have value and purpose." If I leave, they say I will be empty, like the hand that can't welcome the spirit of the dove that alights but once. When that white dove flies away, it will never offer itself again, because straight is the gate, and narrow is the way, and only a very few will ever find it.

I have been raised in this doctrine, so I don't find it difficult to fathom. I know that we are unlike Amish communities in an essential way: the Field does not welcome back wanderers, because God is capricious, because the Lord our God is a jealous God, and he will not tolerate the vain worship of golden idols.

These past couple of weeks, I have hoped to be the exception. I was born, raised, and schooled here exclusively, and my lineage is pure. But now, having been called to this meeting to hear their decree, I fear my appeal will be denied, that I won't be given grace to pursue formal education. At this point, I can't fathom how I will proceed into adulthood either way, how I will navigate a path inside or Outside, how the Field can go on without our Leader, or how I will be able to personally function without this place.

Last year, when my grandfather died, I still believed he was God's son, and patiently, day after day, I watched the sky for signs. I waited for the sun to grow dark, the moon to turn blood red, for war to descend upon us, for the blood to rise up to the horses' bridles. They said that an angel took him, and I thought it was the truth, that his bedside had lit up, "and lo, the angel of the Lord was round about them," and I was surprised the staff hadn't been killed for seeing the backside of God.

Yet here I was, in a world that hadn't ended, an abated apocalypse that left me hanging in perpetual childhood, disappointed, disillusioned, and discredited. I sit in the front, next to my father, the Founder's son-in-law, who calls the meeting to order.

"Brethren, you know straight is the gate, and narrow is the way which leadeth unto life, and few there be that find it."

The members grunt their assent. I try to breathe evenly and inaudibly. Every person in this room has known me since I was in my mother's belly, but they speak of me in the third person.

"Then they will deliver you up to tribulation and put you to death, and you will be hated by all nations for my name's sake."

They speak of *Foxe's Book of Martyrs*, of the heroic courage of the men who were persecuted for their public devotion to Jesus Christ as their Lord and Savior. I tune this part out, having already studied the purported lives of these men and women extensively, holy Christians who were triumphantly flayed, slain, devoured by lions, burned alive, the numerous horrific tortures and executions procured against them for their righteous faith. "If our God, whom we serve, is able to deliver us from the burning fiery furnace, he will deliver us out of thy hand, O King, but if not, be it known unto thee, O King, that we will not serve thy gods, nor worship the golden image which thou hast set up."

The pretentiousness of secular learning is clearly a golden idol of great temptation, leading the young into a den of iniquity. They continue to pontificate.

"What message will this send?"

"If she returns, who else might she lead astray? What sort of precedent would this set? In these dark times, it's not possible to stay true to the path of righteousness while dwelling in the Devil's kingdom."

"Who does she think she is?"

I don't need their permission. This is a simple decision. Stay or leave. But I would wrestle a flaming angel for their blessing.

I have only met one person in this lifetime who walks away more frequently and dramatically than I do, and he was not from the Field. Eric's choice to pack up his car in the middle of the night, leave his job at the Basehor Sentinel and head west in pursuit of a friendship with Henry Rollins, captivated me like an imminent train wreck for two solid years. This fascination, disguised as a romantic relationship, propelled me on an extended exploration of the high desert, a region both geographically and philosophically outside of Los Angeles and its suburban sprawl. The wide spaces cracked open the night sky, the stark sunsets and vivid stars pierced me like a dagger, and the hidden streams and enclaves we took the time to discover together would etch their way into me like a first home.

When Eric's mother, Hannah, re-married just before high school graduation, he packed a backpack and hitchhiked the roads until college, without once calling to notify them where he was. One month shy of college graduation, his girlfriend broke up with him, so he left Brown University, just shy of a degree, and neither apologized for, nor apparently regretted, his flight. When Kansas approved intelligent design theories as legitimate scientific pedagogy, Eric wrote Christopher Hitchens a letter, then ceremoniously left his job at the Basehor Sentinel as a protest, drove through Big Sur to read for three days at the Henry Miller Memorial Library, cruised through Los Angeles to interview Henry Rollins, abandoned his stepfather's car in Covina, and eventually halted in Barstow for a brief gig at the Desert Dispatch.

I was driving back from Las Vegas in a rental car when we collided. I had ridden there shotgun in my date's CRX, for a supposed birthday weekend this potential boyfriend had designed to encourage me to try my hand at gambling, something I had never experienced, though he assured me I should. He suggested I needed to let go more, live in the moment, stop investing so diligently in a future none of us can control. I suspected he thought this would be just the kind of debauched high that might compel me to have sex with him, but I had insisted on separate rooms. Not that it ended up mattering. I left this man dateless in the casino before our first nightfall. He had clearly drunk a few too many shots of bourbon, and when he started shouting at me in a room full of people in a way that reminded me of my grandfather, I unceremoniously walked out, rented a car, and headed back home to Glendora. When I stopped at In-N-Out and got out of the car for my preferred high of Diet Coke coupled with the sugar of a chocolate shake, I saw Eric, a tall, blond man in his twenties, in pleated pants and Doc Martens, his press pass pinned to his crisp dress shirt pocket, intrepidly interviewing public responses to a local fire.

I stood in line, grateful to stretch my legs, and I watched his wide smile and assessed his drawl, which contained a touch of down-home southern manners, mixed with the pretentious vocabulary of northeastern privilege. I noticed that what he scribbled into his small spiral notebook was obviously doodling, not any specific words the people offered, how he practically stomped his foot in impatience with this process, too smart and skilled to be working this kind of beat. He reminded me of my younger brother, and I wanted to intercede, to take him home and make him tea, to tell him he had so much potential, that he could do better than this. When he finished wandering around the tables, he went outside and harassed people in the drive-through, and I stood at the window and watched this too. On my way back out to the rental car, he finally approached me.

"Miss, are you aware of the uncontained fire just north of Hesperia?"

"Indeed. Are you aware that that not a single person here has told you anything anyone will want to read?" I measured his smile and decided to continue, "You might as well just go back to your car and make up responses, because none of that was remotely usable."

He laughed. "Why don't you offer me something more exigent?"

"Hmmm . . . Tennessee?"

"What?"

"Are you from Tennessee?"

"North Carolina."

"You obviously haven't been in California very long. Had a Double-Double yet?"

"Indeed, I have not."

"I'll get you one if you tell me your story."

He raised his eyebrows. "What story?"

As he began to spin his tall tales, we refilled our Diet Cokes over and over, until the associates advised us that they were closing. I looked at my phone. It was one in the morning. I boldly broke the only two rules I religiously upheld; we exchanged numbers and I gave him a ride back to his apartment. He opened the car door, took his messenger bag from the backseat, and sauntered into his driveway without glancing back. I studied him, yearned for his demeanor, thought he was braver than I was, so stalwart in his motions, so direct in his pursuits. I just sat there in the driver's seat and stared in awe. I felt small, like folded laundry set in a basket, and I saw him as everything I was not, all I wanted so badly to be.

But still, eventually I would leave him for the last time, asleep in his bed, with only a note on the table.

My father quotes scripture and gesticulates bombastically. The Council concurs. I lose track of the argument and the approach, consumed by a rising nausea threatening to erupt in projectile vomit. I excuse myself with a mumbled excuse, my hand wrapped around my belly. The door isn't even closed behind me when I begin retching in waves on the floating stairs, my head bowed in shame so heavy, the field below spins like a vortex that can pull with the force of a gigantic magnet. I clench the rail to combat the vertigo, but my hands are slippery from the bile. It doesn't feel like a choice as much as an inevitability, gripping the stairs with slimy hands, acid burning my throat. Eventually, when no one comes out to check on me, I don't know how to go back in, don't know what I could possibly want to hear or say, so I shuffle down the stairs and walk across the field, out the mouth of the cul-de-sac, onto Farna Avenue, all the way up to Ralph's Grocery, where I use the payphone to call my admissions officer.

Not missing anyone would become my only goal, the closest I could get to freedom.

"May I speak to Rachel Carter?" a woman's soft voice queried.

"Speaking."

"Are you acquainted with an Eric Murphy?"

"Yes . . ." I stammered, paused, and then inserted, "But I really don't know how you can reach him."

As far as I knew, Eric hadn't had a residence in years, nor a cell phone, and from what he had conveyed to me, I surmised that he mostly traipsed across the southeastern states, job to job, from Key West to Atoka to Manchester. I got fairly regular emails, detailed stories of people he had met and profiled, but I only heard from him in a personal and emotionally engaging way when he had access to a phone, usually when he was high on DXM, huddled up in a motel on an extended trip. When I stopped answering the phone, he would, for several days in a row, fill up my answering machine with long ramblings, as if we were having an extended conversation. And then I wouldn't hear for him for several months. Between these sporadic outbursts and relatively regular calls on his behalf from collection agencies, I had known his itinerant patterns for over a decade, but hadn't seen him in person all that time. The last time I saw him was the first time I witnessed him fall off his preferred-drug-of-choice wagon, when I saw that he had become someone I couldn't recognize, and I left the aforementioned note on his table. I had hitchhiked my way back the two hundred miles we had strayed from my current Glendora residence, and I hardened my heart to his explanations and pleas.

He still used my number on health and job forms, as both a reference and as his emergency contact, so I never really lost track of his chaotic meanderings. When I got these calls, his presence in my life still felt palpable.

"This is Carla Castanza from the California Department of Social Services. Eric is here in The Ronald Reagan Medical Center in critical condition and he gave us your number. Would you be able to answer some questions for us?"

"I'm sorry, he's where?" I stuttered.

"UCLA," she clarified.

"How long has he been in California?"

"I don't know ma'am. What I do know is that he is consistently consuming Dextromethorphan to the point of discombobulation, passing out in public, exposing himself to the elements, with multiple diagnoses of hypothermia and three separate incidents of broken bones. We have no way to estimate how many emergency room visits he has accumulated, but he has been in here nine times in the past fourteen days. This is the first time we have been able to get him to give us his name."

"I'm not family," I interrupted.

"He said he has no family. Your name and number is the only contact he would give us."

My recent husband looked at me with some concern from across his coffee and I mouthed, "Eric." He shook his head and shrugged amiably, apparently relieved it wasn't of any significance.

"His parents move around. I can give you their names, and his brother's . . . Surely they are traceable?"

She sighed. "Will they take him in? I know this isn't professional of me to say, but he is going to die if he continues this behavior. Each time he comes in, he's connected to social services, rehab, psychiatric counseling. He checks himself out as soon as he can walk and refuses any help."

I considered hanging up the phone. Certainly she wouldn't call back. I had no responsibility here. There was nothing tying me to this man, nothing solid between us, no shared friends or work projects, nothing except perhaps the invisible thread of a shared compulsion to bail.

"I can be there by seven this evening. Shall I meet with you? What should I bring? Is he able to receive visitors? Can he eat?"

He was lean, and so long his feet propped over the metal edge of the bed. His face was significantly weathered and leathered, and it seemed incredible that he hadn't shrunk from his 6'6" frame. When I got close enough for him to identify me, his smile broadened and creased his worn face, revealing a broken left front tooth. I kept my eyes on his, but didn't speak. The memories between us were thick like fog, and I felt the weight of the air wrap tight against my face, viscous as snot, as if it could strangle me. I plodded up next to the bed, and placed my right hand on his concave chest.

"Let me call Hannah."

"Krankstress," he countered, grabbing my wrist with his untethered hand. "It's good to see you."

Time evaporated. It didn't matter that I had settled into a career, a marriage, two children, the necessary accoutrements I accumulated in order to feel like a real adult. Here I was. He was my mirror image, my inverse Dorian Grey, the restlessness I knew was still inside of me, the personification of the ideologies we shared, of lives devoted to running away.

"They say you will die if you keep doing this to yourself."

"We are all dying, Krankstress."

"Not at our own hands."

"Hmmmmph," he sighed. "You say that as if it's an impediment." He coughed lightly into his left hand, but didn't let go of mine with his right. "Not really a better way to go, is there?"

I thought about this.

"Won't anyone miss you? Do you think about how it will affect Hannah and Henry? Don't you care what you are doing to them?"

Eric chuckled and squeezed my hand, the IV needle protruding from his wrist. "Krankstress, it's really good to see you. Did I say that yet? You're still a drug, a drug, baby, my lovely drug, a drug like no other, you know that? If you would come back, honey, I would stop all this nonsense cold turkey."

His eyes rolled back in his head a little and he laid back on the pillow. His breath became even and I watched his eyelids flicker and settle down in apparent harmony. I was told there was Lorzepam in the intravenous drip, so I assumed it had kicked in. I tucked the sheet neatly in around his shoulders and patted him like he was my son. And I waited, as he slept, waited for him to awaken, waited until the nurse returned, to the inevitable news that his heart was giving out, that another episode would likely kill him. She asked me to convince him to meet with CDSS, to agree to the voluntary terms of assistance, to find his way back into society and a social structure that could contain him. I had my doubts, but I let her talk.

He wasn't my problem anymore. The fact that he had held on tenuously all these years to a fetish of me as his savior wasn't my doing. I hadn't encouraged this. I hadn't signed up for his worship or his need. My empathy ultimately wasn't any more helpful than his family's neglect. He had turned down every offer of assistance championed to him, and I didn't think I could dint his nihilism or his determination to self-destruct.

But I sat with him, my hand in his as he gripped onto me, still tense, but more peaceful than I remembered him when we had slept together in random motels, all those stops on all those road trips, those months when I had accompanied him on his pursuit of endless stories. I sat with him now and prayed to a God I no longer believed in. I practiced loving-kindness meditation, and then decided to be proactive. I searched for his family on my laptop, found the necessary connections, left messages on his father's and his brother's machines, gently spelling out his condition, whereabouts, and how to reach him. I called my husband, said goodnight to the children, and then checked into a motel and sat down cross-legged on the bed, reading through the literature and paperwork I had been given. I wrote down a list of steps and contacts that would be helpful to Eric as I fantasized about the ways he would navigate his way back to health, back to the world of the living.

In the morning, I bought a sausage biscuit sandwich from the McDonald's drive-through and carried the small paper sack to his room for breakfast.

He was gone. The staff had advised him not to leave, but he had pulled out the IV and got himself dressed, and they had no jurisdiction to restrain him.

The sun was warm on my face as I left the hospital, and a soft breeze broke through the city haze, lightly tinged with the scent of eucalyptus. I thought of the Field as I pressed the button to lower my convertible roof, of my sisters who were still there, married to men we had known since infancy. I hadn't been invited to their weddings, but I knew of their children and the meal exchanges, the communal playgroups and the scripture that occupied the center of each of these rituals, the soothing sounds of prayer and prognostications. Part of me envied the comfort of their stability, a life that still held assurance of divine resolution.

I sat with my key in the ignition, listening to Elayna Boynton croon from my playlist and thought about all the empty roads I hadn't driven on yet, all the highways that would lead me away from here, away from the urban desert sprawl. I looked in my rearview mirror and carefully wiped the melted mascara away from my under-eyes. Then I backed out of my parking spot, turned my wheel sharply, and steered my car towards home. Received.

MICHELLE DOWD
LOT'S WIFE

Discussion Questions:

1. Compared to several other stories in the collection, how does the setting of California in "Lot's Wife" affect the ideas and actions of the characters?
2. Explain the connection that the protagonist feels for Eric. Why does she feel that they are the same in many ways? To what degree is she correct in this notion?
3. Why does the narrator feel compelled to walk away from so many people and things in her life?

Essay Questions:

1. Compare and contrast Eric in "Lot's Wife" to Bud Barrett in Robert Roberge's story. They are both on similar paths, but does one seem to be more self-aware of his problems? Does one seem more or less tragic?
2. To what degree does the narrator of "Lot's Wife" feel a responsibility to Eric? Should she feel responsible?

Flights

DIBAKAR BARUA

A blue and white jumbo jet shakes free of the earth and roars into an afternoon glare. Shredded clouds, a hard crystalline sheet of water below, and the dotted fragility of the Los Angeles shoreline seem strange and sorrowful.

The last time I crossed the Pacific was five years ago, in 1990, when my wife flew with me to meet my relatives in Bangladesh. The need for this solitary flight came suddenly last week as I tried to cure a bout of mild insomnia by drinking a late nightcap. The phone rang. A raspy voice from the old country crackled through a maze of wires and satellite connections.

"Ah, Bijou!" I yelled, trying to be heard over the bad connection. "Weren't you in Miami?"

"I'm in Bangladesh for a visit."

My most recent encounter with Bijou—our villagers used to call him Fat Bijou—was several years ago. One November, he called me from a cheap motel near LAX to complain about life and American food. ("Everything *smells* here!"). He had sold his father's farmlands and come to LA to attend a religious conference so that he could get lost in America. ("Just give me the plane fare to New York, my little brother. I know a countryman in Queens who'll set me up.")

"Why are you calling me?" I asked him now.

"I have a bit of b-a-d news," he said, drawling out some key words. "Tinku, your niece, has d-i-e-d. She was taken to Calcutta for an o-p-e-r-a-t-i-o-n. Well, her Calcutta aunt can't reach her father in Korea . . ."

Apparently, Tinku, my sixteen-year-old niece died in Calcutta in my sister's house, before she could be taken to a hospital for a scheduled biopsy. Bijou didn't know the long and desperate history of her illness, which I had gleaned over the last several years in increasingly worrying bits and pieces: a defective thyroid gland, then swelling of the limbs, kidney ailment, rheumatic pain, opinions from medical boards, nature cures, a belated attempt at surgery.

I decided then, not impulsively, to fly to Seoul, and see Pranab, my forty-four-year-old college-dropout brother, who worked, illegally, in a textile factory there. I knew, given his circumstances, he'd not be flying to Calcutta for the funeral.

Later that morning, after I broke the news of Tinku's death to Pranab, there was a long moment of shocked silence.

"I'm coming to Seoul," I said.

"Why?"

"To see you."

"Oh, well, I'll be alright," he said. But he didn't sound alright.

"I'm coming," I said. "Just find me a hotel room near you."

The plane's drone makes me drowsy. Closing my eyes, I see images of Noapara—where Pranab and I had spent six years with our mother after Father died in 1965: dusty paths and clumps of mango and date trees, our mud house attic full of wild pigeons and their sad guttural coos, ponds shimmering with lilac-colored flowers of water-hyacinth, monsoon gusts lifting and folding bamboo fences like lily pads, a spectral moon after storms and fallen branches swarming with ants. These lonely images then give way to faces—mother, aunts, cousins, neighbors.

I see Pranab on a sunny afternoon—rushing past me on the dirt road from school, his eyes fastened to a distant point, his body tensed up in flight. Moments later a gang of dusty, barefoot, country boys, with whom Pranab never fit in because of his city ways, his book bag and canvas shoes, come hollering and screaming. Led by Fat Bijou, they give him a chase, calling him a "red boy," a "ripe melon," and other such names.

A few days after this, Mustafa Kamal, our history teacher and an admirer of great nationalist heroes like Subhas Bose of Bengal and Kemal Ataturk of Turkey, took Pranab under his wing. "They're trying to say you're not a man," he said. "Now what can you do to prove them wrong?" Pranab gave one of the boys a black eye and threw another one into a ditch.

Years later, in the early days of the 1971 civil war, Mustafa Kamal would pay for his cultivation of Bengali manhood with his life. A Pakistani soldier from Punjab would shoot him in the back, in front of his wife and children, and Kamal would leap into a muddy pond only to drown.

From this haunting drowsiness, I wake up again to the plane's constant hum. An overhead screen shows a blue-green map of the flight path, an arc rising from Los Angeles over the blue Pacific like a broken rainbow.

At the Kimpu airport in Seoul, a sleepy-eyed man in white waves my passport over a scanner. A page of print flashes on a small computer screen. My passport picture—thin, bearded face, bushy hair—contrasts markedly with my current clean-shaven look and receding hairline.

"Where you going?" he says in English.

I show him Pranab's address. The man peers at it for a long time and slowly shakes his head.

"Chichuk! Kyonggi-Do!" he reads with a rising voice.

"That's my brother's address."

"Your brother Korean?"

"No."

"Chichuk!"

"Yes," I say, losing patience. "What's the matter with it?"

The man leafs through the passport, draws it up against the scanner again, and sighs.

"Five years! Why no travel five years!"

"I didn't have to."

He stamps a page of my passport and lets me go.

Pranab stands in a large crowd of Koreans behind an iron railing. He looks at me for a long second before smiling and waving. Hauling a suitcase, I wave back with my free hand.

"Here you are, after five years," Pranab says in the Chittagong dialect of Bengali we grew up speaking. We hug briefly and talk about the flight and Seoul's weather. He is carrying an extra jacket for me.

Our taxi crosses a bridge overlooking a muddy river and crawls through city streets amid slow but unruly traffic. The sky, some distant hills, trees by the road, shops and construction sites all put on a dusty drab mask, unmitigated by the setting sun. The air is about fifty degrees colder than in Los Angeles.

"You can't blame them for being suspicious," Pranab says after I tell him about the immigration officer. "Too many foreigners coming here illegally."

"I don't see anyone but Koreans here."

"No, not on the streets."

"Well, you should see Los Angeles. Anyway, why would they get suspicious about me? I have an American passport."

"That's why they let you go soon," Pranab says. "The trouble is, you come without any planning. You just buy a ticket and fly." He sounds more envious than critical.

"What did *you* do?"

"I was a businessman!" he says with a laugh. "Had a room reserved in the Hilton. Stayed only one night, though."

We get off at a budget hotel called Hanyang, a building of green tiles, faded red carpet, and rusty brass railings. The dark lobby smells of Korean food from a cafeteria. We check into a darkened second floor room with a small, high window shut tightly against the bitter Seoul cold. Feeling depressed, I lie down on the bed as Pranab washes up in the bathroom. Like me, he has put on some weight and lost some hair. He looks tired too, with dark bags under his eyes and a puffy face.

"I'll bring you something to eat," he says, catching my eyes on him in a mirror.

"Let's go together."

"You won't like the places here. Korean food smells bad."

"All food smells bad to Bengalis," I say, "except their own."

"Oh I can eat Korean now," Pranab says. "But you? I don't know."

He brings back an odd assortment: fried chicken, ketchup, fries, crackers, and apples.

Despite his years and hard knocks, Pranab seems locked into the country innocence of his teens. After dinner, I pick up the phone and dial my wife. "Well, I'm here, eating with my brother."

"How is he holding up?"

"He's fine. Here, talk to him?"

I hand the phone to Pranab without comment. Seated on a vinyl chair, he crosses his legs and holds the phone with a tight, pinched look.

"Yes," he says. "Yes, thank you." And after another minute or two of listening, he says the same thing again and hangs up.

"I couldn't say much to her." He grins in embarrassment. "My English is very poor."

"You could have given the phone to me."

Walking up slowly to a fake cherry dresser, he pulls out a knife from a blue tote bag and begins peeling some apples on a plate.

"When you called me that day," he says quietly, "I knew something was wrong. But I thought it was Mother you'd called about. I just couldn't believe . . ."

"You went silent on the phone."

"I couldn't talk . . ."

Pranab slices an apple, clunking his knife against the plate.

"I keep seeing her on the day I boarded the plane in Dhaka," he says, "her arms around me, asking me to come back soon."

"It must be so very hard for you," I say. "I only saw her that one month in 1990. My memories of her are so vivid. She was so full of life."

"Yes, she was," Pranab says, putting a plate of sliced apples in front of me.

Pranab doesn't stay with me at night. "You need a good night's rest," he says, thrusting an envelope into my hand as he leaves for his factory quarters in Chichuk. The envelope contains several pictures of Tinku—a high-school picture, a teen head-shot, a family portrait. In the school photo, she stands to the far left of five girls, the prettiest in an orange sari, quiet and sad-eyed while the other girls smile. I never knew this more grown-up Tinku.

The family photo shows the girl I came to know, a cheeky eleven-year-old clucking her tongue at the way my wife wrapped her sari, rolling her eyes if her younger sister Rinku, not herself, was the one chosen for a night's camp near Uncle and Auntie's bed. The letters she wrote to us after that visit, four or five a year until '93, took on an increasingly plaintive note—when will you visit again, why don't you write more often. Then suddenly the letters stopped, with not even a response to our New Year's greetings. Did she know she was going to die, I wonder, and put the photos back in the envelope to stop an eerie feeling?

Five years have passed quickly for my wife and me, bringing only minor changes in the middle of the big continuities—the same jobs, the same condominium near the beach, the same car, the same dog. Those same years have sent Tinku hurtling from childhood to a forced maturity that comes from illness and suffering to an absurd death.

Confused sounds wake me around three in the morning. A dull thud thud, a headboard hitting the thin wall in the next room.

A woman's staccato yelps stretching out into shrieks and moans. Then a lull. I almost go back to sleep before being treated again to another series of thuds, yelps, and moans. I go outside and push their doorbell hard. A tinny jingle plays out in the room. The panting breaths, audible outside, hold for a moment. I rush back to bed before anyone sees me.

In the afternoon, I am startled from sleep by the same silly jingle that I set off in the morning, sounding in my room. I take a while before opening the door.

"Come, get ready," Pranab says with a smile. "I've cooked today. Can't feed you our canteen food, really."

Jet-lagged and achy, I put on layers of clothing and thick gloves. The raw Seoul air is full of smoke, vapor, and smells wafting from roadside carts.

Chichuk is only one stop by metro rail from the hotel, the last station at the industrial edge of Seoul. Fringed by brown hills of dead grass and bare trees, it looks like a moonscape.

"You should have come here in springtime," Pranab says. "It's much prettier then."

We follow an asphalt road that winds through tenements, so narrow in places that passing cars use dirt shoulders, raising dust clouds. The tenements give way to spores of metal and plastic green houses in fields of industrial debris.

The textile factory where my brother works bustles behind a big gate with an iron "C" wrought in the middle. We pass warehouses, chimneys, and fork-lifts carrying bales of clothes. Pranab shows me his work station beside a hulking, waving arm that folds long sheets into neat piles. He tells me what he does there, but all I hear is the deafening clatter of machinery.

Out of the gate, we walk down a narrow alley, with rows of mildewed tile roofs on both sides. We take off our shoes before entering the end room of a row house, a squarish room not more than 20> x 15>, dark like a cave, but warm from the heated floor. Cold air seeps in through the closed door.

"You have a lot of those," I say, pointing at a pile of blankets of different colors, patterns and shags.

"Bought them in a thrift store. Cheaper than a mattress, more comfortable."

"So, this is your room," I say, inspecting his things—a chipped green steel cabinet full of clothes, food, and utensils, a small TV and a cassette player, some pictures on brick walls.

"I was lucky to get a room by myself," he says. "Most workers here sleep four or five in a room. Why don't you sit down on this blanket and be comfortable. I'll finish up a few things before we eat."

"Where do we eat?"

"In the office canteen. They let me cook there when I want to make Bengali food. Wait here for a few minutes. I'll come and get you when things are ready. Here, play some Bengali cassettes. Do you have these in your collection?"

He leaves me in the room. I don't play the Bengali cassettes. The TV shows only Korean programs and news about the Simpson trial on the GI station. I switch it off and sit on a warm blanket, waiting for food. The pictures on the walls are pin-ups—not bikini-clad sex kittens, but idealized portraits of feminine beauty: a blonde bride in an elegant satin train, a bejeweled Indian dancer in an ornate dance hall.

Pranab returns to take me to an empty canteen smelling of vinegar and fish sauce, its sooty walls strewn with Korean flyers and notices, its bare cement floor gritty with sand. A batch of workers have just finished lunch, leaving dirty plates and leftovers on Formica tables and even on the seats of some scattered chairs.

Pranab clears a corner table, wipes it with a wet rag, and arranges a feast: rice, kimchi, chicken vindaloo, and curried beef with garlic. Beef and beer, smoking, factory work. I feel concerned about his health. I don't tell him about my practice of Californian style vegetarianism—no meat, plenty of fish. I fill my plate with rice and chicken.

"When did you make all this?"

"This morning," he says. "Take some beef too."

"A little later."

I note a flicker of concern in his eyes.

"So you get weekends off?" I say.

"It's not like that," he says, with a shy smile. "I get paid for the time I put in. No work, no pay."

"Is that so?" I ask. "Do you make as much as the Koreans?"

"I don't know about America," he says, after pausing to take a sip of his beer. "But I've heard a lot about the Middle East and Thailand and Singapore. Believe me, compared to other countries, Korea is a heaven. Now, of course, they have their own bad habits, drinking and such, but they respect what I do . . ."

"That's great," I say. "But don't take time off just for me."

"I have the next few days free," he says.

"Don't give up work for my sake," I say, not wanting him to sacrifice an income just to entertain me. "I'm sure I can do things to amuse myself when you're at work."

"Take some beef," he says.

I take a few pieces of beef; then, like a fool, I begin to chatter about the health risks of red meat and cigarette smoking.

"If I had known I would have got fish," he says.

An awkward silence looms. "You must miss being at home terribly," I say.

"I try not to," he says.

That night in the hotel room, I gear up for what I came to Korea for, a chat with Pranab about his future plans.

"Dada, you should go back home," I say, using the Bengali term of respect for an elder brother. "Your wife and daughter need you. So does Mother. Don't worry about money. I'll send you money for a year, and more if you need it. You'll find something to do by then."

Pranab sits quietly looking at his feet. I carry on, probably with unfounded optimism, about the kind of opportunities he can look into later—renting out taxicabs, exporting garments. He waits patiently for me to finish.

"You are very kind to me," he says. "But there really aren't any opportunities in Bangladesh for honest people."

"How long do you plan to stay on here as an illegal worker making minimum wage?" I ask.

Embarrassed by the edge in my voice, I add, "The money you're making here goes a long way in Bangladesh. But how long can you live apart from your wife and family?"

"Don't worry about me."

"Well, I do worry about you," I say.

"If you want to do something for us," Pranab says, "do it for Rinku. Take her with you and give her an education." Rinku is my brother's second daughter, only twelve years old.

"We can talk about Rinku some other time," I say. "Right now you need to go home and take care of your health. What is it about home that you're dreading? Why don't you want to go back?"

Pranab looks up at me with a flash of anger in his eyes. "What's it about home that *you* dread?" he asks. "Why don't *you* go back?"

A strange question that sounds like a grievance. He knows perfectly well how badly I had wanted to leave the late seventies Bangladesh of military coups and assassinations, how I had pored over university catalogs in the American Center for weeks and had applied to dozens of American universities.

"For better or worse I'm an American now," I say. "Married and settled there. What does your wife say about this? Don't you miss her?"

"I spoke with her on a neighbor's phone just a few days ago," he says. "We had a long talk. I'm trying to get a work permit so I can bring her over here."

"What if you don't get one?"

"Sooner or later I will. If not this year, next year."

We sit silently for a minute or two. Then Pranab takes off his jacket and shirt.

"Are you staying here tonight?" I ask.

"I thought I might."

"This place is noisy. You may not get much sleep. I stayed up much of last night."

"You could ask for a room change," he says. "On second thought, I'll go back to Chichuk. I'll bring you some breakfast in the morning."

"Look, dada. I didn't mean it that way at all. Stay with me."

"I know you don't mean it that way," he says. "But you need a good night's rest."

The night turns out to be noisier than ever. The sexual athletes are gone, but a group of young men take a room a few doors down the hall. They barge in and out of the room yelling at each other, carrying beer bottles.

Giving up all hopes of sleep, I bundle up for a walk. The street is empty, neon signs flickering in the spectral quiet. I walk two blocks to a 7-Eleven store and pick up a bottle of Korean wine. As the clerk rings me up, I notice a pint of Passport scotch in a glass case. I gesture at the scotch. "Ay, ay, sir," the clerk says, stomping the floor with a military salute.

The scotch makes me numb and heavy. With the bottle half-drained, I feel moored to the bed. Invisible hands push me firmly into a vortex of fractured dreams. Phantoms whisper as I drive on the freeways that crisscross in swooping arcs. And the village, of course, with its fragrant mango buds and ponds of lilac-colored flowers.

Pranab comes in the morning to feed me again. He casts a troubled glance at my half-finished bottle of scotch. I make up my mind to atone for an ill-spent night by doing something very peaceful with him, maybe going to a quiet place for a picnic. He suggests the Korean Folk Village, a theme park in Suwon. We pack up and take a train, riding silently across fifty miles of tunnels, roads, houses, viaducts, and bare hills, livened up intermittently by some evergreens or Korean flags.

"It's like the country we grew up in, a village with thatched houses, haystacks, chickens grazing," he says.

February is a slow month at the Korean Folk Village. Some big houses, with pagoda-like roofs of corrugated tile and intricate woodwork in the awnings, flank the entrance. Smaller houses, made of wood, brick, or bamboo, with thatched roofs and barnyards, exhibit the farm life of centuries past. A lane lined with totem poles leads to a row of shops where craftsmen work and wait for sparse visitors.

"Take some pictures," Pranab says. "For your sister and niece."

Obediently, I aim my camcorder at shops, a stream, houses, a small bridge, a woman wearing a *hanbok*, a scholar practicing calligraphy. Pranab walks, seemingly nonchalant, hands held behind his back, and ends up in front of the camera whichever way I turn.

"Enough of this," I say, pointing to the more populated side of the stream. "Let's get over there."

Tourists sit in bunches around square tables and drink home brew from terracotta cups. Hot steam and a musky aroma rise and melt in the thin air.

"I don't like that stuff," Pranab says, as he follows me to a *makkoli* shop selling Korean rice wine.

"You haven't even tried it."

I beckon a server and get two piping hot cups of the drink. Pranab picks up the cup, sniffs and puts it down.

"It smells."

"Smells good," I said.

He takes a small sip.

Later, for lunch, we go to one of the big houses, a restaurant, near the park entrance. We sit near a burning stove and order hot egg drop soup and the only vegetarian plate on the menu—potatoes fried with leek.

"So Fat Bijou is visiting home?" Pranab says. Indoor warmth and spicy soup make him reminisce. "Yes. The last I heard from him he was headed for Miami. Before that he was a busboy in an Indian restaurant in Queens; he got kicked out for stealing waiters' tips."

"He has sent a lot of money to rebuild the village temple," Pranab says. "The temple gate will have his name inscribed. He's doing quite well, obviously."

"Ahh! Fat Bijou, a pillar of society!"

"You and he," Pranab says, "are the two success stories for our village."

"*Oh fuck,*" I blurt out in English and see Pranab turning red in the face.

"Just an American expression," I say in embarrassment. "You remember how Bijou was your tormentor in school . . ."

"I can't hate him," Pranab says, "for doing what he did as a boy. At least he has made something out of himself. The others, like me, are floundering."

"Dada, you are *not* floundering. You don't have to. Money isn't everything."

"Let me tell you about some of them," Pranab says. "You don't keep up with the news from back home. I do. Take Sudorshon, you know the quiet boy who opened a grocery shop. He was killed not too long ago by some robbers. They were going away with his cash box, when, like a fool, he told them that he knew who they were. So the robbers tied him to a post and set the shop on fire."

"That's a tragedy!" I protest. "Not a failure."

Pranab doesn't understand the distinction. He recites a litany of calamities befalling the people we had known as children: loss of property, hard drinking, vagrancy, violent deaths.

"Don't *blame the victims,*" I urge, using an American cliché.

"I am blaming the village. The country too. A dying place."

"It's so alive in my mind."

"It's dying," he says, gently.

"I see why you won't go back home."

"Don't worry about me," he says. "Do something for my daughter."

Pranab becomes rather chatty after that. A gentle and loving man, he dreams of stern measures as a solution for human problems. For Bangladesh, he wants a strong government that would silence the noisy *mullahs*, and jail any bureaucrat, office worker, or businessman caught cheating, malingering, or taking bribes.

"As Kemal did for Turkey," he says, giving his musings a historic precedence.

"Wasn't it Mustafa Kamal who taught us about Kemal Atatürk?" I say, alluding to our school days. "Yes, he was rather proud of his namesake."

"Ah, Kamal Saheb," Pranab says, "a good man."

"What if those who do the judging also cheat or take bribes?"

Pranab seems lost in thought. The slain teacher's memory evokes an irony that doesn't escape him.

"I don't know," he says. "I don't know what to think of anything anymore."

The next day I coax Pranab into working his day shift and play the lone tourist, visiting Gyeongbokgung Palace and museum, buying gifts for my wife in the Itaewon shopping district—a jade bracelet, a celadon vase. This routine makes me tired. My tour book describes Seoul as vibrant and friendly, but its congested roads swarming with grimy Hyundais and Daiwoos, and the incongruous sight of well-dressed crowds rushing about amid a wintry barrenness, depress me. And where are the old and the idle, I wonder. The cold, dry parks are brown and empty. The young and the able, rushing off in business suits, fill the subways and city streets.

That night in a bar called Rock'n'Roll Cafe, Pranab and I sit watching the same young men and women, in T-shirts, jeans, and leather jackets, screaming and bumping en masse to Bon Jovi or The Doors, smoking Marlboros, gulping down Budweisers.

"Some of these girls aren't much older than Tinku," Pranab says softly.

"We're getting old," I say with a laugh. And I can't imagine my brother who is not yet old, who finds comfort even in his one room shack, a few words of Korean, and a low paying job, growing old and making a home in this hard northern clime.

"Go back home, dada," I say. "This is not a country for you."

A look of confusion comes over his face. "Let's get some fresh air," he says, stubbing his cigarette into an ash tray. "I'm getting a headache from all this noise."

Out in the quieter street, braced against the cold night, we walk hurriedly toward a subway station.

"You're so educated, you know the world," Pranab says. "I guess you have a right to tell me what I should do."

"Don't say that," I protest. "I don't know the world any more than you do. I just want you to be happier in some way."

"Yes, I could go home as you suggest," he says. "After you leave tomorrow, it'll be hard to keep going here."

"You'll do fine at home," I say, wondering if that sounds as thin and flat to him as it does to me.

Later, in the warmth of the train, hiding amidst its crowd and clatter, Pranab repeatedly wipes his eyes. When we come to Yeonsinnae, the station near my hotel, I say, "Come, spend this night with me. We'll eat and talk about Tinku."

"Let's say a prayer for her soul," he says.

DIBAKAR BARUA
FLIGHTS

Discussion Questions:

1. Why does Pranab want the narrator to take Rinku to America?
2. Why does Pranab want to stay in Korea away from his family in Bangladesh?
3. Why is Korea so depressing to the narrator?
4. Does Pranab feel shame? Does he seem to believe that failure and victimhood are the same thing? Does this belief add to his feelings of shame?
5. What challenges does Pranab have now that he is living in Korea?

Essay Questions:

1. The idea of foreignness is at the heart of this story. As immigrants to Los Angeles and Korea, how do the characters define the word "home" for themselves and each other?
2. Compare and contrast Pranab's feelings of isolation and otherness to those of Sarah from "The Jizo Statues."
3. To what degree is Pranab's refusal to return to Bangladesh an act of cowardice, or is he motivated by other emotions?
4. What are the primary and secondary reasons the narrator has come to Korea to see Pranab?

The Snack Bar

GRANT HIER

Just a big plywood box with a silver lock and sloping roof, a silent, clunky jungle gym to climb and stand on most days—but as the bleacher seats begin to fill, the hinged window lifts and locks to become a sunshade awning, and inside are moms clad in team colors, eye-candy displays in this Cabinet of Wonder, actresses seen only from the waist up like on the new family RCA color TV (with spinning concentric dials your dad won't let you touch). Inside is a World of Color— unlike the muted neighborhood Helms Bakery Truck displays, smooth sliding drawers of brown and white iced donuts and loaves of bread smelling like manna at the cul-de-sac curb—though these treasures were just as magical, just as anticipated by you and your friends, bouncing in place there, wishing for time to move faster. Then, at last, the communal breaking of ABBA-ZABA bars, the sharing of licorice whips and sunflower seeds poured into upturned palms, even into hands of friends of friends that you never really talked to except here, but it was here that you knew you were part of the tribe, the adolescent church social, a cathedral of chain link casting checked shadows across windbreakers and banana seats on stingrays. Here behind the field of play on Sunday afternoons, relatives long dead now sat and enjoyed the sunlight on their shoulders as if soaking in every detail. Strange treats you would never again know. Sugar dots stuck on paper strips, in rainbow order, sold by the inch. Tiny wax bottles of red nectar, licked out in drips, the empties suctioned to tongue tip and waggled back and forth at that girl you wanted to kiss but could only make laugh at your foolishness. And so she remains there in your memory, forever turning away to watch her brother's at bat, and you chewing the blank wax like flavorless gum, staring across the park, the school playground beyond, the flagpole pinging.

City maintenance workers razed the Snack Bar on a fall morning while you were thinking of something else. Had you been there, you might have protested, or maybe just asked to climb on top of it one last time and carefully rise to stand, on tip-toes, straining to see something more in the distance. And even as you remember it now, it is better in your head than it really was, the paint flakes forgotten, the termite sand accumulating around the studs you never even saw, the façade changing like the faces of all of those friends, those whose names you forget more than recall. Sonny became a car mechanic, but you wouldn't know that. Dennis's sister drowned in a pool. Brad became an alcoholic who recycles forklift flats, and you passed him one day when you were at the mall but you didn't recognize him. They are gone from your life now, like the great monuments of the sport you still study and love more than most people do their religion. Sure, Fenway and Wrigley still remain, and Vin Scully's voice from a radio speaker each Spring you no longer take for granted, embracing its presence as you do your old dog, trying to remember the details, this beauty here all around you now: *remember this now*. It is through the arc of your love affair with the game that you have come to understand the importance of commemoration, the error of sentimentality. History flattens all, one dimension at a time. Team pictures remain in a drawer, but no photos of the Snack Bar, just an imagined outline in the space it once was, like the ghost of Ebbets Field in the minds of another generation still, still floating between apartment towers like a fog. The studs and backstop yanked from their moorings, the diamond paved over to become something else, changed by the world again and again, but sometimes, just before falling asleep, you can still see a detail, catch a glimpse of left field between shadows—just as the billboards and light towers of Tiger Stadium no longer rise, yet flat patches of grass and clay can be found right there where they have always been, waiting like a patient dog to be noticed.

Duffle Bag of Balls

GRANT HIER

Caked in clay dust, splat outlines from a Rain Bird's spray on one side and a sticky island of spilled Slurpee along the zipper. Navy blue canvas with paler seams, thick thread stitched by a whirring machine that was guided by an eight-year-old's hand (not even as wide as a baseball) in clammy heat to a chorus of clicking insects and singing aunts and sisters. The baseballs themselves stitched by hands just as small and brown, but on another continent, the songs sung in a different tongue. But the heat's the same. The sweat. And now they are carried together in the warm sunshine of another country still, plopped down in the chalk of the batter's box, the sound of laughter and shouts filling the air surrounding. The oldest ball inside goes back six seasons, softened now by countless bat cracks and bounces. Three brand new balls stand out for their fresh creaminess against the other dulled and mud-marked cowhides. Several have frayed stitches, one from a chain link snag last August. Another ball still carries the mammalian oil of Jerry Junior's forehead from when Brian, by far the best arm in team history, let go a throw full-tilt from short range, a hard red knob (the sudden focal point of the entire team) welling up and shining like JJ's tears.

Bat Rack

The older city fields (a misnomer, really) had only fencing for teams to stand behind. Newer fields had dugouts (another misnomer, really fenced-in pens) holding teams like restless bonobos in a box, bouncing off each other and yelping with every score—just as bonobos do, only they scored every day. But no boy in these pens had scored. First base, maybe. Some reached second but bragged of third and home sweet home. The bats were either leaned into a corner or hung, individually, handle first, from a single diamond of chain link, angling out at 45 degrees as if half-filled with blood. Something about that last eligible summer of Little League, before Pony, when change marked each day as bold as the X on the calendar between games, the games themselves just seven innings, the moon in the seventh house and the musk of XX chromosomes ascending. That same March the first bat racks were installed, a welded network of circular steel sheaths that made the bats sing as they slid inside and kept them standing upright. That same April your sister had a sleepover and the new girl in school named Natalie (she even looked like Natalie Wood) stayed the night at your house and you caught a glimpse of her putting on her powder blue PJs, the same shade of your favorite sky, the one above the W-shaped roofs of the outfield pavilions, behind the orange Union 76 ball in the parking lot of Dodger Stadium. So much mattered then. Who said what to whom and when and what girls were cute and which had been kissed. Who could swing the biggest stick. Each day defining more.

The power and pride felt when it was your swing that cracked the coach's old wooden practice bat. Richie was first to have his voice crack then deepen by October's playoffs, suddenly getting noticed by your sister. But you were the first to use the new 30" bat and that ping that sent the fastball sizzling back up the middle Opening Day—unforgettable—like the glimpse of Natalie's spine and her half-naked shimmy and that first kiss as you grabbed her wrist and stopped her in the hall in front of your bedroom, the way you could feel the muscles flexing across the shoulders, the firm neck, erect. How strange and tingling this new flesh twitching to life, and your growing. And so you practiced, it felt so good. Practice being just as important as the game (the coach said so) so stroke after stroke you put in the work like a pro, every night and every day, whenever you could, building new muscles in your biceps and forearms. The timing was awkward (like everything then) but you tried it fast and slow, focusing on the form, standing in front of the mirror, seeing the sweat on your chest and imagining Natalie and powder blue cotton skies sliding like the summer days and your slow motion straightening of arms, head down, eye on the ball. And so you learned to swing and shag. A lifelong lesson on the ritual of selection started there as well: the bat pulled from the rack and grabbed mid-way, then hand over hand up the shaft, each fist closer to the knob, the last one to grip it deciding.

Discussion Questions:

1. How does Hier use the imagery of baseball to explore adolescent sexuality?
2. Are the narrators' memories positive only in retrospect in Hier's stories? Were they difficult memories that he has found a way to take pleasure in from afar?
3. What popular culture cues help to set each of these three vignettes in specific moments of time?

Essay Questions:

1. How does Hier use the poetic language to capture a moment in time?
2. Compare and contrast these vignettes to others such as "Chuze Off!," "Terminal Island," and "From Alta Vista High" in the way they present specific moments from Los Angeles's past.
3. Compare and contrast Hier's vignettes to "Preparing to Photograph My Grandparents." How do these authors use popular cultural references to help us understand character and setting?

Pay Phone

MICK HAVEN

"Hello."

The voice was deep, coarse, *male*—not my wife's. I squinted, my vision narrowing until I felt as if I were looking through a four-inch-wide and one-inch-high slit, like the kind on armored cars in old war movies.

"Yes . . . who is this?" I didn't want to give my fear away. My throat was tight, and my voice sounded high to me. Not a good thing when trying to keep cool to have my voice go up a couple of octaves: definitely didn't make me feel large and in charge.

"I'm John."

Visions of my wife kidnapped, hogtied, and held for ransom or having an affair with someone named John—each equally repugnant in its own perverse way—careened around in my head, fighting for dominance.

I pulled my cell phone away from my ear and looked at the screen: yep, definitely my wife's number.

Flipping on my turn signal, I pulled to the curb.

"Look, I've got this phone. I made a few calls on it. I went through the numbers on it. I was just trying to find out whose it was."

"And why do you have the phone?"

"Oh, right."

Pause.

"I found it."

An unbidden image appeared in my mind like a night scene revealed in a camera's flash: my wife dead in some field along the bluffs in Palos Verdes—on her stomach, one leg askew, a shoe missing and her hair fanned out around her head. This guy finds the phone near whatever homeless haunt he lives in. It was lost as the murderer (and probably rapist) dragged her through the field.

I said with all the nonchalance I could muster, "Where'd you find it?"

"It was over by . . ." And John rattled off the name of the restaurant across the alley from the building our condo was in.

"Yeah, I'm not so good with technology and all, so I've just been going down the phone list calling people to see if I could find out whose phone it was and get it back to them."

"Where exactly was the phone when you picked it up?"

"It was in front of an apartment building. The stairs. On the sidewalk."

Now the vision was one that I could live with and much more Elayne-like: she'd dropped the phone in a mad rush to her car from our place because she was already supposed to be at work but was just leaving. And she didn't notice she dropped it because her morning frenzy was akin to, well, a natural disaster like a lahar or something.

"Look, I'm an honest guy, so I just want to get it back to you—"

"Great, thanks."

"For forty dollars."

I laughed. "Forty, huh?" My mind rapidly parsed the angles: we didn't have insurance on our phones, and our plan wasn't up for a while, so we weren't eligible for a new phone right now; buying one would cost more than forty. "Okay, but I don't have the cash on me. I'll have to stop and get some."

"Oh, sure, man."

"Where can we meet?"

"Uh, you know where—" And he named a grocery store a block from our place. "Yeah, so there's a bus stop in front of it. I'll be there."

"How will I know it's you?"

Pause. "I'm wearing a gray sweatshirt and blue jeans."

"All right, let me get the money."

"You're not gonna call the cops or anything are you?"

"No, why should I? You found the phone, right?"

"Oh yeah, yeah, sure."

"All right, then. I'll see you in a few minutes with the cash."

I thought about calling Elayne at work but then figured why? The guy's story was plausible. This was definitely something that would happen to my wife.

So I pulled back onto the road, found a store with an ATM, went in to get the cash and made my way to the grocery store to meet John.

When I got near, I decided to park in front of our apartment and walk to the store. This way as I approached the bus stop I could check it out while crossing the parking lot in front of the grocery store. John sounded cagey, so I thought I should be as well.

It was around 4 p.m. and a beautiful Long Beach SoCal day: warm and balmy, with the hint of a breeze to take the edge off. The afternoon's golden sunlight caused everything to look just a little better than it was.

I walked across the parking lot and eyeballed the bus stop. I saw a guy in a gray sweatshirt and jeans, one of three. Two others were sitting on the bench under the shelter.

I stepped up to Gray Sweatshirt. He was tall and had the skinny, caved-in-face-from-no-teeth, desiccated-and-sunburned, grizzled-gray look I associated with the homeless. Although I hardly ever noticed the homeless anymore because living downtown, I tried to steer completely clear of them, avoiding looking at them, talking to them, noticing them. They were a ubiquitous fixture of the downtown scene, and I still hadn't formulated an effective strategy I was comfortable with using to deal with them.

They made me decidedly uncomfortable as I considered their plight. So I would prefer not to. I didn't even know where the Long Beach Homeless Shelter was if I'd wanted to point them in that direction.

I'd tried a couple of different ways of interacting with them, and nothing seemed to really work. I'd greeted them with a smile, and that just got me hit up for money. I think five times in one day was my personal record. And it was embarrassing because I rarely carried cash anymore: with the advent of ATM cards all I had was plastic. And when I said as much, I always felt guilty, like they didn't believe me, like they thought I was just a cheap bastard. White man's guilt, maybe. Except a preponderance of the homeless I met were white, so I'm not sure how that worked here.

When I occasionally had some money and gave it to them, I felt like maybe I was just sending them to their grave sooner as they went and bought a forty-ouncer or some crack. Sometimes I offered to buy them food but that rarely went well. Outright refusals or comments like "Just give me the money and I'll get it" were the usual responses. Finally, I'd come up with a rule: I only gave money to women and old timers. It was a triage situation.

Plus, a lot of the homeless were crazy—the outright *dangerous* kind, not the neuroses I suffered from—smelled, and shit in the alley beside my condo, which didn't exactly endear them to me. So I never knew how to treat them with dignity because they'd obviously lost a lot of it, and I often felt patronizing.

Although I vaguely remember hearing about some kind of "Ten Year Plan" to eradicate homelessness in Long Beach (maybe I'd read it in the local rag, the *Long Beach Press Telegram*), it still seemed from what I'd seen of their response (none, as far as I could tell) the city didn't really know what to do with them either. That didn't offer me much succor, but at least I didn't feel alone in my puzzlement.

There was a really nice park next to the main branch of the Long Beach Library—downtown, next to City Hall—that had become the de facto headquarters of the homeless. They'd hang out around it and go into the library and take care of whatever ablutions they took care of in the bathrooms. An acquaintance of mine that worked at City Hall told me Long Beach was thinking of bulldozing the park and turning it into a parking lot.

Great fucking solution. It was a gorgeous park with fountains and a bridge and these old shade trees. The public art was mediocre, but, hey, what do you expect? Cities almost always go with safe there.

Speaking of libraries, that was another faction of the civilized world that wasn't really sure what to do about the homeless either: urban public librarians. I'd read in some newspaper or magazine article that at librarians' conferences an issue they confronted was what to do about the homeless that set up shop in their library. There were all sorts of anecdotal stories: bums sleeping in stalls in the restrooms or taking off all their clothes in the bathroom to bathe in the sink, homeless guys looking at porn on the library's computers, exposing themselves in the stacks, scaring patrons and librarians alike, fighting, and the litany goes on.

I asked Gray Sweatshirt, "John?"

He pointed behind me.

I turned, and looked at another guy in the trio: Athos, Porthos, and Aramis. John was definitely Athos. He was big and broad. Well-muscled. His head was shaved down to blond stubble, and he was taller, but not much, than my five-foot-six. Wearing faded but clean jeans, he also wore a collared shirt tucked into the pants. The shirt was kind of groovy, some polyester number that reminded me of the late seventies or early eighties, but all of his attire was clean, and he was clean. And so *not* what I associated homeless people with. A crazy drunk, maybe, but not homeless.

The crazy came through in his eyes: the whites nearly glowed, and his pupils did the same in pale blue. They were open too wide, like a zealot's, and stayed open too long between blinks.

The one detail that kind of gave away his homelessness was a sunburn under his suntan: you only get that look from spending all your time outdoors.

The last musketeer was off to one side and wore a greasy ball cap. Shorter than his pals, he was sucked up and as dingy as his ball cap, with grime visible like a shadow under his wispy beard.

John's age was indeterminate. The other two homeless guys had indeterminate ages as well, but it was different. They could be anywhere from late forties to late fifties, but you knew they got there the hard way: an extra patina of age was layered on top of what they already had, disguising how old they really were.

John, on the other hand, looked like he was older than me, but that was about as good as I could do. However, I had to stop making that assumption since I always assumed everyone was older than me. Now that I was in the twilight of my thirties, that wasn't as true as it had once been, and it was proving false more and more every day.

John's eyes found mine. He reached out a strong hand and said, "I could tell you were a good guy."

I took his hand. It was big and solid. Not coarse but not soft. He gave me a firm grip, no bone-crushing bullshit, although he could've easily powdered the bird bones of my softly civilized writer's hands: that's what my wife's grandmother used to call them, writer's hands. Whenever she'd see me, she'd grab my hand, rub it between hers, turn it over to look at the palm, then look at me and say in broken English (she was Cuban), "So soft. Nice. Writer's hands."

The handshake stopped, and John said, "I knew you wouldn't call the cops."

I shook my head. "Nah. A finder's fee seemed fair." I pulled a couple of crumpled twenties from my pants pocket. I'd thrown them in there so I wouldn't have to pull out my wallet. I'd tried to think ahead, come up with a plan, consider every contingency: just as John had, giving me the description of his boon companion, Gray Sweatshirt. I wondered if he'd run that by the guy or just figured Gray Sweatshirt was a pawn that John was willing to sacrifice to save his royal ass?

I'm a writer, so I make up stories. I find myself filling in a complete history on everyone I meet based on what they look and sound like. It happens automatically within minutes of meeting people. Sometimes faster. In this case, it seemed obvious to me that John was the kingpin. He didn't look like either of these long-time denizens of the street. His eyes gave away the fact that something was amiss, but his physical appearance belied nothing.

I felt like he'd pulled the big fish in the small pond ploy by putting together this cohort with him as the chief. I wondered how he kept his build living on the street? A heavy regimen of calisthenics? What about food? I lifted weights. It took sizable amounts of lean protein to keep a build like John's up. Hot dogs on a coat hanger over a fire under some overpass wouldn't do it.

I held up the crumpled twenties. "Where's the phone?"

John smiled. "Yeah, I knew you were a good guy. I could tell by your voice." He pulled out the phone.

"I'm no good with technology," he said, "So I just started calling. I'm glad I got through to you. I wanted to get the phone back."

I remembered my manners. "I'm glad you got through, too. Thanks a lot."

I held out the money. He took it and gave me the phone.

He folded up the twenties and tucked them away. "Thank you, brother." He smiled again, his teeth white and even in his brown face with its red undertone. "Yep. I knew you were a good person. I'm American Indian. I can tell."

With his pale blue eyes and the blond stubble on his shaved head, this seemed unlikely to me.

"Let's say a prayer."

His non sequitur startled me inert, so when he grabbed my hands and bowed his head, I did the same. Except I kept my eyes open. I wondered what the people in the cars passing by on Fourth Street thought. It was a busy road this deep in the city. Four lanes.

"Tunkashila, thank you for your bounty from this good man. Bless him and protect all of us from harm. Thank you."

He let go of my hands. "Hey, I hope you don't mind but I made a few calls."

I shrugged. "They don't live in China, do they?"

"No. Northern California. Family. Friends."

I looked at the three of them and decided rather than making up my own stories about them, maybe I could get them to tell me how they ended up on the street, what path led them here. I said, "Anyone got a cigarette?"

Dingy Hat said, "No, dude, we're homeless." He shrugged.

Good point.

John and I shook hands one more time, and I started walking back across the grocery store's parking lot, back towards my place. When I got to the front of the store, I had a thought: I'd go in and buy a pack of cigarettes and then give them to the guys and have a smoke with them. I'd be doing a good deed, of sorts, and I'd get to have a cigarette.

I wanted to talk to them. I wanted to find out why they were homeless, what happened to them? Had they simply checked out from society? Maybe they just didn't want the hassles of modern life and all its responsibilities. Were they Vietnam vets? Did they have substance abuse problems? What was their day like? Did they have certain spots they camped at like the hobo jungles in a Steinbeck novel? Did they go to the mission? Was there one in Long Beach? I thought so, but where was it?

Or did they go to the world famous LA Mission?

I'd heard Chuck Palahniuk, the author of *Fight Club*, had decided to go homeless one summer as an experiment to see what it was like, maybe as research for a novel or just life experience.

Did that sound weird? Absolutely. Did it also sound kind of laudable to me? Again, absolutely. If I weren't married and had enough money to take a summer off, it sounded like something I'd do. I'd thought about it even before I heard he'd done it. But I thought about so much. I let my imagination go all the time.

Maybe that was the writer in me. I'd done all kinds of things, either because of books I'd read or flights of fancy in extended daydreaming sessions I'd been going on my whole life.

Anyway, living on the streets: perhaps I could turn it into a piece of Gonzo journalism. Where the reporter injects themselves into the story and becomes part of it. Follow after one of my heroes—of sorts, anyway—of writing, Hunter S. Thompson. Sure, there are drawbacks to the Gonzo school, such as the loss of any supposed objectivity. But, hell, wasn't objectivity a façade, anyway? I seemed to remember from Anthropology 101 that objectivity was an illusion. You couldn't help anthropomorphizing the animals you observed, or, in the case of cultural anthropologists, transposing your cultural mores and biases onto your subjects and their actions.

As I neared the entrance to the grocery store, I looked back. John and his crew were ambling off with John in the lead, gesturing and pontificating. I felt like they might be clearing out in case I changed my mind and decided to call the cops. I wondered if a finely honed paranoia like that worked on the streets as a survival mechanism. But it brought up the question which came first, the paranoia or the streets? And did the paranoia lead to the streets? Too many questions.

Shrugging, I slid by the store entrance and continued heading home. Probably better anyway. Might save me from getting cancer.

I kept walking. Flipping open my wife's phone, I looked at the recently dialed numbers. Just as John had said for some of them he'd simply gone through my wife's address book going down the list in order and calling numbers trying to get in touch with someone who knew whose phone this was. For instance, there was the Coffee Bean & Tea Leaf my wife went to on her way to work. She'd call ahead, so her drink would be waiting for her when she arrived. Or the cleaners she took our dry cleaning to.

But some were 415 area codes, the Bay Area. I imagined those were the personal calls he'd told me he'd made. I wondered how that went. Maybe something like—

"Hey, Mom."

"Son."

"How are you?"

"Good, thanks."

"Can you send me some money?"

Click.

Or—

John's voice is tender and low as he says, "Hey, Son." So low, the oscillating sound waves on the down side have a lacuna, where there's no sound, but the waves are close together, so you don't notice, exactly. But you hear it, these millisecond gaps, these blank spaces, sandwiched in there.

"Hi, Dad."

"How's school going?"

"Good."

"You getting good grades?"

"Yeah, pretty good. Except for a 'C' in math."

"You gotta study harder."

"Okay." Pause. "When are you coming to visit?"

Pause. "Pretty soon. I got some business I need to take care of."

"Really?"

The young man's voice is excited, his next words coming out on top of each other. "Mom says you're living on the streets, but I never believed her. I knew you had a job."

Probably neither of the above. Or both. Or a variation of one. Or the other. Or maybe he called his dad, or his ailing aunt, or his ex-wife, or his grandmother, or his brother, sister, ex-girlfriend, parole officer . . .

Maybe I should give the numbers a call and see? I pushed that thought out of my head. Partially because I was chicken. But also because then I couldn't keep making up the conversations. And I liked making up the conversations.

Getting home, I tossed the phone on the table in the entryway. Later, in the evening, when my wife returned from work, I told her the tale of her phone.

She laughed.

"I just thought I'd forgotten it and meant to check when I got home."

I told her how scared I'd been when I'd answered what I knew was a call from her, but there had been a man's voice on her phone. I told her how my imagination went from affair to kidnapping and rape and murder.

Reaching out, she stroked my cheek. And then she kissed me on the lips.

We weren't quite done with John yet. The next day, while at work, my wife was showing pictures of our cats to a friend, and there was John and his crew, the Three Musketeers. In the first shot they were lounging on the beach beneath a palm tree. From what was around and behind them, I knew exactly where it was. It was next to the snack shack at the end of the bike path near the jetty, two blocks from our place.

It was a sunny day. John was smiling, close-lipped, but he looked happy. And maybe a little drunk or high. His smile and loose-limbed posture made it look like it was a good buzz and just enough. The kind that blunted the sharp edges and made it feel like the whole world loved you. He had his big muscular arms, hands grasping opposite wrists, linked over his knees, holding them up.

The picture was titled "John."

So much for not being technologically savvy.

The other pictures were of his buddies. One was of Gray Sweatshirt, the guy John had described when I'd asked what *he* looked like. Gray Sweatshirt was sitting on a colorful Mexican blanket looking up at the camera—whoever took the shot had been standing. A gap-toothed smile took some years, especially the hard ones, off his life. Beat-up but happy. His skin had that mahogany tone homeless people in SoCal get: the look of too much sun meeting too many days without a bath.

The last one was of both Dingy Hat and Gray Sweatshirt together, sitting on the blanket but this time staring straight into the lens. So to take the picture, John—it had to be him since he wasn't in the photo—must've been sitting or kneeling, right at eye level.

They had an arm draped over each others' shoulders. And they were both smiling.

Why'd they take these pictures? I'm guessing boredom or nothing better to do had to be part of it. But was that it? I mean, they weren't going to get to keep them and put them in a photo album and pull them out and look at them like most people that take pictures do, so why?

Maybe they just didn't want to be forgotten.

We kept those pictures on that phone—never erasing them, pulling them up occasionally to look at them—for a year or so until a new plan came up that gave us new phones, and then, well, I'm not sure what happened to the old phone, the one with the pictures on it, the one I'd ransomed, the one we'd started calling John's phone.

MICK HAVEN
PAY PHONE

Discussion Questions:

1. Is there anything about the narrator's language and word choices in "Pay Phone" that suggests what kind of person he is?
2. How has the narrator from "Pay Phone" experienced the homeless in the past?
3. Why do you think John from "Pay Phone" took the pictures, and why do the narrator and his wife keep them on the phone?

Essay Questions:

1. How and why does the narrator of "Pay Phone" grow throughout the story in his understanding of homeless people?
2. One of the themes that runs through several of the stories in this collection is the way that outsiders live. Compare and contrast John from "Pay Phone" to other characters in this collection in the way that they cope with being outsiders.

Encore Plus

STEPHANIE BARBÉ HAMMER

"Honey, I'll gain today—I just know it," I promise the tightrope walker hopefully as I'm on hold with Room Service. He looks at me with sad eyes, over the corners of his latest issue of *High Wire World*, sprawled—all 350 pounds of him—on our hotel room bed.

The waiter arrives, and I eat a huge breakfast—bacon, eggs, sausage, pancakes, and grits.

Afterwards, I step on the scale. The tightrope walker rolls off the bed, walks heavy like Godzilla, and watches tensely over my shoulder.

157 and a half. 158. I inhale and concentrate. 159. That's the highest I can ever get to.

The tightrope walker shakes his head and sighs.

"Too thin," he says.

These days in New York are our last days, although neither of us says so. I try moving as little as possible, since I can't cram any more into my body. But as soon as I get to the circus, the plan falls apart. I take my seat at Madison Square Garden, but when I see the tightrope walker perform on the wire in the center ring, I jump up and down with excitement, despite my best efforts to remain calm.

I can feel the calories burning me down. Little flames of energy melting our love to sad skinniness.

But at the beginning it was so wonderful. It still *IS* so wonderful. For me. But he gazes down upon me from his great height underneath the Big Top, and I can feel his disappointment in me. In my body.

I watch my tightrope walker and remember how I met him.

It was in St. Louis. I had been very depressed from losing my boyfriend at the University of Geneva. I went to Switzerland for my junior year of college and I met a Swiss man right away, and he was tall and handsome, but still, things didn't turn out as I hoped. I was a really good skier, but the Swiss guy hated skiing, although he was thin and long-legged and built for sports. And after about six months of sex, cheese, and chocolate, he admitted that he loved someone else. A different American. She looked like me, he said, but she was taller, and more *something.*

"More what?" I said, speaking with him in French.

"More something you're not," he replied.

Je t'aime, he told me at the airport. *Mais j'aime l'autre encore plus.*

So I had gone back to college and graduated, and I went to work for a Holiday Inn in St. Louis. I cut my hair and ate macaroni and cheese and a Burger King bacon cheeseburger on Sundays. I went to the circus one night with a friend in Reservations, and I saw my tightrope walker for the first time. He was already pretty famous, and the impossibility of him made the expectant audience hushed and ready to be awed.

"Imagine," said my friend. "A poor white cracker from Texas making it big in the circus. A boy that fat walking the high wire. And he can sing at the same time!"

My tightrope walker came out and began his slow ascent. His chest bulged, and his big belly hung over his tight, shiny red shorts. He carried a red satin hand-kerchief to wipe the sweat from his eyes, and he twisted that around his wrist like a shiny, blood bracelet. He wore eyeliner and he gazed at the audience in-tensely before hauling himself up the ropes, the fat on his arms jiggling in a meaty earthquake of flesh. His long hair hung from his shoulders, and he looked like an exploded, bloated, and totally sexy Jesus. He balanced on one foot and then the other, doing incredible tricks with knives and hula hoops. He opened his mouth, and a rich tenor voice came out. At the end he did a back flip; he turned his huge, heavy self over like a giant piece of fettuccini, and landed hard, the wire twanging like a guitar string as it trembled to bear him up.

After the show, my girlfriend and I went to the Denny's under the famous downtown St. Louis arch, and there was the tightrope walker sitting at a big table with all his circus friends. We sent the table a super-size basket of onion rings with our compliments, and when the tightrope walker went outside to get cigarettes, I followed him. We made conversation by the cigarette machine, and I kissed him, just as the Marlboros fell down into the slot.

He said later that I looked plumper in the darkened doorway of Denny's; I looked more spread out and ample.

I went back to his room with him and quit my job the next day.

I come back to the present. The high wire act hasn't changed. My tightrope walker finishes his song and dives off the wire into the extra strong net.

He bows to the audience. Turns to each side. Bows again.

"It's over," he mouths to me.

What do you do when you want someone so much that you don't even care whether they love you or not?

I don't make a fuss. Since we live in hotels, there's no place to move out of, no furniture to divide, no pets to fight over.

My tightrope walker tours with Ringling and then goes to Russia. They understand and prize fatness there.

I pack a suitcase, and get another job in a big city—the biggest, widest city I can think of.

I work the front desk at the W in Los Angeles now. I'm in the heart of Hollywood, right near the metro and the theater where the *Lion King* plays—where the guys try to take you on tours of the stars that are lying right there on the pavement beneath your feet. At night I walk past the tired tourists on Vine, and the people waiting for a bus that never seems to come, and I walk into my big, unfinished loft just south of Melrose, and I lay my 159-pound body on my king size bed, and I dream of climbing mountains of skin, armed with lengths of wire.

Today, my new fancy hotel colleagues and I go through the smooth white halls and turn on the computers in the manager's office.

The cold, air-conditioned corridors make me think of Switzerland and the Swiss boyfriend. I remember something about my tightrope walker too. Both those men—although physically so different—always kept their eyes squeezed tightly shut when I made love to them. They never saw how I shuddered in the moment, and became—for just an instant—enormous.

I go back to the front desk, and the phone rings. It's a lady—the wife of a famous rock star—who has booked the presidential suite. I click on the buttons and get her set up with flowers, champagne, and someone to play the grand piano so she and the rock star can fall asleep to Chopin.

"Anything else?" I say.

"Yes," she says. "Yes—I need it to be perfect so he'll think I'm really lovely, so he'll think I'm—"

"More?" I say and then just then, even before she answers, I feel an avalanche of hunger.

I disconnect, say I have an emergency and walk out the door. I go down the hill past the stars and tourists to Gower and get six orders of fried chicken and waffles from Roscoe's. Then I go back to the front desk, plop the food down on those sleek counters, tell everyone they are too fucking thin, and call my old girlfriend in St. Louis.

We talk on the phone for an hour. The little red lights of the different reservation lines flicker like flames of wanting on the ice-cold plastic of the oversized phone.

I eat while I talk and slowly, I begin to feel full.

STEPHANIE BARBÉ HAMMER
ENCORE PLUS

Discussion Questions:

1. What is the significance of the last line of "Encore Plus"?
2. Why is it important to the tightrope walker in "Encore Plus" that the narrator be fat?
3. Why is the narrator in "Encore Plus" attracted to the tightrope walker, and is her attraction different than his?

Essay Questions:

1. What does "Encore Plus" suggest about the way women's bodies are viewed by others and by themselves?
2. What is the central argument or theme of "Encore Plus"? What does the story mean to teach us about the world?
3. Compare and contrast "Encore Plus" to "Burying Ellie." How do the women in these stories view sexuality and their places in the world?

The Jizo Statues

CATHY IRWIN

Sarah Shinzuku stood in the laundry room, rolling pairs of socks together. Black, white, pink. Every now and then, one of the sock pairs would be missing, and Sarah would lay the lone sock over the laundry basket. Once Sarah found the missing pair, she would throw the sock pairs in the basket together. Then she would fold underwear, first Jackie's boxer shorts, and then her own Victoria's Secret cotton panties. On some days, her mind would wander and she would remember how she used to fold Hannah's princess underwear covered with faces of Cinderella, Belle, Sleeping Beauty, and Snow White all over each. Sarah knew she had never really needed to fold Hannah's underwear, let alone her own or Jackie's, but she had loved folding and putting her underwear into neat rows in dresser drawers.

Hannah had been their only one. Sarah had wanted more, and they had tried for another baby after Hannah was born. First Sarah was impregnated, then Jackie. Then Sarah tried again and again. Exclusive sperm banks, IVF, fertility drugs, and several attempts with a friend failed. Every pregnancy had ended in a miscarriage.

On nights when she was lonely, Sarah would get angry at Jackie for being so cavalier about having more children, especially with Sarah nearing forty. Before Hannah had drowned, Sarah had worked long hours as a high school counselor specializing in LGBT students. She had loved her job, but she also loved being a mother to Hannah and wanted more, even after serving hormonal teenagers all day and having to commute into Los Angeles.

"If you want to try again, that's fine," Jackie would say after each miscarriage. "But I'm okay with one." She didn't like it when Sarah pressed her for another child. After Sarah's third miscarriage, Jackie could never look her in the eye when they had a conversation about having more kids. Instead, she would stare at her computer screen. Her face had become round over the years, and her body, once taut from self-defense classes, sagged at the belly. Her shoulders now slumped forward even when she was standing. Her black hair had started to turn gray in some places, and colleagues at the law firm joked that it was a sure sign that she would soon make partner. Reserved and confident, Jackie was respected by her colleagues who marveled at her astute observations and practical interpretations of the law that helped her win cases.

As Sarah started to fold Jackie's favorite Los Angeles Lakers' T-shirt, she remembered last month's annual trip to visit Jackie's parents in Seattle, and the day she checked her email. Her t'ai chi instructor had informed everyone that Jana's daughter Tracy, who had just graduated from college, had died in a drunk-driving accident. Jana and her daughter loved to ride horses, and every Sunday morning, after t'ai chi, Jana had a date with Tracy to take their two horses on a long ride in the San Bernardino mountains, enjoying a day among the oak and pine trees.

Sarah had signed out of her email immediately upon reading about Jana's daughter, unable to read her t'ai chi teacher's message any further. It was hard enough for her to leave the guest room to talk to her Filipino in-laws, and now, after reading the email, Sarah just wanted to go home. Jackie was in the kitchen with them, helping them with their taxes, and would soon come to bed and want to cuddle and talk with her about the schedule planned for the next day.

Sarah had turned off the lights and was curled up around a pillow when Jackie joined her in the bedroom. As she curled up behind her, Sarah thought about Jana and how beautiful she looked at their last t'ai chi class when she was asked to demonstrate "white swan cools its wings." When Jackie put her arm on her shoulder, Sarah told her about Jana's daughter and how Jana would never be able to ride horses with Tracy again. She began to weep quietly as she remembered how cold her feet and hands felt that early fall morning when she received a phone call informing her that Hannah had drowned at that slumber party. Jackie remained silent and lay curled around the contours of Sarah's back, the front of her legs against the back of Sarah's knees, calves, feet. They lay there silently, with nothing to think about except a body.

What am I going to do? Sarah thought as she began to put some folded laundry into the basket to transport to different rooms and closets. Usually, she loved the monotony of this chore, loved the sense that she was putting things back where they belonged. And if she focused enough, she felt a temporary sense of control, away from her obsessive thoughts about whether her marriage was going to survive and whether she should have let their six-year-old daughter go to that slumber party.

After she finished putting away the laundry, Sarah went to the kitchen and checked the chicken adobo on the stove, adding the two tablespoons of ketchup that Jackie's mother had suggested. As she stirred the ketchup into the adobo sauce, she began to obsess again about her own survival abilities. If she ever needed to start working full-time again, John, her boss, could probably increase the number of counseling sessions she did with students in the school district. With her teaching credential, she could teach Psychology 101 at the high school or community college level. She could get a job at AIDS Project Los Angeles. If she ever found herself alone, she knew how to survive on very little, the way she did when she was a graduate student at UCLA.

Sarah turned off the stove and text-messaged Jackie to let her know that dinner would be chicken adobo and that she would stop by the supermarket to buy some broccoli and eggs after her t'ai chi class. They would both be home by seven p.m.

As Sarah threw on her sweater and pulled her keys from her purse, she continued to think about her future. I don't need to worry about my health as I am perfectly healthy and have never been seriously injured in my life, Sarah thought to herself as she walked out the front door to her car parked in the driveway. Looking west, the sun and sky were starting to blend into a reddish-orange horizon. Sarah wondered if Jackie could survive on her own in Rancho. If she would miss the smell of lavender on freshly laundered bed sheets. If she knew how to cook her favorite omelet breakfast or lamb chops. Jackie would have to figure things out for herself.

These days, Sarah forced herself to go to her t'ai chi class. She used to love the quiet focus of doing the twenty-eight forms in peaceful unison with a group of LGBT women living in the Inland Empire. Hannah had drowned at the slumber party before Sarah had started taking t'ai chi, so no one knew about her daughter and the class had become a safe haven. But ever since she had heard about Jana's daughter, Sarah braced herself for the moment when Jana would return. Jana hadn't been around for weeks, but today, after class started, Sarah felt a presence in the back of the room and, without looking, knew that Jana was warming up in the row behind her.

After finishing the warm-up exercises, Kai Lu, the t'ai chi instructor, interrupted class and welcomed Jana back. Sarah and her classmates hugged her and echoed greetings, but no one knew what else to say to Jana. Now, when she saw Jana, Sarah thought about how Hannah would have been seven-and-a-half if she were still alive. How Hannah would have started ballet and youth soccer through the local parks and recreations.

"Let's do the twenty-eight forms and concentrate on where we center our *dan tien* and our mind," said Kai Lu.

Sarah and the other women went back to their spots on the floor and stood quietly, gaining stillness, waiting for Kai Lu to begin. With her body and mind so quiet, Sarah could sense the discomfort and energy of Jana behind her. She felt the energy, the tension, the need for release. Finally, she heard feet walking away and out the door.

"I'm sorry," she heard Jana say as she walked away, "I need to go the ladies' room."

Sarah paused and then followed Jana into the ladies' room. She found Jana washing her hands, tears streaming down her face.

"You don't know how hard it is," said Jana. "It's so hard to return to activities that I used to do. To see your faces."

"Believe me when I say that I know," said Sarah. "I once had a daughter too. She drowned accidentally. It was at a slumber party. We hardly knew the people."

Sarah looked at Jana and noticed how much weight she had lost. Her once perfectly tailored shirt and pants were now baggy on her. She remembered meeting Jana for the first time in class and how impressed she was by Jana's carefully applied makeup and hair, her clothing and perfect manners.

"Does it get any better?" asked Jana.

"No," said Sarah. "At least not for me. I'm still trying to figure out what I'm going to do, whether my relationship with Jackie will survive this."

"I was married to a man a long time ago, before I came out," said Jana. "Kyle and I divorced fifteen years ago. I don't think he ever got over the shock. We spoke after the police called to tell us about Tracy and planned the funeral, but that's it. He has his own family and group of friends and lives in northern California."

The two women stood in the restroom, looking straight ahead into the mirror at their reflections, too dazed to pick out anything specific, yet knowing each other's tender pain and unable to fix it. Jana opened her purse, took out a stick of pale rustic brown lipstick, and slowly applied color to her lips.

"Come, we can't stay in this bathroom forever," said Jana after she finished.

"I know," said Sarah. "I still have to go to the store."

"Let's talk soon, "said Jana, as she handed Sarah her card. Jana Peterson. Real Estate Broker.

"Okay," said Sarah, taking the card. "I'll call you."

That evening, Sarah sat quietly as Jackie ate two plates of chicken adobo, rice, and broccoli.

"I can't believe how much work I have right now," said Jackie. "I have to call a client in fifteen minutes, so we can wrap up his case tomorrow."

Sarah sat there as Jackie told her about how many hours she had billed in the past three weeks and how her workload would be getting worse.

"Don't worry," said Sarah as Jackie started to pick up her plate. "I'll clean up."

After dinner, while Jackie spoke to her client in the home office, Sarah went to the den to sit in her favorite sofa chair and drink tea. She liked to sip her tea while gazing at a lit candle on an altar that she and Jackie had set up on a table next to the television. A picture of Hannah as a baby sleeping on Sarah's chest had been mounted on the wall above the altar.

Sarah and Jackie decided to create an altar after both had suffered their miscarriages. At first, the altar was very simple. Sarah had put a plain white candle on a glass plate and had filled a ceramic bowl with sand to place sticks of incense. Jackie had bought a stainless steel candlesnuffer and a wood tray for the matches and a stock of sandalwood incense sticks. Then Sarah had placed three jizo statues on the altar, where they now stood in a line to the right of the candle.

She had bought these statues from a Zen Buddhist monastery in upstate New York. The monastery catalog stated that these baby jizo statues represented a "safe journey to the other shore for babies who had died while being born, who had been aborted, or had been orphaned at birth." In Japan, the catalog mentioned, these statues acted as reminders that a living infant had once been in one's presence.

When Sarah first received the jizo statues in the mail three years ago, she had hesitated before opening the box. She had expected each statue to pop up or fall into her arms. Described as three inches in height, she also expected these jizos to be light in weight, empty, easy to move. Instead, as she unwrapped the first jizo from layers of tape and newspaper, she had found herself holding the weight of a tiny, premature baby, perhaps two pounds, made of cast iron. This jizo was cold to the touch, and as she held the jizo tightly in her hands, she wanted to warm it, protect it, allow it to come to life.

Sarah studied the jizo. Like a tiny monk, its palms were held together in prayer. Its face was round, with eyes shut and a mouth chiseled in a firm, straight line of calm. The statue was sturdy, yet stone cold. Dead. A paperweight. Everything she felt inside. Everything she had dreamed of packed away.

Sarah remembered how, when she was alive, Hannah loved to play with the jizo statues and act out stories with them. Sometimes they were Hannah's classmates if she pretended to be at school; in December, they were the three kings. Sometimes, after dinner, as part of the pre-bath time ritual, she pretended that they were her brother and sisters. Hannah would sit the jizos on the floor next to her and play pretend while Sarah was reading a book to all of them. Hannah would knock one of the statues down and look at Sarah.

"Mommy, he tried to push me and I didn't like it," Hannah would cry. "Tell my brother to stop!"

"Stop it, baby brother!" Sarah would say. "Hannah is upset and doesn't like to be bullied by anyone. Now say you're sorry to each other."

"Oh, sorry! I didn't mean to push you!" Hannah would say back. She would then cradle the jizo in her arms and give them a kiss, resolving the conflict between herself and the jizo. She loved this game and loved playing it until bath time. Sarah would watch the scene unfold between Hannah and the jizo statues, wondering how much her daughter knew, if she had ever heard her and Jackie discussing their options for a second child. She wondered if Hannah had ever heard her softly crying after a miscarriage, whispering the name she had already given her unborn child. Hannah seemed to have some understanding of what was happening and would sometimes just sit in her lap quietly.

After her meditation in the den, Sarah returned to the kitchen to wash her teacup and place it on the drying rack. She put the dried dishes away and made sure the stove had been turned off.

As she walked down the hall to go to bed, Sarah saw Jackie in the den, kneeling at the altar, examining one of the jizo statues and holding it gently in her hands. The shadow of her against the wall had magnified her hands, so she looked like she was holding a creature, perhaps an animal, the size of a baby.

"Good night, Jackie," Sarah said to her.

When she turned around to look at Sarah, Jackie's brow was raised and her forehead wrinkled. When she stood up, her mouth was jutting out, and her tall, stocky body slouched towards Sarah's.

"I don't think Hannah should have played with those statues that you have on your altar," Jackie said. Sarah stood there in silence, wondering why Jackie would suddenly bring this topic up.

"They were too heavy for her," Jackie added. "If they had fallen on her foot, she could have broken a bone."

"Jackie, it's not like these statues are huge," Sarah said. As she walked over to Jackie, her face began to feel hot and her right hand grabbed onto one of the mala beads on her necklace.

"No!" Jackie replied. "These statues should not have been handled by Hannah. They are not toys."

"I know they are not toys," Sarah said abruptly as she snatched the jizo statue out of Jackie's hand. She tried to match Jackie's authoritative voice levels, which made her feel like she was shouting.

"Why did you let her play with these statues in the first place?" Jackie snapped, looking closely at Sarah.

"Hannah and I would draw people in her notebook," Sarah said calmly. "I thought the jizo statues were good pieces that we both could look at while we took turns drawing houses and people. Then the jizos became characters who lived in the houses we drew."

There was a long pause before Jackie let out a long sigh. Sarah returned the jizo to the altar and lined up the statues in a perfect row, each little face looking straight at her.

"How can you be so cruel and selfish?" Jackie asked. "Do you want to keep reminding me of what you want? Of what was? Have you ever thought about what I want?"

"Of course, I have!" Sarah said. "I know you. You want order. You do everything by the book. The law. And when things don't follow reason, you don't know what to do. I loved Hannah and I have tried to be happy with what I have."

"Well, what's with the statues then?" Jackie asked. "If you wanted Hannah to pretend that she had brothers and sisters, then you should have gotten her some real dolls. Not statues that are for altars. Dolls. For play."

"Is this all about play to you, Jackie?" Sarah asked. "Or is it about what we refuse to discuss? Why are you so afraid to talk about Hannah or having more children?"

"Because we have tried to have another child!" said Jackie. "It hasn't worked out. What we had was one child. Hannah. Why couldn't you be satisfied with that?"

"What's wrong with adopting like most lesbian couples? Or trying again?" Sarah asked. The room and Jackie's face began to look hazy.

"Because I can't handle how upset you get when we go to the doctor and find no heartbeat. Because you won't be able to handle what would happen if we adopted—you would probably be thinking of the child in the same way that you see these statues. And that would not be fair to any child."

Sarah stood there in the shadows. Jackie's face was dark, and her eyes seemed to bore through some wall that was behind her head. She seemed to be somewhere else.

"Someone should have been watching Hannah," Jackie said quietly. "She was playing with the dog. No one saw her follow it to the pool. No one saw her jump into the pool. No one saw her go down. No one heard her. No one was there, okay? Our worst nightmare happened. It was an accident. I'm not against you or blaming you, so stop blaming yourself."

"Jackie, I don't know what to say or do anymore," said Sarah. "I'm not sure if I'm with you or against you. I don't think you understand how much I *want* another child. I miss Hannah so much. She is what made me a mother. She is what made me feel normal in this hetero world that we live in."

"Is that all you care about, Sarah?" asked Jackie. "We don't talk anymore. We no longer plan things together anymore, like trips to take during the Christmas holiday or how we might remodel the backyard. It's like you stopped being my partner after Hannah died. What about us? If you want another child, that's fine, but I do not. If you want to be with me, you will have to accept this."

Sarah stood there, looking at Jackie's face, which now seemed hollow and drawn, and as Jackie slowly sat down on the sofa, she seemed to be smaller, more vulnerable than Sarah had ever seen her.

Sarah began to understand what Jackie was saying and couldn't speak. She remembered when they were legally married in 2008 and how gorgeous Jackie looked in her white tuxedo on their wedding night, how her eyes sparkled with excitement as they exchanged vows at City Hall. She remembered how Proposition 8 had kept many of their friends from doing the same, and how Jackie spent years doing pro bono work to help strike down DOMA and Prop. 8.

Sarah stood there with her palms held together. She closed her eyes and pursed her lips. She then took a long breath. Now sturdy and still, she opened her eyes and sat down next to Jackie. They finally sat and looked clearly into each other's eyes, with Sarah knowing what was beyond her grasp.

"Come on," said Jackie. "It's late. Let's go to bed."

The next morning, when Sarah woke up, Jackie had already left for work. Sarah still felt the peace and quiet that had come over her the night before. She had not felt this way since before Hannah was born. She got out of bed, took out two black suitcases from the bedroom closet, and began packing clothes and toiletries. She showered, brushed her teeth, and put on some jeans and a T-shirt. After putting on some sandals, she chose three other pairs of shoes to bring with her and stuffed them into her gym bag. From the nightstand, she grabbed her laptop, went online, and checked how much money she had in her own savings and checking accounts. She then went to their joint checking account and transferred half of what was there to her own accounts. Afterwards, she opened her email to send Jana Peterson a short note. Finished with email, she put her laptop along with other work items into her tote bag for work. Her bags were now packed. She then called up Jana Peterson on her cell phone.

"Hi, Jana," said Sarah to Jana's answering service. "It's Sarah from your t'ai chi class. Listen, I was wondering if you had any time to talk today. I am looking for a room or small apartment, and I was wondering if you could help me. Please give me a call. I just emailed you, so you now have my contact information. Thanks."

After the call, Sarah went down the hall to Jackie's office and picked up the morning newspaper, a roll of masking tape, and a small box from Jackie's stash of office supplies. She made sure the box was small enough to fit into her gym bag. She took a crisp monogrammed note card from Jackie's stationery and quickly wrote a short letter to her. *Dear Jackie, I need time to think about things. Please do not call or try to find me. I will call you when I'm ready. Love, Sarah.* Then, she headed to the den and knelt in front of the altar. She put the jizo statues in the small box, and replaced them with the small note card folded over.

Sarah then walked over to the guest room, a room that used to be painted pink and green with Hannah's name spelled out on a small bulletin board above a desk. Jackie had redone the room a year after Hannah had died when friends from the East Coast came to visit. Now the room was furnished with an old futon bed left over from graduate school, a nightstand with a reading lamp on it, and an empty dresser from IKEA.

Sarah went and opened the closet door. Jackie had hung some of her summer shirts, old pairs of slacks, an old motorcycle jacket and chaps in this closet. On the closet floor were boxes that contained Jackie's books from law school and her psychology books from graduate school. Sarah looked up and noticed more boxes labeled "Tax Returns," "Mortgage Papers," "Warranties," and "Photographs."

On her tippy-toes, Sarah gingerly grabbed the box labeled "Photographs," making sure the contents didn't fall out of the box. She sat down on the floor and opened the lid to pick out photos of Hannah. Sarah then took the jizo statues out of the box, neatly wrapped them in three layers of that morning's newspaper, and wound masking tape around the statues as if making a cocoon. She then placed both the statues and photographs in the small box. Before putting the box of photographs away, Sarah noticed the framed photograph of Hannah that used to hang in her bedroom. Jackie loved this photo.

In the photograph, Hannah stood in her grandmother's garden in Seattle, the soil a rich dark clay color that enhanced the bright pink of her sweater. Hannah was around two years old, standing with her hands triumphantly raised above her head, with wind-swept hair all around her face and her mouth open like an O. The photo emphasized the diamond-shaped, raised flowerbeds, with Hannah standing to the left of one of them that had just been filled with fresh soil and fertilizer.

Sarah stared at Hannah's body and the empty garden bed to the right of her, the plot for the missing ones, the ones that vanished, and the ones never born. She imagined Hannah as a big sister, with little brothers and sisters, showing them how to sing the ABCs. How to plant seeds in a garden. How to move like a swan in water. How to cool one's wings.

CATHY IRWIN
THE JIZO STATUES

Discussion Questions:

1. What is Jackie's objection to the jizo statues? Why does Sarah allow Hannah to play with such expensive items?
2. Why is Sarah leaving Jackie, and do you think she will leave Jackie permanently?
3. Why does Sarah see her motherhood as so important? How does it affect the way she sees herself?

Essay Questions:

1. What are the primary and secondary reasons that Sarah decides to change her life at the end of "The Jizo Statues"?
2. Analyze the jizo statues as symbols in "The Jizo Statues"? What do they symbolize about the characters in this story, what they are missing, and how they relate to each other?
3. "The Jizo Statues" and "Encore Plus" are about relationships in transition and possibly ending. Compare and contrast the reasons the relationships end in both of these stories.

Acrobats

CLINT MARGRAVE

Chuck was always trying to get me to be a Nazi. He had a swastika pin he'd stick to his shirt once the Mexicans went home for the day.

"*Mein Kampf.* Have you read it?" he'd say as we separated the boxes onto pallets.

"Chuck, I'm half Jewish for Christ's sake. I can't be a Nazi."

"I know. You're young. You still want to save the world. Wait until you're my age. Things will be a lot different."

I was seventeen. Chuck was twenty-two.

At lunch, he and Ricky would make fun of me for not eating meat. Both of them were bigger than me, and the three of us were part of the same crew. Our job was to unload the trucks from book fairs all over California and return the carts to their designated spot in the warehouse. But most of our time was spent smoking cigarettes on the loading dock. Sometimes Chuck got picked to do other tasks like labeling packing slips or shrink-wrapping pallets. His mom was the office manager, so he often got special treatment from the higher-ups. When he did this he worked alone and would reapply the swastika pin he kept in his pocket.

"You know Chuck, if you believe in it so much, why don't you just leave the damned thing on?" I said to him one day.

"Do you think I'm crazy? They'd kill me. Ricky'd have his whole damn gang after me."

Ricky belonged to the local Mexican gang. In fact, half of them worked with us. It was good to have friends in high places. Even Chuck appreciated this in one way or another—as long as nobody knew he was a Nazi.

Sometimes all three of us would sneak around the side of the building and smoke a joint. Chuck was always in charge of the supply. We'd get high then go back and harass our supervisor Sean who wore hearing aids. He must have only been about 5'4". Sean fit the short guy stereotype by always bragging about how many women he fucked. He had a sensitive side too, but was dumb as a stone, and we always liked to mess with him. His voice had a twang that made him sound like a redneck from some far-off southern town, but in reality just meant he was from Riverside. He took a lot of grief from the big bosses over the three of us, but for some reason stuck by our sides. Only on occasion would he lose it—his face would turn all red, and he'd start twirling his mustache around. When this happened, he looked like he could burst into tears at any moment.

"Come on you guys, let's get this stuff done," he'd beg. "I got pussy waiting for me at home."

Our favorite way to pick on Sean was to make our voices barely audible so he'd have to keep turning his hearing aids up. We were usually the last ones out of the warehouse, so no one else could interfere. Some days, this would go on for hours, until a phone rang or a truck showed up late to jolt him—which, of course, always sent us into hysterics.

"All right. Real funny. Stop dickin' around," he'd say.

Ricky liked to spend most of his day strolling down the aisles of the warehouse while Chuck and I worked. In each aisle, there was usually some plump Latina with a big ass he'd try to hit on. They all seemed to love him, but not in the way he wanted it. To them, he was more like a big jolly teddy bear than a Don Juan. He didn't see it that way. And when you tried to tell him, his nostrils would flare up and he would squint as if he were going to kill you. We didn't tell him often.

Chuck, of course, wanted nothing to do with these chicks. He was destined for greater things. He wouldn't allow himself to be shelled up in some warehouse, chasing big-assed Latinas around for the rest of his life.

"I won't always be here, man," he said. "You think anybody has a future? Look at 'em. They're gonna die in this place."

In Chuck's opinion, nobody was getting out of there except him and me.

"A bunch of circus clowns, that's all they are. But you and I, we're acrobats."

He had big plans. He wanted to get into USC Film School. He told me he didn't have much time because he didn't expect to live past thirty. At seventeen, I couldn't see myself making it to twenty-five, much less to thirty. Chuck figured he had a good eight years to make his masterpiece. I told him he needed more time. Masterpieces come when they come, if they come. This was not something he could put a limit on.

As it turned out, Chuck and I had similar taste in music. Upon realizing it, we began to monopolize the small ghetto blaster we kept in the loading dock—playing everything from The Jam to Jane's Addiction. Chuck had a game he liked to play called Cool or Lame in which we'd rate everything that came to mind.

"Neil Armstrong?"

"Cool."

"President Bush?"

"Lame."

"Paul Stanley?"

"Lame."

"Stanley Kubrick?"

"Cool."

"Hamburgers?"

"Lame."

"Hitler?"

"Really lame."

Chuck took this as a sign of bonding even if we didn't always agree about what was cool and what was lame.

"You know kid, I like you," he'd say. "It's okay that you're half Jewish."

"I'm only five years younger than you Chuck, stop calling me kid."

The one time I did see Chuck outside of work was at a party his friend threw that for some reason I had been invited to. Chuck was already drunk when I got there. So were most of his friends. It didn't surprise me most of them weren't white, nor did they have any affiliation with the Nazi Party. Even Ricky was there for the occasion, trying to juggle a few ladies he brought with him.

By the end of the night we were all wasted. I had lied about my age to some older chick named Steph, and we had ducked off into the kitchen to make out when I heard Chuck looking for me. Before I had a chance to stop him he stumbled in and yanked me out of there.

"Kid, trust me, that girl's no good for you," he said.

"Jesus, Chuck, I wasn't gonna marry her. I was just trying to get some."

"Listen kid, there are more important things in life than women. You and I are destined for greater things."

Later on, when Steph and I ended up back in the kitchen, Chuck found us out again.

"Let's go," he said. "I told you she's no good. Plus, she's too old for you."

This time I wouldn't stand for it. I got pissed.

"Who do you think you are, Chuck? Get the fuck out!"

Chuck's face turned red. I thought he was going to kill me. But I didn't care. I was too drunk. If it came down to a fight, I'd be ready for it—although I'd definitely get my ass kicked.

"When will you ever learn?"

"Learn what, Chuck? That nobody knows anything but you?"

In my drunken state, I pushed him.

Chuck didn't retaliate.

"You know what I've always liked about you?" he said.

"What is it now, Chuck?"

"Of all the stupid things I tell you on a daily basis, all the wacky ideas I've sprung upon you, all the criticisms I have—you never take my shit."

"Go fuck yourself, asshole!"

By the time the weekend was over and we returned to work, things had cooled down and were pretty much back to normal. As it turned out, Chuck had a crush on this girl Steph but didn't have the guts to tell me. I found out from Ron, another co-worker, who had known Chuck a long time and was also at the party. Ron was an old high school buddy of his who had matted hair and wore the same Joy Division T-shirt to work every day. I figured it was something to do with the girl. Then one day, I saw her drop Chuck off at work, which sealed it for me. As mad as I had been, it pleased me to see him happy.

It wasn't long before Chuck started showing up late or calling in sick on a regular basis. I figured he was too in love to worry about such a novelty as work. Sean was getting pissed, but his loyalty to us remained. The higher-ups were clueless to what was going on, and Chuck's mom seemed to be even more in the dark.

When he finally did come back to work, he looked a mess—unshaven, thin, and moody. I thought for sure he'd be fired, but he had been there so long they just sat him down and gave him a slap on the wrist. He had no real excuse, and his mother helped ease the tensions between him and the higher-ups. Chuck laid the blame on Sean somehow. He told them he requested the days off a long time ago. They bought it, or at least, pretended to.

I asked him where he'd really been and he told me he hadn't slept in four days. He told me he was in love and didn't have much interest in coming to work. He also admitted that he and Steph had been doing a lot of speed and not to tell anyone. This started happening on a regular basis.

One day, a scuffle broke out between Chuck and one of the truck drivers who nearly broke Chuck's foot by catching it under a pallet. Though it was an accident, Chuck took it personally and swung at the guy. Luckily, Sean arrived before anyone really got hurt, or fired, for that matter. From then on, Chuck was even more eager to get the hell out of there. He needed the money, but he knew there had to be somewhere else to go. He really wanted to make films, but the idea of doing that seemed so far away. He felt he needed to detach himself from everything and everyone. Our conversations began to suffer because of this. Whatever bond we had once shared dissolved into simple hallway greetings or an occasional cigarette break together.

"Cool or lame?" I asked him one day about something I can't even remember now.

"It's all lame," he said. "None of this should be happening."

"What?" I asked.

"We are rotting away here."

"It won't be forever, Chuck."

"It won't be soon enough. But then again, what do you know? You still think college is gonna guarantee you a job, someday war is gonna cease to exist—cows are worth saving. Well, I got news for you, kid: it's a lie. Everything is a god-damned lie."

When summer came, they laid all three of us off. We figured this might happen. Our job circulated around the school year. If there were no book fairs, there was no job. On the last day, Sean took us out to a Mexican restaurant as a good-bye present. He told us he would miss us and to come back in the fall and reapply. I knew the hopelessness of doing that, and it didn't really faze me. I just graduated high school and hadn't planned on coming back anyway. Chuck told me he had made up his mind to never lay eyes on the place again.

With a polite handshake, we said goodbye. Chuck and I promised to keep in touch, but it was doubtful we ever would. Sean or Ricky, I didn't think I'd ever see again.

After a while I forgot all about the warehouse. Time passed, and I found myself going to college and working a slew of other odd jobs. Only on occasion would I even think about Chuck as casually as a lot of other people who had passed through my life.

But last night I bumped into Ricky in a local bar by my apartment. He bought me a beer and opted for a game of pool. The way it was brought up, Ricky must have already assumed I had heard that Chuck shot himself. But I hadn't seen or heard from anybody since that day at the Mexican restaurant almost five years before.

"Three days," said Ricky. "It took three days."

Even the doctors were surprised that he had held on so long. But knowing Chuck, this was the way he wanted it. Three days of taunting the wire before crossing it, as the world waited for him to make his move. Like an acrobat. Going no place. Ever.

CLINT MARGRAVE
ACROBATS

Discussion Questions:

1. What clues does Margrave give us that Chuck is self-destructive and suicidal?
2. Do you think Chuck truly believes in Nazism? If not, why is he wearing Nazi symbols?
3. Why is the narrator fascinated with Chuck, whom he also seems to loathe?

Essay Questions:

1. The story is entitled "Acrobats," a reference to a comment Chuck makes. Both the narrator and Chuck seem to be living differently than the other people of the story. In what way are these two characters acrobats? What does the title mean?
2. Compare and contrast Chuck in "Acrobats" to Ellie in "Burying Ellie." Both are annoying and offensive to the narrators of their stories. What is it about these characters that frustrate these narrators?

The Relive Box

T.C. BOYLE

Katie wanted to relive Katie at nine, before her mother left, and I could appreciate that, but we only had one console at the time and I really didn't want to go there. It was coming up on the holidays, absolutely grim outside, nine-thirty at night—on a school night—and she'd have to be up at six to catch the bus in the dark. She'd already missed too much school, staying home on any pretext and reliving the whole time I was at work, so there really were no limits, and who was being a bad father here? A single father unable to discipline his fifteen-year-old daughter, let alone inculcate a work ethic in her? Me. I was. And I felt bad about it. I wanted to put my foot down and at the same time give her something, make a concession, a peace offering. But even more I wanted the box myself, wanted it so baldly it was showing in my face, I'm sure, and she needed to get ready for school, needed sleep, needed to stop reliving and worry about the now, the now and the future. "Why don't you wait till the weekend," I said.

She was wearing those tights all the girls wear like painted-on skin, standing in the doorway to the living room, perching on one foot the way she did when she was doing her dance exercises. Her face belonged to her mother, my ex, Christine, who hadn't been there for her for six years and counting. "I want to relive now," she said, diminishing her voice to the shaky hesitant plaint that was calculated to make me melt and give in to whatever she wanted, but it wasn't going to work this time, no way. She was going to bed and I was going back to a rainy February night in 1982, a sold-out show at the Roxy, a band I loved then, and the girl I was mad crazy for before she broke my heart and Christine came along to break it all over again.

"Why don't you go up and text your friends or something," I said.

"I don't want to text my friends. I want to be with my mom."

This was a plaint too and it cut even deeper. She was deprived, that was the theme here, and the whole thing, as any impartial observer could see in a heartbeat, verged on child abuse. "I know, honey, I know. But it's not healthy. You're spending too much time there."

"You're just selfish, that's all," she said, and here was the shift to a new tone, the tone of animus and opposition, the subtext being that I never thought of anybody but myself. "You want to what, relive when you were like my age or something? Let me guess: you're going to go back and relive yourself doing homework, right? As an example for your daughter?"

The room was a mess. The next day was the day the maid came, so I was standing amidst the debris of the past week, a healthy percentage of it—abandoned sweat socks, energy-drink cans, various crumpled foil pouches that had once contained biscotti, popcorn or Salami Bites—generated by the child standing there before me. "I don't like your sarcasm," I said.

Her face was pinched so that her lips were reduced to the smallest little O-ring of disgust. "What *do* you like?"

"A clean house. A little peace and quiet. Some privacy, for Christ's sake—is that too much to ask?"

"I want to be with mom."

"Go text your friends."

"I don't have any friends."

"Make some."

And this, thrown over her shoulder, preparatory to the furious pounding retreat up the stairs and the slamming of her bedroom door: "You're a pig!"

And my response, which had become ritualized ever since I'd sprung for the $5,000 second generation Halcom X1520 Relive Box with the In-Flesh Retinal Projection Stream and altered forever the dynamic between me and my only child: "I know."

Most people, when they got their first Relive Box, went straight for sex, which was only natural. In fact, it was a selling point in the TV ads, which featured shimmering adolescents walking hand in hand along a generic strip of beach or leaning in for a tender kiss over the ball return at the bowling alley. Who wouldn't want to go back there? Who wouldn't want to relive innocence, the nascent stirrings of love and desire or the first time you removed her clothes and she removed yours? What of girlfriends (or boyfriends, as the case may be), wives, ex-wives, one-night stands, the casual encounter that got you halfway there and flitted out of reach on the wings of an unfulfilled promise? I was no different. The sex part of it obsessed me through those first couple of months and if I drifted into work each morning feeling drained (and not just figuratively), I knew it was a problem and that it was adversely affecting my job performance, and even, if I didn't cut back, threatening my job itself. Still, to relive Christine when we first met, to relive her in bed, in candlelight, clinging fast to me and whispering my name over and over in the throes of her passion, was too great a temptation. Or even just sitting there across from me in the Moroccan restaurant where I took her for our first date, her eyes like portals, like consoles themselves, as she leaned into the table and drank up every word and witticism that came out of my mouth. Or to go further back, before my wife entered the picture, to Rennie Porter, the girl I took to the senior prom and spent two delicious hours rubbing up against in the back seat of my father's Buick Regal, every second of which I'd relived six or seven times now. And to Lisa, Lisa Denardo, the girl I met that night at the Roxy, hoping I was going to score.

I started coming in late to work. Giving everybody, even my boss, the zombie stare. I got my first warning. Then my second. And my boss—Kevin Moos, a decent-enough guy five years younger than me who didn't have an X1520, or not that he was letting on—sat me down in his office and told me, in no uncertain terms, that there wouldn't be a third.

But it was a miserable night and I was depressed. And bored. So bored you could have drilled holes in the back of my head and taken core samples and I wouldn't have known the difference. I'd already denied my daughter, who was thumping around upstairs with the cumulative weight of ten daughters, and the next day was Friday, TGIF, end of the week, the slimmest of workdays when just about everybody alive thinks about slipping out early. I figured even if I did relive for more than the two hours I was going to strictly limit myself to, even if I woke up exhausted, I could always find a way to make it to lunch and just let things coast after that. So I went into the kitchen and fixed myself a gin and tonic because that was what I'd been drinking that night at the Roxy and carried it into the room at the end of the hall that had once been a bedroom and was now (Katie's joke, not mine) the reliving room.

The console sat squarely on the low table that was the only piece of furniture in the room aside from the straight-backed chair I'd set in front of it the day I brought the thing home. It wasn't much bigger than the gaming consoles I'd had to make do with in the old days, a slick black metal cube with a single recessed glass slit running across the face of it from one side to the other. It activated the minute I took my seat. "Hello, Wes," it said in the voice I'd selected, male, with the slightest bump of an accent to make it seem less synthetic. "Welcome back."

I lifted the drink to my lips to steady myself—think of a conductor raising his baton—and cleared my throat. "February 28, 1982," I said. "9:45 p.m. Play."

The box flashed the date and time and then suddenly I was there, the club exploding into life like a comet touching down, light and noise and movement obliterating the now, the house gone, my daughter gone, the world of getting and doing and bosses and work vanished in an instant. I was standing at the bar with my best friend, Zach Ronalds, who turned up his shirt collars and wore his hair in a Joe Strummer pompadour just like me, only his hair was black and mine choirboy blond (I'd dye it within the week), and I was trying to get the bartender's attention so I could order us G&Ts with my fake ID. The band, more New Wave than punk, hadn't started yet, and the only thing to look at onstage was the opening act packing up their equipment while hyper-vigilant girls in vampire makeup and torn fishnet stockings washed round them in a human tide that ebbed and flowed on the waves of music crashing through the speakers. It was bliss. Bliss because I knew now that this night, alone out of all the long succession of dull nugatory nights building up to it, would be special, that this was the night I'd meet Lisa and take her home with me. To my parents' house in Pasadena, where I had a room of my own above the detached garage and could come and go as I pleased. My room. The place where I greased up my hair and stared at myself in the mirror and waited for something to happen, something like this, like what was coming in seven and a half real-time minutes.

Zach said what sounded like "Look at that skank," but since he had his face turned away from me and the music was cranked to the sonic level of a rocket launch (give credit to the X1520's parametric speaker/audio beam technology, which is infinitely more refined than the first generation's), I wasn't quite sure, though I must have heard him that night, my ears younger then, less damaged by scenes like this one, because I took hold of his arm and said, "Who? Her?"

What I said now, though, was "Reset, reverse ten seconds," and everything stalled, vanished and started up once more, and here I was trying all over again to get the bartender's attention and listening hard when Zach, leaning casually against the bar on two splayed elbows, opened his mouth to speak.

"Look at that skank," he said, undeniably, there it was, coloring everything in the moment because he was snap-judging Lisa, with her coat-hanger shoulders, Kabuki makeup and shining black lips, and I said, "Who? Her?" already attracted because in my eyes she wasn't a skank at all or if she was, she was a skank from some other realm altogether and I couldn't from that moment on think of anything but getting her to talk to me.

Now, the frustrating thing about the current relive technology is that you can't be an actor in the scene, only an observer, like Scrooge reliving his boarding school agonies with the Ghost of Christmas Past at his elbow, so whatever howlers your adolescent self might have uttered are right there, hanging in the air, unedited. You can fast-forward, and I suppose most people do—skip the chatter; get to the sex—but personally, after going straight to the carnal moments the first five or six times I relived a scene, I liked to go back and hear what I had to say, what she had to say, however banal it might have sounded now. What I did that night—and I'd already relived this moment twice in the past week—was catch hold of the bartender and order not two but three G&Ts, though I only had something like eighteen dollars in my wallet, set one on the bar for Zach and cross the floor to where she was standing just beneath the stage in what would be the mosh pit half an hour later. She saw me coming, saw the drinks—two drinks—and looked away, covering herself because she was sure I was toting that extra drink for somebody else, a girlfriend or best bud lurking in the drift of shadow the stage lights drew up out of the murky walls.

I tapped her shoulder. She turned her face to me.

"Pause," I said.

Everything stopped. I was in a 3-D painting now and so was she and for the longest time I just kept things there, studying her face. She was eighteen years old, a commandeer of style, beautiful enough underneath the paint and gel and eyeliner and all the rest to make me feel faint even now, and her eyes weren't wary, weren't *used*, but candid, ready, rich with expectation. I held my drink just under my nose, inhaling the smell of juniper berries to tweak the memory, and said, "Play."

"You look thirsty," I said.

The music boomed. Behind me, at the bar, Zach was giving me a look of disbelief, like *What the?*, because this was a violation of our club-going protocol. We didn't talk to the girls, and especially not the skanks, because we were there for the *music*, at least that was what we told ourselves. (Second time around I did pause this part, just for the expression on his face—Zach, poor Zach, who never did find himself a girlfriend as far as I know and who's probably someplace reliving every club he's ever been in and every date he's ever had just to feel sorry for himself.)

She leveled her eyes on me, gave it a beat, then took the cold glass from my hand. "How did you guess?" she said.

What followed was the usual exchange of information about bands, books, neighborhood, high school, college, and then I was bragging about the bands I'd seen lately and she was countering with the band members she knew personally, like John Doe and the drummer for the Germs, and letting her eyes reveal just how personal that was, which only managed to inflame me till I wanted nothing more on this earth than to pin her in a corner and kiss the black lipstick right off her. What I said then, unaware that my carefully sculpted pompadour was collapsing across my brow in something very much like a bowl cut (or worse—*anathema*—a Beatles' shag), was, "You want to dance?"

She gave me a look. Shot her eyes to the stage and back, then around the room. A few people were dancing to the canned music, most of them jerking and gyrating to their own drugged-out beat, and there was no sign—yet—of the band we'd come to hear. "To this?"

"Yeah," I said, and I looked so—what was it?—*needy*, though at the time I must have thought I was chiseled out of a block of pure cool. "Come on," I said, and I reached out a hand to her.

I watched the decision firm in her eyes, deep in this moment that would give rise to all the rest, to the part I was about to fast-forward to because I had to get up in the morning. For work. And no excuses. *But watch, watch what comes next . . .*

She took my hand, the soft friction of her touch alive still somewhere in my cell memory, and then she was leading me out onto the dance floor.

She was leading. And I was following.

Will it surprise you to know that I exceeded my self-imposed two-hour limit? That after the sex I fast-forwarded to our first date, which was really just an agreed-upon meeting at Tower Records (March 2, 1982, 4:30 p.m.) and took us thereafter up to Barney's Beanery for cheeseburgers and beers and shots of peppermint schnapps (!), which she paid for because her father was a rich executive at Warner Brothers? Or that it made me feel so good I couldn't resist skipping ahead three months to when she was as integral to my flesh as the Black Flag T-shirt that never left my back except in the shower? Lisa. Lisa Denardo. With her cat's tongue and tight torquing body that was a girl's and a woman's at the same time and her perfect evenly-spaced set of glistening white teeth (perfect, that is, but for the incisor she'd had a dentist in Tijuana remove in the spirit of punk solidarity). The scene I hit on was early the following summer, summer break of my sophomore year in college, when I gave up on my parents' garage and Lisa and I moved into an off-campus apartment on Vermont and decided to paint the walls, ceiling and floors the color of midnight in the Carlsbad Caverns. June 6, 1982, 2:44 p.m. The glisten of black paint, a too-bright sun caught in the windows and Lisa saying, "Think we should paint the glass too?" I was oblivious to anything but her and me and the way I looked and the way she looked, a streak of paint on her left forearm and another, scimitar-shaped, just over one eyebrow, when suddenly everything went neutral and I was back in the reliving room staring into the furious face of my daughter.

But let me explain the technology here a moment, for those of you who don't already know. This isn't a computer screen or a TV or a hologram or anything anybody else can see—we're talking retinal projection, two laser beams fixed on two eyeballs. Anybody coming into the room (daughter, wife, boss) will simply see you sitting there in a chair with your retinas lit like furnaces. Step in front of the projector—as my daughter did now—and the image vanishes.

"Stop," I said, and I wasn't talking to her.

But there she was, her hair brushed out for school and her jaw clenched, looking hate at me. "I can't believe you," she said. "Do you have any idea what time it is?"

Bleary, depleted—and guilty, deeply guilty, the narcissist caught in the act and caring about nothing or nobody but his own reliving self—I just gawked at her, the light she'd flicked on when she came into the room transfixing me in the chair. I shook my head.

"It's six forty-five. a.m. In the morning. The *morning*, Dad."

I started to say something but the words were tangled up inside of me because Lisa was saying—had just said—"You're not going to make me stay here and watch the paint dry, are you, because I'm thinking maybe we could drive out to the beach or something, just to cool down," and I said, or was going to say, "There's like maybe half a pint of gas in the car."

"What?" Katie demanded. "Were you with mom again? Is that it? Like you can be with her and I can't?"

"No," I said, "no, that wasn't it, it wasn't your mom at all—"

A tremor ran through her. "Yeah, right. So what was it then? Some girlfriend, somebody you were gaga over when you were in college? Or high school? Or what, *junior* high?"

"I must have fallen asleep," I said. "Really. I just zoned out."

She knew I was lying. She'd come looking for me, dutiful child, motherless child, and found me not up and about and bustling around the kitchen preparing to fuss over her and see her off to school the way I used to, but pinned here in this chair like an exhibit in a museum, blind to anything but the past, my past and nobody else's, not hers or her mother's, or the country's or the world's, but just mine.

I heard the door slam. Heard the thump of her angry feet in the hallway, the distant muffled crash of the front door, and then the house was quiet. I looked at the slit in the box. "Play," I said.

By the time I got to work I was an hour and a half late, but on this day—miracle of miracles—Kevin was even later, and when he did show up I was ensconced in my cubicle, dutifully rattling keys on my keyboard. He didn't say anything, just brushed by me and buried himself in his office, but I could see he was wearing the same vacant pre-now look I was, and it didn't take much of an intuitive leap to guess the reason. In fact, since the new model had come on the market, I'd no-

ticed the same randy faraway gaze in the eyes of half a dozen of my fellow employees, including Linda Blanco, the receptionist, who'd stopped buttoning the top
three buttons of her blouse and wore shorter and shorter skirts every day. Instead
of breathing "Moos and Associates, how may I help you?" into the receiver, now
she just said, "Reset."

Was this a recipe for disaster? Was our whole society on the verge of breaking down? Was the NSA going to step in? Were they going to pass laws? Ban the
box? I didn't know. I didn't care. I had a daughter to worry about. Thing was, all
I could think of was getting home to relive, straight home, and if the image of a
carton of milk or a loaf of bread flitted into my head I batted it away. Take-out.
We could always get take-out. I was in a crucial phase with Lisa, heading inexora-
bly for the grimmer scenes, the disagreements—petty at first, then monumental,
unbridgeable, like the day I got home from my makeup class in Calculus and
found her sitting at the kitchen table with a stoner whose name I never did catch
and didn't want to know, not then or now—and I needed to get through it, to
analyze it whether it hurt or not, because but it was there and I had to relive it. I
couldn't help myself. I just kept picking at it like a scab.

Ultimately, this was all about Christine, of course, about when I began to fail
instead of succeed, to lose instead of win. I needed Lisa to remind me of a time before that, to help me trace my missteps and assign blame, because as intoxicating
as it was to relive the birds-atwitter moments with Christine, there was always
something nagging at me in any given scene, some twitch of her face or a comment she threw out that should have raised flags at the time but never did. All
right. Fine. I was going to go there, I was, and relive the minutiae of our relationship, the ecstasy and agony both, the moments of mindless contentment and the
swelling tide of antipathy that drove us apart, but first things first, and as I fought
my way home on the freeway that afternoon, all I could think about was Lisa.

In the old days, before we got the box, my daughter and I had a Friday afternoon ritual whereby I would stop in at the Italian place down the street from
the house, have a drink and chat up whoever was there, then call Katie and have
her come join me for a father-daughter dinner so I could have some face-time
with her, read into her and suss out her thoughts and feelings as she grew into a
young woman herself, but we didn't do that anymore. There wasn't time. The best
I could offer—lately, especially—was takeout or a microwave pizza and a limp
salad choked down in the cold confines of the kitchen while we separately calculated how long we had to put up with the pretense before slipping off to relive.

There were no lights on in the house as I pulled into the driveway and that was
odd, because Katie should have been home from school by now—and she hadn't
texted me or phoned to say she'd be staying late. I climbed out of the car feeling
stiff all over—I needed to get more exercise, I knew that, and I resolved to do it

too, as soon as I got my head above water—and as I came up the walk I saw the sad frosted artificial wreath hanging crookedly there in the center panel of the front door. Katie must have dug it out of the box of ornaments in the garage on her own initiative, to do something by way of Christmas, and that gave me pause, that stopped me right there, the thought of it, of my daughter having to make the effort all by herself. That crushed me. It did. And as I put the key in the lock and pushed the door open I knew things were going to have to change. Dinner. I'd take her out to dinner and forget about Lisa. At least for now.

"Katie?" I called. "You home?"

No response. I shrugged out of my coat and went on into the kitchen, thinking to make myself a drink. There were traces of her here, her backpack flung down on the floor, an open bag of Doritos spilling across the counter, a Diet Sprite, half-full, on the breadboard. I called her name again, standing stock-still in the middle of the room and listening for the slightest hint of sound or movement as my voice echoed through the house. I was about to pull out my phone and call her when I thought of the reliving room, and it was a sinking thought, not a selfish one, because if she was in there, reliving—and she was, I knew she was—what did that say about her social life? Didn't teenage girls go out anymore? Didn't they gather in packs at the mall or go to movies or post things on Facebook, or, forgive me, go out on dates? Group dates, even? How else were they going to experience the inchoate beginnings of what the Relive Box people were pushing in the first place?

I shoved into the room, which was dark but for the lights of her eyes, and just stood there watching her for a long moment as I adjusted to the gloom. She sat riveted, her body present but her mind elsewhere, and if I was embarrassed—for her, and for me too, her father, invading her privacy when she was most vulnerable—the embarrassment gave way to a sorrow so oceanic I thought I would drown in it. I studied her face. Watched her smile and grimace and go cold and smile again. What could she possibly be reliving when she'd lived so little? Family vacations? Christmases past? The biannual trips to Hong Kong to be with her mother and stepfather? I couldn't fathom it. I didn't like it. It had to stop. I turned on the overhead light and stepped in front of the projector.

She blinked at me and she didn't recognize me, didn't know me at all because I was in the now and she was in the past. "Katie," I said, "that's enough now. Come on." I held out my arms to her even as recognition came back into her eyes and she made a vague gesture of irritation, of pushing away.

"Katie," I said, "let's go out to dinner. Just the two of us. Like we used to."

"I'm not hungry," she said. "And it's not fair. You can use it all you want, like day and night, but whenever I want it—" and she broke off, tears starting in her eyes.

"Come on," I said. "It'll be fun."

The look she gave me was unsparing. I was trying to deflect it, trying to think of something to say, when she came up out of the chair so suddenly it startled me, and though I tried to take hold of her arm, to pull her to me whether she fought it or not, she was too quick for me. Before I could react, she was at the door, pausing only to scorch me with another glare. "I don't believe you," she spat, before vanishing down the hall.

I should have followed her, should have tried to make things right—or better, anyway—but I didn't. The box was right there. It had shut down when she leapt up from the chair and whatever she'd been reliving was buried back inside it, accessible to no one, though you can bet there are hackers out there right now trying to subvert the retinal-recognition feature. For a long moment I stared at the open door, fighting myself, then I went over and pulled it softly shut. I realized I didn't need a drink or dinner either. I sat down in the chair. "Hello, Wes," the box said. "Welcome back."

We didn't have a Christmas tree that year and neither of us really cared all that much, I think—if we wanted to look at spangle-draped trees we could relive holidays past, happier ones, or in my case, I could go back to my childhood and relive my father's whiskey in a glass and my mother's long-suffering face blossoming over the greedy joy of her golden boy, her only child, tearing open his presents as a weak bleached-out California sun haunted the windows and the turkey crackled in the oven. Katie went off (reluctantly, I thought) on a skiing vacation to Mammoth with the family of her best friend, Allison, who she hardly saw anymore, not outside of school, not in the now, and I went back to Lisa, because if I was going to get to Christine in any serious way—beyond the sex, that is, beyond the holiday greetings and picture-postcard moments—Lisa was my bridge.

As soon as I'd dropped Katie at Allison's house and exchanged a few previously scripted salutations with Allison's grinning parents and her grinning twin brothers, I stopped at a convenience store for a case of eight-ounce bottles of spring water and the biggest box of power bars I could find and went straight home to the reliving room. The night before I'd been close to the crucial scene with Lisa, one that was as fixed in my memory as the blow-up with Christine a quarter century later, but elusive as to the date and time. I'd been up all night—*again*—fast-forwarding, reversing, jumping locales and facial expressions, Lisa's first piercing, the evolution of my haircut, but I hadn't been able to pinpoint the exact moment, not yet. I set the water on the floor on my left side, the power bars on my right. "May 9, 1983," I said, "4:00 a.m."

The numbers flashed and then I was in darkness, zero visibility, confused as to where I was until the illuminated dial of a clock radio began to bleed through and I could make out the dim outline of myself lying in bed in the back room of that apartment with the black walls and black ceiling and black floor. Lisa was there beside me, an irregular hump in the darkness, snoring with a harsh gag and stutter. She was stoned. And drunk. Half an hour earlier she'd been in the bathroom, heaving over the toilet, and I realized I'd come too far. "Reset," I said, "reverse ninety minutes."

Sudden light, blinding after the darkness, and I was alone in the living room of the apartment, studying, or trying to. My hair hung limp, my muscles were barely there, but I was young and reasonably good-looking, even excusing any bias. I saw that my Black Flag T-shirt had faded to gray from too much sun and too many washings, and the book in my lap looked as familiar as something I might have been buried with in a previous life, but then this *was* my previous life. I watched myself turn a page, crane my neck toward the door, get up to flip over the album that was providing the soundtrack. "Reset," I said, "fast-forward ten minutes," and here it was, what I'd been searching for: a sudden crash, the front door flinging back, Lisa and the stoner whose name I didn't want to know fumbling their way in, both of them as slow as syrup with the cumulative effect of downers and alcohol, and though the box didn't have an olfactory feature, I swear I could smell the tequila on them. They'd gone clubbing, mid-week, and I couldn't go because of finals, but Lisa could because she didn't have finals and she didn't have work either. I jumped up out of the chair, spilling the book, and shouted something I couldn't quite make out, so I said, "Reset, reverse five seconds."

"You fucker!" was what I'd shouted, and now I shouted it again prior to slapping something out of the guy's hand, a beer bottle, and all at once I had him in a hammerlock and Lisa was beating at my back with her bird-claw fists and I was wrestling the guy out the door, cursing over the soundtrack ("Should I Stay or Should I Go," one of those flatline ironies that almost makes you believe everything in this life's been programmed). I saw now that he was bigger than I was, probably stronger too, but the drugs had taken the volition out of him and in the next moment he was outside the door and the three bolts were hammered home. By me. Who now turned in a rage to Lisa.

"Stop," I said. "Freeze." Lisa hung there, defiant and guilty at the same time, pretty, breathtakingly pretty, despite the slack mouth and drugged-out eyes. I should have left it there, should have forgotten it and gone on to those first cornucopian weeks and months and even years with Christine, but I couldn't help myself. "Play," I said, and Lisa raised a hand to swat at me, but she was too unsteady and knocked the lamp over instead.

"Did you fuck him?" I demanded.

There was a long pause, so long I almost fast-forwarded, and then she said, "Yeah. Yeah, I fucked him. And I'll tell you something"—her words glutinous, the syllables coalescing on her tongue—"you're no punk. And he is. He's the real deal. And you? You're, you're—"

I should have stopped it right there.

"—you're *prissy*."

"Prissy?" I couldn't believe it. Not then and not now.

She made a broad stoned gesture, weaving on her feet. "Anal retentive. Like who left the dishes in the sink or who didn't take out the garbage or what about the cockroaches—"

"Stop," I said. "Reset. June 19, 1994, 11:02 p.m."

I was in another bedroom now, one with walls the color of cream, and I was in another bed, this time with Christine, and I'd timed the memory to the very minute, post-coital, in the afterglow, and Christine, with her soft aspirated whisper of a voice, was saying, "I love you, Wes, you know that, don't you?"

"Stop," I said. "Reverse five seconds."

She said it again. And I stopped again. And reversed again. And she said it again. And again.

Time has no meaning when you're reliving. I don't know how long I kept it up, how long I kept surfing through those moments of Christine—not the sexual ones, but the loving ones, the companionable ones, the ordinary day-to-day moments when you could see in her eyes that she loved me more than anybody alive and was never going to stop loving me, never. Dinner at the kitchen table, any dinner, any night. Just to be there. My wife. My daughter. The way the light flooded the windows and poured liquid gold over the hardwood floors of our starter house in Canoga Park. Katie's first birthday. Her first word ("Cake!"). The look on Christine's face as she curled up with Katie in bed and read her *Where the Wild Things Are*. Her voice as she hoarsened it for Max: "I'll eat you up!"

Enough analysis, enough hurt. I was no masochist.

At some point, I had to get up from that chair in the now and evacuate a living bladder, the house silent, spectral, unreal. I didn't live here. I didn't live in the now with its deadening nine-to-five job I was in danger of losing and the daughter I was failing and a wife who'd left me—and her own daughter—for Winston Chen, choreographer of martial arts movies in Hong Kong who was loving and kind and funny and not the control freak I was (*Prissy*, anyone? *Anal retentive*?). The house echoed with my footsteps, a stage set and nothing more. I went to the kitchen and dug the biggest pot I could find out from under the sink, brought it back to the reliving room and set it on the floor between my legs to save me the trouble of getting up next time around.

Time passed. Relived time and lived time too. There were two windows in the room, shades drawn so as not to interfere with the business of the moment, and sometimes a faint glow appeared around the margins of them, an effect I noticed when I was searching for a particular scene and couldn't quite pin it down. Sometimes the glow was gone. Sometimes it wasn't. What happened then, and I might have been two days in or three or five, I couldn't really say, was that things began to cloy. I'd relived an exclusive diet of the transcendent, the joyful, the insouciant, the best of Christine, the best of Lisa and all the key moments of the women who came between and after, and I'd gone back to the Intermediate Algebra test, the very instant, pencil to paper, when I knew I'd scored a perfect one hundred percent, and to the time I'd squirted a ball to right field with two outs, two strikes, ninth inning and my Little League team (the Condors, yellow tees, white lettering) down by three and watched it rise majestically over the glove of the spastic red-haired kid sucking back allergic snot and roll all the way to the wall. Triumph after triumph, goodness abounding—till it stuck in my throat.

"Reset," I said. "January 2, 2009. 4:30 p.m."

I found myself in the kitchen of our second house, this house, the one we'd moved to because it was outside the L.A. city limits and had schools we felt comfortable with sending Katie to. That was what mattered: the schools. Christine and I both insisted on it, and if it lengthened our commutes, so be it. This house. The one I was reliving in now. Everything gleamed around me, counters polished, the glass of the cabinets as transparent as air because details mattered then, everything in its place whether Christine was there or not—especially if she wasn't there, and where was she? Or where had she been? China. With her boss. On film business. Her bags were just inside the front door, where she'd dropped them forty-five minutes ago after I picked her up at the airport and we'd had our talk in the car, the talk I was going to relive when I got done here, because it was all about pain now, about reality, and this scene was the capper, the coup de grâce. You want wounds? You want to take a razor blade to the meat of your inner thigh just to see if you can still feel? Well, here it was.

Christine entered the scene now, coming down the stairs from Katie's room, her eyes wet, or damp anyway, and her face composed. And there I was, pushing myself up from the table, my beginner's bald spot a glint of exposed flesh under the glare of the overhead light. I spoke first. "You tell her?"

Christine was dressed in her business attire, black stockings, heels, skirt to the knee, tailored jacket. She looked exhausted, and not simply from the fifteen-hour flight but from what she'd had to tell me. And our daughter. (How I'd like to be able to relive *that*, to hear how she'd even broached the subject, let alone how she'd smoke-screened her own selfishness and betrayal with some specious concern for Katie's well-being—let's not rock the boat and you'll be better off here with your father and your school and your teachers and it's not the end but just the beginning, buck up, you'll see.)

Christine's voice was barely audible. "I don't like this any better than you do."

"Then why do it?"

A long pause. Too long. "Stop," I said.

I couldn't do this. My heart was hammering. My eyes felt as if as if they were being squeezed in a vise. I could barely swallow. I reached down for a bottle of water and a power bar, unscrewed the cap, tore open the wrapper, drank, chewed. She was going to say, "This isn't working," and I was going to say, "*Working?* What the fuck are you talking about? What does work have to do with it? I thought this was about love. I thought it was about commitment." I knew I wasn't going to get violent, though I should have, should have chased her out to the cab that was even then waiting at the curb and slammed my way in and flown all the way to Hong Kong to confront Winston Chen, the martial arts genius, who could have crippled me with his bare feet.

"Reset," I said. "August 1975, any day, any time."

There was a hum from the box. "Incomplete command. Please select date and time."

I was twelve years old, the summer we went to Vermont, to a lake there where the mist came up off the water like the fumes of a dream and the deer mice lived under the refrigerator, and I didn't have a date or time fixed in my mind—I just needed to get away from Christine, that was all. I picked the first thing that came into my head.

"August 19," I said. "11:30 a.m. Play."

A blacktop road. Sun like a nuclear blast. A kid, running. I recognized myself—I'd been to this summer before, one I remembered as idyllic, messing around in boats, fishing, swimming, wandering the woods with one of the local kids, Billy Scharf, everything neutral, copacetic, life lived in the moment. But why was I running? And why did I have that look on my face, a look that fused determination and helplessness both? Up the drive now, up the steps to the house, shouting for my parents, "Mom! Dad!"

I began to get a bad feeling.

I saw my father get up off the wicker sofa on the porch, my vigorous young father who was dressed in a T-shirt and jeans and didn't have even a trace of gray in his hair, my father who always made everything right. But not this time. "What's the matter?" he said. "What is it?"

And my mother coming through the screen door to the porch, a towel in one hand and her hair snarled wet from the lake. And me. I was fighting back tears, my legs and arms like sticks, striped polo shirt, faded shorts. "It's," I said, "it's—"

"Stop," I said. "Reset." It was my dog, Queenie, that was what it was, dead on the road that morning, and who'd left the gate ajar so she could get out in the first place? Even though he'd been warned about it a hundred times?

I was in a dark room. There was a pot between my legs and it was giving off a fierce odor. I needed to go deeper, needed out of this. I spouted random dates, saw myself driving to work, stuck in traffic with ten thousand other fools who could only wish they had a fast-forward app, saw myself in my thirties, post-Lisa, pre-Christine, obsessing over Halo, and I stayed there through all the toppling hours, reliving myself in the game, boxes within boxes, until finally I thought of God, or what passes for God in my life, the mystery beyond words, beyond lasers and silicon chips. I gave a date nine months before I was born, "December 30, 1962, 6:00 a.m.," when I was, what—a zygote?—but the box gave me nothing, neither visual nor audio. And that was wrong, deeply wrong. There should have been a heartbeat. My mother's heartbeat, the first thing we hear—or feel, feel before we even have ears.

"Stop," I said. "Reset." A wave of rising exhilaration swept over me even as the words came to my lips, "September 30, 1963, 2:35 a.m.," and the drumbeat started up, *ba-boom, ba-boom*, but no visual, not yet, the minutes ticking by, *ba-boom, ba-boom*, and then I was there, in the light of this world, and my mother in her stained hospital gown and the man with the monobrow and flashing glasses, the stranger, the doctor, saying what he was going to say by way of congratulations and relief. A boy. It's a boy.

Then it all went dead and there was somebody standing there in front of me, and I didn't recognize her, not at first, how could I? "Dad," she was saying, "Dad, are you there?"

I blinked. Tried to focus.

"No," I said finally, shaking my head in slow emphasis, the word itself, the denial, heavy as a stone in my mouth. "I'm not here. I'm not. I'm not."

Discussion Questions:

1. "The Relive Box" ends with an enigmatic statement from the narrator. What does he mean when he says, "I'm not here. I'm not. I'm not."
2. Why does the narrator lose himself for days and days in the relive box? What is he missing in his life both physically and emotionally?
3. Discuss how Boyle uses the relive box as a metaphor for the way technology is used today.

Essay Questions:

1. The narrator uses the relive box to go over his best memories at first, but he is soon going over and over his worst memories, reliving them and re-experiencing the pain of those moments. What is T.C. Boyle suggesting about the nature of humanity and our need to fix the past?
2. To what degree does "The Relive Box" accurately depict the ways that technology deprives people of genuine human experience?
3. Compare and contrast "The Relive Box" to "Yoshimi and the Robot." How do these stories deal with the dangers of the rise of technology and are they making similar kinds of statements about it?

Palimpsest

RUTH NOLAN

Pal·imp·sest (noun): a parchment or the like on which two or more successive texts have been written, each one being partially or completely erased to make room for the next.

I drive down the six-lane girth of Washington Road—the quickest off-ramp to the Coachella Music Festival held every April—and cruise past Sun City, a sprawling Del Webb retirement community that squats its fat, golf-course haunches in the middle of a sea of sand dunes and atop an ancient Cahuilla Indian village site. I'm going out to hike at the Coachella Valley Preserve, and even though it's late September 2008, and it's late in the day, it's still over 100 degrees outside.

I drank a few Fat Tire beers at my home in the Palm Desert Country Club not long ago, and now I'm slamming a not-so-cold Diet Coke. Dogs aren't allowed where I'm going, but I'm breaking the rules and bringing my border collie Shasta along. I am just happy she's still alive, because a prominent Rancho Mirage cardiologist found her tied up to a paloverde tree on a remote dirt road in the desert last week and posted her photo on an online animal rescue site, where I found her. She was severely dehydrated and frightened, but otherwise okay.

It turns out that my twenty-four-year-old, live-in boyfriend Paul was the one who tied her up. He confessed to it when I realized that the bungee cord that had been wrapped around Shasta's neck to tie her to the tree had come from my garage, and confronted him, then kicked him out of my house, and he'd yelled at me, and pushed me around, and I'd had to call the Palm Desert Police to help me get him out. But still, Shasta had licked his faced when he'd knelt down to say goodbye to her.

I'm trying to forget all of this, because three days after kicking Paul out of my house, I've realized that he's the love of my life. I realize that in spite of him tying up Shasta and leaving her alone out in the desert to die, I can't live without him. But he won't return my calls. I should forget about him. After all, he's twenty years younger than me, and my twenty-one-year-old daughter, who lives with her boyfriend in Berkeley, hates him. But I can't. All I can think of is Paul.

Shasta. She's been with me for seven years, since just after 9/11, when she was a half-grown pup who could still squeeze through the bars of my front gate. She grew up with my daughter. They loved to swim together in our pool. Shasta always sits beneath my feet when I'm at my desk, grading papers for the college classes I teach. And I'm especially grateful for her company now, since I am already getting lonely. Right now, Shasta is my best friend in the world. She's such a loyal dog that I know she's already forgiven Paul for what he did. If she can forgive him, then so can I.

I accelerate past the entrance to Sun City just in time to miss the red light, and look down at my new iPhone 3. No reception on the cell phone here. I want to call Paul to tell him he left his "Sunshine of My Love" DVD in my car, but I can't get through to him.

Except for Shasta, I'm alone out here with sweeping views of the mountains that encircle the Coachella Valley desert, and I'm exposed, like most of this land, and distinctly lacking the soothing effect of the Pacific Ocean marine layer, something we don't get out here in this shadow desert. We're blocked off from the ocean air flow by mountains that hurl themselves to well over 10,000 feet, and instead are punished by occasional San Gorgonio Pass winds that screech with sand and dirt. And so, I seek the safety and suckle of the oasis.

Shasta sticks her head out the window and barks at a jackrabbit darting wildly through creosote bushes along the road. We're getting out into open desert, her favorite place. She's ready to go.

That day, exactly one year ago, September 21, long before Shasta spent her worst night on earth, alone and shivering with fear, tied up to that leafless, thorny tree, Paul and I had laughingly shared dark chocolate Raisinettes—his favorite snack—and beer at Pushwalla Palms Oasis as the sun went down. This was before we had become lovers, on our first hike together at to the oasis, in the Coachella Valley Preserve.

We hiked deep into a mud-walled canyon and through a mush and tangle of ancient palm trees that seemed to grow larger in the slight breeze of gathering dusk. It's a place of empty whispers and barely-rustling palm fronds, an exotic place where time eases into a slow procession of coyotes, bobcats, and occasional mountain lions moving to and from the small oasis to sip at the faint remnants of water. Even the dinosaurs knew these palms, ages ago when the desert was much wetter, and the reverberation of their heavy stepping can still be felt in the timewarp of eternity that can be felt in this place.

And the oasis was our favorite place to go. This is where we made love for the first time, some weeks after we'd met. This is where we fell in love. And later, this is where we sometimes argued, and where he sometimes slapped me around when he'd get angry, accusing me of having affairs with other men, of still being in love with my ex-husband, Jeff, and always, Shasta would whimper patiently near my side. I'd rinse the sting from my cheeks and tears off my face with water from the small, shallow pools seeping from the roots of the fat-trunked palms in the oasis.

But even when things went bad, it seemed like entertainment, like a fresh adventure where nothing could go *really* wrong. After all, as we always agreed, we were the best of friends. Our disagreements were just minor inconveniences, bumps in the road of true love, as Paul would always say.

That was right before he moved in with me, not telling his parents, or any of his friends, where he was going. He never told them that he'd met me, in fact, something he told me much later. He never told them that he met me through the ad I placed on craigslist, where I'd hoped to find someone besides the elderly, retired men that dominate the Coachella Valley dating scene.

Paul didn't tell me for months that he'd in fact lied to his family and friends, that he'd told them all that he had gone to work and live on a fictional organic farm near Fallbrook, down by San Diego, to pick grapes and avocados and play harmonica in a blues band. None of it was true. His parents didn't even know I existed. He told me this much later, and told me he wanted to keep it that way. I told him that I didn't know why he had to lie.

They'll never get it, he said. *They'll never understand why I'm with you, when you're so much older, plus they want me to go to medical school like my brother and be a doctor. They'll never get me, not at all.*

And then, summer was almost over. And then he moved in.

And then he began insisting on making expensive renovations to my house. He used my credit cards, although I asked him not to.

He had a salt water pool filtration system installed, which cost $8,000.

He ordered a new mattress and headboard, delivered, costing $1,500. He also demanded I move my office into the kitchen area so that he could have his own room and close the door when he felt like it.

I was forced to move my office into my daughter's old bedroom. I thought she wouldn't mind, because she was off living with her boyfriend far away, and had said she was never coming back to the desert, but when she found out, she came unglued.

Paul installed new Berber carpets in all three of my bedrooms, and had my tile floors in the kitchen and living room re-grouted and resurfaced, adding up to a total of $5,000.

And he always bought expensive dog treats for Shasta every time he went to the store, and insisted on feeding her always the most expensive, veterinarian-recommended, organic brands. He kept her water dish filled with clean water, too, often changing it several times a day.

And then one day, while hacking into my AOL account, he found my emails to and from Jeff, who I've remained good friends with. That really set Paul off. From that point on, he blew up at me at least once a day, if not more.

And the more I told him I was sorry—and I truly was—the longer and louder he yelled.

And then he began to take my credit card without asking and go on shopping binges to Costco for cookware, Trader Joe's for organic everything, Best Buy for costly computer and video equipment, and he forced me to put the high-grade gasoline in my car every time we filled the tank.

And then he began to yell at me for hours every day and night.

And we had fantastic sex, three or four or five times a day.

And he told me that I needed to lose twenty pounds.

And then I said, *We should get married.*

And he said, *Yeah, let's go to Las Vegas and not tell anyone! That's what my mom and dad did! We'll surprise them by our rings when we get back.*

And then I'd go to Jeff's apartment in Northridge when the yelling got to be too much, Paul yelling at me for what a whore I was, and I'd have to go to Jeff's because I needed someone I could talk to who was a mature adult. Even if Jeff *had* left me three years earlier for the much-younger-than-both-of-us hospice nurse from Tarzana who now lived with him and paid his rent, instead of me, he said that he still cared about me.

And he'd yell back, *You're lucky I'm not bustin' caps, on you, fucking whore.*

And I'd say, *I told you Jeff and I are still friends, and you said you didn't mind.*

And he'd scream and throw his fists, *That was before I moved in, you bitch!*

And I'd scream back, *Jeff is just my friend, I'm not with him anymore, he's old and fat!*

You're nothing but a slut! he'd yell, and push me to the ground.

And then, on one of the hottest, most suffocating days of the endless, late desert summer, the stock market crashed, and almost overnight, I lost all of the equity I'd so cockily thought I was building up in the house. I told Paul he need-ed to find a job, and he said he would. And he stopped yelling at me so much, because he knew I was so upset about the many tens of thousands of dollars I'd just lost overnight, through no fault of my own, and he promised to forgive me for fucking Jeff.

He said he felt bad for me, because he knew how broke I now was, and what a shame, after I'd worked so hard for so many years.

And then, just a few days later, he tied up Shasta in the desert, and in a blur, he had all of his stuff cleared out of my house, and he was gone. And I don't know if he's ever coming back. Shasta's hoarse bark is now completely well, and I took her to the vet and everything, and I'm sure she's going to continue to do really well. She knows I'm sad. I can tell by the way she licked my hand when I was leaving the house.

I'm here. I'm at the trailhead. I crack open my car door. A blast of heat pulses across my face, and I'm suddenly not sure if I have the heart or energy to hike the three miles to Pushwalla Palms. I stare out the dusty windshield and see the fringed tops of the palm oasis shimmering in a distant, watery blur. It seems that not a palm has moved since I was last here. Things sometimes feel frozen that way here in the desert, like they're stuck in place and have never moved at all. Like they don't even breathe.

I look back from where I drove, across the desert floor of the Coachella Valley. Cars wind their way along the Interstate 10, to the east, to the west. I can't go back to my house. The last spread of sunset beams across the sky behind Mt. San Jacinto to the west, and all at once, the valley falls into a long shadow. There's no music out here, just a deep, pregnant silence, and the inevitable promise of moon and stars.

Shasta whines and paws at me impatiently, then suddenly jumps across me, pushes my door open, and races into the desert. Too late to put her on her leash. I watch numbly as she disappears behind a grove of gray smoke trees. Now that she's broken free, I know she'll probably race all the way to the oasis, cool off, drink deeply, hang out there with a few coyotes for awhile, and only return when and if she wants to. Then again, maybe she won't. Just like Paul.

I look down at my iPhone. There's no phone or wireless service out here at all, just a flood of stillborn memories and Shasta's empty leash in my hand.

RUTH NOLAN
PALIMPSEST

Discussion Questions:

1. What clues in the story do we have that the relationship between the narrator and Paul is not healthy?
2. What does the word "palimpsest" mean and how does it relate to this story?
3. Why is the narrator unsure at the end of her story whether Shasta will return or not? Do you think Shasta will return?

Essay Questions:

1. Why do you think the narrator of "Palimpsest" is willing to forgive Paul for what he has done to her dog? Why would she ever want to get back together with Paul?
2. The last line of the story suggests that the narrator is completely unsure of all of her relationships. What is it about her that makes her feel that the people and animals of her life might leave her at a moment's notice?

Frozen Yogurt

GERALD LOCKLIN

As I enter the popular local Golden Spoon No-Fat Yogurt shop, an old lady sitting by herself at one of the three or four small indoor tables makes eye contact with me and smiles. I don't recognize her, but after you've seen so many of the faces in the world, which all break down into a finite number of types, there aren't many smiles that don't look at least vaguely familiar to you. So I make a habit of smiling back and nodding and sometimes saying "Hi" to just about everyone who meets my gaze these days. It doesn't cost me a cent to perform this courtesy, although many of the recipients of my cordiality probably conclude I am The Village Idiot.

This lady seems pleased to be acknowledged. She beams back at me. She's nice enough looking for someone who may be in the vicinity of eighty. Approaching seventy myself, women of all ages have begun to provoke my interest. As a young man, I was distracted by flaws, blemishes. Now I fix upon the lovely feature—the pretty face of the large woman, the comely bosom of the facially plain. This particular senior citizen is, though wrinkled, petite, with lively eyes and a cuteness that must have captivated many a classmate sixty or sixty-five years ago.

I take a seat outside with my regular-sized cup of unadorned "Just Chocolate" dessert. A few plastic spoonfuls into it, I find the aforementioned temptress drifting through the exit and occupying the other chair at my wobbly metal table before she's even finished asking, "May I join you?"

"Be my guest."

"Thank you so much—it's a little warm out here, but it was freezing back in there."

"It will be just right out here soon. I love warm summer evenings."

"You do? So do I."

"I was in graduate school in Tucson, fifty-five years ago, and I loved it. I never minded the heat, and the nights were perfect for a ball game. Ironically, you could just about freeze to death in the winter. My wife and I would huddle in front of a wall furnace, trying to study."

"Are you still married?"

"Different wife."

"My husband died a year ago. We met in college also. Doesn't your wife like frozen yogurt?"

"She likes it, but she's out of town. We have a cabin in the mountains."

"You don't like mountains?"

"It's pretty up there, but I had some lung problems fifteen years ago and they left me more affected by the altitude. This wife and I have been together so long that neither of us minds a little private time."

"My husband and I were inseparable."

"Some couples grow closer. Some don't."

"But when she's down here your wife joins you for frozen yogurt?"

"Sometimes, sometimes not. Lately it's been more often not. She eats a container of regular yogurt for breakfast every morning, though."

"I suppose that's even healthier."

"But not on a summer's evening."

"No, this is lovely, isn't it?"

"It is indeed."

"Do you live near here?"

"Just north of the freeway."

"I'm just south of it."

"That's even better."

"Yes, it's a pleasant enough place. I'm very fortunate. Except that I'm alone in it now."

"Your children don't live near here?"

"They're both up north. My daughter calls every day now. And brings the grandchildren down on holidays sometimes. My son isn't married. He's a professor. Economics. My husband was a history professor."

"At State?"

"At City."

"I just retired from State."

"Do you miss it?"

"I'm still in my office, and I may teach a course now and then, if needed. It's enough."

"My husband retired early. He said he was burned out. We traveled."

"My wife is counting the days to retirement. She'll be done next June."

"So you will go places together?"

"Or separately, perhaps. Or both."

"It's a shame she doesn't like frozen yogurt."

"Oh, she doesn't *not* like it."

"My husband and I used to go to lots of concerts."

"My wife and I still have a mini-subscription to the opera."

"What else do you do together?"

"We used to go to a lot of movies."

"Not anymore?"

"Not so far this summer. But she watches all the movies on TV. Especially at the cabin. Or, down here, if I'm trying to read or write in the same room."

"Don't you ever watch them with her?"

"Once in a while."

"I don't find many that I like anymore."

"Neither do I. But my wife is good at crafts. Beading and knitting and things. She really is very good at just about any craft imaginable. And she's learned to fix things that I never could. So a lot of time she isn't really paying much attention to the TV screen. But she says she needs the background noise."

"And you don't need background noise?"

"No, I'm from a pre-background-noise generation."

"Me too."

"I think anyone born after 1941 needs background noise. But I don't even like music playing if I can't concentrate on it. Maybe 'concentrate' is not the right word. I don't mean 'study' either. I guess I just mean give myself entirely to it."

"I hear music in my head."

"I do too."

"But so far no voices."

"So far no voices."

"Is there anything good on TV tonight?"

"Actually, there *is*. There's a new series on Masterpiece Mysteries called *The Inspector Lewis Mysteries*. Do you remember Inspector Morse?"

"Oh yes. Oxford. City of Steeples. He was a curmudgeon, but kind at heart. Self-educated. Loved Wagner. Didn't mind a pint."

"Minded two pints even less. Well, Inspector Lewis was his 'sidekick.' Now he's moved up into Morse's rank . . . Chief Inspector, I think . . . and he's becoming more like Morse all the time. And he has his own young assistant inspector whom he treats a lot like Morse used to treat him."

"I think I'll watch it."

"Nine o'clock. PBS."

"Channel twenty-eight?"

"Right-o. KCET. I plan to watch it myself."

"My husband and I both loved Inspector Morse."

"Yes. My wife and I did too."

"He was a very lonely man."

"He was."

"You and I both love frozen yogurt."

"Did your husband like frozen yogurt?"

"I don't think he knew frozen yogurt from meatballs. My husband loved his Scotch."

"Like Morse enjoyed his pint."

"I think Morse liked anything in a glass, didn't he?"

"Well, I did too at one time."

"But no more."

"No, not for fifteen years."

"There are other things."

"Yes, there are other things."

"I don't mean drugs."

"I know you don't."

"Well, I had better start home if I'm not going to miss Inspector Lewis."

"You're not walking, are you? At this time of night?"

"Oh no—I have my car. Do you need a ride?"

"I have my car too."

"Well, then . . ."

Go ahead, I think, *ask me over. I won't hurt you. We'll enjoy watching it together. We don't have to do anything. Well, maybe cuddle just a bit. But only if you wanted to—*

". . . I hope to see you here again."

"I hope so too."

"I don't even know your name. Mine is Jane."

"James Abbey. Jimmy."

"You'd better start home too."

"I will."

"I suppose your wife will come down from the mountain soon."

"Oh yes . . . and go back up and come back down . . ."

"I suppose you have a lot of things to keep you busy still."

"Quite a few. But not at this time of night."

"Maybe we'll meet here again."

"I hope so."

"I can meet your wife."

"She's been kind of off the frozen yogurt lately."

"Let's hope Inspector Lewis is as good at catching crooks as Morse was. Do you think he will be?"

"I think he'll be as good as he has to be. But he won't be Inspector Morse."

"No, we'll not see the likes of Morse again. Is Lewis lonely?"

"Yes. He lost his wife. And you lost your husband."

"But you've not lost *your* wife."

I'm lost for words. Then: "Do you know what Marilyn Monroe said when they asked her how Arthur Miller was as a husband?"

"No. What did she say?"

"Reputedly she said, *He warn't no Joe Dimaggio.*"

"That's sad."

"And funny."

"Which one are you?"

"Neither."

"Do you think our program will be sad and funny too?"

"I'm sure it will be."

"Bye-bye."

"Bye . . ."

GERALD LOCKLIN
FROZEN YOGURT

REVIEW

Discussion Questions:

1. By the end of "Frozen Yogurt," there is almost no description. The story is told as a stream of dialog. What is the effect of this technique and is it effective?
2. How does Jimmy Abbey feel about his wife? How does Jane feel about her husband?
3. Jimmy Abbey wants to watch the television show with Jane. Why doesn't he just ask her?

Essay Questions:

1. Both of the characters in "Frozen Yogurt" feel isolated not only from their spouses but from other people as well. What is the source of their isolation? Are they isolating themselves or are there other forces keeping them away from other people?
2. Jimmy Abbey in "Frozen Yogurt" views Jane as an object of desire, but he writes that he wouldn't have until just recently. How has Jimmy changed? To what degree is this change for the better?
3. The narrators of "Frozen Yogurt" and "Palimpsest" both contemplate their relationships with their significant others. Compare and contrast these relationships. Are they healthy? Do they seem to be happy?

Good Things Happen at Tina's Café

DANIEL A. OLIVAS

During waking hours, Félix José Costa would never allow himself to wonder how different life would be if he were just like everyone else. Average. Common. *Normal.* In that way, he was quite wise despite his relative youth. Even at twenty-six years of age, Félix knew that it was a fool's destiny to expend energy imagining something that could never be.

But in his dreams—oh, those dreams!—he was like everyone else. In his nocturnal visions, Félix would saunter into the Ronald Reagan State Building's entrance on Spring Street and wave to the security guard, a heavyset, middle-aged man who would smile for no one but Félix. *Good morning! How about those Lakers!* And then a manly fist bump, another wave, a jaunty nod from both men. He'd then stroll along to the elevators waving to friends and colleagues, right hand (and sometimes his left) happily and publicly displayed for all to see, another beautiful day in Los Angeles, this grand City of Angels, Lotusland, a magical metropolis where dreams come true.

Compare reality: five mornings a week, after enjoying a cup or two of coffee at a nearby café, Félix enters his building, faux leather briefcase slung over his right shoulder, both hands jammed into his pants pockets, a slight turn to the guard so that he can see Félix's California-issued, laminated identification card clipped to his jacket pocket, a silent dance without emotion, and then on toward the elevators, averting his eyes from passersby. He eventually gets to the eleventh floor, finds his barren cubicle, and begins his day as a legal secretary for three deputy attorneys general and one paralegal, employees in the Public Rights Division of the California Department of Justice.

Félix had learned the word for his "circumstance" when he was relatively young. His mother, Josefina, being quite educated and unafraid of reality, believed in truth regardless of where it might lead one, even her only child. A day after Félix's sixth birthday—after a short life filled with mockery and vicious jibes from neighborhood children and classmates—Josefina wrote the word on a piece of scrap paper and had Félix find it in the family's well-worn *American Heritage Dictionary*. Félix was very good with words and loved the musty smell of their dictionary. He flipped the pages until he came to the word his mother had written down: "pol-y-dac-tyl (pŏl'ē-dăk'təl) *adj.* Having more than the normal number of fingers or toes."

Félix rested his right hand on the page, palm on the cool, smooth paper, six fingers spread wide. There was *that* word: "normal." And he sighed. But Josefina swelled with pride because Félix pronounced it correctly. What a talented boy! What a handsome, promising, smart boy!

Félix's father, Reymundo, was not as educated as Josefina. No, he was a man of the old ways. His son was cursed. Period. And the only way to fight a curse was through magic. One week after Félix learned the word for his condition, and unbeknownst to his wife, Reymundo took his son to visit a childless widower cousin named Tony who lived south of Koreatown on Ardmore Avenue near 15th Street in a rambling, two-story, wood frame house built circa 1910 that was excessively large for Tony. But too many memories kept him in his home. Tony had what people called a sunny disposition, a man who never complained but spent his days appreciating the little things in life. He stayed put, thanked the heavens for his abode, for the many years he had spent with his late, lovely wife, Trini, and lived alone with his memories.

Nevertheless, Tony knew others suffered from loss, and he possessed a gift that could help them. Put simply, he could do wondrous things with mud and a few primordial incantations. For example, if your husband of fifty years finally succumbed to that undetected anomalous coronary artery, Tony could make a new spouse for you, complete with that little paunch and a more or less working male anatomy, out of the deep-brown mud from his backyard. Your beloved beagle got hit by a car? Presto-change-o! A new canine with the same sweet disposition and memories . . . expertly shaped by Tony's elegant, long fingers out of mud. And Tony offered his talents at a bargain, too! If you were hard up, he'd take payment in house cleaning, tree trimming, or home cooked pork tamales. People said that Tony was a saint. One would be hard to argue with such an assessment. But some asked Tony why he didn't make a muddy double of his late wife. Tony would only wave the question away, shake his head, and say: "Not possible." This response could have several meanings. Some thought that he would lose his gift if he selfishly used it for himself. Others believed that Tony idolized Trini so much that he didn't know if he could do her justice with simple mud. Regardless, Tony's friends, family, and neighbors appreciated what he did for them and that was that.

So, one bright Saturday morning, Reymundo told Josefina that he was going to take Félix to hike at Griffith Park knowing full well that his beautiful, brilliant wife did not like to perspire in public. She wished them well. Though the west San Fernando Valley had more than its share of trails that snaked up into the Santa Monica Mountains, Griffith Park sat at the eastern end of that same mountain range and boasted other attractions such as an observatory and planetarium not to mention the nearby zoo, the Autry National Center, and the Greek Theater. Reymundo and Félix kissed Josefina goodbye, hopped in their Honda Civic, and left Canoga Park for nature. But they took a detour to visit Tony who lived just a few miles from their final destination. Though Félix was puzzled when his father stayed on the 101 instead of switching over to the 134, he kept quiet and simply enjoyed the ride. When they exited at Normandie Avenue, Félix knew where his father was taking him. After a few minutes, they parked in front of Tony's house. Félix figured his father needed to chat with his cousin for a few moments just to see how he was getting along in that big, empty house.

But no. Félix's father clearly had other plans. Tony came out to greet them, hands and arms covered in dark mud. Despite his equally muddy Levi's and red T-shirt, Tony could not hide his innate elegance. He had a head full of white, curly hair, a countenance made up of sharp, regal features. Tony could have been an actor, everyone had said, but he loved his magic too much to think of such silliness.

"Vámonos," he said through a broad smile. "Follow me to the backyard. I don't want to hug you two since, as you can see, I am a muddy mess."

Tony's yard was immense, a double lot, with a massive, ancient avocado tree at its center. A grassy lawn covered most of the yard. Here and there were a few small lemon trees, a rose bush or two. Félix's eyes were drawn to Tony's shed at the far end of the yard just to the left of a thick cover of morning glory vines that twined in and out of the chain link fence that separated Tony's property from a well-maintained four plex apartment building. Hundreds of flowers had just opened fully to display trumpets of vibrant blues and purples, dappled with morning dew. To the right of the vines was a vast, wet pit of mud which was clearly the source of Tony's medium of choice.

Tony walked toward the shed as his guests followed. When they entered, Tony clicked on the overhead fluorescent lights and stopped. The loamy smell overtook Félix for a moment making him blink and then sneeze. He had never been invited into his cousin's workspace before.

"Come in," Tony said. He pointed to an ancient, blue velvet couch and nodded to Reymundo who obeyed the silent command to sit.

"Un momento . . . I have little more preparation to take care of," said Tony as he walked to his workbench where a wet pile of mud sat waiting. "Make yourself at home," and he turned to the mud, plunged his hands into it and started to hum a little, nondescript tune.

Félix stood still and scanned the sparsely furnished room. Other than the couch, a lone, metal folding chair stood in one corner. A muddy, white towel hung from a large nail in the wall behind the workbench. Above his father's head was a single wooden bookshelf attached precariously to the wall. Félix could make out a few of the titles. *Sculpture of Africa* by Eliot Elisofon. Paulo Freire's *Pedagogy of the Oppressed. Aztec Thought and Culture* by Miguel León-Portillo. He squinted a bit to discern what other books sat on the shelf but could only make out two that had the word "wrestling" in the titles. Félix's mother had always said that despite Tony's belief in magic, he was quite an intellectual who read two or three books a week on everything from art to philosophy to history. His reading material seemed to support this. Tony also seemed to enjoy the art of wrestling, and judging from the tight ropes of muscle that undulated in his shoulders and arms while he worked the mud, Tony very likely wrestled in his younger years. Félix had tried to watch a wrestling match during the last summer Olympics, but he found it boring and nothing like he thought wrestling should be like. It seemed to him that the two men almost never touched each other but looked more like two cats prancing on their hind legs. Yet the Cuban won the gold over the American. How? Why?

"Estoy listo," said Tony.

Félix jumped just a bit and turned to the workbench. Tony stood to the side of the mud which he had sculpted into the shape of a small sheet cake. Félix walked slowly toward Tony who offered a welcoming smile. Finally, the boy stood in front of the workbench and looked down where he saw what Tony had been doing: in the mud were two perfectly formed imprints of five-fingered hands. Félix's stomach leapt.

"No tengas miedo," whispered Tony. "It won't hurt. Just fit your hands into the mud, palms down."

"But . . ."

Tony understood: "Fit your two outside fingers into the pinkies . . . the mud will give just a bit because it's still wet."

Félix turned his head to his father who now sat at the edge of the couch, elbows resting on each knee, hands folded as if in prayer. He nodded to Félix.

The boy turned toward the workbench and slowly placed his hands into the mud. It felt cool, moist, almost comforting.

"¡Excelente!" exclaimed Tony as he scooped up fresh mud and covered Félix's hands. When Tony finished, he stepped back and admired his work. He then closed his eyes and mumbled something in a language Félix did not recognize.

"Now what?" asked Reymundo.

Tony's eyes popped open. "Now," he said as he reached for the towel, "you and I will go and have a beer in the house while the boy stands here for an hour."

"What?" said Félix unable to hide his alarm.

Tony smiled: "Do you think that great magic can happen in a minute?"

Of course, this made sense. Félix sighed, nodded, and closed his eyes.

"Good boy," said Tony. "Reymundo, I have some cold Buds in the fridge. Let's go."

Reymundo stood and walked to his son. He kissed Félix on the top of his head.

"It'll be over soon," he offered as Tony led him toward the door. "You are a brave young man."

Félix kept his eyes closed for the entire hour falling into what his mother called a self-induced trance, something the boy had mastered when he needed to escape this world. An hour later, the sound of Tony's cheerful voice brought him back to this world.

"Let's see those hands of yours."

Félix's father stood to the side. Tony opened a battered tool chest that sat on the workbench, reached in and pulled out a mud-stained wooden stick that resembled a large, broken spoon. With the sharp end, he slowly chiseled away the now-dried mud. Tony and his father affixed their eyes on the stick and followed it as Tony uncovered first the thumbs, moving outward toward the offending extra digits. When he finally finished, Félix lifted his hands and wiggled his fingers.

Six fingers on each hand. Félix sighed.

Tony turned to Reymundo. "Have you explored surgery?"

"The insurance won't cover the procedure, and it's so expensive."

Tony asked, "How could they not cover it?"

"Look," said Reymundo. "All of his fingers work perfectly. So, they consider it merely cosmetic surgery. Elective."

"Pendejos," muttered Tony.

———

Twenty years later, Tony was three years dead and his favorite cousin, Félix, now lived in his big house. And one Thursday morning, after catching the bus at Pico and Ardmore, Félix sat at Tina's Café enjoying a delicious cup of Yuban, reading the *Times*, a half hour before the workday began. His twelve fingers wrapped around the coffee mug. He felt so at home here. The other customers were not professionals but men and women who had little money and even less hope of improving their lives. Not one of them ever stared at his hands. All offered a smile and a nod, nothing more. But that was quite a gift as far as Félix was concerned.

He had discovered Tina's Café while trolling Yelp for places near his office. He was intrigued by its lone three-star review written by what appeared to be a homeless man named Barney:

Located at 357 ½ S Spring Street. Founded in 2008, Tina's Café has nurtured a loyal following with its dedication to traditional coffee brands such as Folgers and Yuban. Convenient location with some of the lowest coffee prices in town. Decor has a garage sale feel to it, and the lighting could be improved, but the seating is comfortable and encourages random conversations. Unfortunately, the service is poor: Owner is often distant and seems preoccupied with some other venture, but this might be an act. Also, customers must clean up after themselves or else the owner gets very cross and points a finger at the offending mess. Even so, a much better deal than the nearby Third Street Deli.

Félix tried to speak with Tina the first time he came in a year ago, but true to the Yelp review, she was not responsive. She was content to pour coffee and collect money, but not much else. Was she pretty? Maybe. Young? Not certain. Félix suspected that Tina was about five years older than he, but then again, she could be two or three years younger. Was she Mexican? Probably not. Maybe Filipino or Native American. She did not engage any customer in conversation. Tina was Tina, and that was that.

But on this Thursday morning after Tina poured Félix a second cup of coffee, she didn't turn to attend to other customers but, rather, stood before Félix and waited for something.

Félix looked up and tried to smile, but his face wouldn't comply. Tina's face remained passive as she stared into his eyes.

"Yes?" Félix finally said.

"You have six fingers on each hand, you know."

"Yes, I know."

"Good," said Tina before turning away. "Glad you know it."

The next morning, after Tina poured Félix's first cup of coffee, she said, "I have three breasts."

Félix almost fell out of his chair. Tina laughed.

"Not really," she said. "I just made that up."

Félix looked down at the tabletop, and put his hands onto his lap, out of sight.

"But," continued Tina now that the dam was broken, "I'm sure there are women out there, someplace, who do have three breasts, don't you think?"

Félix nodded.

Tina pulled up a chair, sat down with a little grunt, and put the coffee pot down on the table.

"Women just love those hands, don't they?"

Félix looked up at the clock on the wall, pulled out three dollars, dropped them on the table and stood.

"Going to be late for work," he said but didn't move.

"No you're not," said Tina. "You always leave here at 8:15. It's only 7:50. Sit. You have time. I won't bother you anymore."

As Félix took his seat again, Tina stood and walked to another customer. A minute later, she came back to his table.

"I'm sorry," she said. "I was being rude. I have no right to ask such questions, right?"

"Not a big deal," said Félix. For reasons he could not understand, he hoped she'd sit down again.

"Saturday morning," she began, "I think we should meet at the base of Angels Flight. Then we can figure out what to do for the day."

Before he could stop himself, Félix said, "I'd like that."

"Groovy," said Tina. She finally smiled. "Let's make it ten in the a.m., as my papa would say."

"Ten in the a.m.," he said. "It's a date."

"You bet it is," said Tina. "There's nothing else you can call it even if you tried."

Félix stood at the base of Angels Flight at Hill Street. He was seven minutes early so he walked back and forth and occasionally looked up at the two, orange and black funicular cars as they clacked up and down the parallel tracks. Félix looked at the time on his iPhone. Five more minutes. He then noticed a small plaque and took three steps, leaned close, and read it:

Built in 1901 by Colonel J. W. Eddy, lawyer, engineer and friend of President Abraham Lincoln, Angels Flight is said to be the world's shortest incorporated railway. The counterbalanced cars, controlled by cables, travel a 33 percent grade for 315 feet. It is estimated that Angels Flight has carried more passengers per mile than any other railway in the world, over a hundred million in its first fifty years. This incline railway is a public utility operating under a franchise granted by the City of Los Angeles.

"You know they have names."

Félix tried not to show surprise but he failed. He looked up into the morning sun and squinted into Tina's shadowed face.

"What?"

"Sinai and Olivet," said Tina. "That's their names."

"Who?"

"The cars, silly."

"Oh," said Félix. "Why?"

"Biblical, of course."

"Of course."

Tina held out her right hand, palm up. At first, Félix thought she wanted to hold his hand, but then noticed that she presented four, shiny quarters.

"Our funicular fair," said Tina. "We pay the kind gentleman at the top. Fifty cents per person each way."

"I know."

"Oh, you are a wise and experienced man."

Félix blushed and turned away.

"Let's go," she said. "Time is not on our side."

When they got to the top and paid their fair, Tina said: "Must. Drink. Coffee."

"There's a Starbucks right over there."

"Starbucks is evil," she said. "Starbucks was created to destroy small business people like me."

"Oh, sorry," said Félix. "Of course you believe that."

"Yes, you should be ashamed of yourself."

"I am."

"Good," said Tina as she started to walk toward the Starbucks. "Let's go to Starbucks."

Félix didn't move. "What?"

"Starbucks is evil, but I have a hankerin' for a Caffè Vanilla Frappuccino Blended Beverage."

Félix took a step and then another after Tina. "That sounds good."

"Yes, it's delicious," she said with a smack of her lips. "And then we'll sit and talk for a bit about very important things and go to MOCA which opens at 11:00 to look at an exhibit or two or three and then come back here and grab some Panda Express since I am already now craving orange chicken for lunch and we can talk about less important things and then we'll take Angels Flight back down and find a bar or two or three and have a microbrew or some fancy girl's drink and then find some other places to hang out because we are young and the day lies before us like a cornucopia filled with unforgettable and life changing experiences."

Félix smiled.

"It does appear that you like my plan," said Tina.

"I think I do."

Tina stopped walking to let Félix catch up to her. "I repeat: you are a wise and experienced man," she said when he finally stood by her side.

"I guess I am," he said. "I guess I am."

And they spent the day more or less as Tina had planned though it was Félix's idea to walk to Olvera Street to eat dinner at La Golondrina Mexican Café. They spoke of many things, whatever came into their heads, as the hours passed.

For example, at 10:31 a.m. over their blended Starbucks coffee drinks, Tina said: "You know, George Bernard Shaw wrote a scathing review of Brahms, called him a 'great baby' and that he was 'addicted to dressing himself up as Handel or Beethoven and making a prolonged and intolerable noise.' Can you imagine? Brahms? A 'great baby'? Craziness!"

And at 12:57 p.m. as they stood in line at Panda Express, Félix said: "Did you know that Panda Express Executive Chef Andy Kao is widely considered the creator of orange chicken? And they sold over sixty million pounds of it last year. Amazing."

And it was precisely 2:13 p.m. as they rode Sinai back down to Hill Street that Tina offered this: "Wilshire Boulevard was named after Henry Gaylord Wilshire who was from Cincinnati and was known as a bit of a flirt and a definite rabble-rouser. At least that's what I read in a book by this guy named Kevin Roderick."

Their day ended at 10:03 p.m. at the base of Angels Flight, just as it had started. They stood facing each other, swaying in the cool evening, bellies full.

"One kiss?" asked Félix.

"One kiss it is," said Tina.

And they kissed, bodies apart, faces turned in, lips tentative, a flicker of tongue. After a few moments, they pulled back in unison.

"I assume you will come by the very famous Tina's Café on Monday morning," said Tina.

"I'll be there," said Félix.

"I know you will," said Tina.

And they went their separate ways.

It was a foggy Monday morning as Félix stepped off the bus and walked toward Spring Street. He had had all of Sunday to think about his day with Tina. The chilled air allowed him to see his breath. Félix tried not to smile but he couldn't help himself. He would soon be in Tina's Café having a hot cup of Yuban poured by Tina herself.

Félix walked past a storefront with its name, *MIKE'S USED FURNITURE*, in old fashioned, golden script emblazoned across the plate glass. Below the name was: *Est'd 1962.* He stopped and walked back. He looked up at the address: 357

½ S Spring St. The lights were out, the store not yet open for business. Félix pulled his hands from his jacket pockets and cupped his eyes so that he could look into the store. He leaned forward and squinted. Instead of Tina's Café, he saw bureaus and chairs and tables and loveseats neatly arranged and ready for sale.

Félix pulled back, placed his palms onto the plate glass, unable to catch his breath. He closed his eyes and tried to conjure Tina's face in his mind's eye, but couldn't. His legs began to buckle and it took every bit of concentration to avoid falling down onto the cold sidewalk. After a full minute, Félix opened his eyes and focused on his splayed fingers. He blinked once and then again and then once more. Five. *Five!* Five fingers on each hand. He brought his hands away from the plate glass, turned toward the street, mouth open like an empty wallet. And at that moment, every memory of Tina slipped from his mind.

He closed his mouth into a tight smile. And with a little laugh, Félix José Costa raised his perfectly normal hands into the cool, Los Angeles morning.

REVIEW

Discussion Questions:

1. Why does Felix dream about being fist bumped?
2. What is Felix's problem, and why is it a problem for him?
3. Who is Tina, and why does she come into his life? Why does she disappear?

Essay Questions:

1. How does the problem that Felix faces and the solution to that problem reflect the desires and needs of humanity in general?
2. To what degree are Felix's problems real or merely a reflection of social pressures exerted from his family and society?

Torn and Frayed

ROBERT ROBERGE

I hoped the few Valium and Robaxin and the two Ambien I chewed that morning would do what little they could. Crap drugs—far more useful as medicinal side dishes and not main courses, but they were all I had left. Like any pills, they worked better on an empty stomach, so I didn't eat and tried to keep their lame buzz going.

From what Johnny Mo told me, I didn't want food in my system for the job, anyway. We'd clear three hundred each cleaning up this dead guy's apartment in Echo Park. With my half of the money, I'd be able to avoid being sick for a while, and maybe make some money at a poker game later that night.

Johnny Mo's buddy Mac, or Veggie Mac as he was known, hired us for the job. Veggie Mac was called that because he inherited a giant produce warehouse in Torrance. From what I heard he was loaded—had a place in some gated community by Griffith Park where Fatty Arbuckle and Rudolf Valentino used to live in the silent movie days. Los Angeles's first gated community. Johnny Mo told me Mac was the muscle of the produce business.

Mac had a brother who did the buying and selling of the produce. When whoever they sold it to didn't pony up the cash, or when someone screwed them by sending moldy avocados or whatever else could go wrong in the produce business, that's where Mac and his staggering collection of firearms and his unhinged temper came in. People paid up, did as they were told, from what I heard. Ducks got in a row. I's were dotted , and T's were crossed. The way Johnny Mo talked about Mac's violence reminded me of my father, and I was scared of the guy even before we met.

Mac had his fingers in a lot of pies, and one was the crime scene cleanup business that me and Johnny Mo were picking up a few bucks for that day. But Mac's Crime Scene Cleaners cleaned more than crime scenes. And lucky for me, this job wasn't a crime scene. There were protocols for such things, and me and Johnny Mo didn't really know what the fuck we were doing, so there was no way Mac could let us work if there'd been a murder or something at the house. With police involved, Johnny Mo told me, Mac couldn't hire fuckups like us.

This job was just a dead guy with no family. And people with no families, they had possessions that had to be thrown away or boxed and sent to Mac's Public Storage buildings for estate auctions. The guy whose apartment we were cleaning was dead for a while before the neighbors got clued in, so the place was pretty filthy, and the smell was astounding, from what Mac told Johnny Mo.

Two hundred of my cut would buy a generous hundred Percocets from some Russian criminal named Sergei in Long Beach who'd tried to pay me with a nine millimeter the last time I sold him meth. Every time I'd ever tried to sell any opiates, I'd do them all before I could make a dime, so I tried dealing shit I didn't like. The last time I sold him meth, Sergei was cash poor and weapon rich, and offered me the handgun. I told him to keep his fucking gun and that I wanted nothing to do with guns again as long as I lived.

I'd owned a gun during my last six months in The Popular Mechanics but I had no memory of carrying it. People told me I had, though, and I winced at their stories. I read in music magazines and websites about stupid shit I'd done—shit that fans seemed to think was crazy and hilarious and only made my life seem worse for having the poor judgment to have my idiocy played out in public.

I remembered counting the bullets after coming out of every blackout, terrified of what I might have done. I'd become a man I feared, but I had enough miraculous luck to escape without any un-remediable actions.

When Sergei offered the gun, I told him to forget it—take his meth and go.

He said, "You must have gun."

"I don't like guns."

He said, "Guns just like people, except guns have no legs."

I wondered what that could mean and said, "That's cool. I'm not a gun guy, okay?"

He'd said, "Then, with interested, I get you back next time, Bud Barrett, rock star, yes?"

The sharp-dressed black guy next to him said, "With interest, motherfucker."

Sergei said, "What?"

"With interest," the other guy said.

"People know what Sergei says," he said. "Fuck you, piece of shit thesaurus in nice suit, you."

I never thought I'd hear from the Russian again, but since he looked like a mountain of 'roid muscle and scar tissue and tried to pay for drugs with guns, I figured it was stupid to press the issue. I said, "Sure." We shook hands. "Get me back when you can."

And he said again that he'd get me back "with interested next time." Then, he'd called me the night before the job with Johnny Mo and we'd set up a buy for after Mac paid me for this apartment job. Sergei'd get me some great deal, he promised, on Percocets.

The last hundred bucks I'd use for the low limit fifty dollar buy-in for me and my fuck-buddy Jessica at this illegal limit poker game in San Pedro. About a hundred people played the game. If I could make the final table of nine, I'd be in the money and could get more Percs and maybe parlay the winnings into something at a bigger game. Jess had a better chance, luck being equal, at a low buy-in game with a limit, since she played smarter and more conservatively. I hated limit, but you had to play what was there, and I didn't have a bankroll for a no-limit game even if I could have found one.

My style was aggressive. Better suited to no-limit. Some stooge sitting across from you at a table might feel pretty good with middle pair if the most you could bet into him was, say, fifty bucks. It takes no guts to risk losing fifty bucks. That middle pair would start to look a lot shakier—and so would the person holding them—if you pushed their last thousand dollars in the world onto the table. Read the guy who can't afford to lose, focus on him, and he can't beat you unless the cards drop from heaven in his lap. And you had to know he could get those cards, dumb as he might play the game, and that you have to always be ready to lose everything you have. Or else you're him. That stiff who's afraid to lose, who you're looking for at every table.

But the game in Pedro was a limit game, and I'd have to adjust and play tighter, or I could be gone in a hurry. If Jess or I could make the final nine, it was good news.

For the moment, though, I needed the three hundred dollars from Mac's job.

Johnny Mo and I drove over to Mac's to pick up a company van with its cleaning materials and work suits, and then we'd head over to the dead guy's place to clean up.

I thought about this dead guy. "No family?" I said to Johnny Mo.

"Apparently none that want to clean up after the bastard, at least."

"Sad," I said.

Johnny Mo nodded.

"Think about that shit. Living a whole life. All the people you come into contact with. Gotta be a million people you cross."

"You're not friends with them all."

"I'm just doing the numbers," I said. "Years piling up, people in and out of your life. And no one giving enough of a shit to take care of your business at the end."

Johnny Mo said, "I don't want to think about that."

A life filled with people, with the comings and goings of lovers, of friends, of co-workers, of family and no one at the end of that line? If I had died that day, I was pretty sure Jess and my friends would do something about it. Tony and the band might even show they still gave a shit. Hell, they'd tried to put me in rehab, they'd probably care if I died, even if I wondered sometimes if they wanted me in rehab because it cost the band gigs and cost all of them money when I fucked up. None of them had tried to get me into rehab, after all, since they'd fired me.

But friends would care when I died. And, whether these things mattered or not, I'd get some minor notice in the press. I'd probably rank an obit in *SPIN*. For sure, I'd get one in *Pitchfork*. Maybe, but probably not, in *Rolling Stone*. They'd get quotes from ex-band mates. Roll out the same stories for one last go-around, the only difference being this time all the quotes would end with what a shame it was and everyone had seen it coming, but there was nothing anybody could have done. It'd be a clichéd rock and roll obit, for sure. But, then, I'd had a pretty clichéd rock and roll life, in a lot of ways. I was under a decade from being on a major label, but I felt closer to death than to where I'd been.

I knew, though, that I had friends left who'd look after me.

The amount of people who must have been dying alone, living alone, while the wind hit my face and I smoked a cigarette on a beautiful sunny California morning—I stiff-armed it out of my mind.

After a few minutes, I was mildly floating on the Valium, the muscle relaxants, and the sleeping pills. They'd kicked in as much as those crummy pills could, which was always beautiful and mildly depressing, because after the peak of feeling good, even a minor good feeling like this one was the slow glide into feeling bad. Valium didn't really have a peak—I was only on it to slow the sickness of not having any painkillers. But I'd had enough of them to feel decent.

Drug peaks were like a chemical end of summer in your body. Beautiful and sad all at once. For the moment, though, I looked at the other people in their cars in the 405 morning traffic. I didn't like being up early, but the drugs had me in a cushion of peace, and everything seemed to be coming at me slowly enough to deal with it without stress. We had Steve Wynn & the Miracle Three's "Bruises" playing, and I was struck by the beauty of music and how I'd hate to be deaf and not be able to experience it, and I wondered if the deaf know what they're missing or if thinking about it would just drive them insane with despair. I wished I'd been on some pain pills or some heroin. Nothing made music sound better. But I closed my eyes and put my head back and enjoyed it as much as I could.

I said, "Did you ever really think about music?"

Johnny Mo looked over at me. "Are you fucked up?"

"I wish," I said. "Thinking about music. Thinking about how miserable life would be without it."

"Life's plenty miserable with it."

"That's what I'm saying," I said.

"What are you on?"

"Just some fucking Robaxin." There was no way I was going to split my Valium and I was out of the Ambien. The Ambien made days tolerable, though they fucked with your short-term memory. Which was fine, because most of my days weren't worth remembering anymore. Except a shoddy short-term memory fucked with my card game.

I only had five Valium on me, and that was enough, if I stretched them, to keep me from getting too sick for the day.

Johnny Mo said, "Can I have two?"

"You can have one."

Johnny Mo winced. "One does nothing. Shit, *ten* does nothing. Plus, man. I got you this job."

Fair enough. I handed over two Robaxin and he swallowed them down with some Carl's Jr. coffee we'd picked up earlier. "Thanks, dude."

I nodded, feeling bad that I didn't offer him a Valium, but not bad enough to actually offer him one. He was probably the best friend I had left, and I felt sick inside that I would willingly screw him. Then I felt even worse because I knew I'd crossed every line I'd ever drawn and only gotten worse. And I'd keep crossing every new line I'd draw and, no matter how much I hated myself for doing it, I'd keep screwing him and anyone else for more drugs.

At Mac's gated community, we got buzzed through security, and Johnny Mo said to me, "Did I tell you? Don't eat anything out of this bastard's shelves. Out of his pantries."

"What?"

"Dude, he puts acid in his food, in case people try to steal from him."

"Who steals food?"

"No one, if they know what's good for them. That's what I'm telling you."

I said, "Isn't this buddy of yours a millionaire?"

"I wouldn't say we were buddies," Johnny Mo said.

"But he's a millionaire?"

"Pretty much, yeah," Johnny Mo said, thinking for a moment. "At least."

"Who's he inviting over that steals food out of his pantry is what I'm saying."

Johnny Mo lifted his shoulders, took his hands off the wheel, palms up. "I'm just telling you, the man puts LSD in his food."

"What if he wants the food?"

"Then he takes the acid. Mac's always fucked up on something. He doesn't give a fuck."

We rolled down a quiet street, lined with nice new cars and Mac's Crime Scene Cleaner's van we'd be taking for the job and his chopped 1951 Ford in flat black and a front window so narrow it looked like the peep door on a speakeasy. The car looked like it was squinting. Like if Clint Eastwood were a hot rod. Like it was looking to kick some other car's ass. Johnny Mo stopped behind the Ford.

"What about the fridge?" I said. "Is the shit in his fridge spiked, too?"

"Just don't take the man's food."

"I'm not taking his food," I said. "I'm just curious if he does it to shit in the fridge, too."

Johnny Mo looked at me and shook his head. We walked up, me behind him, and he knocked on the door.

"I don't take people's food," I said.

"I never said you did."

"Then why bring it up?"

"As a warning, motherfucker."

This kid, maybe sixteen years old, opened the door. He wore jeans and no shirt. Full sleeve tats—a lot of flames and skulls. No tats on his torso, so he looked like he had someone else's arms sewn on to him, all Frankenstein's Monster. Unfocused eyes, jittery as lamp moths.

"Yeah?" he said.

I let Johnny Mo handle it. Mac was his friend, his acquaintance. I was just along for the money.

"Here to see Mac," Johnny Mo said.

The kid stood at the door. Leaned a little left. A dope head Tower of Pisa. Didn't say anything.

"Here to see Mac," Johnny Mo said and waved a hand in front of the kid's face. "He's expecting us."

The kid focused on Johnny Mo, groggy, like he'd just woken up. "Mac?"

"He owns this place."

The kid said, "Old dude?"

"Is he here?" Johnny Mo said, talking slow and loud like people do to foreigners.

The kid rubbed his nose viciously, like he was on some opiates with histamines. He probably wasn't on dope, the veins popped visibly through the tats, but maybe there were some painkillers around there I could steal. The kid finished rubbing his nose and looked at Johnny Mo. He reached out and gently touched Johnny Mo on the chest, like he was making sure Johnny Mo was really there.

Johnny Mo slapped the hand. The kid didn't pull his hand back, just left it dangling. Whatever he was on had seriously fucked whatever fight or flight response the kid should have had. He looked at his hand like he'd never seen it before.

Johnny Mo said, "Since you're not exactly doing much of a job as a greeter or security, why don't you step the fuck out of our way?"

Johnny Mo walked by the kid and I followed. I look back and the kid was looking out the door as if we were still there, rubbing his hand where Johnny Mo slapped it.

"Maybe he ate something out of the pantry," I said.

"Could be," he said. "Or maybe he's just as stupid as a neck tattoo."

"This friend of yours have pain meds anywhere?" I said.

"Steal from Mac and you could die," Johnny Mo said.

I nodded, but I also needed some pain meds. Risk/reward scenarios argued in my head as we walked inside.

We came to an enormous living room. A living room you could play football in. Fourteen foot ceiling. Three TVs, all on to different channels, lined the far wall, maybe thirty feet away from us, and the room reminded me of Graceland in its tacky splendor. A fire engine red and chrome 1950s Indian motorcycle stood next to a white leather couch that could sit fifteen people.

Mac was in his fifties, gray beard, horseshoe bald, dressed in blue jeans and a Hawaiian shirt. The shirt was really baggy, and I guessed he had a gun under it from the stories I'd heard.

Mac had some remote control thing in his hand, like a Game Boy or something. He abused a joystick, repeatedly. He shouted, "Fuck, fuck, stupid fucking thing! Fuck it to fucking hell!"

Johnny Mo shook his head, leaned close to me and whispered, "That's Mac."

On one of the TVs was a group of Japanese people running across rolling logs and falling into a pond when a giant punching bag pendulumed them into the water. Another TV was on CNN, with some woman polished as wax fruit cheerfully bringing that day's dreadful news to the world. The other had some black and white movie. All the volumes blared. Mac shouted above them all.

"Fuck! Piece of fucking junk!"

Johnny Mo yelled, "Mac!"

Mac looked up. He came up to us and handed Johnny Mo the remote control.

"This thing doesn't work for shit," he said. "I just dropped six hundred fucking dollars on it."

Johnny Mo looked at the box. "What is it?"

"It's a fucking boat," Mac said. He looked at me and turned to Johnny Mo. "Who the fuck are you bringing in my house?"

Whatever sliver of calm I had from my pills took a serious hit.

Johnny Mo said, "Calm down, Mac. This is Bud. The guy doing the cleanup job with me."

Mac stared with primal, unblinking rage at me. I didn't want to look back for long, but his pupils actually seemed to be fluctuating at their rims. I had my answer as to whether Mac took acid.

Johnny Mo said, "We talked about this, dude. I needed a second guy for the apartment cleanup in Echo Park." He paused. "I *told* you about this. It's cool. Everything's *very* cool."

Mac said, "Are you sure you told me about this?" He still stared at me, but at least he'd blinked a couple times. "I do not remember you telling me about this, and my mind is a fucking trap. I remember fucking everything. I can quote the whole motherfucking Bible and I don't even believe one word of that gibberish!"

Johnny Mo said, "Bud is okay."

"I could quote you the cocksucking Warren Report word for fucking word!" Mac closed his eyes and took three deep breaths, but they didn't seem to calm him. He yelled, "I know where every fucking comma goes in every book in this fucking house, do you understand?"

Johnny Mo sighed. "Mac. Bud is cool. He's doing this job with us, okay?"

"A fucking trap!" he said, staring in my eyes. "I forget nothing."

Johnny Mo said, "You were probably really busy." He talked in the tone of a hostage negotiator. "But Bud's cool. This deal's cool. But we need to get to the job so you can get your money, Mac."

The mention of money snapped him to like a cracked amyl nitrate capsule. He nodded, looked away from me, and started doing jumping jacks. "Echo Park. That place is a fucking mess, you'll need respirators." He stopped with the jumping jacks. "But I need your help with this fucking broken boat first." Mac gestured to the remote control.

Respirators?

Johnny Mo looked at the black plastic joystick. "I don't understand how this is a boat."

Mac gestured down to the carpet. On the floor, amidst the mess of fast food bags and beer cans and ashes and cigarette butts from overturned ashtrays was a three-foot version of the Queen Mary. It foundered in a deep shag carpet that reminded me of Elvis's Jungle Room, and it whirled, with the three-inch shag carpet clearly wrapped around and strangling its little propellers. Smoke blossomed out of its rear section. The smell of burning motors. Of something straining to the point of giving up.

"It doesn't work worth a shit," Mac said.

Johnny Mo turned off the remote control and put it on a table. He said, slowly, "Mac. It needs water."

"It's not some fucking flower!"

"Mac," Johnny Mo said with a calm that amazed me. "It's a boat. A *model* boat. It needs water."

"You're not listening! I paid for this. For this fucking, fuck shit. It's not working, the piece of shitbasket shit!"

Johnny Mo said, "You need to put it in the pool. It won't work on the carpet. It's a boat. It needs water to work."

Mac nodded. Like the thought of putting the boat in water was one that wouldn't have occurred to him in a thousand years. He looked down at the boat strangled in the carpet.

Johnny Mo said, "Now, Mac. We need the keys to the truck if you want us to do this job."

"Terry has the keys."

Johnny Mo took a deep breath and let it out. "Who is Terry?"

"He's this kid I hired to take care of shit. He should have been helping me with this broken piece of shit boat." Mac turned an angry three-sixty. "Where the fuck is that fucking kid?"

I looked at my watch. Already near 10 a.m. I needed to get this job done, get some pain pills from my friend Larry and still get to a card table by 9 p.m. I was dizzy from hunger. I said, "Where's the bathroom?"

Mac looked at me. He turned to Johnny Mo. "Who the fuck is this? Who the fuck are you bringing into my house?"

Johnny Mo shook his head and pointed me toward a long hallway. As I walked away, I heard him ask Mac where he could find Terry and the keys to the van and Mac ask Johnny Mo again who the fuck I was and why the fuck was I in his house.

———————————————

The bathroom was almost as big as my whole apartment in Long Beach. I sat on the toilet and read some magazine called *Urban Survivalist* that seemed to be all about security systems and guns and panic rooms. I heard a whirling noise and looked up. At one corner of the room up by the ceiling was a square hole cut out for a model train that came into the bathroom. It chugged on a track above my head and exited out a hole on the other side of the room. I reached the sink and took one Valium and another Robaxin and wiped my face down with cold water and hoped that Johnny Mo had the keys and we could get on with this. I thought about checking Mac's medicine cabinet, but I figured a guy like this had security camera, even in the bathrooms. Plus, the odds that he'd have meds in the downstairs bathroom weren't worth the trouble. People kept their meds in the bathroom closest to their bedrooms—never downstairs or in guest bathrooms. I took deep breaths while the train entered and left three more times before I got up and headed to the living room.

We were in the cleaning van, which was unmarked, and because I didn't have enough drugs in my system, I thought about this guy dying alone and me and Jess and how she wanted to move to Florida to be close to her dying mother. I didn't want to move to Florida, but it seemed important to Jess. She and her mother talked every day on the phone, which always made me think of my mother and how I wished I could talk to her.

The gloom settled, and I wondered whether or not my life was worth two shits and how much I hated, absolutely hated myself sometimes and whether or not that was normal. Did everyone cringe at night, thinking about shit they said or did ten years before? Or was I just wired wrong? My brain a series of rusted and arced connections, firing where it shouldn't, frozen where it should hinge? Junkyards of regret clogged me up. I was sick, diseased. Sometimes I thought this ugliness was just mine. Sometimes I thought it was all of us.

"This could get pretty nasty," Johnny Mo said. "In this apartment."

"I kinda figured as much," I said, though I didn't really know exactly what nasty meant in that context. But, clearly, it wasn't a good job.

"I'm talking shit you don't expect. Like, this guy dies alone, sure there might be plenty of his crap you have to clean up. Transients, though, they come in and they squat and they shit on the walls."

"Isn't there a toilet?"

"What?"

I said, "They aren't squatting in an abandoned building. There's still plumbing."

"How many dead people pay their water bill?"

"You'd have to be dead for a while before they shut your water off," I said, thinking about all the bills I could barely keep track of and how everything was always on the verge of being cut off. "Wouldn't you?"

"This guy *was* dead for a while."

"What the fuck is up with the neighbors?"

"A lot of people don't know their neighbors," Johnny Mo said.

"I mean the smell. You know. The stink of a dead person. Who could live next to that for weeks?"

"I worked with a guy who had no sense of smell," Johnny Mo said.

"So?"

"I'm just saying," he said.

"You didn't work with a whole building of people with no sense of smell," I said.

"What's your point?"

"My point is the odds of no one in that building smelling this dead fucker are not good."

Johnny Mo paused. "Well, you got me there."

When we got there, I saw why, maybe, the neighbors didn't smell anything. It was one of those little bungalow row apartments they built in LA after World War II, and only one unit shared a wall with the dead guy's place. On the door, there was a City of Los Angeles Notice of Non-Inhabitance. It had a couple signatures and an inspection date, two weeks away.

At the van, we put on light blue baggy jumpsuits and booties and gloves. Johnny Mo handed me a respirator.

"Just put it around your neck for now. We may need them, we may not."

I nodded. The sun started to abuse the day, and I was hot already in the suit.

We brought a bunch of five-gallon buckets, some empty, some with a variety of cleaners, over to the door. Johnny Mo had what looked like a pesticide tank.

"What's that one?" I said.

"Enzymes. They get rid of stinks."

I nodded and put on my respirator.

"You might not need that," Johnny Mo said.

"I might," I said, my voice muffled underneath the rubber and filters.

Johnny Mo had the key from Mac and we went in. I don't know what exactly I expected, but the place looked pretty normal. Maybe a little messy, but pretty much like your standard bachelor apartment.

Johnny Mo winced quickly and put his respirator on. "You made the right call."

I wondered how bad it was, because, even through the facemask, it was among the worst things I'd ever smelled. The air was so foul it had a taste like a bad pistachio.

"Let's get an idea of what we have to do," Johnny Mo said.

We walked through the kitchen. There were still magnets on the fridge. A bottle opener with a magnet on its back. A calendar, turned to the month before with black and white pictures of hula girls from the 40s or 50s next to the skinny bachelor stove. It was like someone still lived there.

The living room didn't look bad. Throwing out books and CDs and shit. Johnny Mo took a Marvin Gaye CD for himself, and I took all the guy's blues, including a Lightning Hopkins I only had on vinyl. He had a copy of *Sticky Fingers*, so I got the portable CD player from the truck and put that in, reminding myself to take the Stones CD when we left.

We did the kitchen. Emptied drawers of silverware into contractor bags. Everything was pretty simple until we got to the bedroom.

Me and Johnny Mo walked in, and, at first, I thought the bed was black, or the dead guy had black sheets, but then the fucking room came alive in a swarm of flies. They looked like angry smoke. Puke bolted up from my stomach, and, not wanting to take off the respirator, I swallowed it down and got wobbly in my knees. Sweat pooled at my collarbone and ran all over me and stung my eyes. My throat burned. There was puke in my nostrils.

"Jesus," Johnny Mo said.

Now that the flies were off the bed and landing and taking off and landing again, I got a glimpse of this indentation in the bed, and I saw where the smell was coming from. There was a puss-yellow thick liquid, all banana pudding-pooled up in the rough indentation of a person. The flies swarmed all over it as Johnny Mo got my attention and pointed to the way we'd come in. I followed him out.

In the parking lot, I took my respirator off. The smell didn't go away. I looked to see if Johnny Mo'd left the door open, but he hadn't. It was in my system somehow, and I walked behind the van over by a chain link fence with a purple bougainvillea snaking through it, and I threw up, mostly water and a medicinal acid for about thirty seconds.

I shook my head, knowing I just lost the last few pills I'd taken at Mac's place. The thought of facing the day sober sloshed me with dread.

I turned to Johnny Mo. "How the fuck do we clean that bed?"

"We don't clean it," Johnny Mo said. "Mac has some Mexican dude with a truck on his payroll. Saves the dumpster fees. We just load it in the truck."

"Where does the guy with the truck take it?"

Johnny Mo shrugged. "Hopefully nowhere near my house." He paused. "Hopefully nowhere near kids."

I looked back to the door. "We tip that bed on its side, we're going to spill that goo all over the place."

Johnny Mo said, "Can't do that. Plus, the big shit's gotta leave last, when the truck comes by. We can't have that bed out here stinking like that."

"So we have to work with that in there?" I said.

"Unless you got a better idea."

I looked inside the van. Among the many cleaning solvents were several gallons of bleach on the bottom shelf. I took a five-gallon bucket and dumped two gallons of bleach into it, along with one quart of the enzymes that are supposed to kill odors, along with some Matacide that kills everything except one of the strains of Hep C. I added bacterial soap.

"Look at you, mad fucking scientist," Johnny Mo said.

"If we have to work inside with that bed," I said, "it can't be like it is."

I swirled a gloved hand into the bucket. It soaped up and gave off some fumes that made my eyes tear. I looked away, put the respirator on and carried the splashing bucket into the apartment.

When I got close to the bed again, the room became a swirl of black animation. Flies were on everything and thick in the air.

I poured about half of my bucket into the center of the indentation on the bed. The rest, I swung back and forth over the rest of the mattress and sheets. I made another trip to the van for contractor bags that felt thick as a wetsuit. I dumped all of the bedding I could stand to touch, even through rubber gloves, into the bags. Pillows, a blanket, one very weighed down and soggy sheet. I started to put the pants by the side of the bed into a bag, but I felt something that could've been money in one of the pockets, so I tossed the pants into the hallway.

I carried two contactor bags, knotted at the top, out to the parking lot. The one with the sheets was thrown in with a shitload of flies on the bedding, so the bag faintly buzzed from the inside.

Johnny Mo'd been out in the lot, having a Coke, watching me come in and out for a few minutes.

He said, "You are a fucking cleaning terror, my friend."

I took off the mask, dripping sweat. The back of my throat tasted like bleach, along with the acidy puke. "I couldn't work in there the way it was."

"Well you sure tore that Band-Aid," he said.

I nodded.

"Dove right in the deep end, is what I'm saying."

"I understand," I said. "You going to help me with the rest?"

"Let's do it."

Inside, I took off my respirator, and so did Johnny Mo. It still smelled awful, but it smelled that way anyway, and the masks were making the ninety-five degree day feel worse than I could have imagined. My clothes were soaked under the cleanup suit. "Dead Flowers" started on the CD player, and I turned it up.

I went to the pants I'd tossed into the hallway. I found six dollars in one pocket. In the other one I found an empty pill bottle. Alprazolan, generic Xanax that comes in these little 3 millimeter brick pills that are easy to break and section. It had a refill. I put it and the six bucks in my pocket. If I could find anything with this guy's name and birth date on it in the place, I could call in the refill. Say I was his roommate or something. Most CVS pharmacies, most Sav-Ons, they gave you the script with another person's date of birth.

I was about to check for other scripts in drawers when I heard Johnny Mo scream, "Holy Fucking Shit, you have to see this motherfucker's bathroom!"

I followed Johnny Mo's voice and saw right away there was a ton of porn sort of decoupaged on the walls. On the ceilings and even on the floor. Naked women, very seventies Penthouse beaver shots, legs open, pulled and coaxed vaginal lips swollen and flaring for the camera. All of them under the shiny gloss of some lacquer. And every single one of the naked women had the exact same black-and-white picture of Jackie Kennedy's head on it. No matter what position the body was in. No matter whether the picture was black and white or in color. No matter whether the naked body was Asian, Black, or White—every single one of them had a smiling, blown-up and pixilated head of Jackie Kennedy on them.

"This is fucked up," Johnny Mo said.

I looked at the walls. "Who was this guy?"

"Check this out," Johnny Mo said. He held up a bottle and shook it. "Ambien, baby. You want some?"

I felt bad I'd held out on him earlier with my Valium. "Yeah," I say. "But for later."

"Of course for later. The dude had almost sixty left. You can have half."

Then I felt really awful. "What else is in the cabinet?"

"No idea. I found these in the living room before I saw this." He gestured around to all of the naked women with the Jackie Kennedy heads.

I opened the medicine cabinet. Mostly crap. Nasal allergy shit. Some fluid to drink for a dietary cleanse. Several half-squeezed tubes of various muscle creams and antibiotic ointments and the like. Two prescription allergy inhalers.

I held them up to Johnny Mo, who was still looking around. "You want one of these?"

"How long do you think it took this nut job to do this?"

"There's two of these," I said, still holding up the inhalers. "You want one?"

"And he must have never had any guests, right?"

"I'm taking them both," I said.

Johnny Mo looked at the inhalers. "All yours." He looked back up at the walls and ceiling. "I mean, you couldn't let your best friend see this shit."

"He didn't have a best friend," I said.

"Well, it's a good thing," Johnny Mo said. "Cause this motherfucker would have had some explaining to do."

We let the bleach and cleaning stuff work on the bed as we bagged clothing and dishes, and silverware and posters (Talking Heads, "Stop Making Sense," The Who's "Maximum R&B"). A life ending up in contractor bags. The guy had very little worth taking—though I got an African hand drum that looked cool, and Johnny Mo took this mini-Zen garden from the table in the living room.

The final drug tally was sixty Ambien, which we split. A small orange-brown vial of what smelled like hash oil. We bought a pack of cigarettes at the corner store and each soaked one cigarette in the vial of hash oil and left them on the sun-soaked dash to dry out for a while. I lied down and told Johnny Mo I found a few Valium, and gave him two of my remaining four pills.

We found what looked like eight hits of ecstasy, and a few prozac, which helped with the comedown of E. We split them evenly. Ecstasy was usually cut with speed, so I held onto them for the poker game, where I might need a bump of adrenalin, though I'd have to take a small amount if I wanted to play well.

Johnny Mo wanted nothing to do with the prescription refills I found for the Xanax and some Adderall, which I wanted to fill right away, as it would help keep me sharp at the tables. But I couldn't find the guy's ID, and without his birthday I had no chance of getting the scripts filled. I looked through the apartment for something with his birthday on it.

"Let it go, dude," Johnny Mo said. "You'd get caught."

I nodded. "But if I had his date of birth, I could get them."

Johnny Mo said, "The guy's dead. If they know that, knew him, at the pharmacy, they'd call the cops on you."

"How would they know that the guy's dead?"

"It would be a risk," he said.

"A calculated risk," I said.

"You could still get caught."

I said, "That's the *risk* part of calculated risk." I'd never been caught for prescription fraud at that point, so I didn't really know what to look for from the pharmacy.

I was not tough. I knew my limits, and jail would crush me. The people I'd known before and after jail—it was like someone you knew went in and, with very rare exceptions, a beast came out the other end.

The bags of Richard Bronson's (we'd gotten his name off the pill bottles) belongings sat piled up by the van. Johnny Mo called the Mexican guy with the truck, so I guessed we were close to finished.

Our cigarettes had soaked up the hash oil and dried, and the white paper was the yellow-brown parchment color of old newspapers left in the sun. We each took a hit of our cigarettes, held the smoke, and I felt the immediate swirl in my head. It was the best I'd felt since I'd run out of pain pills a few days earlier. Little light bulbs flickered in front of my eyes, the way they do when you get hit hard and you're about to drop and collapse. My tension drained like someone had pulled a drain plug. My brain exhaled, my body unclenched until my bones were light and my head felt like a hot air balloon.

"Well," Johnny Mo said. "Get that bed?"

We put out our cigarettes to save the rest for when we were done. "Let's do it."

The guy pulled up with the truck just as we were getting the rancid bed out of the apartment. We had to tip it sideways through the doors and it dripped foul liquid onto the floor by the bedroom and the entrance door. We took it across the parking pot and hoisted it into the truck. The guy never said anything to us. He smoked cigarettes while we got the rest of the big furniture. When we were done, Johnny Mo hit the back of the truck twice and the guy drove away.

I took a last look around Richard Bronson's apartment. It was empty and once we cleaned up the mess on the floor, it had that bright promise that an empty apartment has when you're looking for a new place—thinking already of where you'll put your things. I thought about moving to Florida with Jess. I hadn't been back to Florida since the late 80s when the band was based there. I wondered if any of the people I knew in Sarasota were still around. I'd miss LA a lot if I left. But Jess had said that we'd only be going back so she could take care of her mother, who had probably under a year left. Maybe only a couple months. So, I could come back to LA. This left me a little less depressed at the thought of leaving.

Johnny Mo smoked out by the van. He yelled that it was time to get moving. I found a five dollar chip from Caesar's on the mantle and I put in my pocket and closed the door.

I sat at the final table. The guy running the game announced that the final table was no limit, so I could play as aggressively as I liked. I was tired from having played five hours of cards on top of a long day of disgusting work. I took a break and smoked some more of the hash oil. Then, to counteract the down from the hash, I snorted just shy of half of one of the blue ecstasys. Jess got knocked out early and she took the car and went drinking with Johnny Mo. I was supposed to call her when the game ended.

The final table dwindled from nine and eight. It stayed at eight players for a while and then four were gone in a matter of four hands.

At 3:00 a.m., it was down to me and this guy named Rick who wore a cowboy hat low over his forehead and sunglasses and acted like he was one of those idiots on ESPN. I wanted to win the money, but, even more, I didn't want to lose to this guy who'd annoyed me all night. He talked too much. Asked what you were holding and bragged whenever he won a hand. I figured it was all to rattle me, throw me off my game and I suppose it worked, since I'd made it personal, which is always a bad idea.

I got dealt pocket tens. My stack was a little bigger than Rick's, and my hand might have been good enough. I bet a little heavy before the flop, but not too much, as I wanted him staying in the hand, figuring he would because you play hands when you're straight-up you'd never play at a full table. Rick quickly went all-in and stared at me, or at least it seemed he was staring at me behind his wrap-around sunglasses. A stare is usually a sign of a guy with a weak hand trying to bully you out of a hand.

If I called him and won, the pot was mine, and I'd walk with a thousand dollars. Rick had been mostly conservative all night. He'd gone all-in only once at the final table, that time with a king-queen. Earlier in the night, he went all-in on the same hand. He could have had a higher pair than my tens, but I doubted it. Every time he'd held a high pair, he'd limped in and tried to bait the other player.

I called. We turned our cards and, sure enough, he was holding the same hand he'd gone all-in with twice before—king-queen, off-suit. My pair was the better hand, but not by much.

The dealer flopped ten, king, king. I had the full house and he was looking for another king or queen, which would give him a better full house or four kings. The turn was a meaningless three.

Rick stood, which was pretty common for guys who are all-in, after poker got big on TV. Most people didn't used to do it, but after ESPN, all the kids bounced out of their chair at every call, it seemed. I sat, felt under my fingertips, feeling electric and full of the excitement from the game, even if the hash had me a little fuzzy and lightheaded. The ecstasy had kicked in, fighting the hash for keeping me sharp and adding a slight euphoria to my head. The speed it was cut with had me chewing my cheeks, and I tasted a small amount of metallic blood. I was glad it was the final hand—I didn't have a lot of intense focus left in me, but for that moment, I was still sharp.

Rick had four outs—only four cards in the forty or so left, after the ones showing and the ones the dealer burned, that could beat me. He had around a one in eleven chance and he stood there with his sunglasses off and his eyes closed and said please, please, *please* as the dealer started to pull the river card off the deck.

The odds were strong in my favor. Either way, I'd walk out of there with a lot more money than I'd come with. I waited for the final card to fall. I watched Rick begging whatever gods he believed in for his one in eleven miracle and I felt calm—felt the rhythm of my breath and the tingle of anticipation that came with moments where, no matter the odds, no one in the world knew what was going to happen next.

ROBERT ROBERGE
TORN AND FRAYED

Discussion Questions:

1. How does the last paragraph reflect the theme and conflict of Robert Roberge's story?
2. How does the job that Bud Barrett is forced to take emblematic of the loss of humanity that he has gone through?
3. Why does Bud Barrett sell meth rather than opiates? To what degree does this show an awareness of his larger problem?

Essay Questions:

1. Robert Roberge's narrator tries to hide from his reality through constant drug use. Compare and contrast this character's method of escape to T.C. Boyle's character's method in "The Relive Box."
2. To what degree does the final paragraph suggest that Bud Barrett's road will lead inevitably to his death? Is this borne out by other evidence in the story?

Little White Shoes

ZACHARY LOCKLIN

It was just a shoe. Lying on its side off an alley. No foot, no sock.

It caught David's eye as he passed. His head even turned to follow it. But as soon as he was past, it was out of his head.

He was late for the meeting, and his mind was full of contradictory worries. He was new to the city and couldn't get the hang of the traffic and parking, the cracks in the uneven sidewalk and the people milling about or down-rivering against him. It was like his legs couldn't find the rhythm of the pavement. Even thinking about it—he tripped on a peak raised by an earthquake or the root of a nearby tree.

And then he was there, stumbling into the entry of the restaurant, looking around and ducking at the hostess, who didn't even offer assistance, and over her shoulder, just under her left ear, Madison and Jeffries rearing back in laughter.

David edged past the hostess podium with a muttered apology. He unshouldered his bag at the table, apologizing more audibly. He rushed or collapsed into an empty seat. Carol Goddard made her lips into the tightest line yet. Jeffries was more gregarious. "David! Traffic get you down?" Foam stubbled the sides of a nearly empty pint glass in front of him.

"I don't know how any of you park in this city." David tried to simultaneously look at everyone at the table, leaving no one out, and rifle through his bag (already on the floor) for the proper paperwork. He emerged with a pen and notebook but the wrong folder: penned in black on the tab was August and the year. He needed June.

He could almost see the file in the drawer of his desk.

"Gentlemen," Madison proclaimed (two spent pints before him), "and Ladies" (with a polite nod to Carol and Laurel), "now that David is here we can begin. David, we took the liberty of ordering for you, I hope you don't mind, the ladies were getting hungry."

"I'm sure it's fine," David said. "Sorry."

"Not at all, not at all. We've entertained ourselves." He glanced significantly at the August folder. "While we're waiting, why don't we get started. About the requisitions for June—David?"

Everyone looked at him. He was still half-bent over his bag.

"Carol's—hold on—" and there it was—a miracle!—the June folder, somehow slipped inside the July folder. David righted himself, presented the file, pulled out pages one through nine, highlighted in yellow and pink and scrawled over in three different hands. "The Hyatt event, you mean. As far as I can tell—it seems to me we're going overboard on the speakers, but I trust Carol's judgment." Her expression didn't soften. He half-smiled at her.

"Well, as long as we're going to shoot the moon," Jeffries began, and the two faceless men to his left jerked to attention.

Afterwards, slumped and exhausted, David stumbled in reverse to the twenty-dollar parking lot four blocks away. His shoulder bag slapped against his hip. He didn't bother to stop it. Jeffries had ordered him a beer when he arrived—something really dark, nobody would tell him what it was—and now he felt bloated and nauseated.

This time, when he saw the shoe—it was white and tiny—he was trudging so slowly that he really saw it. And what caught him about it was not its loneliness or its desolation—Los Angeles, he thought, was the land of discarded shoes—but the detail of a pink flower over the Mary Jane strap. It was a good shoe. A fancy shoe for a girl's first *Les Miserables* or upscale birthday party. The hard plastic of its body was real leather, David thought.

For some reason, it actively called to him. And he obeyed. Tipsy, tired, nauseated, he stepped into the filthy dead-end alley.

There was the slightest hint of brickish red ink or paint on the toe of the shoe.

A hand touched his elbow. He jumped and spun.

"Jesus, David." Laurel gave him a stern look. "Are you all right?" She was fifty-ish and professional. Her face was set in a practiced professional blank glare.

Yeah," he said. "I got distracted."

Laurel's stern look turned half-concerned. "You're drunk." It was almost sympathetic.

David shook his head. "I'm tipsy. I'm fine."

"They shouldn't make you drink. They shouldn't be drinking at a work lunch anyway. I don't care, but one of these days Carol's going to complain." She stared at him hard for a moment. "You need to get your act together, David. You can stand up to them. But you need to start showing up on time if you want to keep your job. I'm saying this as a friend—"

David had stopped listening. "Look at this," he said.

"It's a shoe." Her voice was flat.

"Is that blood?"

Laurel hesitated. "I think so. Probably."

"Should I be concerned? Should I do something?"

She shrugged. "It's just some kid's shoe, David."

He didn't know what to do with it. A shoe was just a shoe. Laurel was right. He drove back to the office and trudged through the rest of the day. The shoe remained somewhere adjacent in his mind to the paperwork he had to work on.

He had a date in Silver Lake that night. Or Los Feliz, he couldn't tell them apart. It was the third date and he was picking her up at her apartment for the first time. On the two previous occasions, they had met hesitantly at a café and a restaurant, respectively, and parted with, at best, an awkward hug. David had been using an online dating service for more than a year, since before he had left Cleveland, and Rebecca's caution actually comforted him after the frenzy to move forward of most dates. It helped that Rebecca was a full seven years younger than David; women his age didn't have a lot of time left before they needed to get started on having a family.

She lived in a massive Gothic building perched over a winding one-lane road. The parking lot was unpaved; David's wheels nearly skidded in gravel, and once over the entrance, dust erupted around his car until he parked. A metal screen was locked over the open doorway into the peeling lobby. What paint remained was a dingy green. David had to text Rebecca.

"Just a minute," she replied. "On my way."

A long moment later, she was behind the black iron screen, half-visible and fumbling with the handle. It gave, and she flung the door harder than she needed to. She smiled awkwardly at David. "That thing," she said. Immediately, she turned and led David to an angular staircase. "I'm almost ready. Sorry. Come up and see my place."

She was in a thin blue dress that crossed over her small chest, buttoned primly but not very high. Her legs were dark with tights or nylons. This was her hipster way of dressing up. David realized, for the first time, that she wanted him to kiss her tonight.

"That door is a mess, I'm sorry about that. They're supposed to leave it open during the day, but some asshole keeps locking it. I've gotten locked out twice already. That is a conversation I don't like to have with my landlord. I don't like to have any conversations with the landlord."

The stairs led to a poorly-lit, white-painted hall. Directly at the landing, Rebecca fidgeted with another black iron screen and then a dark-stained wood door. David glanced around uncomfortably to find that, to the left, the hall continued on and seemed to bend upwards. He could see another set of stairs clawing towards the third floor.

Rebecca dragged him in and directed him to sit on a couch behind a cluttered coffee table. "Living room," she said. Canvasses were propped against walls beside stacks of textbooks, and a half-finished painting lay face-up on the carpet. She gestured over his head: "Bed." To the right, into a well-lit filthy kitchen. Beside the hall into the bathroom. Behind her, an alcove piled with clothes. "When I moved in, that was like a cage. The guys before me were in a band or something. They put bars on the closet and I guess like locked girls in there. And they raised that area where the bed is, like a stage."

"Huh," David said.

"Let me just get ready." Rebecca was halfway into the darkened hall. "One minute." She disappeared into the bathroom.

Left alone, David examined the coffee table minutely—music magazines, three issues of *Juxtapose*, bits of unused clay, a lighter and two crumpled cigarette packs, assorted razor blades, innumerable pens. The painting on the floor was eerie in its unfinished state: half a face with the wrong half of its features.

Rebecca returned and David stood. Accident placed him too near her at the door. She had put on dark lipstick, and she smelled faintly enough of perfume that he wasn't sure if he imagined it. Tonight she wanted him to kiss her.

He was okay with that.

Rebecca knew a place down Sunset and up a small street. They were quickly seated outside, beside a small koi pond. The fish shared their enclosure with a flowering bush which, David realized, was covered in bees.

The bees didn't help his anxiety. When he ordered, it was with revulsion. But he finished the Coke they brought him in seconds. His hands trembled.

After dinner, she took him to a wine bar in Los Feliz. He joined her in a glass of something red that she ordered. Halfway through her second glass and his first, he excused himself to the restroom, urinated for possibly a full hour, and gave himself a good, stern looking-at in the mirror. "You need to get your shit together," he told himself.

"What?" the guy in the stall said.

Coming through the restroom door, David saw Rebecca down the dark hall, on a stool at the bar, in the dim golden light, reapplying her lipstick.

"She wants me to kiss her," he told himself.

The door opened sharply into his back. "What?" the guy from the stall said, before shaking his head and walking away. "Guy needs to get his shit together," he muttered.

Back at the bar, as David climbed his stool, Rebecca smiled at him silently. It was more than a conversational smile. It was a personal smile, and a secret smile. Private to herself.

"Do you want to get out of here?" she said.

"Uh—sure. Yeah."

Outside it was still light, an early-summer eight o'clock. Rebecca took a cigarette from the pack with her mouth and thought better of it. "Do you mind?" she asked, the cigarette in her fingers and the lighter already out. "Just till we get to the car. I won't smoke in your car."

"I don't mind," David said. "Whatever you want."

"It's early." She exhaled smoke with the words. The car was a block away and they moved slowly so she could finish the cigarette. "Do you want to do something?"

"Sure. Whatever. What do you have in mind?" He felt antsy with her—he had ever since he'd had that glimpse of the future, that she was going to kiss him tonight—but he didn't want to rush things.

"So decisive. There's this art exhibit they've been talking about a lot at school. We have to go to three galleries for my summer class."

"That sounds good."

They were at his car. She leaned backwards against the door, one arm smugly coiled across her, the other perched at the elbow with cigarette in upturned hand. "I warn you though." She grinned. There was a challenge in her squinted eyes. "It's not close. And the subject matter is controversial."

"I have no problem with any of that." He realized that he was farther from her than he should be. He didn't know how to edge forward subtly.

"It's a big deal. Be warned. It's sick shit, David."

"I don't think I shock too easily."

"It's nasty, nasty stuff."

He took the step and put his mouth to hers.

The step was more like a step-and-a-half; he was off balance stooping to her level, and in her surprise, her cigarette almost caught his shirt.

But she came to him. She stretched her neck to him and pressed her mouth upwards to his. Her cigarette hand, recovering from its surprise, came to his head. Her fingers played absently in his hair.

The Krumholtz-MacTarry Gallery wasn't close. By the time they reached it, the sky was nearly dark and it was almost nine. There were no windows; light poured from an open door. A white wall just inside the door hid the exhibit from view.

David parked around the block, in a barren, concrete residential neighborhood. The air had chilled. Rebecca walked with her arm through his, pressing against him for warmth. Her other hand had a cigarette.

"Have you been to this place before?"

She shook her head.

"But you've heard about this exhibit."

"It's nasty stuff, David."

"What is it?"

All she would say was, "Nasty, nasty stuff."

At the door, Rebecca stubbed out her cigarette on a blackened, ashy spot on the wall and dropped it into a sandpit below. David could see nothing past a white-painted interior wall, but a low, throbbing music seemed less to emanate from the room than to hover patiently all the way to the street.

They entered. Rebecca fidgeted with her hair. Painted in a rough courier font on the white wall were two lines:

Doll Parts:
Liu-Wen O'Hara

Rebecca preceded him around the corner and stopped. He ran into her. The room stopped him before he could move away. Her hand clasped the fabric of his pants leg.

It took David a moment, even in his shock, to realize what he was looking at. On pedestals throughout the room, and pinned or wired to the stark white walls, winged, furred, distorted, and dismantled babies' bodies took abstract form before him. Some lacked a head, or arms; a mouth had been supplanted by a beak; wings had been grafted, tails and tail-feathers and tails culminating in tail-feathers; bodies of skunk fur, legs of outsized birds; smooth, pink torsos with ten dark wings, crows' wings, descending the ribs, the face masked in a badger's. Monstrosities. Against the far wall, an emaciated Asian man in a grey hooded sweater on a stool stooped over a touch-screen device. His black hair was arranged in a neat part down the middle of his scalp. David couldn't see his face.

"Those are dolls, right?" David murmured behind Rebecca.

"I don't think those are dolls." Her voice was breathless. Almost a whisper.

She stepped away from David to a podium towards the front. An older couple who had just vacated it moved to the wall and nodded in front of a barely-recognizable form. David thought it was part snake.

He joined Rebecca at the podium. She pressed absently against him and put a hand to his back. Her head was already bowed over a lengthy notice.

"Nope," she said. "Those are not dolls."

David bent to read the notice:

Doll Parts:
Liu-Wen O'Hara
1996-2013

Since a young age, pan-ethnic concept artist Liu-Wen O'Hara has been fascinated by the decay of the physical form. His first exhibition, *Lust Ballet*, a collection of plaster statues of male and female forms left out in heavy rain, was noted
for its bleak hopefulness: the body decays but the form endures underneath. Soon
after the success of that exhibit, Mr. O'Hara became interested in the dramatic
possibilities of taxidermy.

"Taxidermy," he told *Time* magazine, "is the art not of preservation but recon-
stitution." When we embalm a corpse or preserve a dead animal, he seems to say,
we don't restore something previously existing but recreate in our own image, in
the imagery of our own memories. "Memory has no place in the Capitalist world,"
O'Hara told culture critic Inu Hernandez in her blog, *Caligula*, and in a time
of revisionist hegemony and propaganda politics, his words ring more true than
ever. Memory is the captive of power. We remember what we are told to remember. We remember according to our own psycho-political world. "Taxidermy,"
O'Hara told *Interview* magazine, "is a gift to the dead as much as to the living."

For more than a decade, between working on his extremely successful *Houses
of Alterity* and the viscerally romantic *Heart Shaped Box*, a series of crates, bins,
and coolers filled with the preserved organs of thirty species of animal and six
human races, he has quietly collected the materials for what is surely his opus.

The seventeen-year work has paid off in the collection of *Doll Parts*, which Mr.
O'Hara has unofficially subtitled "Procreation in the Age of Death."

The work is legally dubious; O'Hara currently awaits decisions in the courts
of ten states, in none of which have any of the pieces been displayed. Mr. O'Hara
claims that this is exactly the point. "The purpose of art is to challenge the ethics
of the societal structure," he has stated. "In an era of war, abortion, poverty, and
abstract banking, where is the line that we draw? We treasure films of torture
while our news programs force-feed us twenty-four hour footage of explosions
and death at the same time as we throw sheep's blood at the abortion clinics. *Doll
Parts* speaks to this cynicism."

Each of the subjects has been procured legally. Mr. O'Hara himself approach-
es the parents of still-born infants and crib-death victims. To the more destitute,
he offers a cash payment; wealthier clients have paid him more than $100,000 to
immortalize their children. The oldest subject is "Collin—the heart feels free," a
ten-year-old victim of the anti-vaccination movement. The youngest is "Adeline—

God smiles at the grave of innocence," a late-term abortion that took the life of the mother.

It is the hope of this gallery and of Mr. O'Hara that *Doll Parts* helps remind the world of its responsibility to life, to death, and to the beauty of the inhuman form of humanity.

"Jesus," David said. He found that he was breathing heavily.

"This is—incredible." Rebecca looked around the gallery. "All these children."

"Jesus H. Christ," David said.

The older couple had reached the back and appeared to be discussing the price of a particular piece with the artist. David could see his face now: the small, dark eyes that bulged slightly from the deep creases around his mouth and the heavy overhang of his brow. Two young men walked behind David to the door. "It's like, I know I should be disturbed," one of them said. "But I'm not at all."

"They're just so *beautiful*," his friend said.

They both wore skin-tight jeans and plaid shirts, and their beards were monstrous.

Beautiful was the word for it, but David seemed to have side-stepped his own skin. An uncanny chill crept at his nape.

He followed Rebecca to the first wall. They stood before it and said nothing. Her hand found his.

And the two boys were right, in a way. It was disgusting, it was, as Rebecca had said, nasty, nasty shit, but standing before the tragic snake boy ("Armando—in Heaven, everything is fine") with Rebecca's hand in his and the nausea of shock permeating his entire body, he felt something other than disgust.

"Are you okay?" Rebecca murmured, her eyes locked on the body. "Can you handle this?"

"I think so. You?"

She squeezed his hand gently. She half-smiled and didn't take her eyes off of the body.

They weren't all babies, as the notice had said. Next to Armando, a larger torso had been robbed of head, limbs, and gender. No judge of age, David unconsciously assumed it to be seven or eight years old. His mind, translating the unthinkable into the thinkable, had translated all of the pieces into baby dolls.

The torso was titled "Jordan—sexuality in deficit." Urchin spines had been pierced outward through the skin. Otherwise, Jordan was unadorned; beside it, an orange sign announced, "Currently On Trial in Oklahoma." No explanation was provided.

David and Rebecca shifted slowly through the exhibit. Possibly she led him. His own agency had become dissociated from his consciousness. Or was that conscience deserting him?

In the center of the room, slightly raised on a pure white pedestal, surrounded by a spiraling series of free-standing pedestals with undersized works, the centerpiece of the collection bathed in a pure white light.

A single, smudged, child's Mary Jane, white with a pink flower on the strap.

The plaque on the pedestal read, "HOPE"—and nothing else.

ZACHARY LOCKLIN
LITTLE WHITE SHOES

Discussion Questions:

1. Why does Laurel react to David in the way that she does after the meeting? What does she think is wrong with David?
2. How does David feel about Los Angeles? Where do these feelings come from? How does his reaction to the shoe reflect those feelings?
3. Does David grow as a character throughout this story? If so, how does he grow?

Essay Questions:

1. Compare and contrast the way the protagonists of "Little White Shoes" and "Pay Phone" react to and feel about the city.
2. The art show in "Little White Shoes" is similar in many respects to a number of art shows that use Plastination to display human bodies. Is the approach that the artist uses different than these shows? Is there something more objectionable about *Doll Parts* than other shows that have used human corpses as objects of art?
3. How does David's experience in the art exhibit change our understanding of his interactions with other characters during the lunch meeting and his date with Rebecca?

Flutter

ANTHONY STARROS

In the fast lane of the 405, amid Toyotas and Fords, a black Infinity kicked up a piece of something, a cardboard nothing really, spitting it into the air. Gus barely caught a glance of it, and, without even knowing what it was, some dark smudge against the smog, he flinched hard in his seat, jerking the steering wheel to the right, his white Sentra swerving out of his lane and into the next, a grey sedan in the lane next to him also swerving to avoid the action. With all the cars around him, that piece of trash ended up in his way, or he ended up in its way.

The next morning, Gus was getting ready for a trip when a breaking newscast interrupted whatever daytime talk show was on as background noise. This exclusive stopped him mid-pack, and he stood motionless in his bedroom next to a black duffel bag filled with warm clothes, a half-folded long-sleeved t-shirt hanging from his hand. A mudslide had destroyed a groundskeeper's home at a youth camp in the San Bernadino mountains, the same camp where Gus went as kid. Rain had been dousing the southland for three days and only just broken that morning, the skies outside his room still dark and overcast.

A few months before, the biggest forest fires in decades had burned down acres and acres of forest in those same mountains, clearing land once-thick with evergreens. The fires burned all around the perimeter of the camp, close enough to singe the walls of the cabins where Gus had slept as a camper. Countless other kids had also slept out there over the thirty years since the camp was built. The fire had burned so much away that when the same area was hit with this deluge, these three days of rain, there were no trees to absorb the water and dissipate flow. There was no forest left on that part of the mountain, no brush to clog the water from picking up momentum and gathering mud and rocks, then stones and boulders, some "the size of Volkswagens" he heard a voice say, his attention now back to an interview on TV.

A female reporter in a red storm jacket was talking to a firefighter. Her warm breaths, steaming through the cold, punctuated the interview as they stood on a huge concrete slab, rain-slicked and muddy, random bits of rebar sticking up like broken bones, the only remnants of a four-bedroom house that Gus knew all too well. He could see what used to be there, even though there was nothing but black-brown wet earth and huge grey boulders glistening with rain and floodwater to be seen on the TV. The house had washed completely away, leaving stones and mud surrounded by a dozen soaked figher fighters in yellow jackets with reflective stripes, some poking and prodding into the ground and around the muddy brush, some holding coiled ropes, one just standing still with his hand to his head.

"Well, as you can see, there's absolutely nothing left here," said the rescue worker. "The slide followed the natural path of the creek that ran through the camp grounds right to this house." He raised a gloved hand and pointed at the concrete as a quick stream of water ran over it. "The only way you can even tell there used to be a house there is from this foundation right here."

"And this was the only house that had people in it?" The reporter was hunched over, almost hollering now as helicopter blades punched the air overhead.

"Yes, well, so far we think this was a kid's camp in the summer, and the caretaker was here . . . living here in this house with his family."

"And these other buildings," the reporter turned her hooded head about in forced amazement. "All these other buildings are fine, not even a broken window?"

"Yeah, it's really unfortunate. If these people had been in any of the other buildings on the premises, they wouldn't have even been hurt at all. We've heard that there were supposed to be some kids up here, but we haven't gotten that . . . we have no confirmation of that yet. We're still trying to find out if there were campers up here or not. Cars have been found by the camp, and we do have one survivor, the um . . . the caretaker's cousin who was visiting for Christmas. Unfortunately, his family is also currently missing and he's in shock and confused right now. Other people could be missing too, we just don't know that much about it yet."

Just that summer, before the fire and before the rains, Gus had gotten a phone call from the camp director and was asked to work at that camp one last time. Since he had been there so recently, as an adult, there were new memories from there still fresh in his head, mingling with the memories of the camp from his youth.

That creek that grew so massive was where Gus gathered campers and counselors to take "creek showers," fifteen kids and two adults in bathing suits and soapy heads, all singing campfire songs and scrubbing up, the water running cool and benign around their ankles and calves.

It was by that same creek where he'd chased a bear away from a pack of scared kids, running around the grass field banging a big stew pot with a metal ladle and hollering, scared to death the bear would turn on him. After the bear ran off up the side of the mountain and disappeared into the brush, Gus hunched over by the wooden bridge that crossed the creek, panting, his hands resting on his knees, the pot and ladle on the grass by his feet. He remembered looking at the rickety brown bridge as his chest heaved and his heart raced. On it, over the thirty years it existed, under the darkness of summer nights, boys would sneak away in the night and meet up with girls, lips touching while feeling the span flexing under their shifting teenage weight as they timidly held one another, the sound of running water loud beneath them the whole time, almost too surprised that they were kissing to enjoy the moment fully. Gus had been one of those teenagers.

That same creek rose with earth and swelled, pulling trees thirty feet tall from the ground, ignoring roots and foundations, and it rose with fury until it was a rocketing torrent, roaring past six empty cabins, tearing through a steel swing set cemented into the ground and mangling it like a twist-tie, then swallowing up a twenty-foot water tower and crumpling it like some leftover tin foil. Carrying six-foot boulders and entire trees, it smashed into the only building where people lived in the off season, where, with his wife, George, the ex-El Salvadoran soldier, forty-four years old with a gold tooth, lived. Where dark-skinned Raquel, his nine-year-old daughter with long black hair and huge dimples when she smiled, lived.Where Theresa, his nineteen-year-old daughter, was visiting just for the holiday. Where Jeremiah, his six-month-old son, lived. The torrent exploded into them like a cement dam sliding a hundred miles an hour. It scattered them about the mountain. Jeremiah and George were found right away, Raquel not until three days later, five miles down the mountain. Her mother is still missing to this day.

Gus finally sat down in his comfortable chair, in his heated bedroom, still holding the half-folded T-shirt. The aerial footage of what used to be George's house was shown all across the southland while soccer moms cleaned up torn wrapping paper and plotted re-gifting, not even acknowledging what they'd seen or heard, background noise to the stress of the holidays. He watched the overhead footage from a helicopter, circling the cement slab doused with mud. Gus knew when the newscasters didn't that it wasn't campers who were washed away, but that it was George and his family. He also knew when they reported that a man watched his wife and daughter get swept away from his grasp, that the girl's name was Raquel, and that she put her hair in a ponytail, and that she wore a pink bathing suit when swimming in the pool with the big kids, and that Gus had bought her a pink backpack from Smart and Final for her birthday just a few months before.

Gus also knew first-hand that George was thankful for his job and for the house provided to the caretaker so he could live at the camp year-round and keep the grounds that would ultimately swallow up his wife, his daughters, and his son. Gus and George had spent a lot of time together that last summer, mending fences, clearing fields, building wooden targets for paintball wars. Early each day, George hollered "goood morning" into the staff area with a deep drill-sergeant's voice, rolling his Rs thickly. Everyone knew when he was close by since he whistled everywhere he went. When the camp was again dealing with a bear that tore through their trash every day, it was George who got a black-and-white dog named Captain from a friend. They often sat together on the porch of this house, Captain lying sideways on the door-mat and George in a chair cradling his son in his arms while feeding him. Amid all the cabins and other buildings on that hill, it was George's house that ended up in the slide's way.

Gus finally dropped the half-folded shirt onto the duffel bag that he'd no longer need. In it were gloves and beanies and jackets packed for a trip up to the camp where the slide had hit that morning. Eighty-five other people were going too—two dozen children, packs of teenagers, and a handful of adults—all to pour from yellow busses, sleeping bags and pillows in tow. A bus-full of near-misses.

Gus would have been there by two p.m. that day, a few hours late for mortality. His cell phone began ringing in the other room. He was so close to being right next to George on his patio, playing with Captain, the bear-dog with a blue bandana around his neck, all of them sitting unflinching with the earth swelling behind them, with their backs to death. Eighty-six people spared at the cost of a few. Gus's chest thumped hard. He felt relief. Then he felt disgusted with himself. Thump. The TV was still on, but he could only stare at the bag he'd packed for the mountains, straps dangling to the side. Thump. He looked at his feet wrapped in thick, clean white socks, not a speck of mud on them as his home phone also began ringing from the nightstand beside him. He ignored them both.

———

Only then did he remember that piece of cardboard he'd seen on the freeway. The 405 is infinitely busy. Cars constantly fly along creating wakes and exhaust. That cardboard might have been carried for miles without ever having been touched by anything, a wisp floating violently amid tons and tons of barreling steel and horsepower. It began as a tree somewhere but ended up as a box, was used, crushed, torn, and finally tossed. It lay for who knows how long until the wake that traffic causes disrupted it, until a gust carried it to wherever and it fluttered about jaggedly, barely missing for who knows how long until, finally, one day it didn't. And that was just it.

Months later, when Gus drove up to see the place for himself, he stood at the foot of the camp. The whole property looked like it had been parted down the middle with a muddy comb then left to bake under the sun, cracks like the desert forming on the deposit. He stood squinting as the warm spring sun shined on his head, and he saw that on either side of George's house everything was intact: the cabins, the bathrooms, the mess hall and pool on one side, the staff area on the other. They all stood undisturbed while splitting the camp in two was a vast deposit of now-dried earth and stone. Gus then walked over to and stood before the patio where he and a summer crush had stolen away to sleep under the stars some twenty years ago. Ten yards behind him was the flat dirt area that was once a house, but the building in front of him was eerily untouched, all the windows boarded up. Gus stared at the abandonment, so much destruction just behind him. A thin layer of caked-hard dirt covered half the patio, also dried and cracked. He stood in the spot where he had slept side to side with a girl who he had once pined for, a distant memory, a one-time source of sadness that now seemed so unimportant. He kicked a pebble lying on the deposit and exposed a divot of earth, a small hole in the ground that may have been formed the day a family washed away.

With all the emotions he felt that December while standing in his bedroom rising back up, standing at the cemetery that bore no bodies, so many other problems again became insignificant. They just floated away, like some piece of cardboard above the traffic that lives cause. The non-stop movement that, like a night-time photo with the shutter left open, seems a synchronous stream of light. But it was no longer a blur to Gus. The long, smooth red line of tail-lights suddenly became separate and vivid images of each car, truck, and van. In each Infinity and Navigator, Gus now saw love and death and hate distinct to each empty passenger seat. All shared a spot in that line, contributing in some slight way to the stream of light caused by non-stop movement, until, one day, they didn't. And that was just it.

ANTHONY STARROS
FLUTTER

Discussion Questions:

1. The phrase, "and that was just it," repeats itself throughout "Flutter." What is the significance of that line? How does it help to reveal the characters' problems?
2. What is Gus's relationship to the camp that is destroyed, and how is he reacting to it?
3. What has led to the destruction of the camp?

Essay Questions:

1. This story explores the random nature of the universe and how helpless people seem to be in it. What are the forces that are shaping the lives of Gus and the people he knows and how does he react to these forces?
2. Compare Gus's reaction to the death of his friends in "Flutter" to the imagined dangers of "Spirals and Epicenters." How and why are the characters in these stories reacting to the world in the way that they are?

Spirals and Epicenters

RYAN SAREHKHANI

Sometimes it's easier, he thought, to function in a world where actions and reactions—equal, opposite, or otherwise—are made inseparable by some unobservable current that smashes all things together until they're ground into the same fine grain. A world in which he could blame his shoddy understanding of thermodynamics on an inability to read about it because the bumps on any given road make him carsick.

For now, this ouroboros of tragic causality had descended on the traffic cones outside the bus window, framing them as the object of his thoughts for the moment. They sat there, redirecting the world around them, providing a service to the world that only requires that they take up some amount of physical space, creating the channels by which the rest of us can collide in new and creative ways, narrowing the highway to three lanes. The cones, which he had thought to be standard procedure for funneling traffic into Pudong Airport, turned out to be placed there in response to a car wreck, the third he'd seen this weekend.

A jerky merge into the right lane pushed him and a nearby passenger together. It was apparent at this point that a conversation was imminent, the type that happens in a close proximity between people who are worried what they must look like bumping shoulders with a perfect stranger.

"Where you from?" asked the passenger, a local.

"Los Angeles," he answered, not because he was, or because he was familiar with the area, but because the word holds a certain weight or currency in the world that Covina, county, or suburbs don't. The answer seemed to befuddle the passenger, and, for a moment, he looked down, pressing his chin to the right side of his collared Polo. Then, an epiphany.

"Ah, you mean *Luo San Ji*? Bang bang! Haha!"

"Yes." He responded with the enthusiastic half laughter of someone who missed a punch line.

Wondering who had come out on top of the conversion, he now felt like he was on the shit end of the currency exchange. There was a tension building between the passenger's forearm and hand; his fingers were in the shape of a gun.

The weight of his statement, which, through an assumed quality of common-place, was meant to smother the chance for any more small talk, now sat on him in the form of a sour expression that he didn't know he was wearing. Shanghai, he thought, Shanghai couldn't be any safer. How else could the word *shanghaied* be coined?

He set out to make a point about stereotypes, media representation, and globalization, but, before his conviction could hit the tip of his tongue, he realized that he wasn't current on any Shanghai crime statistics. For that matter, he couldn't conjure up any LA rates either. To some extent, any city can stand in for any other city, but the analogy was failing, crashing in on itself. The numbers were there somewhere, just unavailable. The tension in the passenger's forearm was moving to his mouth, pushing out a tense smile at the thought of a possible social fault.

"It's not the guns you have to worry about, actually, it's the . . ." Car crashes.

"Earthquakes."

"Yes, I see. I'm sorry." The passenger looked away for a moment, exposing the side of his face so he could tend to some subconscious itch on the edge of his jaw.

"Well, the earthquakes," he explained, "aren't really a problem either. They're something we kind of just ignore out there, nobody ever gets hurt. Sometimes they wake you up at night, but they break the routine enough to get a good adrenaline rush, and you feel great for getting through something like that. Honestly, you don't even notice them until you're cleaning up broken glass the next day. They say we have dozens a week, but I'm convinced those are just trucks ripping by my house."

There was a screech under their feet, and the passenger nodded. The bus stopped. They parted ways with what felt like a "Happy travels" or "Good luck."

He saw the man walk toward someone soliciting money for some sort of relief fund. The man dropped a few coins in and gave a nod of acknowledgement. He decided to follow in suit and approached the solicitor himself, dropping the last of his Chinese money into the bowl.

The airport was at a steady rumble, the kind that accompanies the slow churn of a lava flow that never seems to dry up. The people were always on their way out, moving somewhere else, but the rumble always stayed in the same place at the center of it all. A particularly volatile group, excitable children, was adding a distinctly un-ignorable frequency into the whole of the composition. The sound was growing louder from behind him, but he couldn't bring himself to look over his shoulder, so he began to count. The time between hushed *squee*s was shortening, and this made him sure. They were coming closer. He stood up and began to step away, but the leader of the children snared him with an introductory speech token and a sense of common courtesy.

"Hello. How are you?"

"Hello. Busy. In a hurry."

He put on a decent performance, occasionally looking over his shoulder at some invisible companion pointing at her watch and beckoning him to the terminal.

"You are American?"

"Yes."

They looked at one another, newly and obviously enthused.

"You have money?"

"What?" Were there beggars even here?

They smiled and pulled out some money, RMB, of their own.

"Can we trade?"

He didn't want to. He had been very careful to spend all of his RMB so he wouldn't have to convert it. He had a lucky break with the relief fund outside that allowed him to unload every one of his unwanted cents. He didn't want to bring anything back with him, nothing but what he came with. Relatives were disgruntled, and his friends had gotten used to it even though they thought he was crazy. Kaily would think he was crazy. Kaily, his neighboring apartment dweller, who always seemed to be hovering in the peripheral space outside his door, who always seemed so interested in his travels, who wouldn't take any money in return for watching his place while he was gone. Shit. The only payment she would agree to was some sort of souvenir, something tacky and inauthentic like a straw hat or a mass-produced fan, something that you couldn't find in an upscale airport, something he'd forgotten.

"Yes."

He gave them a five and took whatever they gave him without thinking about the exchange rate. It didn't matter. The children thanked him and shuffled off somewhere. He knew it wasn't enough to buy anything here, and even if it did, she would know that he bought it from the airport, or worse; she could assume that he bought it when he got off the plane at LAX. He was formulating a plan, though.

She wouldn't take money. That was the problem in the first place. But would she take this? Surely, she wouldn't spend it. It's colorful, exotic, worth almost nothing back in the US. In theory, it's the perfect little travel trinket. He could sell her the culture. He could sell her something she didn't know. He could sell her a story.

It wouldn't work. Fifteen minutes until his flight and he knew that. It's too lazy, and it would look like he was giving her the first thing that he found in his pocket. It'd be better to just tell the truth rather than pawn off some Monopoly money on her. She would make a dumb joke about hiding a rotting fish in his apartment and not telling him the location until he produced a gift, and she would chuckle, and they would move on.

He walked into a convenience store, bought a drink, and told the cashier to keep the change. Before he could turn around, the cashier rolled his eyes and dropped his change on the counter. Obviously, some sort of cultural faux pas had been committed, so he scooped up the change and hoped for another relief fund. He was about to hand it over to a kid and make his day, but he noticed something. One of the coins in his hand was of a glinting silver, a bit larger and thicker than a quarter, with smooth wavy edges that gave it the form of a flower. He held it between his finger and thumb, and the child perceived it as display. The kid wasn't happy when he didn't get to keep it. "This," he thought, "I can sell."

He didn't look at it again until he got situated on the plane. He began to formulate, figuring his thoughts would take off with the plane that was posturing for flight. He needed something mystical but not too far from commonplace. Like a folk tale in a foreign land and a lesson learned. A beggar came to mind, or one better, a fortune teller.

In the market, a fortune teller, a negligibly blind woman, would approach him and tell him that the threads that hold all life together are crossing at this moment and that the stars and planets themselves were all looking down and their vision was converging at one point. The fortune teller would relay that he, the foreigner, had always avoided these strings, slipping through their geometric web with masterful ignorance. But now, she would say, he is trapped in the cosmic limelight, and he will soon be faced with a change of fortune, but the nature of that change would be entirely dependent on the clarity of her counsel.

"And how could I compensate you for this advice?" he would rightly ask, knowing the tropes of this type of exchange. "Well," she would respond, "there is no price for bad news, but, if the news is favorable, what does the price matter?" He would meditate for a moment before offering his terms, "Okay, but you must share with me in all aspects of my good fortune." Taken aback, she would answer, "Ah, a wise man indeed," before inviting him to turn his eyes to the crowd growing behind him.

The crowd would approach him with cameras, pose with him, take pictures, and offer money for his time. By the time the crowd dissipated, he would have amassed a small fortune. At the moment in which he was alone, the fortune teller would return and ask, "Your fortune was good, then?" to which he would reply, "Yes, and I would be fortunate to keep my promises," and he would give to her every piece of currency that he had just been gifted, and the fortune teller would smile. He would ask, "And why would these people treat me this way?" and the fortune teller would respond with a veiled "Why else?" Wryly, he would postulate, "They thought I was from Hollywood."

She would leave him with one more cryptic message before leaving him: "Your humor serves you well, as there is some truth in every joke. The answer is simple. You knew your particular place in this world at this particular time, a sentiment not many in your position share. Remember, though, that it was not something you knew yesterday, and you may not know it tomorrow." She would hold out her hand, and, in its center, would lie a coin of glinting silver, a bit larger and thicker than a quarter, with smooth, wavy edges that gave it the form of a flower. "This," she would say, "is for you, in case you forget."

"Perfect," he thought while staring at the flower engraved on the coin. Not only had he crafted a story for her, but he had created a mystery and an invitation, and he had saved himself. He would hand it to her and say, "In case you need any good advice. I can watch your place while you're gone." Proud of himself, he began to flip the coin around in his fingers, scanning its artistry. He noticed an inscription on the flower's reverse side. Written in plain English. "Hong Kong." Shit.

She knew that he didn't go to Hong Kong. "It's practically just a city," he thought, "Does it really need its own currency? Do countries even need their own currency?" His story was falling apart. Shanghai locals wouldn't bat an eye at a foreigner, let alone take his picture and give him money. But she couldn't know that. For all she knew, Shanghai was a completely different animal than LA. The fortune teller could be from Hong Kong. It could add a touch of romanticism. She could even be Indian. It didn't matter. His narrative was crumbling, and he stopped trying his hardest to arrange the pieces logically. The pieces would add up on their own if he just let them be and took himself out of the equation. The least Kaily could do was appreciate the story, which, at that point, was more trouble than actually just buying something.

He was done with the story even if the story wasn't done itself. He needed to be alone in his thoughts without the interference of fortune tellers, crowds of fans, or tenement mates. He attained his goal, he thought. He was returning from his journey, and he was still himself, without anything new in hand but a coin he wouldn't keep for more than a few days and a loosely crafted story, which, because he couldn't literally carry it, didn't really conflict with his code. The plane was a few hours into flight, and, with no more mental chores to run, he turned his thoughts to more pressing and immediate matters.

Ironic, he found it, that contrails are put on display to the world, with the exception of the passengers on the planes that create them. Modern flight, on its most basic level, is a science of slicing air. It's hard to believe, then, that the innumerable vortices spiraling outward into streams of crystal and vapor are simply a side effect of a wing's sharp edge, instead of its function. The world's heaviest glass spinners, working delicately enough to design ice sculptures on the scale of dust, still suspended in air above the world of jagged tectonics and rigid canyons. This reaction, he thought, must be the only phenomenon that can't be felt or seen from the point of its origin. On other planes of existence, effects are most violent and severe at ground zero, but something felt disconnected here, fell short in areas of zero ground. Why then, had nobody resolved to install just one more window in the back of the airline?

There was a line forming at the rear of the plane about twelve hours into the flight. People's bowel cycles must sync up after they spend a prolonged amount of time together. He formulated this theory through the transitive property of another that he heard in passing once. He wondered if it would pass patent. Something lit up on the overhead display; the plane's innards were heaving. It hadn't been a smooth flight.

Since the plane took off there had been a constant shuddering along the walls and ceiling, but the sound was compounded by the noise and commotion of the passengers currently inhabiting the aisles. They were bracing themselves against the storage cabinets. The person sitting to his right looked pale, and her stomach was contracting. The environment suddenly became unaccommodating to his sensibilities.

Luckily, he had been blessed with a window seat, so he redirected his attention to the world just outside the writhing mess. What stood out to him now was how quiet the sky seemed to look. The clouds, which seemed to be rising in uniform, did so without the slightest noise. The tremors in the plane had become more frequent and severe, and people were asked to return to their seats. The sounds of shuffling feet, chatter, intercoms, and the incessant shuddering, he thought, wouldn't carry outside the window. There were no sound waves at that altitude, he assumed, but it could've been outer space that he was thinking of. Still, he longed to be outside of his steel coffin, with nothing but the sound of air rushing by his ears.

Falling, the plane is falling, was the only thing running through their minds. Some were weeping, some praying awful prayers that welled up from the bottom of the stomach, there were wild yells—all of which were being muffled by the overbearing sound of the plane's plastic shell crumbling. The plane must have been hit by a jet stream, or a storm, or a pressure change. Either way, he assumed it must've hit the plane like a wall, causing it to shatter and come apart at the junctures that seemed to be held together only by screws. Luggage was falling from overhead, and he shook his seat to make sure it was bolted down. The vast openness that he had always seen in the world was compressing and constricting around him, and, for the first time, he felt claustrophobic. Soon, he knew, this invisible force would send him spiraling toward the ground, to the land of epicenters and rear view mirrors, where he and everything around him would be smashed into powder and ash.

His thoughts of symbolic destruction dissipated. His mind had accepted his impending death surprisingly quickly. His body, however, was still clinging to life, and it let him know it. More incorrigible than the nausea and tears was the twisting pain of his bones bending beneath his tensing muscles. He couldn't seem to hold onto anything tightly enough. The shoddy nature of his seat's arm-rest couldn't provide him the strong base he needed, so he began to clench only his fists. It felt like his joints were pulling apart, like twenty years of arthritis had set in to make up for the old age that he wouldn't experience.

Even in the fit of nihilism that permeates these types of situations, the pain became unbearable, and he unclenched his hands. The first thing he noticed was a clean rush of air hit his palm. It was the kind of feeling that normally accompanied taking a bandage off for the first time in a week. Oxygen on raw skin. He removed the coin from his hand, and he began to bleed. A wound in the shape of a flower began to bloom, and quickly wilted, in the palm of his hand.

For the first time in hours, there was silence in the cabin aside from the standard shuddering, and the plane felt to be leveling out. The pilot came on the intercom and said they had just hit turbulence, but not the worst he'd ever seen. There was laughter and embraces, but mostly just breathing after that. Of course, he reasoned, the plane couldn't crash into the ground, turning everything into a collective debris; it was flying over the ocean. The plane's collision point would be much closer to the Southern California coast. Really, all landings are a sort of gentle crashing.

He hadn't slept right since the crash, even if it was just an internal one. They told him that everyone felt like he did after a sixteen hour flight where orange juice, beer, and peanuts were the only means of real sustenance. He couldn't sleep on the plane, not after the turbulent affair got his adrenaline pumping to the point of complete transcendent awareness, but, when he reached the ground, his body dumped on him. Stumbling away from the rabble, he felt as if his walk across the aerobridge was the longest he had ever taken—a feeling he knew had to be absurd, but he humored himself anyway.

When, he thought, does one walk end and another begin? Does anyone ever walk more than once, or are the paths that they take all part of the same continuous motion? Does sitting down break the sequence? What if your feet stay on the floor? The specifics didn't matter because, at that moment, he knew that he had begun a new walk, and it ended at the waiting area in the terminal. He spread himself out across a row of seats, firmly grasped the pole that held them bolted to the ground, and fell asleep without having to try. It was morning in LAX.

A week later and there was celebrating. His friends had found it in them to commemorate his safe arrival and muse about his near-death experience. They felt his battle scar to be fashionable. Kaily had attended. Things were going swimmingly enough until she brought up her fee. When he couldn't produce anything, she joked, "I left the stove on one of those days and it pretty much scorched the walls. I painted over it, but it's gonna flake off soon. I was going to fix it for real, but now . . ." and so on and so forth. That's when he left. They tried to stop him, they told him that he was doing that thing that he does, and it left a sour taste in everyone's mouth. He didn't understand their distaste in him. He had every intention of returning. He just needed to get Kaily's coin that he left in his car.

He didn't realize until ten minutes into his walk that it was 2:10 a.m. Everyone was getting ready to leave anyway when he decided to make his statement. There would be no return to the bar. They knew that, and now he knew it too. He would spend the rest of this night alone, and perhaps sneak in an apology tomorrow, but it didn't matter because night was no stranger to him. No stranger, at least, than the things that happen in daylight.

Unseen forces and invisible currents, he knew, always swept people along the inconceivable channels of their day to day; it didn't matter whether they were lit or not. The friction caused by these channels, however, could always be felt. While these undercurrents must all run to the same place for everyone, they tend to linger, swirl, and crash routinely in areas and times of higher population. This is where he felt he was now, dragged undertow through some confined aquifer, one that ran on a cyclical circuit that attempted to shear him down to his most basic element.

Of course, he wasn't completely closed off to the idea that his problem was what his friends told him it was earlier in the night—simple jetlag—but he had his doubts. They told him that travelling from West to East doesn't cause problems, but travelling from East to West almost unavoidably induces his current condition. He found this to be problematic, as he had resolved long ago that, in the vast fluctuating openness of space, directions are inherently arbitrary, or at least relative. Why, then, would travelling one way be any different than travelling another? What mattered wasn't where trajectories began or where they sought to end, but where they intersected others—where he was now. This reaffirmation of his old musings led him to something new.

The friction that he felt, the currents, the entropy, the chaos, the channels churning beneath the surface—these elements perpetually clash with such fearful magnitude and extremity that any single life is expected to be crushed in the crossfire or thrown into the spectrum's periphery, but they do not operate with the intent to destroy; they are necessarily creative forces. On their grandest level, the cosmos, and, on the most miniscule, biology. Surely, he was somewhere on that spectrum.

If the clashing of human trajectories is responsible for the creation of sprawling metropolises, then these same collisions must be responsible for the creation of something within him as well. East to West, Northwest to Southeast, these things didn't matter, for he was constantly in the center of things, and he knew it. He found it no coincidence that his revelation descended upon passing Señor Fish. With its subtitles scrawled in Katakana, it was the imminent and somewhat apocryphal product of

---

South and East—Spanish and Japanese—which culminated in a language that resembled something like English. This language and culture was in transition. He too, he thought, was in transition, only resembling the man he was just a few minutes earlier.

On the walk back to his car, he wondered if he would even recognize himself in a mirror. Luckily, fate had seen it fit to provide him with a multitude of them laid out in front of him. For a moment, the tension that he had always felt fell from his shoulders, retreated beneath the surface of the earth where it could stew, boil, and grind until it could force out more of the reflective towers that surrounded him. Volcanic glass, with its smooth, dark, crystalline sheen, seemed to coat the buildings that he slinked in between. They must have sprung out of the ground incredibly quickly, he thought, and cooled off far too fast. For once, though, he was not interested in the elements that conspired to create the things around him. His attention focused on the image reflected in the mirror, himself.

There must have been hundreds of office windows in view, but in each of them resided an image of himself, a new vignette, an untaken path. In one, he was a grinning fool who tempted fate; in another, he was a maudlin wanderer, but, in most cases, the glass held the image of a man protected by sincerity from the weight of responsibility that he had just taken upon himself. It was the last window on the block that made him stop.

Its tint was a deep black, and two strips of duct tape stretched from corner to corner, crossing in the center. Most peculiar was the fact that it was not broken, not cracked, not shattered—nothing that would necessitate its seemingly patchwork appearance. It was black. It could have been a slab of stone, or it could have been a hole in the wall that allowed the perfect darkness beyond the sill to be seen. Either way, it was hypnotic, and he froze there, too afraid to lift his hand and touch the anomaly that sat in front of him. Here, he let his eyes do the prodding, and one thing became clear; this surface, if it was a surface, reflected nothing.

A car ripping around the corner shook him from his trance. He wasn't paying attention earlier, but, somewhere in the back of his mind, he felt as if it was the car's second time around the block, and he couldn't tell if it was slowing around him or simply slowing sporadically before accelerating again and again. The driver must be drunk, he thought, and he just wanted to get home; they were in the same boat. His car was close by, just across the street, and he only wanted to get to it.

He turned the corner into the parking structure, and the car passed by, catching a glimpse of him from behind. The passengers yelled something, something that sounded like a name; he couldn't make it out, but it wasn't his. They must be looking for someone, and now they were sure to make another pass; next time, they would enter the structure. Being careful not to make a scene, he passed by the empty security guard's booth on the way to the stairs, and he began to climb.

His car was on the fourth floor, and on the way up he heard many loud, raucous voices emanating from the second, which, in a parking structure at 2:30 a.m., isn't terribly uncommon, but he could not help but interpret them with a sense of malignancy that fueled a newfound sense of agoraphobia within him. His stride began to increase. He firmly grasped the handle of his car door with his entire hand, and, with a shaky sigh, some of his anxiety left him. Upon stepping into his car, he felt a tremor, but he could not discern its origin.

Perhaps it was only a small quake, or perhaps it was a car starting, or, most likely, he thought, he had had a long night with a lot of walking and the weight of a new but liberating burden, and his legs simply began to give out. But this minor vibration, to him, signaled some sort of omen of things violent to come, and he decided his home, or at least the road, would be a safer place to contemplate it. He noticed the coin glinting in the cup holder. He picked it up and grasped it with the closest thing to sentimentality that he had. He was going to leave with it.

Before he could turn the key, a loud noise resonated through the halls of the parking structure, making it sound distant and muffled even though its epicenter was so immediate. The sound was like a bang. He knew the sound. He knew it was a gunshot.

There was a lot of screaming after that, a lot of yelling coming from the street entrance. It was a good thing he didn't start his car, alert them of his presence. He got out of his car, left the door ajar, and simply stood there and stared out at the building opposite the structure, trembling in a fit of adrenaline. He was in the wrong place at the wrong time, and he had put himself there. The constant presence of the yelling made it hard for him to think. He began to wring his hands.

No current would push him along this time, no unseen force would pull him to safety. The currents, though, now rushed within him, carried along with the same force, and burned with the same intensity that they always had. His hands grew warm. He had possibilities. They were not infinite, but they were there. He feared, though, that many of them ended in nothingness, in perfect black, in his own end.

He could not drive out the front because they were there, and he couldn't rightfully run them over—he didn't have it in him. Besides, they had at least one gun. The elevator would be a safer bet, but, when it opened, it might give him away, and, in the confusion and heat of the moment, he might end up being shot out of sheer jerk reaction. The stairs seemed like a viable alternative, but, on the way out, he might actually have to see them, or sneak by. If he could fashion some type of rope, he could climb outside and avoid having to see them or sneak by, but he knew that was a stupid idea the second it came to mind. He resolved himself, kept his head low, and made for the stairwell.

Within an arm's reach of the stairwell door, he heard the sound a car door slamming. Of course, he thought, he had left his door open, and he was parked on an incline. He wanted to throw up. He brought his hands to his face and drowned in his failure for just a moment. The warmth was somehow comforting, and he began to bask in it, feeling lighter. There was just a moment of silent inquiry that came from below, and then another bang, and then more yelling, this time, coupled with the sound of running.

All paths led upward, and, if they kept on their current paths, they would reach him soon. He couldn't formulate any longer; his legs would not allow it. He was full of fear and disarray. He began to sprint, forgetting about the stairs just beneath him. He toppled headfirst down one flight, leaving him between the third and fourth floors. The coin had fallen out of his hand, and it beat him to his resting place. He didn't see which side it landed on. He gripped the bottom of the handrail to help himself up, but it was too late. His body gave out, and he lost consciousness, still firmly grasping the rail with one hand while the other fell short of the coin.

When he came to, there were sirens outside, and smoke. There was no more yelling. There was a pounding feeling at the top of his neck and the back of his skull, and he pulled himself out of a puddle that he could only guess was his own vomit. There was a lot of pressure behind his eyes, and his walk was executed as more of a stumble. His face and hands were covered with blood. He scanned his skull, but he couldn't find a wound. It took a while, but he noticed that, somewhere during the ordeal, he opened the cut on his hand. He picked up his coin, forgetting to check which side landed up. They hadn't found him, and, if they did, they must have thought he was already dead. The police had taken care of the situation, and there was an ambulance on the street. He figured they would have room for just one more.

He looked like he was just in a wreck. Unsurprisingly, an officer stopped him.

"Hold on. Which car were you in?"

Still hazy. "Mine."

At his wits end. "The car that approached from the street? Or the one exiting the parking lot?"

"Parking lot . . . fourth floor. Thank you for . . ."

"Wait. The what?" He beckoned one of the drivers over. "Was this guy with you?"

"No, there were only four in the collision," the paramedic confirmed.

"The hell are you doing here, sir?"

That was a more complicated question than it seemed to him at first. He thought. He turned his palm upward and presented the officer with his prized coin.

"Jesus Christ."

The officer reached into his pocket, gave him some change, and moved him along. He stumbled back to his car, the best dressed vagrant in Los Angeles.

REVIEW

Discussion Questions:

1. How does the man the protagonist talks to at the beginning of the story react to the idea of Los Angeles?
2. Discuss the structure of the story. It is broken into three sections. How does the protagonist of "Spirals and Epicenters" grow through these three sections?

Essay Questions:

1. When the protagonist of "Spirals and Epicenters" is finally in Los Angeles, he exaggerates the violence of the car crash, imagining that someone is shooting. Why do you think he makes this kind of assumption? What events and ideas have led to this assumption?
2. Both "Spirals and Epicenters" and "Flights" deal with the emotional disconnection that immigrants sometimes feel. Compare and contrast the ways and the reasons that the characters from both stories make or avoid human connections in their lives.

Under the Radar

SUZANNE GREENBERG

It was hard for me to pretend it was fun riding around on the back of a golf cart. Guy liked to fly under the radar. That's what my mother said whenever I complained about it.

"What's flying got to do with it?" I asked.

"It's an expression," my mother said. "A figure of speech."

We were washing the dog in the backyard and up to our elbows in soap bubbles. Last summer, before he left us, I used to look out the kitchen window and see my father soaping up the dog, talking to him all the while. *You're a good dog*, he'd say. *What a dog.* But my mother didn't talk to Ernie. She washed him the same way she scrubbed the shampoo through my hair when I came home from a day at the beach. It didn't exactly hurt, but it didn't feel good either, her fingernails so close up to my scalp.

"It's not even legal," I said, "riding around on a golf cart."

"It might be," my mother said. "Guy likes to keep them guessing. The police don't know whether they should ticket him or not. Haven't you seen how they look at him?"

I'd seen. Where else was I going to look? I was always the one stuck in the back seat facing them when the police edged up behind us, elbowing each other and laughing. I'd put my hand under my shirt like I had an itch and give them the invisible finger.

"He's a clever man," my mother said, turning the hose on Ernie now, full force and cold.

I was twelve, and no one would hire me for a real job, so I was stuck babysitting every afternoon at the mail-order bride's house. Mrs. Gallop spoke Russian to

Nikki before she left for the gym. The words sounded thorny, like Nikki was in big trouble, but Mrs. Gallop always gave me her same quick smile before she left, so I knew it was just the way her language sounded in my ears. *Mail-order bride,* my mother said every time I went over there to baby sit. *Why not just call it prostitution and be done with it?*

"Be a good girl for Sally," Mrs. Gallop said.

"Don't worry about us," I said. I listened to my words extra hard when I spoke to Mrs. Gallop, wondering how I sounded to her.

Sometimes Mrs. Gallop flipped on the music she worked out to before she even left the house, and I could hear the Russians singing loud in her tiny headphones. She hated America and California in particular. *It's unnatural to have this much sunshine,* she told me once with her accent. Even on a cloudy day, Mrs. Gallop made a little visor above her eyes with the side of her hand when she walked outside.

I thought she could benefit from sunglasses, but Mrs. Gallop always put big gray earmuffs over her headphones and headed out the door. *Like she's still in Russia,* my mother said. *Like she might be headed off on her dog sled.*

"Play treasure hunt," Nikki said as soon as her mother shut the door. "Close your eyes."

I shut my eyes while Nikki hid toys. Sometimes I'd cheat and peek, but it didn't really matter since Nikki always hid them in the same spots—under the kitchen sink, under her small bed, and under her mother and father's bigger one. I got sick of this game before we even hit July. Still, it kept Nikki happy, and I was too lazy to come up with something better.

"Let's see," I said when she was done hiding everything. "Where should I start?" I looked under the couch pillows in the living room, and then I went into the kitchen and looked in the refrigerator because I was hungry. I opened the vegetable bin and the cheese bin. The food in this house looked nothing like our food. The vegetables were twisted-looking roots, and the cheese was wrapped in white paper. When Nikki wanted a snack, I'd dig around until I found something I recognized, like an orange.

"You're not really looking," Nikki said, behind me now.

I reached in my pockets and pulled out one of the gummy bears I always brought with me for bribes. "Open wide," I told Nikki. Then I popped one in her mouth.

I heard the metallic-sounding horn of Guy's golf cart, and Nikki and I went to the living room window and looked out. Guy was at the wheel, and my mom was riding shotgun and waving big like she was a beauty pageant contestant sitting in a convertible. "Come on out here, girls!" she said. "We're going for a ride."

I had never left the house with Nikki before when I was babysitting, but I figured it would be all right as long as we got back before Mrs. Gallop did.

"This is cool," Nikki said when I lifted her onto the back seat of the golf cart.

"Who wants to go for ice cream?" Guy said, taking off before we could answer.

"Where's the seatbelt?" Nikki asked. "Do I need a helmet?"

"It's okay," I told Nikki. "We're flying under the radar."

At Rite Aid, I held Nikki up so she could study her ice cream choices. I could hear my mom and Guy kissing behind us, and I hoped that no one I knew was going to walk in. *Be happy your mother's finally happy,* my mom said when I made a face at her one morning while Guy was singing in our shower. *Be happy someone's still interested in the old nag.*

"Rainbow sherbet," Nikki said. "On a pointy cone."

Even though I wasn't that hungry anymore, I ordered a double rocky road because I wanted to see if my mother would change my order to a single scoop the way she would have before Guy came along. But my mother was studying the ice cream choices like she'd never seen them before and whispering something to Guy that made him laugh.

"Strawberry cheesecake," my mother said. "In a cup. Two spoons."

We had parked in a regular space in front of the store, and when Nikki and I sat in the back, I reached my feet out and touched the headlights of the car behind us with my toe. We drove down the street, past the gym where Mrs. Gallop worked out. I put my arm around Nikki to hide her from the big glass window everyone faced while they exercised.

When Nikki's sherbet fell off, it landed on the street in such a perfect ball that for a minute I thought about jumping off and picking it up, sticking it right back on her cone. But instead I watched the car behind us flatten it with its tire before turning the corner. I stared at the curved rainbow left behind on the street. I had never seen Nikki cry before, and she did it so quietly, at first I didn't even notice. "Take mine," I said.

But Nikki shook her head. "I don't like brown ice cream," she said.

Guy kept driving, his hairy elbow leaning out his window, my mother feeding him spoonfuls of strawberry cheesecake.

"You didn't even look under the beds," she said. "You have to finish when we get home."

A cop came around the corner and Guy beeped his tinny horn and waved. *DUI,* I'd heard my mother tell her sister on the phone. *It could be worse. At least he's not taking me out on the handlebars of his bike.*

"Scenic route time, girls," Guy said, turning by the marina, away from our neighborhood.

"I want to go home now," Nikki said.

I thought about Nikki's mother, the mail-order bride, getting home from the gym, taking off her earmuffs and then her headphones, the way a house feels when someone's missing from it. I reached in my pocket and took out two gummy bears, one for me and one for Nikki.

"Enjoy the scenery," I said to Nikki, feeling like I was forty years old. "You'll be home before you know it."

SUZANNE GREENBERG
UNDER THE RADAR

Discussion Questions:

1. What do the mother's observations about Mrs. Gallop say about the mother?
2. Why does Mrs. Gallop feel so out of place in Los Angeles?
3. What does Guy's reckless behavior both on the road and socially say about the mother's choices?

Essay Questions:

1. How does the narrator of "Under the Radar" feel about the foreignness of the other characters? Does she see them as lesser or different? Are these attractive qualities for her?
2. Compare and contrast this story to "Chuze Off!" To what degree is the characters' otherness the source of their problems?
3. What does the mother's view of her relationship with Guy reveal about her values and her sense of self?

The Empire Sky

DANIEL HOLLAND

In the distance, a thunder clap echoed across the warm Arizona night. A moment later, as though shook loose by the chaos, a thorny branch of white light skipped atop the mountain's black silhouette. My uncle's wife, Naomi, and I leaned back in our wicker deck chairs and waited. Nothing else came, so we resumed our talk.

"What is it about Stone and work?" I asked. At half past eight, my uncle Stone was apparently still in the office at his automotive repair shop.

"Work and faith are his tonics, his way of . . ." Naomi mused, "Well, his way to . . . they help him burn off some of the extra . . ."

As she struggled to finish her thought, I gazed off at the bleached sun deck that wrapped around their ranch, The Empire Sky, then up to the imposing tri-level home itself. First erected by my great-great-grandfather in the 1890s, the house embodied a certain Western ideal; it was a relic from a time when family was first and the cowboy was king.

But as my dad so often reminded me, nothing is true at first sight. To Dad, Cody Rider, my great-great-grandfather, wasn't the straight-laced rancher that my uncle made him out to be. He was just the beginning of something bad.

"Angst?" I offered.

"Energy," she answered firmly.

Something in her down-turned lips made me shiver and look away. A Hopi Indian and accomplished painter, Naomi had an upturned chin that was both understanding and intimidating when it leveled itself in your direction. Her cheeks were wide-set and soft, her eyes clear and intense.

Rotating clouds lined up over The Empire Sky, and a warm rain ticked downward. "I've got a bit of extra energy myself. Runs in every family, I guess," I said.

She nodded vacantly, then raked a hand through her graying mane and tugged her jean jacket overhead as an umbrella against the circling drops. She knew about these summer storms in August; the rain came first, then as the pent up electricity coiled, fissures of lightning bled across the plains.

The domed sky glowed as a bolt opened up directly above us. In the backyard, a gnarled oak stump and the tattered marker beside it sparkled, then died away.

"What was the name of my grandfather's horse again?" I asked, pointing to the grave marker he'd dug for the animal so many years ago.

"Don't know. Stone doesn't talk about those things much."

I didn't believe her. "He loved that horse. Pictures of it all over."

"I guess," she whispered, then patted my knee—it was change-the-subject time.

"Well, you know, Uncle Stone and I talked about the cycle. I'm here to break it. I'm no dumb victim anymore, and I promise that my dad—"

"Don't do that," she admonished, "Don't promise, just leave it."

She slid the jacket back onto her shoulders and tried unsuccessfully to smile. "I'm sorry," she said.

"For what?"

The phone rang and she padded inside. "For you," she called out.

As I passed, Naomi's smile tightened a notch, and I wondered if she was going over my whole sordid tale and reconsidering Uncle Stone's decision to save me. "A lost boy of the lost father," he'd called me. I was again out after another two-year stint in the LA County Jail. SUVs this time. ("They're a major fucking contributor to global warming," Dad contended). Even though Uncle Stone believed I was a thirty-two-year-old "victim" whose "victimizer was a slippery bastard masquerading as a social do-gooder," he decided to help me anyway, and I wasn't going to let him down.

Inside, on their sunken living room couch, I studied the way the rain divided the bay window into jagged partitions. Hesitantly, I picked up the phone, knowing it was him. "Are you better?" I asked.

"What from?" Dad spat. "Faked it until they let their guard down, then kicked myself free. That's the key." Though he'd avoided the cops on the SUV collar, Dad found still himself in an Orange County psyche ward two months later. He'd been caught spray-painting radical anti-government epitaphs on a city courthouse. Even at sixty-two, he couldn't stop railing against a country that he believed was built on half-truths and outright lies.

"What's the key?"

The living room was lined with thick oak paneling, and on the high ceiling above a heavy brass chandelier creaked to the left and right. A musty coolness hung in the air that made me want to sleep.

"Faking it's the key, just ask your uncle. Pretend you don't have any ideas of your own. That's another trick."

"What if I don't?"

"Don't what?

"Have any ideas of my own."

"What are you doing out there anyway?"

Running from you, I wanted to say—running away from you and California, just as you ran from Grandpa and Arizona. But to tell him that would have been to say too much. To him, Uncle Stone and this ranch were symbols of everything he was against. But maybe to heal old wounds we come back to where they were first opened?

"Stopping this . . . pattern, I hope. How's the hand?"

Dad had gotten two fingers of his left hand badly crushed in a protest against world trade years back. "Some of it works, some of it doesn't, everybody's life story." Then he added, "You're being fed the lie, Ernie."

"I know what I'm doing," I replied.

"You do? What did Descartes say about knowing?"

Here we go again, I thought, over-thinking everything. What Uncle Stone called "playing with yourself." These thoughts started it all—as far as my uncle was concerned—they led to Dad's depression, his outbursts, and his breakdowns.

"I'm tired, Dad. Can we talk later?"

"What did Descartes say?" he hissed.

"Skepticism. Don't trust anything. What a shitty way to live."

Throw pillows stenciled with old stage coaches and jagged tomahawks layered the couch. I leaned my head back, exhausted.

"You're not like them." I knew by "them" he meant everyone connected to The Empire Sky, but he especially despised my grandfather. On one hand, Grandpa George was the great horseman who had the misfortune to shatter his leg falling from his favorite Mustang; on the other, he was said to be liberal with the crop and some—my dad again—even thought him a spiteful martyr whose burning anger pulled everyone around him down. In all the narratives he was a womanizer, though Uncle Stone seemed more inclined to forgive his dalliances than my dad, who felt those other women contributed to Grandma Laura's heart attack.

Naomi was leaning in the doorway watching me, so I attempted a reassuring wave. I trusted her, for the most part. Uncle Stone had found a real partner in this regal woman, while my mom couldn't hang on to the spiraling mess my dad became. A lasting feminine influence was what our side of the family tree needed, but it was too late now.

"How do you know where I belong?" I shot back at Dad.

"Who knows you better?"

"What was it Descartes said about knowing again, Dad?"

Lightning darted across the bay window, its radiance shimmering in my head long after its light had faded. I could actually feel the redness in my eyes.

Naomi turned on a lamp, and Uncle Stone's favorite portrait of Grandpa materialized on the far wall. He was astride his trusted black Mustang, looking confident and youthful.

"Dad, what was the name of Grandpa George's horse?"

A door slammed. At the end of the hall, Uncle Stone secured his enormous white golf bag in its special rack, and then he hooked his Stetson softly atop the wall mirror. I thought I saw him wipe a red smudge from his cheek before Naomi hugged him. Then she stepped back onto the patio and allowed the huge frame of my uncle to claim the doorway. "Got in a bucket before the rain got bad," he bellowed.

"Dad, I have to go," I said, hating the whiney sound of my voice.

My father was insistent: "That uncle of yours, he's not the hard worker you think. He's just like your grandpa. Don't fall for the cowboy act of his! Who do you think started this dance to begin with?"

I hung up the phone, but my uncle had gone upstairs, so I wandered outside and stood under the overhang, watching the serrated line of rain tatter the deck. Stepping forward, I raised my face to the sky. Heavy drops flattened my hair and split across my nose and cheeks. Naomi appeared and guided a hand to my neck, her fingers warm and soothing. "Get some sleep," she said, "You look tired."

That night my room echoed with sounds from the hills. From my backpack, I pulled out the copy of *A Course in Miracles* Uncle Stone had given me. I read the passages he'd underlined about the victim/victimizer cycle and listened to the crickets buzz. I read about how we often adopt the stance of the victimizer after "we are forced into being a victim ourselves." Strangely enough, all the talk of victims sent me to dreaming. Dad and I had stolen the black SUV from the tri-level house on Mulholland again. Pounding the steering wheel in triumph, he lost control of the car. As the lights of Los Angeles pinwheeled around us, he jumped out, while I wrestled with my seat belt. The steering wheel spun so fast that the world fell away. I was in the middle of a storm, riding inside pockets of light and darkness, tumbling down. I awoke tangled in covers, stumbled to the bathroom window, and stood absently glaring at the storm. In a glint of lightning, a jagged stain shimmered on the oak stump. Intrigued, I flicked on the light and peered out, but it was gone.

At six a.m., I stumbled groggily into the shower; I had to be at the auto shop by seven. It was to be my first day working for my uncle. Cranking the handle on high, I let the scalding water cleanse me, then scrubbed myself hard. While combing my hair, I stared through the back oval window at the low, flat land dotted with Saguaro cacti. Uncle Stone's backyard featured looping ridges and dry washes falling off as far as the eye could see. My heart was pounding so hard, I knew I needed to meditate—something else I'd picked up from my dad.

On the beige carpet, the light broke through the windows in two long rectangles of sunshine. The sun layered me in its stark yellow glare. Sweat surfaced on my brow and cheeks, collecting in pools that didn't run unless I moved. I sat still. I wanted to sweat *it* out—whatever was inside me. "Help," I whispered into the ringing silence. "Help me."

"You gonna work hard?" Uncle Stone asked when I arrived at the shop fifteen minutes late.

"I'm sorry, I just—"

"Hard work," he repeated, as though it was some kind of new and untested philosophy that he'd just sprung on the world.

The shop was in a huge Tempe strip mall; it had seven car bays, a handful of overworked mechanics, and an endless supply of steaming sunshine. It was also the cleanest repair shop I'd ever seen.

Uncle Stone caught a reflective look on my face and examined me closely. "What? You got idle time?" he asked.

"No, sir," I answered. Just the type of conformist BS that Dad would have crucified me for. Hell with him. Maybe Uncle Stone was right about thinking. What real good had it ever done anyone?

Stone thrust a seven iron, his constant companion, into my face.

"Take a swing," he'd commanded, "You got monkey mind. You got cancer of the skull."

Feeling ridiculous, I'd gripped the club and took a weak little swing. "Harder," he'd commanded. "That brain is busting you. Swing hard now!"

I reared back, winding myself up, and let her rip, the flat iron's follow through clipping the tip of Stone's white Stetson. "Jesus Christ!" he'd snorted, "Be careful, fool!"

As he snatched the iron back, my eyes rested on a pristine '64 Thunderbird in the second bay. It sparkled like a black diamond. "Is that all original?" I couldn't help asking.

"All original and untouchable. Get it?"

I almost laughed just thinking what dad would say to that. He had a thing about Thunderbirds. When Stone's eyes caught mine, I dropped my head. "Got it," I said.

"Pair of overalls in the office. See Matius about your day."

My day was cleaning every dirty nook and cranny in the shop while Stone meandered about swinging various clubs and barking out orders. Matius, the head mechanic, went about his business with a quiet efficiency I found unnerving. But the fact that my uncle had hired a Mexican as his second-in-command was a sign that my dad was wrong about Stone. He wasn't just another "exploiter of cheap labor." Though, by day's end, Matius' T-shirt, a quagmire of grease and oil, seemed to argue otherwise, and, as he futilely scrubbed his hands in the stained black sink, I found myself back in the middle again, comparing Uncle Stone's system to my dad's.

On the second day, Stone promoted me to cars. It felt good changing oil and swapping brake pads. At last I had a rhythm going. Around seven that night, Stone tapped my leg, and I rolled out from under a 4Runner. He looked me over with that steady gaze, the way that people who have never done much wrong look at the people who always will. "Easy," he said. "Take it easy. Let Matius finish up."

That day I realized Stone couldn't be moved to trust me. He kept fingering his seven iron nervously, and I knew he was waiting for my pressure valve to break. That hurt. The man who gave me *A Course of Miracles* didn't have any faith in me. I was working hard and sweating hard—but he just shook his head, weighing his club on his left shoulder like it was a burden. I shrugged. What could I do? I worked how I worked. It was all I knew.

One week later, as I was changing some bushings on a corvette, I saw the weathered sandals. I whacked my forehead on part of the axle and nearly swallowed my torque wrench. As I rolled out, Dad gripped my hand and pulled me up. He shoved me backwards and looked me over. "I missed you, Ernie!" he sighed.

I just stammered.

"I didn't mean to leave you, but when it comes to cops, it's every man for himself. You know that."

"Sure," I said, smiling down at his usual attire, a worn Grateful Dead T-shirt and cutoffs—but the crutches were new. "What the hell happened?"

"Had an argument with a guard. He wanted me to keep both legs in formation."

"What did you want?"

"I wanted to see how far I could shove one up his ass."

I laughed, shocked at how good it was to see his stormy gray eyes.

"Evening," Stone said. He was standing in the office doorway, a fake smile trembling on his lips. Chipping an imaginary annoyance with his seven iron, Stone paused and gave up half-way.

Dad nodded. "Afternoon," he said.

They walked towards each other, then stopped abruptly ten yards apart.

"So you're Ernest's new boss, eh?" Dad inquired, "His teacher?"

"Get out of here," Stone muttered.

Dad clawed a bottle of pills from his pocket. "Water anywhere I can borrow? Got a hell of a headache," he said. "Same damn Arizona weather."

"No water," Stone said flatly, "No nothing. Get out now."

Dad swallowed the pill dry and reared up on his crutches. "I need one night. That's all. Look at me. I'm broken up. What am I going to do?"

Stone glanced at his crutches. "God only knows."

"I'm your brother. We're still family, aren't we?"

Stone twisted his hat between his thumb and forefinger doubtfully.

"One night," he said. "One."

I followed them to the ranch in Dad's beat-up Mercury. They drove in the black Thunderbird, engaged in a heated discussion the entire way. In the ranch's circular driveway, Dad jumped out before the car was fully stopped. I couldn't decipher his face. He just stood there on pause, looking at The Empire Sky like he couldn't believe it was still standing.

Surrounded by Naomi's oil paintings of Arizona people and places, we ate but said little. In a huge portrait above us, a couple waltzed happily over a cliff's edge. The man appeared in control, but the woman's head was spinning towards the chasm that awaited them. She had a dreamy expression, hopeful but sad.

Naomi, who'd seen me staring at the painting, broke the silence. "My parents didn't understand me marrying Stone. They thought he was . . . They didn't get him . . . I gave them this painting to prove that things change and—"

"Did it work?" Dad asked.

"Not really. But they're at rest now."

"My apologies."

Stone shifted in his seat and threw his fork onto his plate. The conversation was a little too deep. Dad dug into his overcoat hanging on the chair and brought out a little bottle of Jim Beam. "Your wife's too good for you, Stone," he said flatly, touching the bottle to his lips.

Naomi leaned forward but said nothing.

After wiping his mouth with his three good fingers, Dad handed me the bottle. I wanted to pass, but I knew he wouldn't allow it. I took a light sip and set it in front of Naomi. She glanced up, surprised, and then gingerly passed it back to Dad.

Smirking, my father set it in the center of Stone's plate. With a strange intensity, Stone glared down at the bottle. "Same damn ass."

"Forgot about that problem of Stone's," Dad said, beaming at me. "Turns mean after a few, just like—"

"Dinner's over. Get out."

My dad winked at me. "After dinner, I'm gone. Poof. I disappear forever. Leave you here to become a responsible drone. That's what you want, right?"

I felt a growing pressure churning inside my chest.

Stone snatched the bottle, got up, and poured it into the sink.

"That's just unfriendly," Dad snorted. He got up, steadied himself on his crutches, and swung on his jacket. Soundlessly, we followed him out through the open patio door and onto the deck. He stopped and peered up at the gathering clouds. "Well, Empire Sky, I leave him to you." He turned, slapped my shoulder, nodded, then clopped off. "Dad" was all I could say.

"Good night, Bryan," Naomi sighed.

"Goodbye, brother," Stone purred.

When Dad got to the stairs, he spun, dropped his crutch, and walked carefully backwards as though negotiating a tightrope.

Stone, like a crazy man, grabbed a golf club that was leaning on a deck chair. "Liar!" he spat.

Dad did a little hop, then whirled around on his heel and said, "Truth-tellers use falsehoods to kill lies."

"Wait. No. Naomi," I pleaded, "We have to—" But she seemed to be edging further and further away.

"You can still do this right," Stone insisted. "We'll give him everything he needs—"

Dad drifted up the side of the deck and peered over. When he gazed back, his pallid cheeks were crimson. "Give him this."

Stone walked over to the edge and I followed. Dad was still gazing straight ahead. "Tell him about that horse named Sky."

"You could have years ago. Why didn't you?" Stone's mouth twitched, and he put his arm around me. "Say your goodbyes now."

"Some truths are so hard they hurt to tell, but I'm ready now. Tell him how much Grandpa George liked to brush those black haunches . . . with his whip!"

Dad's eyes rode heavily across the landscape, resting on the oak stump and the marker, re-seeing the memory as though it was happening once again. "George loved that horse until he got bucked off. Wasn't even Sky's fault that the rabbit ran under him. A fool rabbit spooked from a lightning flash. Action and reaction, cause and effect, cycle after cycle."

"Doesn't matter." Stone turned and took my wrist. I didn't move.

"A shattered man who couldn't accept God's plan. What would your *Course in Miracles* say about that? About a cane? You remember that cane, Stone?"

Stone let go of me and turned away.

"Sure you do. He used it that night. After he drank himself into a stupor. Hobbled the horse because it kept circling backwards around the tree. Caned it and caned it and caned it. Even when it was dead, he kept caning it. Like all that blood was going to change anything."

The stain I'd seen: Sky's blood.

Stone spun the seven iron in his hand. "What a liar says is never heard."

Dad walked back and picked up his crutch. He lobbed it over to me. "Did you forget, Stone? You're the son of a horse killer. Great-grandson of a horse thief turned empire-maker!"

"And you're the family victim, who gave your own kid your weakness."

"The weakness started way before me," my father said, glaring up into the shifting night air.

My mind was spinning, and my chest hurt. In the turbulent sky, the red clouds were stretched to their breaking points. Though I was standing, I felt myself falling through those same pockets of light and darkness.

Stone's eyes glowed with a fixed hostility, a look more desperate and dangerous than I'd ever seen on his face.

Dad turned to me. "Pay close attention, now. You see. Do you see! This is what's below the mask."

Stone's skin was turning a maroon purple; perspiration beaded his upper lip. He squared himself in front of me: "Give me that goddamn crutch!"

I held it up high.

Dad howled with laughter. I looked away, tried to concentrate on the breeze, the looping ridges, the dry washes falling away, the open road below, and the mountains beyond it.

Stone spun and slammed Dad across the ear with his seven iron. Instantly, Dad's knees buckled and he fell.

"Give him the crutch," my father hissed from the ground. "Now!"

I felt a tremendous electricity course through me.

Without hesitation, I raised the crutch up and whipped it down, lacerating the tip of Stone's scalp. He doubled over in a succession of falls: his head sank to his chest, his butt to his heels, his arms to his lap. He slumped forward until his bloody scalp rested right on my dad's shoulder. Dad nudged him and my uncle crumpled backwards onto the patio, his mouth a crooked line of pain.

I couldn't believe it. My ears pounded. I shook my head, trying to understand what I'd just done.

Naomi stepped from the shadows, arms crossed as though preparing to scold three little boys. Her eyes held no surprise in them, only a sad recognition. This wasn't the waltz she wanted, but it was somehow the one she expected. I stumbled towards her, trying to think of any way to explain what had happened, what was still happening, what would always happen, but she seemed to already know.

"Go!" she spat out, leaning down and rolling Stone into her arms, her beautiful chin crinkling under his weight. I couldn't gauge her face. It might have been sadness, hate, indifference, or all three.

She checked his head and pulse.

"I . . . had to," I pleaded, "but we . . . my Dad . . . I didn't . . . all of us. I . . . we . . . didn't want any of this."

She just watched the cloud shards' riotous struggle.

"Is he okay?" I asked.

"Of course not."

"I just want you to understand . . . I'm not . . ."

"I know what you are," she whispered.

I glanced around. Dad was gone. A thunderous rumbling shook the earth and I looked up and then realized the sound was coming from the car port. I ran to the other side of the deck and looked down. Dust clouds billowed up both sides of the '64 Thunderbird. My dad looked up and waved for me to jump in.

I turned to Naomi. "Go on," she said, "run."

It came out as a challenge.

REVIEW

Discussion Questions:

1. What is the symbolic power of naming the ranch Empire Sky? How does the ranch's name contrast with its current and former owners?
2. What do you think the narrator should do: go with Naomi and Stone or go with his father? Why?
3. Why does the narrator keep Stone's crutch?

Essay Questions:

1. In "Empire Sky," to what degree is the father's assessment of Stone's character correct?
2. In "Empire Sky," is the father's quest to convince his son that Stone cannot be trusted a good one? Is the narrator in any danger if he stays with Stone? Does he have a chance for advancement with Stone?

From Alta Vista High

KATHY SILVEY HALL

April 29, 1992

She awoke to the phone ringing.

It was still dark, but her hand knew where the receiver was before she was entirely awake.

"Hello."

She suddenly realized the voice on the other end was accustomed to groggy voices, that it woke people for a living.

It was her first empathetic gesture of the day. Before her feet touched the ground, they wore someone else's shoes as if by reflex.

"This is the subfinder for the Centennial School District. Are you available to sub today at Alta Vista High?"

"Must be difficult to get people today," she said. She was entirely awake now, and the problems of the voice on the other end of the phone were clear to her.

People who didn't know her often misconstrued her empathy as kindness, but it was, primarily, a survival mechanism. The voice on the other end of the line might be more inclined to call her for future jobs because she had treated it like a person, although it was more likely to call her again because she was saying yes today than for any other reason.

"We're needing quite a few subs, and I've had a few refusals already this morning."

She lit a cigarette. It was technically morning, but one of the disadvantages of substitute teaching was that mornings tended to begin before dawn.

"I'll be there," she said. "What classes do you want me to take?"

"The one I'm filling now is Basic Math, but you might have to float."

"I figured I wouldn't get a prep," she said.

She took down the details, then showered, dressed, and drank a cup of coffee, pouring another to take with her.

She drove to the school in the red daybreak.

Over her left shoulder, Los Angeles burned.

She arrived at the campus to find it strained, crackling with tension and repressed violence.

You never have to take your pulse at a time like that. She liked that, that feeling of life close to the bone, of being plugged into something and feeding on its energy.

The administrators were trying to pretend it was just another Thursday, but they could see how few students had bothered to come to school. The absent students didn't bother her, but she was deeply offended by the number of truant teachers. Their fear disgusted her. She tried to forget their names, but a decade later she would still know who had left these children to process the injustice, the fires, the looting, the breakdown of civilized society, with only strangers to guide them.

As the day went on, several students went home while others arrived late, showing off their new clothes.

"Nice," she said to one giddy young man who had bounded in to announce that he had new Nikes.

"My dad jacked them for me."

For his child, she thought. Looters were presumed to be selfish.

"Your dad really loves you. Those are very nice shoes."

"It doesn't bother you?"

It was bait. She'd been baited this way all day.

"I can't think of a single reason you shouldn't have nice new shoes like that."

He regarded her closely, trying to decide if she was afraid of him, but she had spoken calmly. She had not hesitated. And there had been no sarcasm in her voice.

"So all this makes sense to you?" he asked.

She smiled. Smart kid. She suddenly liked him. It made no sense to him. It excited him, but it made him nervous too. If he could have those shoes, anything could happen. Literally anything.

"I understand the anger. The verdict was wrong and racist and evil. The beating was terrible and also wrong. I am not going to tell anyone that if the law doesn't apply to those cops it should apply to anyone else. Taking some shoes for your son is not nearly as bad as beating a man half to death, and letting those animals get away with beating him like that, to my mind, that was worse than them beating him in the first place."

The students started talking, telling stories, mostly about the men in their families, fathers, uncles, cousins, taking clothes, shoes, televisions. They did not say they were angry, but it showed. They were trying to sound overjoyed with their recent acquisitions, but they were all angry and scared.

She let them talk, and soon they had just about forgotten she was there. She could feel the room relax as the kids created a calm space in which they could say what they needed and withhold what they were not ready to say. When they were spent, one student, quietly and without emotion, said what everyone had been thinking but no one had said.

"They shoulda burned Beverly Hills."

She smiled. "I hear you," she said. "But they should have burned Simi Valley."

They laughed bitterly. Children that young should not know how to laugh bitterly.

A few minutes later, the principal walked in. She had been trying to get to all the classes where substitutes were teaching. The kids had been out of control, and the subs had been helpless. The sober faces and the quiet of this room surprised her. "Hi, I'm Ana Martin. I don't think we've met."

"Nicole Silvers. How's it going?"

"I think we'll make it through the day."

"No reason we wouldn't."

But an hour later, there was a reason.

She walked into the principal's office.

"The surplus store on Hawthorne has been looted."

Ana looked up. "Is that a problem?"

Such intense denial. "Only a few blocks away an angry mob has just armed itself. I thought you should know."

Within twenty minutes, the school was closed for the day.

REVIEW

Discussion Questions:

1. Why are the students in "From Alta Vista High" surprised by Nicole Silvers's reaction to the new shoes?
2. Why do the characters in "From Alta Vista High" feel that the riots are justified?
3. How does Nicole Silvers react to violence?

Essay Questions:

1. At the end of "From Alta Vista High," Nicole Silvers's class is calm and quiet. The students are sober. How has Silvers created this calm?
2. Several of the stories in this collection deal with people who are trying to make sense of violence. Who in this collection seems to have the best method for dealing with a violent world and why do you believe what you do?
3. Several of the stories in this collection such as "Chuze Off!," "From Alta Vista High," and "Continuation School" use the classroom as their central location. How do these authors portray these classrooms? Do they have a central problem in common? Do the characters find any comfort here?

Chuze Off!

MARCIELLE BRANDLER

"Diana," murmurs my mother. I flinch. She only attacked me once in front of the twins, when we lived in Hollywood, but my flight reflex is still strong. She continues. "I want to you to strip Angie and Annette's beds and dust their room." Mother has me up early, but the twins, who are only one year younger than me, are just waking up. I start picking up their dirty clothes while they stretch and put on their robes. I pull their sheets from the beds, which are still warm from their bodies.

"Why do ya let Mom treat ya that way?" yawns Angie.

"Yer so tall, ya look like the Statue of Liberty. Ha ha ha," Annette guffaws. Then, I hear a low whisper, "Li-ber-teeeee," behind me in my ear. I turn, and Angie twirls away in delight.

"You guys are idiots," I say.

"We'll tell Mom you said that," says Angie, but she's distracted by Mother's voice calling from the kitchen.

"And you had better air out their room."

I click my heels and salute her with the finger. Angie and Annette gasp and smile, because here is the goody goody of the family being disrespectful. I have spent my life forever trying to please a woman who despises me. Now, I realize that she's never going to love me. I'm just her slave. My sisters pad off to the dining room where their Cheerios have already been poured and sugared by Mother's loving hands.

I'm wiping off their dresser when the softness of morning is broken by, "What in the Lord's name is this?" It's Mother's voice coming from the hallway. I have to keep working, but I listen. She's coming from the laundry room with a pair of their jeans.

"Are these reds and whites? You girls are taking drugs?"

Angie and Annette are strangers to me. We live in very different worlds, they in their Hells-Angels-wannabe world and I in my tortured desperation, clinging to Jesus as my only hope.

"Annette, I found these in your jeans. Did you get these drugs from that Preacher Riley person?"

Annette's voice booms, "So what? You act like such a good Mormon, when ya treat Diana like that. Yer just a bitch." Her spoon clanks in the bowl.

"What did you call me? Your father will hear about . . ."

"He's a hypocrite, jus' like you. Ya act like yer so 'worthy,' but yer not."

I can't wait to leave this house. Now, I am afraid she will take out her anger on me, as she did so many times when I was little.

Then Annette's voice interrupts my thoughts, "You use' ta smoke and drink."

"We gave that up for the Church," whimpers Mother.

The house is now silent. Six a.m. Everyone's asleep except me. I am ready to go to Seminary, now standing on the porch in the chilly fog of the morn, my favorite time of day, waiting for my ride. Absolute Quiet. Ahhh. Then I'll go to my high school. I am glad Mother no longer hangs my dad's belt over my bedroom door as a way to say, "You've got a whipping coming." I knew the Mormon Church would bring some sort of peace to our family. It forces my mother to calm down. I love studying the *Book of Mormon*, the *Pearl of Great Price*, and the Bible. I love the deep ethical discussions we have with other young brothers and sisters in the Church. Ah, here's my ride.

"She's a Hell's Angel. Don't mess with her." Magdelena seems to know about everyone on campus, who are cholos and who's running for class president.

"But why do they say, 'Chuze off' and start pushing each other?" I ask.

"Oh, that's just how they fight," she murmurs. "'Chuze off,' means, 'wanna fight?' like saying 'F you.'" Cholos drive low-rider cars and wear low-rider jeans. They lean way back when they walk and swing their arms way forward. They call that walk "truckin" and smile a gold-toothed smile and say, "Keep on truckin."

There's Preacher Riley, a white guy. He's a senior, but the rumors are that he stayed back twice so he could sell drugs. He always wears the same black, high-collared Nehru shirt. He is dark-haired, handsome, tall, and confident. Sexy. How can such a great-looking guy with so much going for him get into all that? What a waste! Part of me wants to get to know him, but I live in a different world than he does. Another guy is called Chainer, an angry loner who wraps a thick chain around his waist under his shirt. My friends claim that he hides a knife in one of his black Beatle boots. They say that Chainer goes to downtown LA and gets into gang fights using his chain and knife. I thought white gangs were only in *West Side Story*. Why would a guy go out of his way to find trouble?

"A fight! A fight!" someone is yelling. "Let's go see." Maggie is pulling my arm. "Why?" I'm mumbling, "We should stay away from trouble." In spite of all this "excitement," I can't stop yawning. Trying to do my homework at night, when I need glasses, and getting up early for Seminary, always leaves me drained by lunchtime.

Maggie's all excited, "Oh, come on. We'll be far enough away. I just want to see." Almost all the tables in the cafeteria are abandoned. How eerie. Students are cheering on the fighters. They're two *girls! Girls fighting.* I don't get it. What's the point of fighting? Actually, one is doing all the pushing and scratching while the other girl is trying to pick herself up from the table and chair she's just been slammed against. "Chuze off, bitch!" She starts towards her prey, but stops. "Don't you ever mess with me!"

The smaller girl says, *"Como se dice?"* but this seems to enrage the other girl. "You think you are better than me, speaking Spanish. You don't speak no Spanish when I'm around."

"That's weird," says Maggie. "Those two are best friends. That's Luz and Brenda"

One cholo yells, *"Orale pues! Chingasos!"*

"Hey. Isn't that the same guy who taped a mirror to his shoe so he could look up girls' dresses?" murmurs Maggie.

"Ew. Yes," now glued to the fight. Egged on, Brenda growls, "I'll show you who you are!" Some boys yell, "Tear her dress off! Yeah. Pull it over her head." I hear "Hit her. Come on, Brenda. Hit the bitch."

It seems more of a show than anything else. Brenda isn't very forceful.

"I don't get it," I say. They are both Mexicans, so why . . . ?"

"Because Luz speaks Spanish and Brenda doesn't."

"But still . . ." Then, I find myself yelling, "Why don't you girls act like ladies?"

The room goes silent. Brenda drops Luz and stalks towards me. "You sayin' I'm not a lady?"

"I . . ."

Now, students are running from the room. I assume it's because some of my friends are in the crowd, and they don't want to defend me, but I'm wrong.

"Let's go!" says Brenda. "What's . . . ?" I turn to Maggie, but she is gone.

Mrs. Zardov, the Girl's Dean, a tall lanky woman in gray, whisks towards us silently. The crowd is down to four or five now. I back stealthily toward the farthest doorway.

"You kids, go to class. Brenda and Luz, come with me." The girls comply and she takes the two girls away in silence.

I wonder what's going to happen to them. The bell rings.

Today, I ask Maggie, "Why are the buildings on this campus round?"

"They designed them that way so it would be harder for gangs to get together and start fights." Maggie knows a lot about school history. "Will you still be here at Bassett next year?"

"I think I am going to El Monte High next year." I have no clue about other schools.

"Órale, that's a great school. Two swimming pools. Huge campus."

Angie is in the distance motioning me to one of those blue silo-type buildings. "Maggie, I gotta go see what my sister wants."

Angie's very anxious, "Please, stay with me. Liza's gang is around the building. She punched me in the stomach."

"Okay, I'll stay." It takes only a minute for the gang of girls to appear. I walk up to Liza Krause, the leader of the Hell's Angels girls, and say, "You girls better leave my sisters and me alone." I am not afraid, because we are still on campus, and I feel a sense of authority.

Linda hisses, "What if we wanna beat ya up, eh?"

"Oh, you could beat us up. Look at you. You're huge." I'm completely calm. Teachers are patrolling for just this kind of thing, ". . . and there are more of you, but I'll tell my mother, and she'll have all of you sent to juvenile hall."

I feel a finger gently tapping the back of my right shoulder. I turn. There hovers Denise, a lanky coal-black girl of medium size saying, "I don't wanna go to no juvnal haaall."

"Well, then, you'd better leave us alone." The gang seems to disappear right before my eyes, and so do my sisters. You would think that, at least, Angie and Annette would stay with me for protection, but I never can figure those two out. Why are they friends will Hell's Angels anyway?" I shake my head, "Oh, well."

A few days later, Liza Krause swoops across the campus right toward me. "She must see someone behind me," I think. I turn around, but there's no one there.

"Hey, chick," she breathes, "I saw you staring at me in class."

"Huh? I can't even *see* that far." I place my hands on my hips trying to look confident, while queasy inside. She's even taller than me. Her long, straggly brown hair hangs in little strips down her shoulders. A huge purple pimple with a white middle peeks out from under her red bandana. Her weather-beaten face is caked with blush, and she reeks of patchouli oil. Those sinewy arms could really do some damage. Liza Krause coos like Marilyn Monroe, in contrast to her tough-girl look. "Well, we're just going to have to take *care* of this."

No time for me to get too nervous. "I don't want to do anything on campus to get in trouble with the teachers. Where do you people meet?"

Can this be more stupid?

"You know where the ice cream truck is around the corner on Maple Street?"

I have to think a minute, almost laugh, "Yeah."

"I'll meet you there after school. Two thirty." Then, she's gone. I must admit that I did watch her in class as she caressed her legs. Pantyhose were just invented, and girls have all sorts of ways to show off their newly-acquired leggy freedom. One well-to-do girl I used to walk home with always uses her very long fingernails to slowly scratch up and down, up and down her legs in class. No more girdles with those lumps that garter fasteners make under skirts. But Mrs. Zardov still checks girls' hems. If they don't cover the knee, the girl is sent home to change.

So here I wait by this doggoned ice cream truck that I never noticed before on my way home. How am I going to handle the situation if Liza Krause hits me? My mind just stops. I do not ponder it. I just wait. The ice cream man waves a cone at me. Do I want to buy? I shake my head, "No thanks." I never have money. I wait and wait.

A lady begins watering her lawn with her shaky old hands. Shadows are moving, like I should be, as the sun glides sideways in the sky. That's my cue. It's 2:15, and I *have* to be home by 3:00. I'm more afraid of my mother whipping me with Dad's belt if I don't get home in time to clean the house. She only had to tell me once, "Get it all done and be in your room before your father gets home. And don't tell anyone, or I'll have you sent to juvenile hall." My great fear is prison. I know that I am already in prison, but someday I'll be free. Even Christmas and birthdays are a farce.

I see a group of students walking on the other side of the avenue. No, it isn't anyone from the Hell's Angels. In fact, it's Preacher Riley, surrounded by girls. They stand looking at me. They seem to be waiting for something. Do they know about me and Liza Krause? Since junior high, I've never been in any trouble. This is such an odd situation to be in—me, an active Latter Day Saint, fighting with a gangster. Hey, there's that Chainer guy swinging his chain. It's 2:35. Chainer walks over to Preacher Riley and reaches towards a girl, who pulls away. He moves closer to Preacher. I look at my watch. I close my eyes and face the sun letting the insides of my lids turn red then yellow with amazing patterns. Then I remember where I am. When I open my eyes, I see a huge crowd of kids from campus watching me. They all stay across the street. It's 2:40. I'd better go. I'm worried that I might look like a coward and have to fight Liza Krause later, but I don't dare infuriate my mother. As I walk, two girls follow me, but from the other side of the street. It's Maggie, and she's with that girl, Luz. I hear someone yell, "Fight!" and Maggie and Luz run back.

LA FICTION ANTHOLOGY   269

Angie and Annette are waiting in the living room. I know Mother won't be home yet, and I rush to catch up on my chores. Angie follows me outside. As I begin pulling the laundry off the clothesline, she says, "You were supposed to fight Linda today, huh? She chuzed you off, huh?"

"How did *you* know?" I must look puzzled. I drop a towel on the grass.

I rush to my room and begin folding the clothes. Angie enters my room and Annette stands in the doorway, an unlit cigarette dangling from her lips.

"Know why she didn't show?" Angie gazes at me in awe. "Do ya know, huh? She's *scared* of you."

It would be a triumph if those girls meant anything to me. I can see that it means a great deal to my sisters. I'm their hero. I am glad I'm able to save them. I just wish someone could be my hero and save me from living in this house with these people.

MARCIELLE BRANDLER
CHUZE OFF!

Discussion Questions:

1. How does Diana's relationship with her mother affect the way she deals with other people?
2. How does Diana fit in at home? How does Diana fit in at school?
3. What are the major social or cultural forces that are helping to isolate Diana?

Essay Questions:

1. How do the various groups of students on campus help to create identity and how is the narrator's sense of identity defined in relationship to those groups?
2. What does the narrator think about violence? How does she react to it? How does she use it for her own purposes?
3. Compare and contrast the way the characters in "Chuze Off!" and "Flights" deal with the fact that they are outsiders.
4. The last paragraph of the story deals with heroism. How does Diana seem to define "hero" and to what degree has she become one according to her definition?

Terminal Island

STEPHEN COOPER

On the Friday after the pre-induction letter came, I drove my mother down to Long Beach. She had to see the doctor about her eyes, which were going bad. She had been going every week, though it didn't seem to be helping much. I would wait in the waiting room to drive her home. The waiting room was always full of old people who wore dark glasses and held on to their canes. I would skim magazines or nod off if I was loaded.

I wasn't loaded though on this day. I'd been staying straight since getting that letter. I didn't want to show up for my army physical all loaded out. So I found a *National Geographic* with a colored map folded up inside. The map went with an article about this country up in some mountains. The old men there marked their birthdays riding horses through the fields. You could see how fast they galloped by the way the pictures blurred away. These people lived to be a hundred and ten or even twenty and they took great pride in riding as fast or even faster than when they were young.

I was turning the page to read to the end when the door to the waiting room eased open. My mother was feeling her way out along the jamb with both hands. She had skin tone patches over both her eyes held down with perforated tape. I put the magazine down and gave her my arm to guide her out.

"You get her home and draw those drapes," the doctor said from behind the reception counter.

He was shuffling papers, not even looking out through the glass partition. He was a credit doctor and he worked fast, through lots of patients, in and out. Most of his patients were old. But my mother was still young, only forty-two that summer, even if she was a widow with only one son left, and failing eyes.

"Your hand's so cold," my mother said.

I got her around the plants and the jutting canes and the coffee table, then down the cement stairs outside, one at a time. Out in the parking lot the wind was kicking papers and rocking an empty half-pint back and forth.

"You know what they say about cold hands," she said. She drew her legs inside the car. "My, but it's boiling in here."

We drove then for a while without her talking, which was strange. She usually talked an awful lot with those patches on her eyes. She would talk about the weekend, or the weather, or her book collection of Blue Chip Stamps, anything, just to keep from saying nothing. And when we got home I would draw the shades and let her rest. The doctor was putting drops in her eyes which he said might make them burn. But she never said a word about the burning, then or after.

At the railroad crossing near the Edison plant, we had to stop for the flashing light. The bell was ringing and the arm was down but there was no train. A gust of wind hit the car broadside. You could feel it lift from the rocker panels.

My mother said, "Raise the roof back home in Texas, that old wind would. Plywood ceiling. You'd see it give, then suck away, like it was breathing."

As if to show me, she took a breath. She held it in for quite some time. When she let it out, the bell was ringing and still no train.

"This wind out here, it's pretty stiff but not so gritty," she went on.

"Less dirt out here to blow," I thought to say. "All this blacktop everywhere."

The bell stopped ringing, and the light turned green, and the arm finally hoisted itself back up. I eased my foot back off the clutch, and we crossed the tracks.

"There's plenty of dirt out here," she said. "How many thousand acres of Signal Oil?"

She must have smelled the oil fields coming up then. The road went along the fields for quite a ways with the working wells and the gumdrop tanks. The air always smelled like they had just repaved the road. Of course they hadn't repaved anything, not one crack or jagged hole. High above the refinery buildings, the giant chimney flames burned slanting, pale and almost smokeless against the sky. The air around them shimmered. My mother rolled her window up and folded her hands on her blue print dress.

"Is it true you've gone and joined up in the army?" she asked.

I hadn't told her because I didn't think she'd want to know. I had joined up on the 120-day plan 118 days before. We hit a pothole. The whole seat jerked.

"They got this program," I tried to explain.

"They got a program," she said back.

"It's this deal they got for joining. You learn a trade."

A fancy tank truck cut in front of us. We appeared in its curving, shining chrome. My mother was facing straight ahead with her face held tight that way of hers.

"I told them I want to learn a trade. They said there's no better place. Building bridges. That kind of thing."

The tank truck pulled ahead. Our reflection disappeared. I don't think I believed any more of what I was telling her than the recruiting sergeant who had told me did. He had sat there with his cigarette burning while I figured how I was going to die for joining up. But it's what he had told me, and I had listened, and now I was telling it to my mother. She sat there by the window taking it in behind those patches. I guess she'd heard it all before, from Pat and Jamie.

"So when's the swearing in?" she said.

"Not till next week," I said. "Monday morning is the physical. They give you time to get all ready and stuff."

We drove then for a while not talking about that or anything else. For once I wished she'd just go on the way she usually did after the eye doctor. The oil fields stretched a long distance behind the razor-top chain link, a thousand wells all pumping steady in the wind.

Finally, she raised her hands up in the air and folded them tight in front of her mouth. She held them folded there with her knuckles against her lips.

"I've got an idea," she finally said. "Let's don't go straight home just yet."

Fact was we were already getting pretty close to the projects. I could see across the oil field to the smudged gray line of cinder block. I was pretty sure my mother knew exactly where we were.

"Your eyes don't need the rest?" I said. "You know you're supposed to rest them."

"I've got all night to rest my eyes," she said. "Don't you feel like going someplace different for a change?"

"Sure," I said. How could I blame her? There were just the shades to draw at home. "We go straight home all the time. Today we'll go someplace different."

"So where do you want to go?" she said. "Is it your pick or mine?"

"Anywhere," I said.

"Then let's get away from these fields. Too much of that tar smell and you just can't think. We'll go someplace with a view, as dumb as it sounds."

So I turned around and drove us past the last of the Signal fields. The smell thinned down in the gusty heat. Sidewalks reappeared with walking people. There were discount houses and barbershops and places that would cash your paycheck with no ID. We passed the shot-up arrow pointing out to the prison on Terminal Island.

"That's better," she said. "I know. Let's drive up the hills there in Palos Verdes, past where all the rich people live. I'll show you a special spot I used to know." She sounded better, not so tight or now-or-never.

"A special place for what?" I said.

"Where you can see across to Catalina," she said. "Clear to the world-famous Avalon Ballroom. They turn those lights on and when the night's clear you can really see it."

I said, "Fine." The Avalon Ballroom was where you sailed across to dance cheek-to-cheek. It was one of those places from back in the old days, nothing I cared enough about to see its lights. And Catalina was just an island. Nothing special. But I was doing this for my mother, what little I could do, her youngest son. I turned off the boulevard up the winding hill toward Palos Verdes.

The commercial district fell behind and the air turned sweet with eucalyptus. The open hillsides were gold and yellow in the slanting light. We passed some stables and a tile fountain misting rainbows in the wind. I realized how often I must have driven past that fountain and never seen it. My last year in school, I would drive up nights to park with girls I hardly knew, Mexican girls who kissed me back and one or two who even let me touch them, though never once did I do what I bragged of back at the projects. That was the other thing I thought would happen in the war.

The last of the guard-gate fancy houses gave way to rolling open country. We turned a curve and the ocean sparkled into view. You could see the whitecaps angling in and a big black tanker steaming south, and when I looked back down at the side of the road there was a peacock.

"We just passed a peacock," I said to my mother. I had seen peacocks at the zoo. "Standing right back there by the side of the road, up on a rock."

My mother sat forward in the seat, as if she could see its folded colors.

"Oh!" she said. "That's lucky. Was he spreading?"

I said, "It was just standing there, looking back."

"Even so," she said, "it's something. Wouldn't you say? I'd say it was."

I was glad I had told her, for it seemed to please her some way deep.

"You know my daddy kept a pair of peafowl back in Texas," she went on. "You didn't know that? Those noisy buggers. They'd keep us up nights with their singing, but he always said they were worth the trouble, just to see."

She was talking easy now, as if she had something to look forward to on the way home later on. She touched the tape around her eyes and then my shoulder with the same two fingers, then she put her arm up on the seat behind my head.

"We're getting warm now, I can tell," she said. "We're almost there."

"You'll have to tell me when," I said. "You're the one who knows the way."

"It's where I used to come out with your father on Sunday afternoons. Back before you were born, if you can believe that. Pat and Jamie were little boys. We'd bring them along, and they would play like crazy. We'd been out from Texas long enough for your dad to find some work. He was working swing there at the tire plant, six days on, Sundays off. We'd come up here different Sundays when we could. I'd pack a picnic, thick ham sandwiches and soda pop for your brothers, and chips, and Pabst Blue Ribbon beer in can for the two of us. Ice cold. Your father would drink most of the beer himself and I'd drink a can or maybe two and the boys would play and we would take a nap out in the sun."

She leaned back against the seat with the sun now full upon her face. The sun was striking the ocean, making it shine like broken glass. My mother had never spoken much about my father or about her own life, how it was, and so it was strange to hear her talk now as we drove. My father had been killed in an accident at the Goodyear plant when I was two and when Pat and Jamie were seven and six, and she had raised us on her own there in the projects. She'd had some boyfriends but none for serious.

"Tell me when you see the lighthouse coming up," she said. "It'll be to the right, off on a point. Where the US Coast Guard used to have its rifle range."

"If it's tall and white, I guess I see it," I said. "A couple miles, give or take. Though I didn't know the Coast Guard had anything to shoot at."

"Now find the place where the road dips down."

I slowed down so I wouldn't miss it. The lighthouse was coming up, no work to do on such a bright clear day. I started thinking my mother must be remembering things all wrong. Then the blacktop dropped from under us, sharp and sudden, so your stomach felt it.

"We're here," my mother said. "Now you can park, just anywhere. It's just a stroll to where I mean. You'll see."

I parked the car down off the road and cut the engine. It was quiet. A bird chirped off somewhere, then another, higher pitched. A whirring bug noise rose and fell upon the wind. My mother opened her door and started to get out. I went around to give her a hand.

"Now," she said. "The wire. There's still wire, isn't there?"

A three-stand fence ran between the road and an unworked field. The field sloped down toward a jagged cliff. After that the ocean stretched for miles.

"There's wire, and a little path," I said.

"You hold the wire and slip me through."

I pressed down the middle strand with my foot and held the top one with both hands. She felt for the top strand and hiked her dress and in one quick down-and-up smooth motion she was through. She stood there for a moment holding the dress up in the wind, waiting for me to climb on through the same way she had. She seemed different than I was used to seeing her back at home. She looked younger standing there with her long legs bare and that waiting look. Maybe I had never looked at her very close before, but now I did. With those patches on her eyes I could look, and I stood there looking, for a minute, maybe longer, I don't know. I think she knew what I was doing but she didn't say. She just kept standing there.

"Come on," she finally said. "We're almost there."

I climbed through the wire, nearly snagging my shirt. She let go of the blue print hem as I stood up. The wind pressed the flower pattern against her thighs and flung her hair.

"Can you see the island?" she said.

"It's out there."

"You know that song. Let's sing that song."

She took my arm and we walked together down the brushy slope. She sang, *"Twenty-six miles across the sea, Santa Catalina is a-waiting for me."* The ocean sparkled and a rabbit jumped and a pair of quail smacked the air breaking cover, and for a time there I almost forgot about the war.

"One time," she said, "your father brought up his little .410 pump and shot a quail when it flew up in front of us. It flew right straight up in front of us and he shot it down with one good shot. But it was too little to do anything with. The boys, they had to touch it, and when I got it home it was just nothing, this little shot bird. He never brought his .410 with him after that."

Burrs were catching in my socks and on my mother's dress around her knees. The edge of the cliff was coming up off to the side. It curved around in a wide half-circle above the dark blue of the bay. You could hear the breakers down below and the wind.

"Now wait," my mother said.

She held me back. The edge of the cliff was still ten yards off. A wheeling seagull banked and held upon the wind.

"To the left is where it should be. Down level with the ground. It's dug in deep so they couldn't see it from on the ocean."

"Who?" I said. "See what?"

"Our place."

To the left was just more brush, a bed of cactus, a slashed-up tire, broken bottles, rusting beer cans. There was a circle of dirt with heat-cracked rocks made black by years of matchbook campfires.

"I don't see anything," I said.

"Look for concrete."

She let go of my arm. I took some steps off to the left. The seagull's shadow hung in front of me, then veered away. It crossed something light-colored, flat, and solid—a slab of concrete, I finally saw. It was overgrown and almost hidden in the brush.

"You mean this thing?" I said. "This concrete slab down here?"

"You found it!" She seemed excited. "Help me over."

"Watch that cactus."

"There's a ladder in the cement we used to use."

There was an opening, three feet square, near one square corner of the slab. I kicked a tumbleweed out of the way and saw some numbers. It was a date formed in the concrete, *1942*. I leaned over the opening and saw an iron handhold leading down.

"This is it?" I said. "Your spot?"

"Not up here. Down inside. The view's in there, what you see by looking out."

I could see the space beneath the slab. It was a bunker, square and dim. There were rags and cans and bottles on the floor.

"You go down first. Then you can help me down."

She had one hand behind her head to hold her hair down in the wind. With the other she was clutching at her dress. Right then I wished we'd gone home and pulled the shades like we usually did, back to the projects where there wasn't any view. I was going off to the war and was going to end up getting killed, but I didn't want to touch those rusted rungs down in that hole. Below the cliff, the ocean crashed. Another stiff-winged gull streaked by. The wind felt cold even with the sun, though inside my skin burned hot with fear. But it's all for her, I told myself, and clambered down.

As soon as I climbed down there, it got cool and damp. I stepped off the bottom rung onto a piece of glass and felt it crack. What light there was came mostly from the slit in the seaward wall. You could see through the slit how thick the concrete was, and then the ocean, a hard, bright slash.

"Okay now," my mother called. "Help me down."

She was standing at the edge of the hole in the low slab ceiling, holding her dress down against the sky. She felt forward with the toe of her sandal until it touched the edge. Then she sat down and swung her legs. She was quick even with those patches. I held her waist while she climbed the rungs down next to me. I could see what the rags were on the floor now, rotten blankets, cast-off underwear. I could barely control the trembling starting up inside.

"What is this place?" I said. "It says 1942."

My mother said, "It was for the war. The Second World one. They built these places to keep an eye out."

"An eye out for what?"

"For the invasion they thought would come but never did."

She stood there just in front of me. The wind sifted in through the concrete slit. I didn't know one war from the other. She touched her throat.

"Let's go look out on the view," she said. "You can tell me what you see."

I cleared a way and walked her over. The slit ran right about the level of her eyes. A band of light cut across her face. Her hair tossed back and forth in the shining light.

"Are we there?" she said.

"We're here."

"Then tell me what you see."

I had to stoop. The light was blinding.

"Okay. I see the sky. It's really blue. There's not a cloud. And I see the ocean. Mostly ocean, no invasion. Not today."

She squeezed my hand and said, "Go on. But don't be silly. What else do you see?"

"I see Catalina," I said. "Clear as a bell and long and dark."

She stood there listening while I went on. But I wasn't looking out there anymore. I was looking at my mother, her streaming face in that band of light. In all the years I could remember I had seen her cry only twice before. Once for Pat and once for Jamie, when they were buried. They were buried a year apart, but she stood there crying by each one's grave when everybody had left the VA cemetery but her and me. Now all I could see were those patches and that stricken, listening look.

"You can see it as clear as if we were almost there. By boat—by the Big White Steamship. You can see the mountains, and the town of Avalon, and I'm pretty sure you can see the Avalon Ballroom."

"Without the lights even?" my mother said. "It's not dark yet. Is it, Johnny?"

"No, it's not dark. It's awful clear."

"Oh, baby," she said. "Oh, Johnny. We made you here."

I didn't know what to make of that, or how it mattered, or if it did. But this was her day. We'd come out here instead of going home. I put my hand around her waist and kissed her eyes where they would have been and she didn't turn or take my trembling hand away. I remembered Pat then when we were young and he was the biggest, playing war, and how he and Jamie always ended up in bloody fights. I would stay quiet where I'd been killed while they would argue over whose side won and come to blows before my mother could come rushing out. She would come rushing out and pull them apart where they were rolling around in the thick green ice plant and say, "No moaning!" to whichever one was crying loudest.

The ocean echoed on the walls and the wind blew in like my brothers' ghosts. My mother kept saying, "I loved you all so much. I loved you all." Even when it got dark she kept on saying it, and when we were in the car again driving home, past the Signal fields with the giant chimneys jetting flame. The sky was orange. It rolled and pulsed, the color of night where I'd always lived. I thought of that peacock staring back at me with its feathers folded. I was going off to war. I thought I was ready for anything. I got us home and pulled the shades and started packing.

STEPHEN COOPER
TERMINAL ISLAND

REVIEW

Discussion Questions:

1. At the end of "Terminal Island," the narrator pulls the shades before he starts packing. Why does he do this? What does this action suggest or symbolize?
2. The narrator's mother at the end says that she loved them all, meaning that she loved her family. She uses the past tense for the narrator. What do you think she means to suggest through the use of the past tense?
3. Why is this place so significant to the narrator's mother?

Essay Questions:

1. "Terminal Island" and "The Jizo Statues" both explore the idea of a mother dealing with the loss of her family. How do the differences in point of view affect the ways in which we understand the theme?
2. To what degree does the narrator understand what his mother is going through? To what degree does the mother seem to understand the narrator? How does "Terminal Island" develop the theme of isolation?
3. The story is set on an old World War II site and the narrator is about to go to the Vietnam War where two of his brothers have died. The idea of war pervades this story, but what is "Terminal Island" saying about war?

The Appropriation of Cultures

PERCIVAL EVERETT

Daniel Barkley had money left to him by his mother. He had a house that had been left to him by his mother. He had a degree in American Studies from Brown University that he had in some way earned, but that had not yet earned anything for him. He played a 1940 Martin guitar with a Barkus-Berry pickup and drove a 1976 Jensen Interceptor, which he had purchased after his mother's sister had died and left him her money because she had no children of her own. Daniel Barkley didn't work and didn't pretend to need to, spending most of his time reading. Some nights he went to a joint near the campus of the University of South Carolina and played jazz with some old guys who all worked very hard during the day, but didn't hold Daniel's condition against him.

Daniel played standards with the old guys, but what he loved to play were old-time slide tunes. One night, some white boys from a fraternity yelled forward to the stage at the black man holding the acoustic guitar and began to shout, "Play 'Dixie' for us! Play 'Dixie' for us!"

Daniel gave them a long look, studied their big-toothed grins and the beer-shiny eyes stuck into puffy, pale faces, hovering over golf shirts and chinos. He looked from them to the uncomfortable expressions on the faces of the old guys with whom he was playing and then to the embarrassed faces of the other college kids in the club.

And then he started to play. He felt his way slowly through the chords of the song once and listened to the deadened hush as it fell over the room. He used the slide to squeeze out the melody of the song he had grown up hating, the song the whites had always pulled out to remind themselves and those other people just where they were. Daniel sang the song. He sang it slowly. He sang it, feeling the lyrics, deciding that the lyrics were his, deciding that the song was his. Old times there are not forgotten . . . He sang the song and listened to the silence around him. He resisted the urge to let satire ring through his voice. He meant what he sang. Look away, look away, look away, Dixieland.

When he was finished, he looked up to see the roomful of eyes on him. One person clapped. Then another. And soon the tavern was filled with applause and hoots. He found the frat boys in the back and watched as they stormed out, a couple of people near the door chuckling at them as they passed.

Roger, the old guy who played tenor sax, slapped Daniel on the back and said something like, "Right on" or "Cool." Roger then played the first few notes of "Take the A Train" and they were off. When the set was done, all the college kids slapped Daniel on the back as he walked toward the bar where he found a beer waiting.

Daniel didn't much care for the slaps on the back, but he didn't focus too much energy on that. He was busy trying to sort out his feelings about what he had just played. The irony of his playing the song straight and from the heart was made more ironic by the fact that as he played it, it came straight and from his heart, as he was claiming Southern soil, or at least recognizing his blood in it. His was the land of cotton and hell no, it was not forgotten. At twenty-three, his anger was fresh and typical, and so was his ease with it, the way it could be forgotten for chunks of time, until something like that night with the white frat boys or simply a flashing blue light in the rearview mirror brought it all back. He liked the song, wanted to play it again, knew that he would.

He drove home from the bar on Green Street and back to his house where he made tea and read about Pickett's charge at Gettysburg while he sat in the big leather chair that had been his father's. He fell asleep and had a dream in which he stopped Pickett's men on the Emmitsburg Road on their way to the field and said, "Give me back my flag."

Daniel's friend Sarah was a very large woman with a very large Afro hairdo. They were sitting on the porch of Daniel's house having tea. The late fall afternoon was mild and slightly overcast. Daniel sat in the wicker rocker while Sarah curled her feet under her on the glider.

"I wish I could have heard it," Sarah said.

"Yeah, me too."

"Personally, I can't even stand to go in that place. All that drinking. Those white kids love to drink." Sarah studied her fingernails.

"I guess. The place is harmless. They seem to like the music."

"Do you think I should paint my nails?"

Daniel frowned at her. "If you want to."

"I mean really paint them. You know, black, or with red, white, and blue stripes. Something like that." She held her hand out, appearing to imagine the colors. "I'd have to grow them long."

"What are you talking about?"

"Just bullshitting."

Daniel and Sarah went to a grocery market to buy food for lunch and Daniel's dinner. Daniel pushed the cart through the Piggly Wiggly while Sarah walked ahead of him. He watched her large movements and her confident stride. At the checkout, he added a bulletin full of pictures of local cars and trucks for sale to his items on the conveyer.

"What's that for?" Sarah asked.

"I think I want to buy a truck."

"Buy a truck?"

"So I can drive you around when you paint your nails."

Later, after lunch and after Sarah had left him alone, Daniel sat in his living room and picked up the car-sale magazine. As he suspected, there were several trucks he liked and one in particular, a 1968 Ford three-quarter ton with the one thing it shared with the other possibilities, a full rear cab window decal of the Confederate flag. He called the number the following morning and arranged with Barb, Travis's wife, to stop by and see the truck.

Travis and Barb lived across the river in the town of Irmo, a name that Daniel had always thought suited a disease for cattle. He drove around the maze of tract homes until he found the right street and number. A woman in a housecoat across the street watched from her porch, safe inside the chain-link fence around her yard. From down the street a man and a teenager, who were covered with grease and apparently engaged in work on a torn-apart Dodge Charger, mindlessly wiped their hands and studied him.

Daniel walked across the front yard, through a maze of plastic toys, and knocked on the front door. Travis opened the door and asked in a surly voice, "What is it?"

"I called about the truck," Daniel said.

"Oh, you're Dan?"

Daniel nodded.

"The truck's in the backyard. Let me get the keys." He pushed the door to, but it didn't catch. Daniel heard the quality of the exchange between Travis and Barb, but not the words. He did hear Barb say, as Travis pulled open the door, "I couldn't tell over the phone."

"Got 'em," Travis said. "Come on with me." He looked at Daniel's Jensen as they walked through the yard. "What kind of car is that?"

"It's a Jensen."

"Nice looking. Is it fast?"

"I guess."

The truck looked a little rough, a pale blue with a bleached-out hood and a crack across the top of the windshield. Travis opened the driver's side door and pushed the key into the ignition. "It's a strong runner," he said. Daniel put his hand on the faded hood and felt the warmth, knew that Travis had already warmed up the motor. Travis turned the key and the engine kicked over. He nodded to Daniel. Daniel nodded back. He looked up to see a blond woman looking on from behind the screen door of the back porch.

"The clutch and the alternator are new this year." Travis stepped backward to the wall of the bed and looked in. "There's some rust back here, but the bottom's pretty solid."

Daniel attended to the sound of the engine. "Misses just a little," he said.

"A tune-up will fix that."

Daniel regarded the rebel-flag decal covering the rear window of the cab, touched it with his finger.

"That thing will peel right off," Travis said.

"No, I like it." Daniel sat down in the truck behind the steering wheel. "Mind if I take it for a spin?"

"Sure thing." Travis looked toward the house, then back to Daniel. "The brakes are good, but you got to press hard."

Daniel nodded.

Travis shut the door, his long fingers wrapped over the edge of the half-lowered glass. Daniel noticed that one of the man's fingernails was blackened.

"I'll just take it around a block or two."

The blond woman was now standing outside the door on the concrete steps. Daniel put the truck in gear and drove out of the yard, past his car and down the street by the man and teenager who were still at work on the Charger. They stared at him, were still watching him as he turned right at the corner. The truck handled decently, but that really wasn't important.

Back at Travis's house Daniel left the keys in the truck and got out to observe the bald tires while Travis looked on. "The ad in the magazine said two thousand."

"Yeah, but I'm willing to work with you."

"Tell you what, I'll give you twenty-two hundred if you deliver it to my house."

Travis was lost, scratching his head and looking back at the house for his wife, who was no longer standing there. "Whereabouts do you live?"

"I live over near the university. Near Five Points."

"Twenty-two hundred?" Travis said more to himself than to Daniel. "Sure I can get it to your house."

"Here's two hundred." Daniel counted out the money and handed it to the man. "I'll have the rest for you in cash when you deliver the truck." He watched Travis feel the bills with his skinny fingers. "Can you have it there at about four?"

"I can do that."

"What in the world do you need a truck for?" Sarah asked. She stepped over to the counter and poured herself another cup of coffee, then sat back down at the table with Daniel.

"I'm not buying the truck. Well, I am buying a truck, but only because I need the truck for the decal. I'm buying the decal."

"Decal?"

"Yes. This truck has a Confederate flag in the back window."

"What?"

"I've decided that the rebel flag is my flag. My blood is Southern blood, right? Well, it's my flag."

Sarah put down her cup and saucer and picked up a cookie from the plate in the middle of the table. "You've flipped. I knew this would happen to you if you didn't work. A person needs to work."

"I don't need money."

"That's not the point. You don't have to work for money." She stood and walked to the edge of the porch and looked up and down the street.

"I've got my books and my music."

"You need a job so you can be around people you don't care about, doing stuff you don't care about. You need a job to occupy that part of your brain. I suppose it's too late now, though."

"Nonetheless," Daniel said. "You should have seen those redneck boys when I took 'Dixie' from them. They didn't know what to do. So, the goddamn flag is flying over the State Capitol. Don't take it down, just take it. That's what I say."

"That's all you have to do? That's all there is to it?"

"Yep." Daniel leaned back in his rocker. "You watch ol' Travis when he gets here."

Travis arrived with the pickup a little before four, his wife pulling up behind him in a yellow Trans-Am. Barb got out of the car and walked up to the porch with Travis. She gave the house a careful look.

"Hey, Travis," Daniel said. "This is my friend, Sarah."

Travis nodded hello.

"You must be Barb," Daniel said.

Barb smiled weakly.

Travis looked at Sarah, then back at the truck, and then to Daniel. "You sure you don't want me to peel that thing off the window?"

"I'm positive."

"Okay."

Daniel gave Sarah a glance, to be sure she was watching Travis's face. "Here's the balance," he said, handing over the money. He took the truck keys from the skinny fingers.

Barb sighed and asked, as if the question were burning right through her, "Why do you want that flag on the truck?"

"Why shouldn't I want it?" Daniel asked.

Barb didn't know what to say. She studied her feet for a second, then regarded the house again. "I mean, you live in a nice house and drive that sports car. What do you need a truck like that for?"

"You don't want the money?"

"Yes, we want the money," Travis said, trying to silence Barb with a look.

"I need the truck for hauling stuff," Daniel said. "You know like groceries and—" he looked to Sarah for help.

"Books," Sarah said.

"Books. Things like that." Daniel held Barb's eyes until she looked away. He watched Travis sign his name to the back of the title and hand it to him and as he took it, he said, "I was just lucky enough to find a truck with the black-power flag already on it."

"What?" Travis screwed up his face, trying to understand.

"The black-power flag on the window. You mean, you didn't know?"

Travis and Barb looked at each other.

"Well, anyway," Daniel said, "I'm glad we could do business." He turned to Sarah. "Let me take you for a ride in my new truck." He and Sarah walked across the yard, got into the pickup, and waved to Travis and Barb, who were still standing in Daniel's yard as they drove away.

Sarah was on the verge of hysterics by the time they were out of sight. "That was beautiful," she said.

"No," Daniel said, softly. "That was true."

Over the next weeks, sightings of Daniel and his truck proved problematic for some. He was accosted by two big white men in a '72 Monte Carlo in the parking lot of a 7-Eleven on Two Notch Road.

"What are you doing with that on your truck, boy?" the bigger of the two asked.

"Flying it proudly," Daniel said, noticing the rebel front plate on the Chevrolet. "Just like you, brothers."

The confused second man took a step toward Daniel. "What did you call us?"

"Brothers."

The second man pushed Daniel in the chest with two extended fists, but not terribly hard.

"I don't want any trouble," Daniel told them.

Then a Volkswagen with four black teenagers parked in the slot beside Daniel's truck and they jumped out, staring and looking serious. "What's going on?" the driver and largest of the teenagers asked.

"They were admiring our flag," Daniel said, pointing to his truck.

The teenagers were confused.

"We fly the flag proudly, don't we, young brothers?" Daniel gave a bent-arm, black-power, closed-fist salute. "Don't we?" he repeated. "Don't we?"

"Yeah," the young men said.

The white men had backed away to their car. They slipped into it and drove away.

Daniel looked at the teenagers and, with as serious a face as he could manage, he said, "Get a flag and fly it proudly."

At a gas station, a lawyer named Ahmad Wilson stood filling the tank of his BMW and staring at the back window of Daniel's truck. He then looked at Daniel. "Your truck?" he asked.

Daniel stopped cleaning the windshield and nodded.

Wilson didn't ask a question, just pointed at the rear window of Daniel's pickup.

"Power to the people," Daniel said and laughed.

Daniel played "Dixie" in another bar in town, this time with an R&B dance band at a banquet of the black medical association. The strange looks and expressions of outrage changed to bemused laughter and finally to open joking and acceptance as the song was played fast enough for dancing. Then the song was sung, slowly, to the profound surprise of those singing the song. I wish I was in the land of cotton, old times there are not forgotten . . . Look away, look away, look away . . .

Soon, there were several, then many cars and trucks in Columbia, South Carolina, sporting Confederate flags and being driven by black people. Black businessmen and ministers wore rebel-flag buttons on their lapels and clips on their ties. The marching band of South Carolina State College, a predominantly black land-grant institution in Orangeburg, paraded with the flag during homecoming. Black people all over the state flew the Confederate flag. The symbol began to disappear from the fronts of big rigs and the back windows of jacked-up four-wheelers. And after the emblem was used to dress the yards and mark picnic sites of black family reunions the following Fourth of July, the piece of cloth was quietly dismissed from its station with the U.S. and State flags atop the State Capitol. There was no ceremony, no notice. One day, it was not there.

Look away, look away, look away . . .

REVIEW

Discussion Questions:

1. What is the meaning of the title of this story?
2. At different times in the story, characters are offended or angry. The frat boys in particular become angry. What is the source of this anger and what is the point that the author is making with this anger?
3. What is the mission of the protagonist and to what degree is he successful in this mission?

Essay Questions:

1. Analyze the use of language in the narrator's dialogue. He is trying to accomplish something through people's perception of both symbol and language. How does he use language and the reconceptualization of particular words along with the standard use of other words to create meaningful re-evaluation of concepts?
2. Compare and contrast the themes of this story to the themes of "From Alta Vista High." How are they similar and what makes them essentially and importantly different?

LLOYD AQUINO teaches composition, literature, and creative writing at Mount San Antonio College. He lives with his dogs Charlie and Brady.

DIBAKAR BARUA's poems and stories have appeared in literary magazines such as *Puerto del sol, West/Word, Ibbetson Street, Short Story International*, and *Arts.bdnews24.com*. His book of poems, *The Womb of Memory*, was published in 2008 by World Parade Books.

SEAN BERNARD lives in Southern California, where he teaches at the University of La Verne and serves as editor of the journal *Prism Review* and fiction editor of the *Los Angeles Review*. His fiction has appeared in numerous journals, and he is the author of the collection *Desert sonorous* (2014 Juniper Prize) and the novel *Studies in the Hereafter*.

T.C. BOYLE is an American novelist and short story writer. Since the mid-1970s, he has published fourteen novels and more than one hundred short stories.

MARCIELLE BRANDLER's poems have been translated into Czech, French, Arabic, and Spanish. She has judged poetry competitions and directed workshops for California Poets in the Schools and Performing Tree. Brandler lives in Pasadena.

MICHAEL BUCKLEY is a widely-published short story writer whose work has appeared in national journals such as *The Alaska Quarterly Review, The Southern California Review*, and *Clarkesworld*. His work has been anthologized numerous times, including in *The Best American Non-Required Reading, 2003*. His debut collection of short fiction, *Miniature Men*, was released in 2011.

RON CARLSON is the award-winning author of four story collections and four novels, most recently *Five Skies*. His fiction has appeared in *Harper's, The New Yorker, Playboy*, and *GQ*, and has been featured on NPR's *This American Life* and Selected Shorts as well as in *Best American Short Stories* and *The O. Henry Prize Stories*. His novella, "Beanball," was recently selected for *Best American Mystery Stories*. He is the director of the UC Irvine writing program and lives in Huntington Beach, California.

STEPHEN COOPER is the recipient of a National Endowment for the Arts Fellowship and the author of *Full of Life: A Biography of John Fante*. While researching Fante's life he discovered and edited the manuscript for Fante's last book, *The Big Hunger*. He lives in Los Angeles with his wife and their two children.

MICHELLE DOWD is Professor of English and Journalism at Chaffey College and the founder and faculty adviser of *The Chaffey Review*. She is honored to work with young people who are actively exercising their voices, and she floats around southern California literary communities courting and supporting this process. Her students' and her own work can be heard in spoken word venues, and found in multiple literary journals, as well as in the occasional anthology.

PERCIVAL EVERETT is a Distinguished Professor of English at the University of Southern California and the author of nearly thirty books, including *Percival Everett by Virgil Russell, Assumption, Erasure, I Am Not Sidney Poitier*, and *Glyph*. He is the recipient of the Academy Award from the American Academy of Arts and Letters, the Hurston/Wright Legacy Award, the Believer Book Award, and the 2006 PEN USA Center Award for Fiction. He has fly fished the west for over thirty years. He lives in Los Angeles.

JUDITH FREEMAN is an American novelist frequently dealing with Western and Mormon themes. She has lived with her husband, artist-photographer Anthony Hernandez, in the Rampart District of Los Angeles since 1986.

SUZANNE GREENBERG's novel *Lesson Plans* was published by Prospect Park Books in May 2014. Chosen as a Library Journal Editor's Pick, *Lesson Plans* was named "One of 7 Great Books from Small Presses that are Worth Your Time," by Reader's Digest. Her short story collection, *Speed-Walk and Other Stories* (University of Pittsburgh), won the 2003 Drue Heinz Literature Prize. She's the co-author with Lisa Glatt of two children's novels, *Abigail Iris: The One and Only* and *Abigail Iris: The Pet Project*, (Walker Books). Her creative work has appeared in *The Washington Post Magazine, Mississippi Review*, and *West Branch*, among other journals. Her work on creative writing pedagogy appears in *The Authority Project*, and the forthcoming book *What We Talk About When We Talk About Creative Writing*, both edited by Anna Leahy (Multilingual Matters). She's the co-author of *Everyday Creative Writing: Panning for Gold in the Kitchen Sink*, (McGraw Hill). Suzanne teaches creative writing at California State University, Long Beach, where she's a professor of English.

KATHY SILVEY HALL teaches composition at Mt. San Antonio College, Cerritos College, and El Camino College. Her story is part of an unpublished novella, *Alta Vista High*, a different chapter of which appears in the Lists column of McSweeney's Internet Tendency. Her work is concerned with the miscommunications, disruptions, and imbalances of power and privilege between the varied cultures which make up Southern California.

STEPHANIE BARBÉ HAMMER has published short fiction and poetry in *Mosaic, The Bellevue Literary Review, Pearl, NYCBigCity-Lit, Rhapsoidia, CRATE*, and *Hayden's Ferry Review*, among other places. Her prose poem chapbook, *Sex with Buildings*, was published with Dancing Girl Press in May 2012. She is the recent recipient of an MFA from the Northwest Institute of Literary Arts and she is currently working on a series of novels about a secret branch of Anabaptists who use puppets for their rituals. A former New Yorker, Stephanie divides her time between Los Angeles, California and Coupevillle, Washington. She lives with her husband, Larry Behrendt, at least two unfinished knitting projects, and a bunch of cookbooks whose covers she has never cracked.

MICK HAVEN graduated with BUD/S Class 150 and was assigned to SEAL Team 4. He was a mediocre SEAL but served with some great ones. He writes and teaches writing. Besides the story he has on Amazon now, *Operation Road Warrior*, his writing has appeared in *Playboy* and *Inked* as well as newspapers and literary journals. He's a staff writer for an alternative paper. And he's got a story coming out in an anthology on Los Angeles being published by Red Hen Press in early 2016. The collection's going to feature T.C. Boyle and Percival Everett too, so that ain't bad.

GRANT HIER was named winner of Prize Americana for his book *Untended Garden—Histories and Reinhabitation in Suburbia* (The Poetry Press, 2015), which has also been nominated for both the Kate Tufts Discovery Award and an American Book Award. He was recipient of the Nancy Dew Taylor Prize for Literary Excellence in Poetry (2014) the Kick Prize (2013), and several of his pieces have been nominated for a Pushcart Prize. His poetry has been anthologized in *Monster Verse—Human and Inhuman Poems* (Knopf/Everyman, 2015) and *The Barricades of Heaven: A Literary Field Guide to Orange County, California* (Heyday, 2017). In addition to writing, Grant is a musical artist, visual artist, and former graphic designer and art director. He is Professor of English and Chair of Liberal Arts and Art History at Laguna College of Art and Design where he teaches creative writing and various other courses.

DANIEL HOLLAND loves stories. He holds an MFA in Creative Writing and has published short stories, opinion editorials and poetry in various magazines and newspapers. After finishing his first feature film, *Reclaiming Friendship Park*, he has found a new medium of storytelling to obsess over. He teaches at Mt. San Antonio College, where he tries to infect, uh teach, his students to love stories as well.

CATHY IRWIN is an Associate Professor of English at the University of La Verne in California. She grew up in Los Angeles, received her BA in English from the University of California at Berkeley, and both her MA and PhD in English from the University of Southern California. Besides her work in poetry and literary scholarship, she is the author of *Twice Orphaned: Voices from the Children's Village of Manzanar*, an oral history anthology that focuses on the 101 orphans of Japanese ancestry sent to an internment camp for Japanese Americans during World War II. She currently lives with her family in Claremont, California. She can be reached at tirwin@laverne.edu.

DANA JOHNSON is the author of *Elsewhere, California* and *Break Any Woman Down*, which won the Flannery O'Connor Award for Short Fiction and was a finalist for the Hurston/Wright Legacy Award. Her work has appeared in the literary journals *Slake*, *Callaloo*, and *The Iowa Review*, among others, and anthologized in *Shaking the Tree: A Collection of New Fiction* and *Memoir by Black Women, The*

Dictionary of Failed Relationships, and *California Uncovered: Stories for the 21st Century*. She lives in downtown Los Angeles.

GERALD LOCKLIN has published over one hundred volumes of poetry, fiction, and literary essays including *Charles Bukowski: A Sure Bet* (Water Row Press) and *Go West, Young Toad* (Water Row Press). Charles Bukowski called him, "One of the great undiscovered talents of our time." *The Oxford Companion to Twentieth Century Literature in the English Language* calls him "a central figure in the vitality of Los Angeles writing." His works have been widely translated and he has given countless readings here and in England. He is a Professor Emeritus at California State University, Long Beach. Visit Gerald Locklin's website at www.geraldlocklin.org.

ZACHARY LOCKLIN is the author of *My Beard Supports Nothing*, a collection of Facebook poems published by *Weekly Weird Monthly Press*. The Facebook Poems is an ongoing project inspired by Tennyson's newspaper poems, believe it or not, and all the bad poetry that shows up on Facebook. Zach is a graduate of the Master's of Professional Writing program at the University of Southern California; he currently teaches composition, creative writing, and literature at California State University, Long Beach.

CLINT MARGRAVE is the author of two poetry collections, *Salute the Wreckage* and *The Early Death of Men*, both published by NYQ Books. His work has also appeared in *The New York Quarterly*, *Rattle*, *Cimarron Review*, *Word Riot*, *3AM*, *Bartleby Snopes*, and *Ambit* (UK), among others. He lives in Los Angeles.

RUTH NOLAN writes about California desert culture and the environment for *KCET Los Angeles*, *News from Native California*, *Inlandia Literary Journeys*, and *Sierra Club Desert Report*. Her writing has been published recently in *Rattling Wall*, *New California Writing - Heyday*, *Lumen*, and *Pacific Review*. Ruth teaches creative writing and American Indian literature at College of the Desert, where she is Professor of English. She is editor of *No Place for a Puritan: the Literature of California's Deserts* (Heyday Books, 2009.) She holds her M.F.A. from the UCR Palm Desert low residency Creative Writing & Writing for the Performing Arts program.

DANIEL A. OLIVAS is the author of seven books and editor of two anthologies. His books include the award-winning novel, *The Book of Want*, and the landmark anthology *Latinos in Lotusland*, which brings together sixty years of Los Angeles fiction by Latino/a writers. Daniel has written for many publications including *The New York Times*, *El Paso Times*, *Los Angeles Times*, *Los Angeles Review of Books*, and others. Daniel received his degree in English literature from Stanford University and a law degree from UCLA. By day, he is an attorney with the California Department of Justice in the Public Rights Division.

CYNTHIA ADAM PROCHASKA's work has appeared in the *Santa Monica Review*, *The Florida Review*, and the anthology *Literary Pasadena*. She was a professor at Mount San Antonio College in a previous life and currently devotes her time to writing and fighting the urge to watch cat videos online.

ROBERT ROBERGE studied writing at Emerson College and Vermont College where he received an MFA in the early nineties. In 2013, Roberge released his fourth book of fiction, the novel *The Cost of Living* (Other Voices Books). Previous books include the story collection *Working Backwards from the Worst Moment of My Life* (Red Hen, 2010), and the novels *More Than They Could Chew* (Dark Alley/Harper Collins, 2005) and *Drive* (reprint, Hollyridge Press, 2006/2010). His stories have been featured in *ZYZZYVA*, *Chelsea*, *Black Clock*, *Other Voices*, *Alaska Quarterly Review*, and others. Since 1995, he has lived in Southern California.

RYAN SAREHKHANI is hard to describe, but the image of a sloth burdened by the maladies of the world in an economy class plane seat wouldn't be terribly off base. He generally takes a good amount of prodding before even producing the clumsiest of animal metaphors. It was pure cosmic luck that he earned his M.A. in Twentieth Century American Literature and Rhetoric at Cal Poly University, Pomona.

Los Angeles Times bestselling author **STEPHEN JAY SCHWARTZ** spent years as Director of Development for film-maker Wolfgang Petersen, where he worked with writers, producers and studio executives to develop screenplays for production. Schwartz's novels, *Boulevard* and *Beat*, follow the dysfunctional journey of LAPD detective Hayden

Glass as he fights crime while struggling with his own sex-addiction. The series was optioned by producer Ben Silverman (*The Office, Ugly Betty*, and *The Tudors*) for development as a television series. Schwartz was a judge for the 2012 Edgar Awards, the 2012 ITW Awards, and is currently judging the 2015/2016 *Los Angeles Times* Book Prize in the Mystery-Thriller category. His work has been recognized by authors as diverse as Michael Connelly and Elie Wiesel. Schwartz recently completed his MFA in Creative Writing from UC Riverside and, in addition to editing an anthology for Rare Bird Books, is busy writing his third novel, a standalone thriller set in Los Angeles.

ANTHONY STARROS began college as an Art major but finished with a Master of Fine Arts in creative writing in 1999. During his last year of graduate school at CSULB, he won the James I. Murashige Scholarship for his short story "Papou." He then worked as a freelance copywriter and began teaching at various colleges around the Long Beach area: Goldenwest College, Cypress College, Orange Coast College, and CSULB. He accepted an invitation to become full-time faculty at LBCC in 2002. He has had poetry and fiction published in various small presses and periodicals over the years. He currently teaches composition and creative writing, is Chair of the Jacaranda Essay Contest Committee, and Co-Chair of the Distance Learning Task Force.

PAUL KAREEM TAYYAR began writing poetry in his early twenties, placing his work in journals like *Ibbetson St., Into the Teeth of the Wind, Chiron Review, The Chaffin Journal*, and *Pearl*. His first book, *Everyday Magic* was published in 2007. In 2009, he published *Scenes From A Good Life* and *Postmark Atlantis*, the latter of which was an Amazon Poetry Bestseller in the United States and Germany. He holds a B.A. in English from the University of California, Santa Barbara, an M.A. in English from California State University, Long Beach, and a Ph.D. in English from the University of California, Riverside.

ABOUT THE EDITORS

JOHN BRANTINGHAM is the Writer-in-Residence at the dA Center for Cultural Arts, and his work has been featured on Garrison Keillor's *Writer's Almanac*. His books include the short story collection *Let Us All Pray Now to Our Own Strange Gods* (World Parade Books, 2013) and the crime novel *Mann of War* (Dark Oak Mysteries, 2013). His newest poetry collection is *The Green of Sunset* (Moon Tide Press, 2013). He teaches at Mt. San Antonio College in Walnut, California, and is the president of the nonprofit San Gabriel Valley Literary Festival.

KATE GALE is the Managing Editor of Red Hen Press and Editor of *The Los Angeles Review*. She is author and editor to several books, most recently *The Goldilocks Zone* (University of New Mexico Press, 2014) and *Echo Light* (Red Mountain Press, 2014), and her work has been featured in a variety of literary journals and blogs. A resident of Southern California, she teaches in the low-residency MFA program at the University of Nebraska.